I0682443

ADMINA'S ARGUMENT

STORIES FROM THE WORLD OF THE WIZARD
AND THE WARRIOR

VIVIENNE LEE FRASER

Admina's Argument

Stories From The World Of
The Wizard and The Warrior

Vivienne Lee Fraser
www.viviennelfraser.com.au

Copyright © 2021 Vivienne Lee Fraser
All rights reserved.
ISBN: 978-0-6488860-7-5

Cover design by KILA Designs

Cover image: ©depositphotos.com

Map and Drawing of Admina ©James Simpson

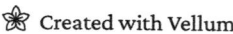 Created with Vellum

This book is for all the minor characters in The Wizard and The Warrior series who clamoured in my head for their stories to be told. And for Sam, who inspired series two.

Seamus' Map of Aria

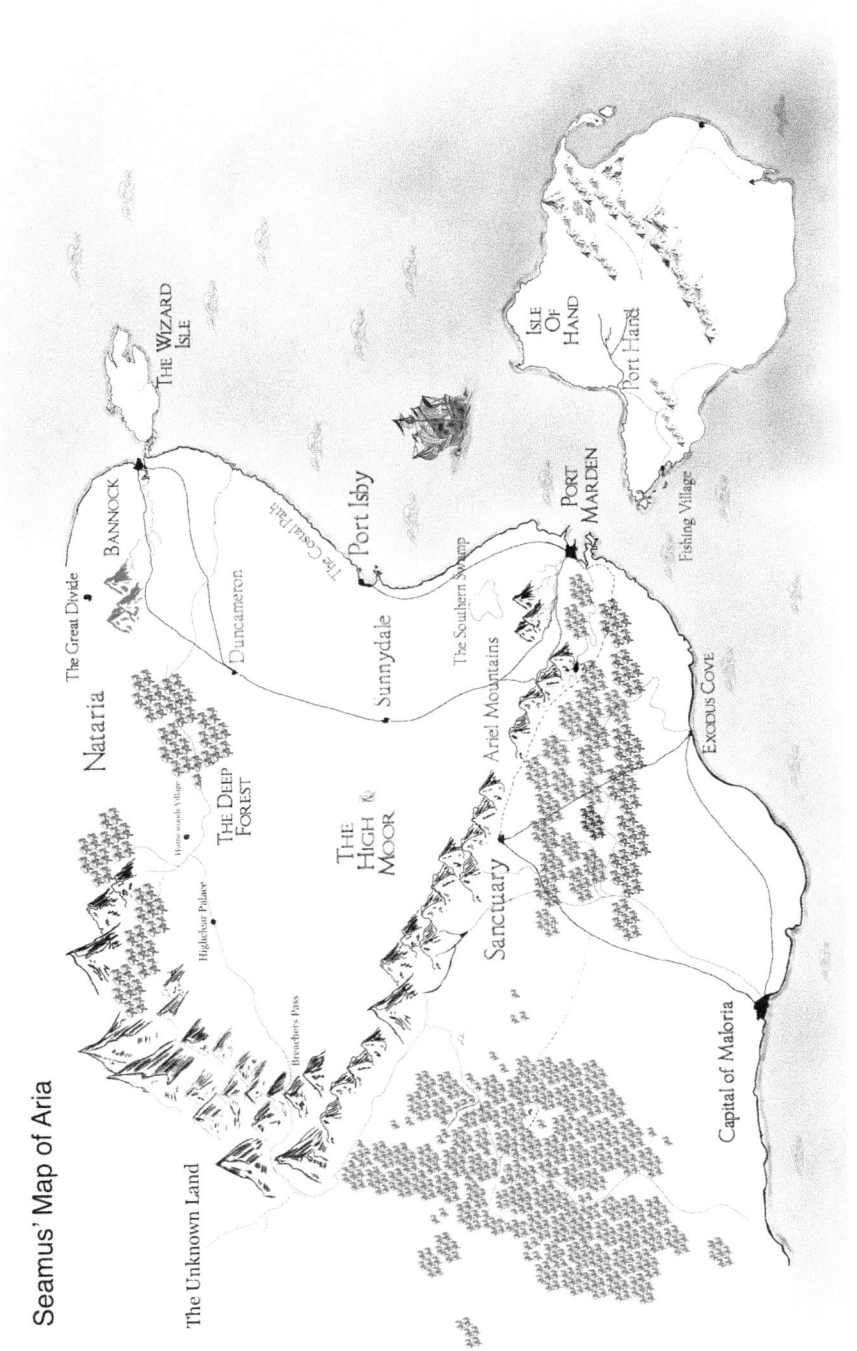

PART ONE
DESTINY

CHAPTER 1

WHY ME

T he door slammed. 'This is the final straw.'

Dominic stopped writing and raised his head to find out why his wife was causing such a commotion. Aliah flopped into the seat in front of his desk in a most unladylike way, which appeared more so because the wide skirts of her formal, blue court dress did not quite fit into the narrow-armed chair. The stiff fabric rustled as she attempted to make herself more comfortable.

'I assume you mean the straw that broke the cart wheel, and from the look on your face, I'm going to guess you're referring to our beloved daughter and potential heir to the throne of Aria?'

Flicking her head to the side as if she were sending a plait back over her shoulder, the crown on her head wobbling precariously amid the elaborate curls holding it in place, Aliah huffed. The gesture was a sure sign of his wife's agitation, and it was all he could do to bite back a smile.

'That girl is in real trouble this time,' Aliah said.

And that approach will go down well with Admina, Dominic thought but didn't say. Used to standing between a headstrong wife and an equally stubborn daughter, his verbal response was more measured.

3

'Rather than going and making Mina's life more of a misery than she believes it already is, maybe we could discuss her most recent transgression and think of a way through this—together.'

His wife glared at him, her blue eyes stormy and full of anger. She drew herself to her feet and leaned forwards as if about to make some cutting remark. She paused before sighing deeply. Sitting down, she placed her hands in her lap and raised her eyes to meet his.

'Mina didn't turn up to her first class this morning. When another student went to fetch her, they found her room at Wizard Isle empty. A search of the isle and the castle turned up neither our daughter, nor her belongings.'

Aliah looked expectantly at him, and Dominic made sure he hid his smile. Years working as a spy before becoming joint ruler of Aria taught him the value of not showing his reactions.

Aliah partially rose, placed her hands on the desk, and locked eyes with him. 'You're pleased about this, aren't you? You're happy, because you told me sending her to study with the wizards on the isle would not go well if she didn't agree to it beforehand. Now that you've been proven right, a part of you is celebrating.'

Wondering what small tic or change of facial expression gave him away, Dominic grinned. Mina was less likely to do something when ordered—on principle. However, what amused him was what his wife called "independent thinking" when it came to her own actions, Aliah labelled as "disobedience" when it came to their daughter's antics.

'Aliah, please sit down.'

She didn't move a muscle.

'All right, I do find this amusing, but that doesn't mean I don't want to sort it out. We both agreed that Mina attending the first classes aimed to licence magic users without their having to join the wizards was important, not only because it would allow her to have more options for the future, but because it would also demonstrate to the country that women with magical abilities have an alternative to becoming hedge witches and using their gifts illegally.'

Aliah sank back into the seat behind her, almost as though his words had taken some of the wind out of her sails. She fiddled with a strand of hair that worked its way loose, twisting it around her finger. Letting it go, she straightened up and placed her hands demurely in her lap. 'I know you; there's more you want to say. Go ahead, you may as well get it all out now.'

His wife was the very picture of a child waiting to be admonished, and Dominic had to use all his self-control not to say the first thing that popped into his head—*Goodness, Aliah, could you be any more reluctant to discuss this?* Instead, he said, 'The only thing we disagreed on was whether or not Mina would appreciate the benefits of attending classes. Your approach of ordering her to go has not worked; perhaps now it is time to try my way and persuade her to agree to return.'

Aliah opened her mouth as if to say something, then closed it again. She tugged at her hair, a sure sign she was thinking things through, or plotting something. He hoped it was the former, but when she smiled, Dominic's stomach sunk—definitely the latter.

'Perhaps you're right, Dominic. I failed. Maybe it's time for the master to deal with this thorny problem. I'm sure you'll handle it much better than me.'

'Flattery won't always get you what you want, Aliah, and in this instance, it definitely won't work.'

A smile played at the corners of her mouth, and Dominic realised she baited him into a reaction. She was getting quite good at this; he would make a diplomat of her yet. 'Of course I can talk to Mina, and she might return to the isle and resume classes, but that will only solve one problem. It won't sort out the issues between you and your daughter. If we are to train her to be our heir, you will need to be able to discuss many, often quite sensitive, things with her. You'll also both have to learn to listen to each other.'

'Humph.' The almost smile disappeared.

'If you don't make the effort now, she may never accept the Heir's Ring and the responsibilities that go with it. Then all we did to fight for female children to be treated the same as their male counterparts will have been for nothing.'

He waited for her to respond. He understood how hard she fought to be more than merely someone's potential wife when she was a princess, and this was the one thing that might actually encourage her to shift her position slightly.

'Aliah?'

'All right, I'll deal with her.' Aliah crossed her arms. 'I'm just not sure how to go about it.'

'Manage her as if she were one of your dukes, one you wanted to do something they wouldn't normally agree to. You always find a way to win them around to your way of thinking.'

'I charm them,' Aliah answered, face deadpan.

Dominic snorted. When Aliah's eyes twinkled with amusement, he relaxed; he had won the battle.

Chewing on her lip for a minute, she nodded and said quietly as if to herself, 'Yes, that might work. Now if I could only find her.'

'You know exactly where she's hiding. She's where she always is when she doesn't want to face the consequences of her actions.'

Aliah stared at him blankly, then grinned. 'Of course. I'll go speak with her now.'

'Um, are you sure?' Dominic asked, a laugh tinging his words as he imagined his wife climbing an apple tree in her current attire.

Looking down at her dress, Aliah chuckled. 'Well, perhaps I might change first.'

***

A WORN BROWN-LEATHER pack leaning up against one of the oldest apple trees in the palace gardens was the only indication Aliah correctly guessed her daughter's whereabouts. Rounding the tree, she found the foothold carved into the trunk by a much younger version of herself. She had spent many an afternoon hiding amongst the leaves, escaping from the demands made on a princess of the realm, feeling sorry for herself.

Climbing into the broad branches was more difficult nowadays, but she managed it—just—thanks to her regular training with a weapons master. Not too far up, she found her eldest child, legs on either side of a stout branch, her back against the trunk. She followed Mina's gaze. A guard platoon was running through their drills in the practice yard, and they had her daughter's complete attention.

Once she had taken a place on the opposite branch, Aliah waited for her daughter to speak first. In their peaceful, leafy cocoon, the sound of metal crashing against metal wafted up, interspersed with birdsong and the buzz of bees. She closed her eyes, making the most of this moment of respite from the court life she sometimes found stifling, thinking to herself she should do this more often.

'Aren't you going to yell at me, Mother?'

Aliah sighed and opened her eyes, her break from the pressures of being co-regent and parent all too short. 'Would it achieve anything if I did?'

Mina didn't answer immediately, and Aliah marvelled at how changing her normal instinct to go on the defensive when attacked altered the dynamics between them. She grimaced; how she loathed it when Dominic was right.

'No... I guess not,' Mina admitted. 'I'm not going back though, so you may as well allow me to train as a guard and let me do my service to the country my way.'

Aliah clenched her fists and took some calming breaths, willing herself not to respond by telling her daughter her disobedience would not be rewarded by giving her what she wanted. Closing her eyes, she imagined herself talking to Duke Damon, her closest ally and leader of the Southern Duchy. Although they were friends, the duke had his own mind and often had to be persuaded to act in the interests of Aria as a whole.

'Mum, aren't you going to say anything?' Mina sat forward and stared at her mother.

Her daughter's eagerness for her parent to agree with her might play to Aliah's advantage. Focused on her end goal, she might not notice a more subtle approach, and in the meantime, she could teach Mina to build a better argument—one not based on "I want".

'Yes, Mina, I have plenty to say on this matter....'

Mina took a deep breath, as if preparing herself for another long lecture. In response, Aliah closed her eyes and relaxed against the tree, enjoying the warmth of the day and planning the best way to approach her argument. While she was thinking, Mina's impatience prodded her like tiny needles pricking her consciousness.

'Mum?'

'Maybe we can start by me admitting it was wrong to force you to attend school on Wizard Isle.' Aliah opened her eyes long enough to catch the startled expression on her daughter's face before it returned to its usual, sullen mask. 'I didn't do you the courtesy of treating you like an adult, and you responded by running away, just as a child would... so I shouldn't be surprised.' Voicing her apology caused some of Aliah's own anger to dissipate.

'I am not a child!' Mina spat, and an image of a cat arching its back ready to fight popped into Aliah's mind. Instead of telling her daughter if she wanted to be treated like a grown-up, she should start behaving like one, she said, 'Your father's and my reasons for sending you to school on the isle were not only aimed at benefitting Aria. It's true we wanted you to become a role model for others by becoming the first female licenced magic practitioner in the land—'

Mina snorted. Aliah ignored her.

'We believed learning how to use and control your magic would open more choices for you in the future.' Holding up her hand, she forestalled Mina's usual comments at this stage of the argument. 'When we discuss this, you always say, "I don't want to use my magic. I want to be a guard and serve my country in a troop somewhere in Aria".'

'Yes.' Mina's tone was weary, as if she did not quite trust this reasoned approach from her mother.

'You'd follow that up with something like "You're turning me into a slave to the nation, trampling on my free will," and other such things. Have I summarised correctly?'

'I guess... mostly.'

'What did I miss?' Aliah raised an eyebrow.

'I am not sure I want to be heir to the crown, or ever rule Aria, so all this is moot.'

Mina's sulky tone set Aliah on edge, and she imagined giving in to her initial reaction to shake her daughter until her teeth rattled. Unfortunately, that would not do anyone any good. Aliah closed her eyes again and prayed to the goddess for patience before answering. 'You're a moon-turn away from your seventeenth birthday, when you are required to begin your year's service to the crown. Let's sort the next twelve moon-turns out and worry about the future later.'

'All right, if it will make this go more quickly.'

The concession was given grudgingly, but Aliah was happy to take the small win. Gritting her teeth, she attempted to build momentum. 'So now that we are agreed the focus will be on your service to the crown, let's look at this problem a little more closely. Why do members of the royal family offer themselves to Aria for a year?'

Again, a dramatic sigh preceded Mina's answer. Clearly, discussing this with her mother was almost too much for her to bear. 'We've been over this a thousand times.'

'We have, but please indulge me.'

'You always tell us "We grow up with many privileges, and it is our way of paying Aria back before we set out on our chosen paths as adults", but *you* never did it, did you?' Mina blurted out.

Goddess! Aliah couldn't decide what to do. Should she allow herself to be side-tracked, or should she carry on as planned? It would be easier to ignore the outburst, but she was aware if she didn't respond, Mina would continue to use this as an excuse to back out of anything they agreed to. 'When I was younger than you, I was forced to leave for a faraway land to wed a foreign king I'd never met—'

'But you didn't marry him.'

'No, I didn't, thank the goddess. However, the barons and the council thought risking my life to save Aria from the Carsten invasion more than counted as my service to the crown.'

'Of course, how could we forget... you're The Great Warrior, saviour of Aria.'

Bitterness laced Mina's words. Ordinarily, this would cause Aliah a mass of guilt, followed by her either giving in or getting angry— because she was mindful of how having ballads sung about your mother's bravery could not be easy on a child. This time though, she pushed her own negative emotions aside and struggled on. 'Mina, I am talking to you as a mother and your queen, not as The Warrior. Being Aria's saviour is my past—and I'm happy for it to remain history. Besides, it has no bearing on what we're discussing now. You grew up a princess in this palace, well educated and well cared for. In return for all you've received, we ask you to give something back to the people of this country.'

'But—'

Aliah pressed on. 'In the past, for princesses, this meant cementing Aria's ties either internally or externally through marriage.'

Mina groaned under her breath. Aliah continued as if she hadn't heard. 'Your father and I convinced the king's council to change the laws and allow for female royal children to do something for Aria, just like their brothers would.'

'I have no problem with that, and I appreciate not being forced to marry some power-obsessed male who only sees me for my title. I just don't understand why my year can't be spent in the guard.'

'Because so far, the only benefit your father and I can identify is you want to do it, which totally misses the point of giving service being about what Aria *needs...* not what you want.'

Aliah realised she had pushed too hard too fast when she saw the stubborn set of her daughter's face.

Mina folded her arms and leaned back against the trunk. 'Perhaps you should marry me off then, if this is all too difficult for you.'

Opening and closing her fists to release the building tension, Aliah fought the urge to lash out in the same way her daughter had. Only her experience from their previous encounters held her back. Reacting to the taunt would not get them anywhere. Stretching, she said, 'Perhaps I have been remiss in passing on some of our family history. Maybe you would not be so quick to become a bride if you had experienced what it feels like to be treated as chattel.'

'I don't believe you could tell me anything that would make marriage less appealing than spending a year on Wizard Isle.'

'Challenge accepted, although I think the branches of a tree are not the best place for storytelling. While you take your belongings back to your room, I'll organise some food and join you. Then I can tell you about the first Natari princess to come to Aria.' In the following silence, Aliah wondered if Mina had taken the bait.

'Okay, see you soon.' Mina swung down to the ground and threw her pack over her shoulder. As she ran towards the palace, a mass of dark, unruly hair escaped its bindings and caught in the straps of her bag.

Taking a more measured approach, Aliah climbed down and stretched her limbs before walking back through the castle.

***

AFTER THE CALM of the apple tree, the kitchens were a mass of frantic activity. Aliah stopped a serving boy to ask for food to be taken to her daughter's room, before heading upstairs via the servants' passages to the first floor, where most of the work managing the realm took place.

She ducked her head into Dominic's office to find him finishing up with a messenger. He waved for her to wait. 'You might be interested in these,' he said as the man closed the door behind himself. 'They're the latest updates from Duke Hubert.'

Aliah picked up the documents and perched on the edge of a chair as she read. As Duke of the Western Realm, Dominic's brother was a strong supporter of the crown, as well as caring diligently for his subjects. Of late, his dispatches had been increasingly full of details of unrest on the borders to the Unknown Lands, and today's were no different.

'He still doesn't want us to do anything?' Aliah glanced up in time to catch Dominic shake his head. 'He's being ridiculous. This is the third attack on a patrol since his initial reports of people settling in the Ariel Mountains.' She dropped the papers on Dominic's desk. 'We should send a guard troop regardless of what Hubert advises.'

'Is that wise? I mean, our barons don't look kindly on the crown throwing its might around, and Hubert is no different, even if he is my brother.'

Aliah reached for her plait and tugged it gently. 'The safety of the realm and the people of Aria must come first,' she insisted.

Dominic frowned. He was close to his twin brother and always felt conflicted when, as his king, he had to go against him. 'I think we should wait before acting. I'd like to hear how his delegation is received and consider the settler's response to it.'

'Won't waiting put our border settlements more at risk?' Aliah asked.

'I don't believe so. Also, I would like to find out more about what's going on in the Unknown Lands, what's making people flee for their lives, before we go stomping in with hobnail boots.'

Aliah's thoughts finally caught up with her husband's. 'Ah, so you're thinking about the news Seamus sent in his latest reports from Sanctuary. Do you think these two problems might be linked?'

Dominic smiled at her. 'I do indeed. The edge of Sanctuary's holdings is not far from the Unknown Lands, and I'm worried there's something going on there that is causing people to flee for their lives.'

'I always thought it stupid to call somewhere the Unknown Lands,' Aliah commented. 'They have always discouraged visitors, even traders, and they've never attempted to make contact with any of their neighbours. Their isolationist approach means when something like this happens, the surrounding countries become suspicious. The lack of official channels for communication means we have gone straight to border skirmishes rather than discussing the issues and agreeing on a solution.'

'The inhabitants of Sanctuary originated from the area, as did most of the population on Hand, so we're not totally in the dark about the people fleeing over the mountains,' Dominic reminded her. 'Even I've read a little of their history. In fact, I believe records in Sanctuary name the region as Talagria.'

'You've been speaking with Seamus,' Aliah accused, unsure why she was annoyed her husband had kept their conversation from her. Sure, she and Seamus had joined forces to save Aria as The Wizard and The Warrior. And yes, he was like a brother to her, but he was also Dominic's friend.

'A couple of times. Between us, we have enough strength to mind speak for short periods. I asked him to find out what he could from records in the Sanctuary archives. You're not angry, are you?' Dominic's voice sounded uncertain, which it only did when he thought Aliah was winding up into one of her rants.

As a young girl, she had allowed her passions to rule her better judgement, especially when she believed others didn't respect her opinion. As an adult, she tried to control her outbursts. Now, they mostly only happened with her husband, and only in periods of intense stress. Instead of flying off the handle, Aliah reached forward and took her husband's hand. 'No, I'm not. Although I am a little taken by surprise,' she said. 'Normally, we'd talk these things through together, but thank you for taking this off my plate.'

Dominic gently squeezed her fingers. 'You were so preoccupied with the trade representatives from Carsten, not to mention our daughter's headstrong behaviour, so I thought I would handle this myself—check out what was happening before I brought it to your attention.'

'And now you believe there's something more here; otherwise, you wouldn't be speaking to me about it now.'

A grimace passed over her husband's face, quickly replaced by a wry smile. 'Unfortunately, I do. I need a longer conversation with Seamus to confirm my suspicions—'

'And you can't mind speak for long without me,' Aliah finished for him.

'Now that I have a more complete picture of activity in the borderlands, I want to talk with Seamus to clarify some details, and the sooner the better.'

Aliah closed her eyes, picturing the rest of her day: afternoon tea with Mina, before changing for dinner with the Carstenites. She would be weary after attending the state function, but if the dinner finished early, she might be able to squeeze it in later this evening. 'After the meal tonight?' she offered.

'You won't be too tired? These formal things can be so wearying.' Dominic's concern was heart-warming.

'Yes, they are, but perhaps we can arrange for a messenger to interrupt us during dessert—one able to act suitably worried. Then we'll have an excuse to leave a little early to attend to an urgent matter.'

'I *do* love the way your mind works.' Dominic's eyes sparkled.

'Now, if I am to have any time free tonight, I must go and spend a few candle marks with our wayward daughter.' Aliah rose.

'How's it going, dare I ask?'

'Mmm...,' Aliah said as she opened the door. 'Let's say it is a work in progress. I must hurry. I need to find something in our rooms before I meet with her.'

TIGHTLY GRIPPING THE SLIM VOLUME, Aliah pushed open the door to her daughter's room. At least Mina had changed into a gown, albeit a plain one. She leaned forward in her chair, stuffing honey cakes into her mouth. Fortunately, good manners, or perhaps years of training, forced her to sit up and attempt to hide her gluttony as her mother sat opposite.

'I see you started without me,' Aliah said as she placed the book on the table before pouring tea for them.

'I didn't get breakfast or lunch today,' Mina said, reaching for another honey cake.

Aliah glared at her daughter with a stare perfected during sixteen years of motherhood.

'All right, missing meals was my own fault, and hunger is no excuse for bad manners.' Mina placed the cake on a plate and added a couple of small sandwiches before proceeding to eat her meal with a little more decorum.

Looking through the open window at the distant mountains, Aliah wished she were anywhere but here. It was a perfect day for a ride through the forests, or perhaps some hand-to-hand combat would work out some of her frustrations. Swallowing her sigh lest her daughter take it the wrong way, Aliah sipped her tea and studied Mina over the rim of the cup.

Her bright blue eyes and jet-black hair marked her as her father's daughter, but her features and her stubbornness were all from Aliah. If only the potential heir to the throne had inherited her father's diplomatic skills and less volatile nature, this situation would be so much easier.

'Why are you looking at me like that?' Mina paused with a sandwich halfway to her mouth.

'No reason. I was just thinking how grown up you are. I can't believe it is time for you to give your year to the crown already. When your father and I first came up with the idea, your seventeenth birthday seemed so far away.'

Mina shrugged. 'I always thought it was more about saving your sister from a horrible marriage, rather than anything to do with me specifically.'

'It was... sort of. Cece was a lot younger than me, and you were only a month or so old when the council proposed a suitable marriage for her. Given their last foray into the field of forging diplomatic alliances using royal children saw my father betrothing me to the king of Carsten as a way to prevent them from invading—'

'This isn't news,' Mina interrupted. 'You escaped when you found out they were going to invade anyway, and you and Uncle Seamus saved Aria not only from the Carstenites, but also from a god taking over our world. Every child in the land is forced to read *The Wizard and The Warrior Chronicles* in class.'

Aliah clenched a hand and tried to release the anger building inside. When she and Seamus fought against the Carsten army headed by a god, it had been so much more than the story written in the chronicles, but this was not the time for that discussion. Her lesson today was far more important than her own ego. 'I used my experiences and the repercussions to convince my father to agree Cece could decide whether or not to marry to further the interests of the crown. He spoke before the council and talked them into writing into law that princesses were not bound to give their lives, instead—'

'I remember this bit. Father came up with the idea of tithing one year in service to Aria like the boys.' Mina looked at her mother, blue eyes glittering like sapphires. 'Cece chose the marriage option, and come to think of it, I would rather marry a complete stranger than spend my time on Wizard Isle with its supercilious inhabitants.'

'You're only saying that because your father and I would not force such a situation on you.'

'No, I'm not.'

'I don't think you appreciate what a change this was for Aria, allowing a woman to have some say in her own future. Perhaps learning what some of your ancestors gave up for Aria might help you understand why this seemingly small concession was so important, and why your tithe year, the first female one to be given in service in Aria, must really mean something.' Aliah's voice sounded stilted and harsh to her own ears. Her helplessness at being sold off to the highest bidder for the benefit of Aria had changed her, and she thanked the goddess every day she had not been forced to go through with the marriage. 'How about I tell you something of the first Natari princess to set foot in Aria?' She attempted to lighten her tone to encourage Mina to open her mind and listen to her.

'If you must,' Mina responded, her gaze staring through the open window. 'Is this going to be a long story?'

Aliah knew she only had a short time before her active daughter grew impatient. She hoped the parts she had marked in the book would hold Mina's interest and inspire her to learn more. Still, she didn't want to appear desperate, so she refilled their cups before answering.

'The story is short, but my hope is, however forlorn, you will think on what you hear long enough to allow her experiences to inform your decision.'

Picking up the book from the table, she flicked to the first entry she had marked. The pages were well worn, as many before her had found comfort in the words between the covers.

'What's that?' Mina's voice was even, but the way she leaned forward as she spoke showed her rising interest.

'One of your ancestors' diaries.'

Mina slumped back in the chair. 'I'm not sure some angst-ridden ramblings of a teenage girl will convince me to change my mind.'

'I don't expect you to think differently after this. I only want you to consider what she says.' Aliah hopefully hid her irritation at her daughter's pig-headedness. 'And don't worry, I'm not going to read the whole book. I've selected a few little snippets to give you an idea of her life.' Picking up her cup, she leaned back in the chair and began reading from the story her mother first told her when she was old enough to understand what her future was likely to be. The queen had intended the writings to prepare Aliah. She, on the other hand, read them to her own child to illustrate what she had saved her from.

CHAPTER 2
PROPHECY

A NEW LIFE

The blustering wind-filled sails cause the ship to lurch to the side. Josina and Edmund shiver. I can't tell whether from fear or because of the cold air piercing their clothes.

The journey has been an arduous one. The farther south we travel, the greater the distance from our homeland, the colder the weather becomes, almost as though it mirrors the chill in my heart.

I stiffen my resolve and stand tall, unwilling to let the others see my fear. As a princess, it is up to me to show them how much I am looking forward to our new life. I can't let them know how nervous I am, journeying across the sea to marry a complete stranger to seal the alliance between two powerful nations.

For as long as I can remember, I've been told that, as a princess of The Blood, I have one job and one job only—to marry to strengthen the state and our family's hold over it. I've always known this was to be my fate, but I had hoped not to be sent so far from Nataria. Although, to be fair, I had grown up with most of the single Natarian nobles, and I would not choose to spend the rest of my life with any one of them.

At least coming to Hand is a sort of adventure. No one knows me or my past. It is a perfect opportunity to become the person I want to be. Surely that will make up for the cold weather and the aching loneliness in my heart.

This is a new start, I tell myself over and over, and it helps calm my nerves, and my stomach begins to settle. The ship lurch again, and my breakfast threatens to make a reappearance. The straight between Hand and Port Marden was rumoured to be treacherous even in the best weather, and it's living up to its reputation.

Gripping the rail, once again, I straighten my spine and force myself to stand proud. When I arrive, I want the people on the Island of Hand to see who a princess of The Blood really is.

After what feels like an age, but is probably only a few minutes, a landmass draws closer, and activity around me increases. The Captain advances over the rolling deck, feet as certain as if he walked on land.

'Your Highness, it's best if you return to your cabin now as I need everything clear for docking.'

I open my mouth to object, but his lips tighten in anticipation of my argument, so I paste a smile on my face. 'Thank you, Captain. Please let us know when we may disembark.'

The Arian words sound odd coming from my mouth, but I am thankful Edmund has been helping me brush up on my pronunciation during the journey.

Below deck, the motion of the ship is magnified, and as I enter my cabin, I groan in frustration. My future husband's first glimpse of me will be of a woman laid low by sea sickness. I want him to see me as the strong, independent person I am, not someone who needs to be coddled and cared for.

I lie on my bed and close my eyes, imagining myself back on the balcony of my room at home with the sun warming my skin, and the time passes more quickly. I sit up at the sound of a knock on the door. It's the ship's boy.

'Captain says you can come back up now.' He turns to leave, but my maid Josina reaches up from her seat on the bunk and touches his arm.

'We can leave the ship?' she asks him, forming the words slowly in the unfamiliar tongue.

'No, ma'am. The Harbour Master must check the paperwork before we can begin unloading. After that, you can leave. Captain says he will send a man for your things, but you can wait on deck.'

As we make our way into the fresh air, the ship shudders one final time as it nudges the wharf below, and I get my first sight of the place I am to call home. The houses sprawl from the flat land behind the docks, up the sloping edges towards a palace that sits atop one of the hills surrounding the harbour. The dwellings closest are mostly grey stone, but the ones higher up are whitewashed, and some are painted in blues and yellows and reds, lending a little colour to the otherwise dull day.

While the ropes are thrown down to secure the ship, I survey the people who are to become my new subjects. Their clothing is sombre, but their faces are warm and friendly as they move back and forward while they work.

The docking process is swift, and I soon find myself leading our group down the gangplank and to a plain black carriage with a gold insignia on the side, which I take to be the coat of arms of my betrothed's family—the insignia of the ruling family of Hand. The door is opened by a liveried official, and I am surprised there is no one inside.

'The duke sends his apologies, Your Highness. Something came up that required his immediate attention. He extends an invitation for you to join him in the family quarters for a meal this evening.' He bows and ushers us inside.

'Well, I—' Josina starts, but I hold up a hand to silence her. Even though her words are Natarian, that is no guarantee they will not be understood.

'Thank you,' I say to the man and take my seat with as much dignity as I can muster, having not yet regained my land-legs. Once I am seated, the door closes, and we are on our way to our new home.

'This is not a good sign,' Josina says as the carriage starts to move and no one can overhear us.

'The duke may be dealing with an unavoidable situation,' Edmund answers. He is always the voice of reason.

I say nothing and work at keeping my face impassive. I do not want anyone, not even Josina and Edmund, to know how bereft I am, entering my new home alone rather than on the arm of the duke. I am very aware I am a symbol of the people who conquered Hand, a duchess forced on them as part of the peace treaty at the end of a long, bloody invasion. Their acceptance of me relies totally on my new husband's support.

Before I left home, father assured me the duke was a fair and caring man—a man who promised to treat me with respect. He trusted this foreigner's word, and that trust bolstered my resolve to travel to Hand and to do my duty. As the carriage made its way through the streets to the castle, I hoped my father's trust had not been misplaced.

Through the window, I watched as the houses grew more ornate and realised we must be close to our final destination. I schooled my face into a polite smile as we passed through a gate in the defensive wall around the palace precinct. The carriage sweeps in a wide circle and pulls up.

The footman jumps down and opens the door, and I glimpse marble steps leading up to the main entrance. A carpet in the blue of the Natarian royal family has been rolled out, and a tall, gaunt man with tufting grey hair moves forward and bows stiffly before offering his arm.

'Your Highness, I am Bertram. I offer the sincere and heartfelt apologies of my duke. Please be assured that only a matter of the gravest importance would prevent him from being with you today.'

I nod once, accepting his apology as custom dictated, and place my hand on his arm. Holding my head high as we walk, I hope I am hiding the hurt and worry churning my stomach from the crowd who has gathered in the courtyard to catch their first sight of the new duchess.

'I will escort you and your companions to the guest chambers.'

As Bertram leads us up the main stairs and along the first-floor corridor, he wears the blank mask of a professional diplomat. It was from the faces of the servants we passed on the way that I draw the conclusion we are not welcome in here.

'Your Highness,' Bertram said as he stopped and opened a stout wooden door.

The rooms inside were sumptuous. The fire in the grate welcomed us, as did the light snack waiting on the table by the window. I could make out two doors leading from the main sitting room. I turned to Bertram to ask about the rest of our accommodation to find he had moved across the hallway and opened the door opposite.

'If your companions would sleep in here tonight, we can find them suitable quarters after the ceremony tomorrow when we move you into the family rooms.'

'Thank you, Bertram. This will suit us well.'

He bowed and backed away. 'I will leave you to settle. His Grace hopes to come and escort you to dinner himself just after sundown. I will send one of the maids to prepare a bath for you.'

'Thank you, that will be most welcome.'

As he left, Josina took control of the servants who had followed us bearing our belongings from the ship. In an effort to keep out of her way, Edmond and I retreated to my sitting room, and we each filled a plate with food, then warmed ourselves by the fire.

After maintaining formalities for the first few days of our travels,

I fast learnt we would get along much better if we dispensed with them when we were in private.

Josina had been my personal maid since we were both little, no more than children. The only person closer to me had been my older sister. Edmond had been my tutor, and I was grateful he had agreed to come to Hand as my personal advisor. Until I found my feet, these were the only two people I trusted in my new home, the only two people I could be almost myself with.

We were nearly done eating when Josina joined us, and I excuse myself, retiring to my bedroom. My bath is ready, and I intend to make the most of the hot water, adding some bath salts I brought with me before stepping in and allowing the rose-scented liquid to soothe away my tensions.

Once the water cools, I towel myself dry, and wrap a warm lounging gown around my shivering form. Not wanting to rejoin the others, I slip under the covers and curl into a ball. The next thing I know, Josina is knocking and calling through the door.

'Your Highness, Bertram is here with some news.'

I rub the sleep from my eyes and sit up. After checking in the mirror to ensure I'm presentable, I open the door. Bertram straightens himself before bowing.

'Thank you, Bertram, but I am sure we can dispense with these formalities unless it is a state occasion,' I say. 'Is there news for me?'

'Your Highness. The duke has sent word that he will be tied up for the evening. Everything.... Things were worse than he first thought.'

'Is it anything I can assist with?' I ask. I do not want to become the wife who sits at home waiting for her husband, when she can aid him in his duties.

Bertram wasn't quite quick enough to hide his shock at my offer. 'Thank you, but I'm sure everything will be under control before the ceremony tomorrow.'

'The men who brought our luggage from the docks said the council was meeting today. Some of the nobles vehemently objected to your wedding and threatened to expel the duke, intending to replace him with one of his cousins,' Josina says in Natari.

'It is not as bad as it sounds,' Bertram blusters, confirming my suspicions that he can understand our language. 'A few details need to be ironed out before tomorrow, that's all.'

Although disappointed at not being able to meet my husband before our wedding day, at least I now know why he's not with me. He's fighting for the very peace I had come here to cement.

'Thank you for letting me know, Bertram. We will take our supper here.'

I returned to my room and close the door before anyone can see the tears threatening to spill from my eyes.

'I AM TOO YOUNG FOR THIS.'

The thought goes through my head as I stand in the doorway to the great hall. Angrily, I push it away. This is not the time for doubts. Concentrating on putting one foot in front of the other, I move between the lines of nobles, deftly navigating the aisle they create for me. I walk the length of the throne room.

In the style of Natari, I am covered from head to foot in the palest of blue silk. As a princess of Imperial Blood, a golden diadem studded with sapphires sits on my head, holding the veil in place—a visible sign I stand above those I walk between.

Although I am fully clothed in the manner of my people, I have never felt more naked. The gazes of Hand's nobles penetrate the royal persona I present to them. It is as though they see right through me, and their barely conceal hatred caused my hands to tremble. I lift my eyes and stare proudly ahead, and I continue walking as if I was attending court at home, where I am adored.

Standing on the platform in front of me is the man I married by proxy at my grandfather's command. The emperor decreed I, his favourite grandchild, would be bound to tall, proud King of The Old Blood to seal the peace between our two peoples.

Sean, Duke of Hand, with his dark curling hair, swarthy complexion, and almost black eyes, looks so strange and foreign. Still, his face radiates compassion, and my heart melts a little as he smiles his encouragement.

Nearing the end of his twenties, he is in his prime—a handsome and powerful man. As if it has a mind of its own, my body shivers in anticipation of tonight. After the celebrations, our marriage will be consummated, and I no longer find that thought distasteful. In fact, the thought crosses my mind that this barbarian might one day make a suitable consort, but only time will tell.

Ignoring the cold stares and whispers surrounding me, I keep my gaze fixed on him as I walk proudly through my enemies. They may not want me here, but I will do my duty to my emperor and family. I will bring peace to these lands.

For a moment, the duke's gaze waivers, and his eyes sweep the room. A frown draws his brows together, but he is smiling again when he looks back at me. He holds out his hand, drawing me forwards. Both my body and soul respond.

Perversely, at the exact moment when I begin to believe I might find some personal happiness in this marriage, someone yells, 'Die foreign whore!'

From the corner of my eye, I catch something metal flying across the room. Instinctively, I hold up my hand, stopping the weapon mid-flight a mere handspan from my face. I release it, and the knife clatters to the ground accompanied by a collective gasp.

The silence that follows my action is eerie, and it takes me a moment to realise why. They are not appalled by the fact that someone attempted to murder me. The nobles of Hand are astounded, because they just witnessed magic used in their halls for the first time—ever.

I slump as I remember Edmund's most often repeated lesson. When their forebears arrived on the island, they decided all would live by the hand alone and banned all use of sorcery. Now, not only have I broken a generations-old prohibition in a very public arena, but I announced my magical abilities to the world.

The air around me thrums with the wrath of the nobles. It was of no matter to them I had done this to defend myself.

I look to my husband. His face is a picture of dismay as he leaves the dais and makes his way through the crowd to my side.

***

MY FORMAL WEDDING ceremony is a blur. I repeat some words, I am given a ring, and the next thing I know, I am standing on the deck of a boat, watching the Port of Hand recede. My wedding finery is covered by my husband's cloak, and he holds me close as he talks, almost as if he is afraid I will blow away in the wind.

'Your maid is organising your things to be packed. I will send the boat back when we dock, and she and your advisor will be with you by morning.'

I incline my head, indicating I hear his words. I still do not understand why I can't spend my wedding night in my new home.

'I am sorry it has to be this way.' My husband rests his cheek on my head. 'I spent all day yesterday soothing my nobles, reassuring them that by marrying you nothing on Hand would change. Sure, we will get a new overlord, I told them, but my marriage means he will trust us to run Southern Aria ourselves.'

The consequences of my actions hit me as he spoke, and I whispered, 'And then I, on my first introduction to your court, break one of your oldest laws. I am so sorry. I didn't think.'

His arm tightens around me. 'No, it is I who should apologise. I didn't realise the level of risk I placed you in so soon after their outburst. If I had only realised how far some people would go to stop the wedding, I would have changed the ceremony, making it more private, and had you more heavily guarded. Will you ever be able to forgive me for placing your life in danger?'

'There is nothing to forgive,' I say. 'But tell me, why do we flee from these traitors? Would we not be better served to stand together and show we are not afraid of them?'

'Normally, I would be in agreement with you, but the man who threw the knife was one of my own household staff. Until I find out how deep this treachery goes, I cannot vouch for your safety on the island.'

'I am not afraid.' I am, but my pride will not let me admit to this. 'I can defend myself.'

He chuckles, and I can feel the rumble in his chest as he does. 'I bet you can. Unfortunately, there is much more at stake than your physical wellbeing, and I cannot take the risk that something might happen to you. After having negotiated peace with your family, it would quickly unravel should anything happen to you. We would be back killing each other, and I fear it would be worse than before.'

'I see.' And I do. I am more than a person. I am a symbol—a symbol that can both bind our people or tear them apart again. 'So where do we go now?'

'I have a house in Port Marden. Truth be told, it is more modern and more comfortable than the palace, and I prefer it there. We can stay tonight and plan our next steps. I think though, for the foreseeable future, it will become your new home.'

DUCHESS

Rain drizzles from a grey sky, turning the cobblestones on the street below a darker hue of slate. How cold and dreary this inhospitable place is compared to Nataria. Yet, standing in the window overlooking the street below, I realise over the past year I have grown accustomed to Port Marden.

The port town is always bustling, and there are a number of other foreign-born women living here, and they have welcomed me into their community with open arms. Together, we managed to secure a lease on a building and hope to open an orphanage in the new year.

Although I am far from my home and my family, at least here I feel useful. In fact, I would go as far as to say I would rather be here than anywhere else.

It is market day today, so despite the inclement weather, the street is still quite busy. Many of the figures huddled against the cold cross to the other side of the road rather than walking past the house where I live; a couple actually spit on the pavement outside. These are the people who arrived on the ferry from Hand, and their behaviour does not surprise me. What does interest me is that they chose to walk down the street where the "Natari Whore" lives at all. Perhaps the cold makes them think twice about taking the more circuitous route to the main square.

In recent months, their anger towards me increased. In their eyes, not only has their beloved duke been forced to marry a witch, but now the Natari nation was foisting my baby on them as the next heir to the ducal throne. The bloodline of the leading family on Hand would be tainted forever. It was because of the outbursts from some of the more vocal nobles that my husband had put off my return to the island. To him, my safety and that of our child was more important than anything.

I argued this course of action was giving in to our enemies. Not only did they continue to keep me from the palace, but it also gave them licence to question the legitimacy of our child as heir. Some of our friends supported me, but the memory of the knife being thrown at my head was too vivid an image for my duke to change his mind.

As if my baby senses I am thinking about it, it kicks as it moves inside me. I place my hand on my stomach and rub gently. 'Calm down, little one. I know you are eager to join us out here, and you will, soon. Just one more moon turn, and we will meet in person.'

I glimpse a familiar figure turn the corner. He glances up, and his eyes lock with mine just as they did the first day we met, and my heart skips a little as I smile. 'Look, little one, your father is here.'

My eyes follow his progress until I can see him no more, but I stay at my look-out, unmoving, until I know he is finally with me. I feel a cool breeze at my back as the door swings open. My heart beats faster, but I do not rush into his arms as I long to. I wait until he is almost beside me, and I turn to allow him to kiss me on both cheeks as Arian custom demands, before throwing myself into his arms.

My protruding stomach comes between us, but he bends down and gives me what I consider to be a proper kiss before tucking some wisps of hair behind my ear. He places a hand on my stomach.

'Our baby is active today. I think she will be like her mother, with honey hair and violet eyes and more energy than is sensible for one person to have.'

This is our little game, and I answer as I always do.

'Our son will be tall and strong like his father and will have dark eyes and black, curly hair, so your people will accept him as the next duke of the Southern Duchy and king of his people.'

Ours was not a love match, but standing together against the people of Hand had forged a strong bond between us. Although it was not the custom here, my husband consults me when making major decisions. He has a wit and intelligence that match my own, and I am growing more than fond of him, and I believe he has similar feelings for me.

I spy papers in his hand, and ask, 'You found out more about the prophecy?'

'I ordered refreshment brought up. The documents can wait until we relax and catch up on all the other news.'

He can be infuriating too, but I play this game. I follow him over to the two chairs placed either side of the fire, taking the one closest to the window. He tells me all the news from Hand, and I tell him the marketplace gossip from Port Marden. We drink our tea, but I cannot take my eyes off the papers. I fidget in my chair, and he raises a single eyebrow.

'I can wait no longer. Show me, please.'

He leans over and takes the scrolls off the table, then hands them to me. 'There is another in my bag. I found them precisely where I dreamed I would.'

I take them from him and eagerly begin reading. For a moment, I forget everything except the words in front of me, although I am sure my face reflects my joy. When I am finished, I look up. 'This is word for word as you recounted from your dream,' I say, brushing the tears from my eyes. 'We were fated to marry and fated to begin a line that would fulfil a great prophecy.'

He simply nods and passes me the final scroll. 'This one is not quite so certain as the others. It hints at the possibility of your line from Nataria fulfilling the prophecy alone. I guess the art of prophecy and foreseeing are not always so clear cut.'

I cannot stop myself frowning. I would hate for someone to be able to use this information against us. As I read, I realise this document is not as detailed as the others, and the arguments are not as strong. 'Is this enough to convince your dissenters that our marriage is in the best interests of Hand?'

There is a tightening of the muscles around his mouth, and I know the answer before he speaks. 'For the majority of my subjects, nothing we give them will ever be enough. You displayed your magic in public, and that will not be forgotten, or forgiven—ever.

'I do not ask forgiveness, only that they allow me to return without endangering my or our children's lives.'

'Many of those of the Old Blood say you should be put to death. The fact that you are here in Port Marden, where they allow spell casting, drives them crazy. Not even the knowledge we are likely to be starting a line that will save our people in the future will change their minds. In fact, many of them may never accept our child as heir.'

Too agitated to remain seated, I stand and pace out my frustrations.

'That's so hypocritical. You use your foresight for the good of your people all the time, and I am sure I sensed others on the island using small spells and glamours.'

He sighs and takes me in his arms. I know he would do anything to take away my hurt, but there is nothing he can do.

'So long as no one uses their gifts in public, there is no evidence they have them. And to prove it, you would have to use magic and—'

'And that would be used against me.' I bury my face in his jacket, and he holds me tighter.

'And if anyone found out about my powers, I would lose my position as duke, and those in Hand with magical abilities would be worse off.'

My shoulders slump, my anger spent.

'If I was not duke, then I would not have been able to sue for the peace that stopped the war—a war that decimated my people and yours. There are many who still resent me for giving in, sure we would have won our independence if only we had continued fighting.'

'I know.' My voice is muffled, but I am sure he hears me.

'And if I were no longer duke, we would not be able to place our son on the throne and thus meet the conditions of the prophecy.'

I push away from him so I can see his eyes. 'If our baby is a boy, will they accept him?'

'I believe if we do not parade the fact that you are his mother in front of them, then I think they will not question his being my heir.'

'So, even though you found the scrolls stating our marriage was destined, it is now our destiny to live our lives in separate houses. Not only that, but I must be separated from my children.'

The pain of this knowledge cuts deep, and again tears fill my eyes.

'I know I ask a lot of you, but I will ask it anyway, for the sake of our children, and for the sake of both of our peoples.'

The pain in his eyes mirrors my own, and I wonder what sort of life we would have had if I had ducked instead of using magic to save myself. I shake the thought away. We cannot change the past; we can only control how we live from now.

'Come, our guests will arrive soon, and we still have to dress.'

I HOLD my son's hand as we wander through the market, trailing behind Josina. He is back for a rare few days holiday with his father, and I do not want to let him out of my sight. He, on the other hand, is fascinated by the fact that he is going to have a brother or sister and keeps reaching up to touch my stomach.

'Will they like me?' he asks, for perhaps the millionth time. Like his father, he is reassured by these ritual games.

'They will love you, and you will look after them, because you are bigger and older, and they will need your help while they grow up,' I tell him.

'But how will I do that, when they are here and I am at the palace?'

Every time I hear it, the question wrenches my heart. 'You will visit them, and they will visit you. You will spend plenty of time together, I promise.'

'I will miss them when I am not here, like I miss you.' His solemn brown eyes are too old for a five-year-old as he looks up at me.

'And I miss you too, my love.' I bend and kiss the top of his head. 'Now, we must not lose Josina.' I scan the crowds for signs of her.

'Oh, look, there is Annie. She cares for me sometimes when Nanny is busy. Annie, Annie,' he calls before I can stop him.

The woman standing by the vegetable stall looks up at the sound of his voice, starts to smile, sees me, then spits on the ground before turning away.

I glance down at the face of my son, catching sight of his anguish before his face returns to its usual smiling mask. 'She must not have recognised me,' he said, not quite masking the tremor in his voice.

'I am sure she didn't,' I tell him, allowing this untruth so he is not pulled between his two lives. 'Look, there's Josina.' I point out my friend and companion, and as we walk over to her, I cry inside. My son is too young to be dealing with this.

A LIFE WELL LIVED

I hold my beloved's hand, knowing I can do nothing more to take away the pain. All I can do is make him physically comfortable in these final hours. The hurt in his heart, I can do nothing for either.

I smooth the hair back from his forehead. It is now more salt than pepper, and his once smooth skin displays the patterns of the life he has lived. To me though, he is still the most handsome of men, and he is my one true love.

'Always, I seem to be asking something of you, something more than anyone should be asked to give. You arrived in my life as a beautiful, proud Natari princess. Because of your love for your people and your children, and I hope me, you lived most of our life together alone in this house. It is not the life I promised your father I would give you.

'In return for my mistreatment, you gave me more than I ever hoped for in a wife—support, love, and children. It is my greatest sadness no one will ever know how much I love you, or of all the work you did for the good of Hand and for the people of Aria. If only they had taken the time to look beyond their prejudices and get to know the real you. Now, I am leaving you to face the rest of this life alone.'

'I regret nothing,' I tell him. 'I never expected to love the man I married, nor that he would respect me and offer me an equal partnership. And I have found a certain amount of pleasure in my work with the orphans on the mainland, making some friends along the way. We produced three children who brought joy into our lives. There is nothing to apologise for.'

My husband manages a weak smile and squeezes my hand. 'You are right to remind me how fortunate we have been. It is easy to focus on the bad things, yet you remind me we had happy times. For people such as us to find love within our marriage is more than we expect. I will leave this earth a contented man.'

I lean over and kiss his forehead.

'I leave knowing we produced something that will live beyond us. We set in motion events leading to the rise of The Wizard and The Warrior—the two destined to defeat a great enemy and save both our peoples.'

His eyes close and his hand releases mine. My tears fall freely, as I know the end is near. My heart is breaking. I don't want him to leave me, but I cannot bear for him to continue like this.

Lying beside him, I wrap him in my arms one last time. His breath is a mere flutter against my cheek, and I hear him whisper, 'When the new power rises and The Wizard and Warrior meet, old and new blood will combine to save one and all. It has begun. I love you, my princess.'

Then he is gone.

***

JOSINA PLACES an arm around my shoulders and draws me closer. I sense Edmund move in behind me as if to protect me from the gazes of the strangers who watch the procession of my husband's coffin through the streets of Port Marden to the docks. From there, his body will be returned to Hand.

I taste the salt of tears flowing unchecked down my face and am thankful for the black lace veil hiding me from prying eyes. In the crowd, I am just one of many saying our final farewell to our duke.

As the cart carrying the coffin passes, my eyes linger before I raise them to meet the gaze of our eldest child—the one who is no longer my boy but Duke of the Southern Duchy. Responsibility sits well on his shoulders, but to me, he will always be the boy with the serious eyes who made me laugh.

My lips form a smile. Those who shunned me now crow at how fortunate they are to have the emperor's grandson leading their nation. My wily grandfather ensured a favourable reception for the new duke, bestowing some concessions on the Southern Duchy to come into force on the day he is crowned.

Yet, while they accept my children, it is as if I don't exist. In the end though, I will have the last word. I will not run away like they expect now that my partner as gone. I will remain and support my children, and carry on with the work I began years ago helping the poor children of the duchy—but that will not be my only solace.

I turn away. I've had enough of this charade.

I FEEL a gentle pressure on my shoulder, then strong arms lift me to my feet.

'It is done?' I ask.

My youngest child nods. 'The coffin now resides in the family crypt on Hand.'

I incline my head, and my gaze slips to the nondescript gravestone in front of us. On one side, the inscription reads **Sean of Hand. Beloved husband, father and son.** The other side is blank.

'Until tomorrow,' I say as I slip my hand into my youngest son's, and he helps me inside.

In death, we will no longer be apart, I silently add.

CHAPTER 3
THAT'S HISTORY

Having flicked through some of the most compelling entries in the book her many-times-great grandmother brought with her from Nataria, Aliah placed it on the table. She intended to "forget to take it with her" in the hopes Mina might be interested enough to read the whole thing—the passages speaking of the princess's loneliness, her hunger for a life she could never have, and feelings of powerlessness she hoped to save her own daughter from ever experiencing.

'I'm not sure what you want me to take from that,' Mina said as she stood and stretched. 'In essence, it's a story of love growing out of an arranged marriage.'

Aliah suppressed a smile; that was precisely what she wanted her daughter to pick up from the extracts. The idea was to give her enough to make her interested and to think she may have found a way to counter Aliah's arguments. If she was curious enough about her ancestor's life, she might read the rest for herself and learn something different. 'I guess you could look at it that way.'

'How would you describe it?'

'As a tale of two people who loved each other, kept apart because the needs of their countries and the threads of prophecy forced them to live a life contrary to their own desires.'

'So you only read the bits that reinforced your own view of the world?' Mina challenged her.

Working hard not to smile as her daughter walked into the trap she had laid, Aliah stood. 'Sadly, your reaction is not unexpected.' She pretended to be angry. 'I am sorry I can't discuss this further. I'm already late for dinner.' She stalked to the door as if she were indeed annoyed. 'Even though you have heard it all before, I hope you will think on the words of your ancestor in light of what you're facing, and perhaps we can spend some time together discussing it tomorrow.'

'You mean you want my decision then,' Mina shot back.

Pausing in the doorway, Aliah's head cocked to the side as she wondered how far she might safely push her daughter in the direction she wanted her to go. 'That's not what I said nor meant. We can talk for as long as it takes for all of us to feel comfortable that what you decide to do meets Aria's needs.'

'All of us?'

'Yes, you, me, and your father,' Aliah explained.

'He knows about this?' Mina's face screwed up in confusion.

Yes, my dear, so don't go crying on his shoulder, hoping he will rescue you from me. To her daughter, she said, 'Yes. In fact, it was his idea we spend some time talking—to give you the chance to put forward your thoughts. Then he expects you and I to work together to reach an agreement about your future.'

'Oh.' Mina's eyes widened.

'Today's tale was genuinely meant to give you an idea of what your ancestor was prepared to do for her country. My hope is it will help you think about how what you're proposing measures up to what she gave up.' Before her daughter could speak again, Aliah closed the door.

'SHE MADE me so angry with her "how does your plan stack up against the sacrifices others made for Aria in the past."' Mina paced about her brother's room while he sat in a chair by the fire, his eyes following her.

'She left the book behind when she went to dinner. I'm sure it was on purpose. Well, I think it was. I did needle her, and she got annoyed. So, maybe it wasn't on purpose after all.'

At the sound of suppressed laughter from her brother, Mina stopped midstep, turned, and glared at him. He laughed so much he couldn't get a word out. Hands on hips, she tried to maintain her anger, but she felt it slipping away.

A few minutes later, when Gabriel's laughter was under control enough for him to speak, he said, 'Do you ever listen to yourself? You sound like you're angry for the sake of being angry, and Mum just happened to be your target.'

Sinking into the chair opposite, Mina snorted. 'What would you know? You're her golden boy and can never put a foot wrong.'

'Really, Mina, thinking before I act doesn't make me her favourite, merely less troublesome than you.'

Gabriel brushed his fringe out of his eyes. He looked so like their mother, with his honey-gold hair and blue eyes. It was uncanny. All her friends thought he was quite the catch. Squinting at him, she couldn't see the attraction herself. Only a little over a year younger, he was smart and thoughtful, but he still could not best her in a swordfight, even though he was bigger and stronger, and she could outrace him on any four-legged animal. Still, he was a prince, and she guessed that went some way to make up for his lack of physical prowess.

'Mina. Mina!'

Shaking her head, she refocussed. 'Sorry... what?'

'I said, you read the rest of the book, didn't you? That's why you're so annoyed with Mum.'

Taking a deep breath, Mina said, 'Yes, of course I read it.'

'And you learnt something from it?' When Mina did not answer, Gabriel prompted her. 'Mina?'

'God's breath! Yes, I learnt something. That poor woman. I don't even know her name, yet I'm so angry over what she was forced to do. She married a complete stranger, then his people banished her from his home. She spent the rest of her life in exile from her family in Nataria and her children in Aria, snatching what time she could with a husband she grew to love—and all because she was expected to do what she could for her country.' Mina's eyes filled with tears.

'Her name was Edisha.'

'Sorry? What?'

'She was called Princess Edisha. She was the mother of the ruling family on the Isle of Hand, the matriarch of the southern dukes. And as the Natarian emperor's granddaughter, she is one of our many-times-great grandmothers,' Gabriel said.

Mina smiled. 'I might have guessed you would have come across her in your studies. Thank you for telling me. Finding out her name is recorded somewhere and that she was not forgotten by history makes me feel a little better.'

'So, what about her story roused so much anger? I mean, it can't be simply because she was expected to marry for the good of the realm—thanks to Mum and Dad, you dodged that arrow—so what is it?'

'When I think of everything Edisha went through for Nataria and Aria, and I think about my desire to spend my year of service in the army, and the fuss I've been making—it's like I'm a spoilt brat or something.'

'What makes you say that?'

'It's because I want to be a guard. I've wanted to since I first took up a sword. I realise now if I spend a year joining a troop as my service, I'm serving my desires rather than considering what it will contribute to Aria.'

'Why does coming to this realisation make you angry?' Gabriel leaned forward, as if to better hear her answer.

'Because I believe it's the lesson our mother wanted me to learn from Edisha's diary. She manipulated me.' As her anger dissipated, so did her energy. She knew with all her heart she didn't want to return to Wizard Isle, but she now also realised her parents were right; it might actually be the thing she needed to do to meet her obligations and secure her future.

'And you think that means you must go to the wizard school?' Gabriel asked, guessing her thoughts.

'Yes,' Mina whispered.

'Mina, you're smarter than that.'

'Sorry?' She shook her head, trying to clear the fog.

'That isn't the only option you have. All you need to do is find a way to convince our parents spending a year in the army will benefit Aria as well as you, in the same way attending the wizard school would have.'

Mina stared at her brother, allowing his words to sink in. Slowly, she nodded. He was right; this battle was not yet lost. If she could buy some time to pull together a half-decent argument, she still might win.

'Good,' Gabriel said, 'now the real Mina's back. Let's come up with a plan.'

As ALIAH UNDID the buttons on her blue formal gown, she regretted dismissing her maid earlier that evening. Although perfectly capable of undressing herself, it was awkward reaching all the fastenings, especially when exhausted from her long and tumultuous day. Just as she was about to give up, the door opened, and Dominic entered their bedroom.

When the messenger arrived, calling them away from dinner with the Carstenites, Dominic allowed Aliah to go ahead while he dealt with the formal goodbyes. His eyes twinkled when he saw her half-dressed state.

'It's a shame we have other business to attend to tonight,' he said as he undid the rest of her fastenings with the ease of practice.

Leaning back into him, she luxuriated in his embrace before pulling away and heading to their dressing room. Returning moments later in a loose robe, she found her husband lying on the bed. He had draped his royal blue jacket over the back of a chair and placed his boots neatly by the fire before closing his eyes to the world. Reluctant to invade his rest, Aliah nevertheless asked, 'Are you sure you want to do this tonight? Maybe we'd be better off getting some much-needed sleep and talking with Seamus in the morning.'

Running a weary hand over his forehead, Dominic sat up. 'No, we'd best do this now. I arranged an early meeting with the guard captains first thing tomorrow. I want their input on Hubert's report. It would be useful to have Seamus paint a fuller picture of the region before we meet.'

Resisting the urge to curl up beside him, Aliah moved instead to a chair by the fire. 'And I guess since Sanctuary observes the Sixth Day as a day of rest, he might not appreciate the interruption.'

Dominic pushed himself off the bed and headed towards the balcony doors. They had been opened to cool the room, but now the air was chilly, and he pulled them closed before stopping at the table to his left. Aliah's maid had thoughtfully arranged a pot of caffe and some mugs for them before retiring, and Dominic filled two cups before joining her.

She took a few sips of the drink while her husband sat. When he was settled, she placed her cup on the hearth and picked up the sword leaning against the chair. Placing it on her lap, her right hand gripping the hilt, she asked, 'Are you ready?'

Dominic nodded, and she closed her eyes, allowing the power of the gods-given sword to flow through her. Reaching inside, she found the core of her magic and imagined pushing it out of her body in a long strand. As she did, she gathered a little of the light-blue energy Dominic extended towards her. Merging their magical strands together, Aliah paused to take strength from her husband's presence before casting their awareness outwards.

In the darkness, she threaded them through the sparks of consciousness, which appeared as something akin to stars in the night sky. Keeping herself in check, she resisted the urge to gravitate towards the brightest lights, instead focussing on the gossamer thin line that would lead her to Seamus. A blink later, she arrived at Sanctuary, and her pathway forked. One path was a mass of swirling colours that led to Seamus's aunt, Amelia. The brightness of her link indicated she was dreaming a foretelling. With hardly a pause, Aliah followed the single gold thread that would lead her to her friend.

She slowed down as she reached the bright ball of Seamus's essence, and whispered, *Seamus, are you awake?*

Mm... what? Aliah? Is that you? And Dominic too? This must be important.

Aliah sensed warmth as Seamus opened his mind to her. He was sitting by a fire with a book in his lap. She chuckled as she remembered when they had first started mind speaking how he had taken over her consciousness, and it had been difficult for her to even think, let alone speak while they were connected. Nowadays, he imagined a room—Aliah supposed it must be much like his living room in Sanctuary—so they could meet and talk in comfort, almost like they were visiting in person. Having created the link, Aliah relaxed a little, which Seamus translated into her taking the other seat by the fire. He also imagined Dominic sitting at the nearby table.

Although Dominic could mind speak well over short distances, he was unable to maintain a conversation from far away for any length of time. After years of trial and error, they found Dominic could link with Aliah and could hear what was being said, but he could not participate directly. He could, however, voice his thoughts to Aliah, and she would mind speak for them both.

Closing his book and placing it gently on the floor, Seamus said, *I take it this isn't a social call?*

Unfortunately, no. We had another report from Duke Hubert today about unrest in the border lands. It appears the problem Sanctuary has been dealing with for the last few years is now spilling into Aria. We were wondering if you noticed any increased activity?

Seamus stroked his beard and waited some time before answering. *I wouldn't say we're experiencing more raids than usual, but some of the people I speak to are concerned about the ferocity of recent attacks.*

Are you able to give us more details? Aliah asked.

Since defeating the god and freeing Aria from invasion, Seamus's life had taken a different course than his warrior partner. He had set up a school to train magically gifted children in Sanctuary. Making use of the community's extensive archives, he spent the rest of his time helping his aunt's husband, Walter, research and codify the various types of magic found in their lands.

The eldest son of the southern duke, in his adoptive home, he held no rank and had to rely on reports from his cousin Liam, Aria's Ambassador to Sanctuary, or his aunt Amelia, the chief seer, to gather his information. However, while his intelligence lacked the detail of official updates, he kept his finger on the pulse, and his news was often delivered in a more timely manner.

No specifics, just gut feelings. When these attacks first started a few years ago, the guard felt we were being tested to find out how easily we would roll over. When we retaliated, their efforts died down, but not long after, we found Talagarian settlements around the base of the Ariel mountains.

Is there an actual purpose to this history lesson? Aliah asked, her tiredness allowing her natural impatience to surface.

'Let him finish,' Dominic said. 'You've been friends with Seamus long enough to trust he has a reason for rehashing this.'

I take it from the look on your face that Dominic told you to be patient with me. Seamus grinned, before saying to Dominic's ghost-like figure, *Thanks, old friend.*

I'm sorry for being rude, but this is taking a lot out of me, Seamus. Things are busy at court, and I have very little energy left over for midnight catch-ups.

I am sure the delegation from Carsten is eating out of your hand.

If only my daughter was as biddable. Aliah sighed and ran a hand through her hair. *But we can talk more about her another time.*

I did offer to train her magical abilities here, Seamus said.

And I appreciate that, truly I do, but I would like her to be able to use her magic legally in Aria—the Wizard Council will not yet recognise male Sanctuary-trained wizards until they have undergone considerable testing. So I doubt they will consider licensing witches trained in your school any time soon.

The offer still stands. Anyway, back to our Talagrian problem. You're aware we strengthened the settlements on our borders to deal with raids from the new Talagrian camps, setting up local garrisons to protect our outlying farms.

Yes. I'm also aware that after, although there were occasional raids, the Talagrian's retreated with very little to show for their efforts. If I remember correctly, those encounters caused very few casualties on your part, Aliah said in the hopes of speeding things up.

Mm... well... over the last moon turn, casualties have increased. In fact, in the past two six-days, the guards have repeatedly requested additional healers from the school be sent out to our settlements.

That doesn't sound good. I thought you said the number of attacks hadn't increased, Aliah said, her tired mind finding it difficult to see where all this was leading.

They aren't. But as I said before, the Talagrians have been attacking with increasing ferocity. Not merely raiding, but it's almost as though they want to break through our lines of defence—almost as though someone or something is chasing them out of their homes.

Aliah considered Seamus's words, then asked Dominic, 'What do you think?'

'I think this sounds very like what Hubert is experiencing. He said the refugees in the mountains no longer feel safe and want to leave—urgently.'

Seamus, Hubert is sending someone to talk with his Talagrians. Have you had any success with diplomatic missions to the ones living on your borders?

We tried early on, but with these new attacks, I am afraid the council is no longer interested in talking. Because of our history with Talagria, they will never consider opening our doors to refugees from there, so I guess they don't see much point in opening lines of communication.

Is that because they believe the Talagrians are still using battle magic? And because they have taken part in magical attacks, they have transgressed the basic laws of magic, and they've likely brought this on themselves? Aliah asked.

Yes, but also because they don't want any practitioners of battle magic within our territories, Seamus said. *Sanctuary's ancestors gave up a lot a long time ago to make sure our people were clear of any magical taint.*

Do you think the council would be interested in our dealing with this problem together?

Seamus considered her question, then shook his head. *I am pretty sure their views are entrenched. I can ask Liam to raise it at the next meeting though, if you want.*

If you wouldn't mind. I can send the formal dispatch in the morning, giving him authority.

The room fell silent, and Aliah closed her eyes, enjoying the brief moment of peace. Unfortunately, she had much to do in the morning, and she made a move to stand.

Seamus leaned forward and placed a hand on her arm. *Aliah, before you go, there's something I believe Amelia would want me to tell you.*

Something she couldn't tell me herself? Aliah asked. *We talk at least once a moon turn. Can't it wait until we next catch up?*

This is something from a vision she had yesterday, and she is still struggling with sorting out the true meaning. She and Walter have immersed themselves in old scrolls trying to find answers. When I tell her tomorrow that we spoke, I am sure she will ask if I've warned you.

Warned me? Aliah's stomach tightened with dread. *Of what?* A warning from the Great Seer was not something she relished. The last time a Great Seer was interested in her, she had become involved with a prophecy, and her life had been placed in danger.

Her recent visions appear to show our prophecy is somehow linked with another. She believes destiny has not finished with The Wizard and The Warrior.

Aliah stared at her friend's face, checking he wasn't pulling one of his pranks. The concern and worry in his eyes told her this was all very real. Her hands grew clammy, and her heart began to race. *But, Seamus, we're old,* she protested.

Speak for yourself, he shot back.

Too old for this malarky, at least. I'm not sure I have the strength or resilience to go through what we went through again.

Tears welled in Aliah's eyes as she remembered her childhood friend Daniel. Her wounds from losing him in their battle with an errant god had never completely healed. *Surely we gave enough last time.* She allowed the thought to escape into Seamus's mind.

I don't relish this any more than you do. My children lost one parent to the will of the gods. I'm not going to let them lose another. But I think it is better to be prepared when Amelia consults us once she has figured every-thing out.

Thank you, Seamus. I will pray to the goddess that she misread the messages and we are able to spend the rest of our days dealing with nothing worse than rebellious children.

Goodnight, Aliah, sleep well. And you too, Dominic.

Aliah found herself outside Seamus's mind. Following the white thread back to her body, she resisted the urge to take a detour and talk to Amelia about her new seeing. Besides, she needed all her remaining energy to face her daughter in the morning.

Back in their bedroom, Aliah slumped in the chair. 'So we wait. We wait for Hubert to report back and for Liam to send official word about whether or not Sanctuary will help us,' she said, and Dominic nodded confirmation.

'Do you want to talk about what Amelia's seen?' he asked.

'No,' she said tentatively. 'No.' This time more firmly. 'I have enough to deal with here at the moment, and Amelia's vision is one particular fire I don't want to rush into.'

'Mm, but you do realise it is something we will need to face sooner or later?' Dominic's eyes searched her face as if trying to read her true feelings on the matter.

'I know, but not yet. All right?' She held his hand, beseeching him to allow her to dodge this for the moment. It was not like her to hide from a challenge, but Aliah was not ready to resurrect The Warrior from the annals of history. 'Come on, let's get some sleep. There are enough real problems for us to face tomorrow without inventing more.'

She tugged his hand, but Dominic didn't move. He stared intently at her, and she could almost hear the words he wanted to say, but in the end, he gave in to her entreaty to leave the subject alone. 'You're right, my love. Time to take these weary bodies to bed.'

Aliah sighed with relief as he rose and walked towards their dressing room. Pulling back the covers, she slipped between the sheets and was asleep before her husband joined her. It was not a restful night, and she awoke the next morning tangled in bedclothes and wishing she could roll over and ignore the knock on the door signalling it was time for the king and queen to rise and begin the day.

PART TWO
IF IT'S GOOD ENOUGH FOR YOUR FATHER

CHAPTER 4

'I UNDERSTAND DUTY, BUT...

Aliah's eyelids started to droop. She blinked twice then refocussed on the man in front of her. Blast it, what had she missed? Carsten's ambassador bowed his head and kept his eyes on the floor, waiting for her to speak.

Smiling back at him, she looked over his head at the richly dressed courtiers filling the ancient audience chamber. The rows of wooden seats were full, and the banners of Aria's great noble houses hung from the ceiling, indicating each had a representative present. How could she have dozed off during such an important meeting?

What had they been talking about before her mind had wandered? Ah, yes, trade agreements. They were getting down to the nitty gritty now. How much and at what price were the people of Aria prepared to offer in return for the precious metals and gems from Carsten?

A quick glance of the faces in the room told her whatever the ambassador had proposed was not being well received. Then again, few Arians had lost their enmity towards Carsten, and fewer still were in favour of opening up any relations with their previous enemy at all.

Scanning around in the hopes of finding at least one person on her side, Aliah's eyes were drawn back to one face in particular. How interesting. Sitting in the back of the room was the last person she expected to attend this meeting—Admina.

'Your Highness, we have another appointment,' Tiana, her steward, prompted.

Aliah returned her attention to the ambassador. 'Your proposal provides much food for thought. I will need to go through the details with my advisors before offering an official response, and, of course, we will need to make some changes here and there. All in all, though, I can tell you the crown looks favourably on your mission and your suggestions.'

The ambassador swept into a flourishing bow. 'As Your Highness wishes, but can you give us an indication of the areas of immediate concern so I can have my staff work on some alternatives?'

Aliah fought not to purse her lips. In Aria, once the monarch made a pronouncement, all discussion would cease. After their failed invasion when a god took over the body of their king, Carsten now had an elected government, and their approach to dealing with the crown head of Aria was completely different to what she was used to. Her subjects were also not pleased with the ambassador's audacity, and some even went as far as to gasp audibly.

'As I said, the crown looks favourably on this trade agreement. However, I still want to run through details with my council of ministers before commenting officially on any specifics.' Aliah stood, signalling an end to the session. As she turned to leave, she caught some of the muttered comments of the people closest to her.

...I'm still paying the carpenters for repairs to my... son never returned from the war... for ten years we had to support those refugees...

Anger over the failed Carsten invasion, and the resulting problem caused by Carstenites who did not want to return to their homeland, clearly ran deeper than she first thought. Although the histories told how a god had possessed the King of Carsten, most people did not truly believe in any deity but the goddess any more, and they blamed the people for following their deranged leader. That meant she would likely be forced to push harder for recompense during the negotiations.

However, she didn't want to press so hard she offended their new allies. With problems on another border, she wanted to woo the Carstenites, not only to remove a potential threat, but also because of the vast quantities of iron included on the list of goods they were keen to sell.

Before anyone could approach her to request a private audience, Tiana announced there would be no further public interviews today as 'Queen Aliahanna is required in an important meeting and will not be available until this evening's state dinner.'

The guards bustled everyone out of the room as Aliah retreated via the door behind the throne. The corridor led to her private office, but she had no intention of staying there long. Depositing the state crown on the desk, she speedily changed into her riding clothes. If she hurried, she just about had enough time for a ride along the coast before she was scheduled to meet with Dominic and his newly appointed Captain of the Guard.

The door from the audience chamber opened, and Aliah bit back a sigh as Admina slipped through it. Her daughter's eyes widened with surprise as they found her mother mid-change, pulling on her riding boots.

'Important meetings of state?' Mina raised an eyebrow.

'I have to take these moments when I can. Your situation is high on my list of priorities, and you clearly want to talk, but can it wait until after lunch? There isn't another space in my schedule long enough for a ride for another few days, and I need to feel the wind in my hair for a while.'

'I can come with you if you like?'

Aliah's stomach dropped. For most of the time, she was either queen, wife, or mother. The moments in her life when she could be just Aliah were few and far between; was she prepared to let this one candle-mark she had eked from her week go?

Shaking her head, she said, 'We won't be able to talk, Mina, not on the ride I have planned. We can walk and talk on the way to the stables, or you can wait until I return and we can have a quiet lunch together. Or we could discuss this at teatime as we arranged this morning.'

Anger sped across Mina's face. Before she could voice her displeasure, Aliah said, 'Let's do the "walk and talk" now, and after my ride, we can have lunch. I'll be quick, I promise.'

Her daughter didn't move.

'Come on.' She grabbed Mina's arm and led her out through the other door, the one leading to the palace's private rooms.

Striding through the back corridors used by the castle staff, she turned and asked, 'What is so urgent it can't wait until lunchtime?'

'You know, Mother, you having to sneak off for a ride in the middle of the day doesn't exactly sell becoming queen to me.' Mina's tone was sour as she reminded her mother she had not yet agreed to take the Heir's Ring if it was offered.

Aliah bit back a sigh. 'Mina, you'll soon find that no matter what role you take on as an adult, there will be very little time for life's pleasures. That doesn't make growing up bad; it just makes you appreciate them all the more when you get them.'

Ignoring her mother's comment, Mina ploughed on. 'And that farce in the council chamber doesn't help either. How can you be so pleasant to the people who invaded Aria? To men who hurt and killed our people—killed one of your friends. All I could think of while I sat watching was how much I wanted to remove those men from our castle and our lives.'

'Another thing I hope age will teach you is there is more than one side to every story—more than one version of the truth. Not all Carstenites are monsters, any more than all Arians are victims. Many of our own people benefited from the invasion, and in fact some of our subjects actually helped them attack.'

'Humph.'

'I also have to look at the bigger picture. Some of the things going on in Aria at the moment mean that I view their delegation in a different light to you, and most of my court from what I can tell.'

Aliah stopped by the door leading to the stable yard. 'Is this truly what you wished to speak to me about, because I'm quite happy going over all the ramifications of the Carsten proposal with you over lunch if you would like.'

Not waiting for an answer, she pushed open the heavy wooden door and stepped outside, confident this conversation was a preamble to Mina's real reason for wanting to speak with her.

'No, thank you very much,' Mina said sourly as she followed her mother to the stables. 'I'm not Gabriel. I have no interest in those sorts of details. He would not only be eager to hear them; he would even have some insights you haven't considered.' Mina sniggered.

A groom led Aliah's already saddled horse out and handed the reins to her. As she waited for her two guards to emerge from the building, she pinned her daughter with a direct stare.

'So?'

Mina struggled to hold her gaze, signalling to Aliah something more was going on inside her daughter's head. Her tired brain groaned; couldn't anything in her life be simple?

'I had a think last night, and I want to look into something. Before I do though, I want to double check I understood you correctly when we last spoke. If I find something to do that will benefit Aria, and I can demonstrate how, I won't have to spend my year on Wizard Isle?'

Aliah considered the question for a moment, attempting to identify the obvious trap. Well, not so obvious, because she couldn't find it. She would have to dance well to avoid the hidden pitfalls. 'In essence, yes, with two restrictions.'

'But—'

Aliah raised her hand to silence her daughter. 'Firstly, you must have some form of training to manage your magical ability. If you don't, it will become a hinderance to you later on in life.'

'But I don't want to use magic. I find the whole thing rather creepy.' Mina shuddered, adding emphasis to her words.

'I didn't say you had to be taught how to use it. I said you must learn how to manage it, so you don't come to, or cause, any harm later on in your life.'

Mina shuffled her feet. 'All right, that sounds sensible. What's the other condition?'

'The second is either your father or I must give our full support to your plan.'

Dominic and Aliah agreed to this last thing as they spoke over breakfast earlier. Aliah was concerned Mina would view all her objections as her mother simply denying her what she wanted. Aliah was also certain Mina believed her father could be manipulated into agreeing with her, not fully understanding the strength of his resolve in this area. They decided Mina should spend some time with her father to find this out for herself; otherwise, she could always use the possibility of his changing Aliah's mind to evade making a good decision.

'Done.' Mina was quick to agree. 'Enjoy your ride.' Her daughter turned on her heel and rushed back into the castle.

Aliah knew exactly where Mina was going, and she had a pretty good idea what she would find when she got there. She gently nudged her mount, even more ready to enjoy her ride now Dominic would have the joy of dealing with one of her more pressing problems.

MINA GRINNED as she made her way through the castle, happy now she had a clear path to getting her own way. The guard outside her father's study door did not move a muscle as she approached, a sure sign the king was busy with something that could not be interrupted. Taking a seat by the window, she tapped her foot restlessly as she waited.

What seemed like ages later, she was still sitting there. Turning in her chair, she tried to catch the guard's eye, but he ignored her. Someone important must be with her father if his doorman wasn't even prepared to engage with the princess. She stood to leave just as the door opened.

'And you don't want to tell me who you have in mind for our new captain?' a voice Mina recognised asked from inside the room.

Newly appointed sergeant, Casey, had been part of the palace guard up until her promotion and reassignment to a field unit a few days ago. The troop had returned for reinforcements after having fought off some pirate raids in the north. With most of their members patched up and their vacant positions filled, they were almost ready to head out on their next assignment. All they needed now was a replacement captain for the woman who retired at the end of the mission.

Casey's figure appeared in the doorway. Catching Mina in the corridor, she gave her old pupil a broad smile. The sergeant was only a few years older than Mina and had been her sword master and sparring partner for the last couple of years. Casey was her mentor and idol, and one of the main reasons she wanted to join the guard.

'Did I hear you have your first posting?' Mina asked.

Casey nodded towards her father. 'Can't talk about it.'

'Oh, all right.'

'Do you want something, Mina?' Her father interrupted.

'Yes, if you have a few minutes. And if Casey doesn't have anything more pressing to do, would she be able to join us?'

Dominic raised his eyebrows, and Mina simply smiled.

'I guess we can both spare you a little time.' He held the door open and waited for Casey and Mina to enter before closing it.

Mina took a seat as Casey stood to attention beside her chair. Realising her mistake, having the guard in attendance made this meeting public not private, Mina stood. Once the king was seated behind his desk, she again took her seat, with Casey joining her this time.

Now that she was sitting in front of her father, Mina didn't know exactly where to start. All the great ideas swirling round her head as she left the stables had disappeared and her mind went blank.

'Well?' her father asked as he steepled his hands in front of him. 'What is this all about?'

Instead of marshalling her thoughts and constructing a reasoned argument, Mina felt words tumble out of her mouth, pushed into the room by a confusion of emotions. 'I want to spend my year in service as a guard, and I want you to help me convince Mother to let me.'

Casey snorted, and Mina swore her father was trying hard not to laugh. Realising they were not taking her seriously, her anger began to build.

'No, listen to me. I don't mean I want to play at being a guard. I intend to join a company as a new recruit, just like any other Arian, and work as a trainee for a year. In return, I would learn more about the lives of people in Aria, and our guards in particular, which would surely be of benefit to me, and therefore Aria, in the future.'

The room was silent. She turned and glared at Casey, willing her to speak in support of the idea.

'You said I was a better swordsperson than most of the new recruits. Was that a lie?'

'Whoa, calm down. I don't lie. Nor do I give false praise. But there is more to joining a company than being able to wield a sword.'

'Like what?' Mina challenged her friend.

Out the corner of her eye, she saw her father sit back and nod once, gesturing for Casey to speak freely.

'Like, for instance, you have to be prepared to do the grunt work: dig latrines, serve food to senior guards, help groom the horses—'

'I can do all of that,' Mina said.

'Tell me, when was the last time you tidied your room or cleaned out your horse's stall?'

Mina paused. 'Of course I can do those things. It's just someone else always does it before I get around to it. I do groom my horse though... most of the time.'

Casey stared thoughtfully, and Mina could sense her weighing her words before she next spoke. 'You need to be able to follow orders without questioning them.'

'I can do that too,' Mina protested.

'Like you did when you were ordered to attend the wizard school?'

'But that was a stupid... Oh.'

'Not to mention a year's pay for a soldier wouldn't even buy that pretty outfit you're wearing.'

Mina looked down at the plain blue, ankle-length dress her maid had put out for her this morning. There were no embellishments and no fancy frills. Many of the castle servants dressed better than she did.

'But—'

'There is another stumbling block Casey has been too polite to mention.'

The two women turned at the sound of their king's voice. 'Even if you joined a company for a year, you would still be "Princess Admina". You'd be treated differently, whether you wanted to be or not, simply because no soldier is going to be comfortable commanding their monarch's daughter.'

'And, if we engaged an enemy, our first thought would always be to protect you first and worry about the mission second,' Casey added.

Mina stood, and her chair scraped back across the wooden floor before getting caught on the edge of the large rug in the centre of the room. 'You both sound as though you don't want me to do this. I would be a good guard, and I want to spend my year of service in a troop. Why won't you help me?'

'Admina, please sit down.' Her father used his king voice, and she sat automatically.

'Neither of us think you wouldn't be a great asset to any of the guard corps. In fact, I believe you would be great at anything you put your mind too. It's just....'

'If I may, sire?' Casey waited for the king to nod his agreement before continuing. 'Your being there would cause disruption in any unit. So, although you are already well trained, a complete novice would be of more value to us, because we would not have to manage concerns of rank, nor would we need to consider their safety.'

Mina thought for a moment. 'What if I were to renounce my position?'

Casey snorted, then turned an embarrassed face to her king. 'Apologies, sire.'

'No need, we are all being frank here. While I understand the joke, perhaps you would like to explain it to Admina.'

Casey closed her eyes before drawing a deep breath. 'You don't get it. Even if you are no longer called princess, you're still noble born. You can't join the ranks as a common guard, because the others will not accept you. You can't sign up as an officer like the other nobles, because you haven't had training in military strategy and the rules of war.'

Anger at being dismissed, and embarrassment at not having fully done her research, warred inside of Mina. In the end, neither emotion won as she felt her dream of earning glory as a guard captain fade into the ether. 'So, I can never be a guard?'

'That was not what we said.' Her father smiled.

'But you both pointed out I can't sign up, because they won't have me.'

'I believe we said there is no place for you in the guard ranks, or as an officer. Think, Mina, who in the guards are accepted for their skill and are treasured and protected by the other troop members?'

Mina studied her father's face as if the answer might appear there. Shaking her head, she finally said, 'I have no idea what you're talking about.'

'Scouts, Mina,' Casey said. 'A scout who can plot our route or search out an enemy, whether it be in the wild or in a town, is worth their weight in gold.'

'But most scouts train for years before they get a position.'

'Some don't have to wait. They come to us with special skills, skills such as those you possess,' Casey pointed out.

'But... but I've never used them.... I couldn't...'

'If you attended the Wizard School as your mother and I wanted, you would have developed your magical ability to send your senses into different places, then the guards would welcome you with open arms.'

'It always comes back to the school on Wizard Isle, doesn't it?' Mina's shoulders slumped.

'I don't understand why you don't want to use your magic. If I were able to sense where people were, or weren't, I'd be using it all the time.' Casey leaned forward to catch Mina's eye as she spoke. 'If I could be a scout, I wouldn't have had to attend all those boring classes on military history and strategy to earn my promotion.'

Avoiding Casey's earnest gaze, Mina said, 'I don't use my magic, because it's another way for me to be different from everyone else.' She took a deep breath and spoke directly to her father. 'So, if I developed my magical abilities and made myself useful to the guard, you and Mother would allow me to renounce my claim to the throne and sign up?'

The king laughed. 'The two aren't mutually exclusive. Your mother and I are not planning to vacate our positions any time soon, and we would be happy for you to be a guard once your commitments to the crown have been met... and if they'll have you.'

'To have a chance of becoming a guard, I have to first do what you want—which is something I really don't want to do?' Mina frowned, trying to realign her thoughts to this new way of thinking.

Nodding at Casey, the king said, 'I think we can take it from here. If you could ask Cook to send up some refreshments on your way through the kitchens, I would appreciate it.'

As her father waited for Casey to leave, Mina's fingers fiddled with the seam of her dress as she tried to find a way out of her current dilemma. She had been so sure her father would support her; she had not considered what she would do if he didn't.

The door clicked as it closed, and her father spoke, 'When we are young, sometimes we don't realise the thing we want the least is the very thing that will make us happy.'

When Mina did not respond, he continued. 'You're growing up fast, and you're old enough to make your own decisions, but the problem with being young is you don't know what you don't know.'

The room remained silent. 'You think the ills in your life are because you are considered to be heir to the throne, even though we haven't named you as such, and because you have magical abilities. You believe because of these things, you're treated differently, and all you want is a normal life.'

'Is that so wrong?' Mina could not summon the energy to be truly defiant, but she felt the question needed to be asked anyway.

'No, I guess not. While we're still finding out who we are, we all want to be many things, and most of those are not who we already are. Your mother was the same—'

'We've all heard Mother's legend—numerous times.' Mina realised she had mis-stepped when her father's face reflected his impatience with her sniping. Attacking her mother was not the way to win him over.

'Yes, Aliah's story is well documented, from everyone else's perspective but hers. Perhaps one day you might ask her what she thought about being pulled into saving the world.

'Anyway, I was going to say I felt the same as you when I was younger. When I was growing up, all I knew was I didn't want to be my father's son, and I definitely didn't want to fall in line with the plans he had for me.'

'You don't talk about when you were a boy very often.' Mina sat up a little in her chair, hoping to find out something more about her family's mysterious past.

'No, I don't. It wasn't a pleasant time for me, but I think it's time I told you a little story about why I left home. Maybe it'll help you appreciate the irony of my spending years fighting against becoming the husband of a powerful, wealthy woman, only to find that in the end I chose to follow that path of my own volition. I'm not sure where to begin. When I think back, I guess it all started with a horse race.'

CHAPTER 5
INTO THE SHADOWS

A GAME OF HIDE AND SEEK

Dappled sunlight danced over the thick rug covering the wooden floor. Dominic curled up in the chair by the window, waiting for his mother to arrive. Each day she would spend time with her sons, teaching them to read and about the history of their country. Soon, a tutor would take over these duties, but until then, this was the best part of his day.

Sometimes the duchess was late though, as she had many other duties to attend to. On those days, he loved to sit in her chair and stare out the window, watching the comings and goings on his father's estate.

He was brought back from daydreaming by the squeak the door made as it opened. When he asked his mother why no one oiled it, she replied she liked to know when someone entered her rooms.

In a playful mood, Dominic decided to duck behind the chair and play a trick on his mother. As he settled in to his hide-y-hole he heard not his mother's light footsteps, but the solid footsteps of his father, followed by the creak of his mother's bed.

He ducked his head around the corner of the chair in time to catch his father gently place his mother on the coverlet, then arrange the pillows behind her.

'Gamina, please, you have to stop exerting yourself this way. You know what the healer said, the more strain on your body the shorter your time with us.'

Dominic sunk back on the floor and huddled into a ball. His whole world was crumbling around him, and he did not know what to do. How had he not known something was wrong with his mother? Staying as quiet as possible, he continued listening in.

'Pierre, I refuse to live my life wrapped in cotton wool, that is no life at all.'

'But, what will I do when you are gone? You are my world.'

Was his father actually crying? Dominic snuck a peek and saw tears running down his father's cheeks. In all his twelve years he had never seen his father show one iota of weakness.

'You will carry on and raise our boys to be fine young men.'

'And when that is done, what will I have left? Nothing.'

'You could always marry again, Pierre. You are still young.'

He knew his father had married later in life, grandfather had never found anyone good enough for his precious son. Weeks after his death, Duke Pierre had met Lady Gamina, and she saw something in the gruff man no others did. It was a true love match, especially for the duke. When his wife was in the room it was as though everyone else ceased to exist.

'Never.'

'Then put all your love into the estate and our boys.'

'I worry, Gamina, about the boys. My father... well... he was never really a father to me. What do I know of raising sons? Without you here to show me the way ... I fear for our boys.'

'Oh, Pierre, if only you would trust the goodness inside of you. I know you want only the best for our sons. Perhaps you should think, "what would my father have done here?" and do the complete opposite.'

His mother's attempt to lighten the mood worked, his father chuckled. 'Yes, I guess that is one option.'

The bed creaked again. 'Now you must rest, Gamina. I have sent for the healer to check you over and I will come and sit with you again later.'

As the door snicked closed his mother said, 'You can come out now, Dominic.'

For a fleeting moment, the boy considered staying where he was, but his mother always seemed to know when he was hiding, and could find him even when others could not. Not wanting to make her angry, he unwound himself and stood up.

'You know it is bad manners to eavesdrop on other's conversations?'

'If I had not, would you have ever told us you are ill?' he asked defiantly, raising his head and looking her in the eye.

He lowered his gaze again, frightened by what he saw. So drawn and grey was she, her liquid brown eyes dominated her face, and her usually tidy hair was dishevelled. Her appearance warned him of how ill she truly was.

Sighing, she reached out and took hold of his hand, drawing him nearer. 'What good would it have done to worry you? There is nothing you or anyone else can do.'

Dominic sat on the bed in the same spot his father occupied moments before.

'Is it bad?'

In spite of all he had heard, he needed to hear it from his mother's own lips, even though he was afraid of the answer. Unable to look at her, his toe scuffed at the floorboards.

'I will not lie to you, son, it is not good. There is something not quite right with my heart. I have been taking a potion, which helped for a while, though I think maybe I need a stronger one now.'

A tear leaked from his eye as a range of emotions warred inside of him. He had wanted his mother to tell him everything would be fine, but he could tell from her voice that, although she was putting on a brave face, things were far from all right. Not knowing what to say, he said nothing at all.

His mother pulled him further onto the bed and wrapped him in a hug. Safe in her arms, he could forget for a moment that she was not well and had just turned his world upside down.

Sometime later, he pulled himself back into a sitting position. A little colour had returned to his mother's face, and he could almost believe this had been a bad dream, except for the weariness around her eyes and the bluish tinge to her lip.

Taking her hand in his he asked, 'What can I do to help?'

His mother placed her other hand over the top of his before she answered. 'My big, brave, boy. How proud you make me. I need is for you to treat me as you always have. Every moment of life is precious and should be lived to the full, and we should always behave it as though it will be our last.'

He nodded solmenly.

'Also, I need you to keep this to yourself.'

'What? You mean I shouldn't tell Hubert?' He and his twin shared everything, how could he keep something this important a secret?

'You and your brother are close, so you must have realised he is not as strong as you are. I can see how much this is hurting you, but you will not break. Hubert might. So I want you to promise me to keep this between ourselves.'

He knew her words to be true, still his agreement was given grudgingly.

'Thank you. I know that was difficult. Now, I need to rest for a while, my love. Go and find Hubert, take him for a ride and forget about all of this.'

He followed her request, more or less. He saddled his horse and rode like the wind though the woods, trying to erase the last candle mark of his life, and swearing he would never eavesdrop again.

The sun was setting as he returned his horse to the stable. Grabbing some bread and cheese from the kitchen on the way upstairs, he ate alone in his room. When his brother came up some time later he pretended to be asleep, sure if he spoke to his brother Hubert would see how his secret weighed heavy on his heart.

THE RACE

Wind whipped his hair across his face as he urged his horse Dawn on. Behind him he could hear the hoof beats of another horse drawing closer. His friend Thalia laughed with glee as she passed him just as they came into the stable yard.

'I did it. I beat you.'

Her brown eyes sparkled with merriment as she tugged at some stray hairs, attempting to force them back into her plait.

'You did, fair and square.'

Her joy over the rare win made it difficult to remain grumpy at his loss.

'Where is Hubert?'

He wandered back to the yard gate and searched for his brother. There he was, on his own horse, coming in at a slow jog. Although he loved riding as much as they did, and was most certainly the better rider of the three, he rarely took part in their hare-brained races, preferring to just enjoy his time away from their tutor.

Since the tutor had arrived two moon turns ago the brothers had found their routine changed beyond recognition. Their heavy academic workload had reduced the amount of time they had for outdoor pursuits. Today had been a gift. Thalia's father, Lord James, arrived to discuss business with their father, and the boys had been pleased when Duke Pierre requested they keep the lady entertained.

They spent the afternoon riding the trails around their home, lying on the riverbank talking and laughing, and when they realised the time, finished off with a race home.

Having made sure Hubert was all right, Dominic returned to his mount and began to unsaddle her, just as Thalia's father emerged from the stables with his horse saddled for their journey home.

'Come, my dear, we must be away home. Dominic, Hubert, leave those horses for the stable boy. I think you father needs you more at the moment.'

Thalia made a face over her shoulder as she followed her own father out the gate, causing the two boys to smile. Dominic did not think anything of Lord James' abrupt departure. It was no secret he did not get on well with the duke, and often left feeling less than satisfied. What was unusual was his request the boys attend their father.

Heeding his word, they handed their reins to one of the servants and rushed up to the house, just catching a glimpse of his father's back as he slammed the study door behind him. Sharing a worried glance, he and Hubert went in search of their mother.

As they reached the top of the stairs a familiar figure emerged from their mother's door, pulling it gently closed behind him. The healer had been a regular visitor this past moon turn, and the look on the man's face told Dominic all he needed to know.

'I am sorry boys. If it is any consolation, she passed quietly, without pain. I am sure your father will want to talk to you about it. Err, I must be on my way.'

Hubert looked a Dominic questioningly. He wanted to turn away and deny any knowledge of what was going on, but the tears streaming down his face gave him away.

Leading his brother to their room, he explained everything he knew, and listened while his brother railed and yelled, then finally burst into tears. Lying side by side on their beds, each wrapped in their own grief, they waited for their father to come to them.

Long after the sun had gone down Dominic roused himself. Grabbing his brother by the arm, he led him to the kitchen. Food was waiting for them, but the sorrowful gazes of the servants made him uncomfortable so they took their plates back to their room.

A few days later, their mother was buried. The ceremony was

attended by many from the local area and some from further afield. Duchess Gamina was well loved. Their father was conspicuous by his absence. It was many more moon turns before he stirred from his study and began to take up the reins of his duchy again, but he was clearly not the man he once was.

EAVESDROPPING

Dominic entered the room like a whirlwind. The wooden door shuddered as it banged into the stone wall as he flung his sword and scabbard into the far corner of the room before flopping down on his bed.

'Humph.'

'So, father found you?' the room's occupant asked from the desk by the window, not bothering to raise his eyes from the book he read.

Dominic did not respond, scared if he opened his mouth he would not be able to stop the flow of angry words once he started. Hateful words he would not be able to take back once spoken. A sigh escaped as he turned his back and stared morosely at the wall.

'Sometimes I wish he had never come back out of his room,' he finally admitted. 'At least while he stayed in there, he left us alone.'

'I swear I said nothing.' The mattress dipped as his brother joined him, his tone bitter as he continued. 'I was too busy defending myself. After lunch he found me in here reading a history book and abused me. Asked why I was not out practicing with my sword like a future ruler, learning how to lead my people into battle should the need arise.

'Then he rants because you are out doing exactly what he wants me to do. What was his reasoning? No rich woman will want to marry you with sword calloused hands, I guess you need to be in perfect condition to be displayed as someone's pet husband.'

As he rolled back over his brother's sad brown eyes met his. 'You and I both know a duke is more than a man holding a sword. That is why you will be a much better leader than him when your time comes.'

Hubert forced a wan smile. 'The irony is, you are closer to father's ideal replacement. Every lecture he starts by reminding me of future duties and always finishes with wishes you had been born first.'

By a quirk of fate, Hubert preceded Dominic into the world by only few minutes, crowning him the heir. They looked so alike many people had difficulty telling them apart, but on the inside they were two very different people.

Hubert, the studious introvert, was prone to weighing up every action before proceeding. He was shy and kept to himself, having only a few friends.

Outgoing and friendly, Dominic was quick of mind, and quick to action. The only thing keeping him balanced was his sense of duty and his love for his brother.

They were unsuited for the roles their father planned for them, something he relished reminding them of at every opportunity, but the duke would not considering changing his mind about their futures.

'At least neither of us is our father, we have that in our favour.' Dominic hauled himself off the bed. 'I am not waiting for father or the dance master to find me. I am in no mood to strut around to music.' He walked over to the door and stopped, hand on the handle. 'Are you coming?'

'No, I am not as brave as you. Go. Should father come back, I will say you are looking for the dance master.'

'What if Dance Master Jaingo comes?' Dominic laughed.

Infected with his brother's lightness, Hubert played along. 'Why, you are searching for him, of course. Did he not pass you in the hall?'

'Thanks,' Dominic said and the door clicked into place behind him.

Aimlessly wandering down the draughty dark corridor, he

paused to touch his hand to the door of his mother's room. A ritual he followed every day since her death the year before.

The duchess never fully regained her strength after giving birth to twins, her heart had been compromised.

She had often stood between her husband and the two boys, protecting them from his excesses while counselling him to be more understanding. With her ability to influence him, the duke had joined many family outings and evenings by the fireside, getting to know his sons better. Without her to intervene no one curbed their father's actions, and he had become brooding and introverted. All his time was spent building his duchy and planning for the future; it was as if he no longer wanted to live in the here and now.

A sense of loss washed over Dominic. Closing his eyes, he spent a brief moment with his memories as he touched his forehead to the wood. Letting the world back in, he continued on with renewed courage, wondering where his father or anyone else might be unlikely to search; the library. Unimaginative, and viewing his offspring only as imperfect reflections of himself, a place devoted to reading would be an excellent spot to wile away an afternoon.

Inside the library's sunlit emptiness, Dominic went straight to his favourite section; the one containing stories of travels to other countries. As he ran his finger along the titles, looking for something to lose himself in for a candle mark or two, voices, and the click of a latch, broke his concentration. The door creaked open, and he ducked under the desk as footsteps approached.

'No one will disturb us in here,' his father said. 'The only reason people come in is to clean, or perhaps the tutor must getting material for instruction. Useless to dedicate a room to storing books, but I guess someone in my position must cultivate a certain image.'

Dominic barely caught the mumbled response as his eyes focussed on his father's feet, which appeared right in front of him as his father prepared to sit. In a heartbeat, he would be discovered.

'The seating by the window is much more suited to our business,' the other voice said. 'Cosier and less likely to be overheard by someone passing by.'

His father tensed, reluctant to allow someone else to dominate the situation. The squelch of leather echoed through the room as the other man sat. Forced to join him, his father moved away from the desk. Dominic relaxed a little and made himself more comfortable, as it looked as though he would be here a while.

'So, you wish to buy my services?' the other voice said as a chair creaked and his father settled down.

Surprisingly, the strange man remained in charge. Under normal circumstances, Duke Pierre blustered and bullied, barely allowing others to speak, to ensure he got his own way. This man must be able to give his father something he desperately wanted or ... or maybe he scared his father.

'Quite so,' the duke responded. 'I have never done this sort of thing before. I am not quite sure how this works ...'

'Tell me what your problem is, and we'll discuss options to make it go away.' The matter-of-fact tone told Dominic the visitor regularly took part in secret dealings such as this.

His father's voice shook. 'Mmm, well, there is a vassal who does not agree with my new levies. Says they are too high. Claims people would starve if they pay. He flatly refuses to collect any more taxes from his estates. Now the other lords are following his lead. They have the gall to ask me to account for why I need the extra money. How dare they question what I do.' Duke Pierre's tone changed to petulant, sounding much more like he had done over the past few moon turns.

Unable to place himself in anyone else's shoes, he could not contemplate anything other than his own needs. The thought others would be worse off if they paid extra to line his coffers would never cross his mind, he was so focussed on his own plans.

'I assume the first lord you spoke of is the one we are talking about here?'

His father obviously agreed, as the guest continued. 'So, all I need now is a name, and for you to tell me what you want done. The cost depends on the job. Destruction of property being the cheapest, maiming of the man or a family member the mid-point, death being the most as expensive.'

Dominic froze. His father would not go as far as to hire thugs to keep his lords in line, would he?

'Oh, no. No,' Duke Pierre protested, and Dominic let out a tense breath. 'Death is a bit extreme, I think? I want this man to realise everything he has, even his life, is because of my generosity, so he should do my bidding without question.' By the end his father sounded a little flustered.

'Does he have children?'

'Yes, three.'

'One who is dearest to him, perhaps?'

'His daughter, Thalia. A young girl of about fourteen, I think. She plays with my sons.'

Dominic bit back a snort. They did not play with Thalia. They hunted or rode together when he and Hubert happened to sneak out.

'My suggestion is we take and hold her until your man sees sense.'

His father was discussing having his childhood friend kidnapped. The girl his brother spoke of so often Dominic had begun to think Hubert soft on her.

'All right, leave it with me. My initial fee is ten golds, in advance. A further ten gold is to be paid when we return her, or we can rene-gotiate the fee if the final outcome changes.'

Shivers tingled up and down Dominic's spine at the coldness running through the man's words.

'That is agreeable.' More like his blustery self, the duke took back control. 'Let us go and meet with my chamberlain. You are now employed as my new trading representative in Duncameron. That should be a good enough cover so when this is over, I can dismiss you without anyone taking particular note.'

The floor underneath Dominic vibrated as chairs scraped back and the men rose to seal their monstrous deal with gold. He poked his head out to catch a glimpse of the man with his father, at the same time repeating to himself, 'Please do not turn, please do not see me.'

Unfortunately, a long black cloak with a hood hid the man from view. Should anyone ask for a description, he could only state the man was taller and slimmer than his father, which was not very useful at all.

<hr/>

WHAT NOW?

Dominic uncurled his body. The conversation had upset him so much his afternoon of reading was pushed to the back of his mind. He needed to act—and fast. Though for once he realised the importance of thinking through his next moves rather than blindly reacting on impulse. Too much was at stake, he coin not afford any missteps.

His agitation mounted as he paced around the room, considering his options. In the end he sat down at the desk, attempting to calm down and think the situation through rationally.

Stopping Thalia's kidnapping was a priority, but no one would believe what he had overheard. Even if he did manage to convince someone of the danger his friend faced, what would they be able to do without details of the kidnapper?

Perhaps he could talk with Hubert? No, since their mother's death, he had been even more fragile, worrying about the smallest things. He could not add to his brother's burdens.

After much internal debate, he decided to tell Thalia's father of the plan. The lord might think his tale a work of fiction, but he had to do something, and this was the best option he had.

After exiting the library, he ran through corridors and out into the courtyard. All the while he kept to the shadows, avoiding areas of the palace where he would likely run into servants. As he moved, he wished for people not to look his way and, to his surprise, no one stopped him.

At the stables he slipped through the main door and paused. Inside men and boys went about their business, and he implored them not to glance his way as he walked the least populated route to his horse's stall.

The bolt was pulled back and, without questioning why, he entered before spying his friend Thom busy hanging up newly waxed tack in the back. Surprised and annoyed at himself for not checking the stall first, Dominic stopped worrying about people seeing him. The startled groom let out a shocked cry and dropped a halter. Dominic looked around to identify what had scared his friend, before realising it was him.

'Ahh! You about gave me a heart attack. How did you do that? Just appear behind me?' The flustered boy grumbled as he strived to restore some dignity, bending to pick up the bridle he dropped.

'Sorry, I didn't mean to frighten you, Thom, although it was rather funny when you jumped.' He could not help but smile at the memory of the groom's feet actually leaving the ground.

'I wasn't frightened. You were not here, and then you appeared, like some sort of ghost. I must have been so engrossed in what I was doing I missed you come in. What a horrid trick to play.' Them picked up the bridle and hung it securely over a free hook. 'What are you up to anyway?'

Throwing a blanket over his horse, and reaching for his saddle, Dominic answered, 'Going for a ride.'

'The afternoon break is soon, and you want to head out now? Without eating?' Thom, whose stomach was the centre of his world, could not understand why anyone would miss a meal for any reason.

'I need to be by myself for a bit.' Dominic reached for the bridle Thom had just stowed away, and fitted it over the hire's head as he spoke.

Ofttimes the older boy experienced the duke's mistreatment of his sons. Later he would voice his sorrow, and wish the boys had a father as good as his own. In a show of solidarity, when one or other of the boys needed to escape from their father's overbearing presence, he would keep their destination secret for as long as possible. It was a small enough kinds, but one the boy's appreciated.

'Please don't tell anyone I am riding, or the direction I took. Well, unless they ask a direct question you cannot avoid answering,' Dominic requested, aware he could rely on Thom to keep his confidence, but feeling a little guilty at asking him to take the risk.

Once again he began thinking, 'please do not notice me,' as he led Dawn outside and over to the mounting block. Without assistance, he swung into the saddle and rode off towards Lord Ericsson's estate.

THE CHASE IS ON

A little over a candle mark later, Dominic came upon the outlying buildings of the Ericsson estate. Tucked in behind, a grand manor house over-shadowed them all. Dawn wound her way towards their destination, wearily stepping with care, now they had slowed from their earlier manic pace. Dominic patted her neck affectionately.

'You can rest soon, girl, and I'll make sure there is an apple waiting in the stall for you. You have done well getting me here so fast.'

As Dominic dismounted in the yard, a surprised man grabbed Dawn's reins. A small tug of guilt pulled at him as he gave instructions. He took pride in the fact he normally attended to Dawn himself, but he had more pressing matters today.

'Give her a rub down and go easy on the water for a while. She deserves a juicy apple if you have any handy. Can you tell me where your master is?' Dominic absent-mindedly stroked Dawn's neck as he waited for an answer.

The groom called over a stable lad and handed him the reins before responding. 'He's in the estate office, I believe, with his chamberlain. He won't want to be disturbed.'

'Where Thalia?'

'She went out riding with a guard not that long ago.' He tossed the words over his shoulder as he headed back to work.

Dominic's heart pounded and his anxiety added speed to his feet as he ran to the manor house, leaving an astonished groom in his wake. Although he crashed into the house only moments later, it felt like an eternity. He skidded to a halt inside the door, thrown off by the thunderous face of Lord James Ericsson of Homewoods.

'What is the meaning of this interruption? You barge in here like you own the place....'

Dominic held up his hand and tried to calm his breath before he spoke.

'Apologies... sir. I... have some... some... disturbing news.' Dominic gulped some air into his lungs. 'I believe your daughter may be in some danger,' he spouted the last words out in a final rush.

Lord James' face turned from anger, to surprise, to fear, all in the blink of an eye before settling on suspicion. 'Is this some prank...' he started, but Dominic interrupted before he finished the sentence.

'Please, sir, if you would just send someone after her to bring her back, I'll explain while we are waiting.'

Perhaps the desperation in Dominic's tone changed the man's mind. He nodded to his chamberlain, who left to do his bidding.

'All right, young man. Tell me what this is all about.' Thalia's father rested his chin on his hands, his fingers getting lost in the line of greying hair framing his ears.

'May I please sit?' Dominic's legs suddenly wobbled with fatigue.

With a sweep of his hand, the older man directed him to a chair in front of the desk he sat behind. After collapsing into the seat offered to him, Dominic recounted all the details he could remember from the conversation between his father and the unusual visitor.

'Are you sure of this?' Lord James' face wore a bored mask, almost as though this type of thing happened to him every day

Dominic nodded once.

'Well,' Lord James expelled the word as he thought. 'It appears at the very least, I need to be wary over the next few days...' The thud of a door banging and loud footsteps interrupted his musing.

'My Lord! My Lord! Your daughter's guard just returned gravely injured. Lady Thalia has been taken.'

Not stopping to think, Dominic bolted out of the house towards the stables. A black gelding was tied beside one of the mounting blocks, and one of Thalia's brothers was was walking towards it. Dominic untied the reins and swung up into the saddle before anyone moved to stop him.

'Which way?' he asked. No one responded. 'Which way did Lady Thalia go?'

A servant pointed, and Dominic took off at full gallop.

'Hey, that's my horse,' he heard as he rushed through the gate, but he had no time to explain.

Not far into the ride, he stumbled across the scene of a struggle on the riverside path Thalia had taken. While he rode, he searched the growth at the edge of the path, and soon picked up her abductor's trail.

The tracks became fresher, and their direction indicated the kidnaper's destination was likely to be Homewoods Village. Every now and then he slowed his pace and listened to the sounds of the forest. Sure enough, the furore made by horses crashing though scrub, and the murmur of voices soon filled the air.

They have no idea of how to move quietly through a forest. Dominic grinned. *Most helpful of them to be so inept.*

He followed, guided by the noise, keeping as quiet as possible. His borrowed mount had been trained to hunt, which made his task easier. The gelding made little more sound than a woodland creature as he picked his way through the heavy vegetation.

The trail led round the outskirts of the hamlet before the change in tone of hoofbeats signalled the kidnappers departure from the woods.

On foot, Dominic led his horse, searching for signs of their exit point. When he found it, he tied his mount to a tree, making sure to tie him loosely enough to allow him a nibble of lush grass. With the horse catered to, he turned his attention to the shacks in front of him.

To call them cottages was generous. They were the meanest dwellings used by the poorest people. Set apart from the main village, many of the buildings had been abandoned by their owners years before. Some of the houses had been tidied up by new inhabitants to the best of their meagre abilities. Still others were occupied by vagrants and vagabonds, giving the place the air of a temporary camp.

Outside one of the dilapidated buildings a man stood, holding the reins of five horses. The dwelling behind him appeared a little more solid than those around it. A mix of new and old timber on the door suggested recent repairs had been carried out. Fortunately for Dominic, the windows had not received any attention. They were only covered with a thick, dark cloth, meant to keep prying eyes and some of the weather out.

Concealed in the bushes, he waited while two men exited the building and placed a stout piece of wood across the exterior door. This bar was designed to keep people in, rather than strangers out.

The three men left on foot, leading their steeds. Only one man left inside. Dominic sat down to think. He was strong, but he would not be able to beat a grown man in a fight. Should he go to the guardhouse on the off-chance the duty officer would recognise him and do as he asked to simply because he was the son of the duke? Or should he return the way he had come and hope he came across some of Lord Ericsson's men? By now everyone would be out looking for Thalia.

At that thought he wondered, should he have waited and left with the main search party? No, if he had delayed he wouldn't have caught up with the kidnappers, and he would be left searching for signs of them, rather than knowing exactly where they were. Still, it would have been nice to have some help about now.

He ran his hand through his curly, dark hair. Retuning was risky, but so was trying to rescue Thalia by himself. If he was able to free her, then together they might go to the authorities and ask for protection until her father's men could escort her home.

He rose to his feet. Debating his next steps was not doing anyone any good. More information was what he needed, and the only way to gain that was to get closer to Thalia's prison.

A RESCUE PLAN

From the edge of the woodland he studied the back of the building. The one window on this side stood high enough up to be useless as a vantage point for sentries. Crouching close to the ground, he left the shelter of the trees, and upon reaching his destination he flattened himself against the mud and wattle wall, his head a hand span or two below the sill.

'What was that noise?' A gruff voice came from within.

No one answered so Dominic made ready to move, pausing as heavy footsteps followed the scrape of chair legs against wood. Out of the corner of his eye the curtain above him swung as someone attempted to gain a better view. The pounding of his heart filled his ears.

'I am not here, do not see me,' he said under his breath.

The covering dropped back into place. 'Must be hearing things,' a deep voice muttered, almost drowning out the creak of floorboards. Dominic waited. 'Humph,' the owner of the mutterings dropped back into his chair, and Dominic breathed a sigh of relief. Nervously calming his breathing, he inched to the right towards the corner. Back to the wall, he leaned around to assess this side of the dwelling.

A window stood about head height, the afternoon breeze fluttering the frayed cloth—a perfect place to try a quick peek inside. As he moved, a young boy emerged around the corner of the home opposite, stopping in surprise as he spotted an unfamiliar figure next door.

With his finger to his lips in the universal sign of silence, Dominic rushed over and led the boy back behind the building he had emerged from, out of view of the window. Squatting down until his eyes were level with a pair of serious brown ones, he introduced himself.

'Hello, I am Dom.'

Remembering how, as a youngster, he loved when people treated him as a grown-up, and especially when they shook his hand, he thrust his own hand forward.

'I am John, sir.' The boy solemnly took the offered hand.

The oddness of being treated like an adult threw Dominic for a moment, but he forced himself to concentrate on the problem at hand. He chose his next words with care so as not to cause alarm.

'John, do you know the men next door?'

'Mother said they are bad men and to keep away from them.' Although his face was fearful, his tone was conspiratorial.

On the assumption all boys were similar, Dominic guessed his new friend ignored his mother's advice and made finding out about the goings on next door his new game. Keeping his own tones hushed, he tested his theory.

'But we are brave and are not afraid of bad men, are we?'

The boy shook his head.

'So, you wanted to find out what they were doing?'

A nod of the head confirmed his suspicions.

'You spied on them. How exciting.'

John grinned, 'It was.'

'Can you tell me anything about what is happening inside there today?'

Again, the boy nodded.

'Before, when they took a girl in, I peeked out the window. She cried,' he whispered as he lowered his eyes. 'I think she was scared.'

Placing his hand on the boy's shoulder, Dominic spoke quietly. 'The girl is my friend, and I am worried those bad men might hurt her. I'm here to try and take her back home.'

'Can I help?' A gleam at the thought of an adventure sparked in his eyes.

Dominic thought the boy to be about six or seven, thin and wiry. Despite the fact an extra set of eyes would be a help, he was concerned about placing the child in danger. Then again, what about the risk the scallywag would attempt to do something regardless of his instructions to stay away?

Hurrying to think of something useful without putting the boy in harm's way, he inquired, 'Can you draw where the girl is?'

In response, the boy picked up a piece of wood and drew a square on the ground, and added a door and some windows. He partitioned a bit off, and placed a small rectangle against the wall at right angles to the window.

'The girl is on a bed in the sleeping room at the back. They tied her up.'

Astonished at the detail, Dominic asked the boy, 'How do you know this?'

'When they went inside, I dragged a crate over to find out what was going on.' Leading him by the hand between the buildings, John pointed to a wooden box. 'I was coming back to look again when I ran into you.'

Against his will, Dominic's face broke into a wide grin. At first, he thought this boy would scupper his rescue operation, but perhaps he might be able to provide something to help instead.

'Can you show me where the man is?'

With the stick in his hand, he marked an "x" in the front, beside the door.

Before he asked the next question, Dominic took a moment to think of what other information he needed for his budding plan to work.

'Where is the door into the bedroom?

The boy pointed.

He tapped his lip with an index finger as he studied the drawing. If he understood the layout, he should be able to slip in through the window without being seen by the man.

'The window is here?'

'Yes.'

Excellent, I will be out of the guard's line of sight when I enter. If I am quiet, I can be in and have Thalia out before he realises anything is amiss.

Dominic stood, and the boy trailed after. Surely he did not think he was coming too, did he? Making it clear the boy's involvement ended now, he asked one last favour. 'Thank you for everything, but I can do the rest by myself if I can borrow your box?'

'I can help you get her out.' The stubborn lad stood his ground.

'What I'm planning is risky, if we get caught, there is a chance those men will hurt us.'

'I'm not scared.' The child thrust out his chin. 'I crawl in and out of the hole all the time. No one worries about a small boy. Sometimes they chase me away, but most times they let me stay with them, if I'm quiet that is.' John stood taller as he bragged about his exploits.

'Hole?' In spite of his concern for the boy, he was intrigued.

'All the cottages have them. For the boxes.'

He went around the corner and indicated an opening a little larger than the crate, with a flap over top.

'After dark is not a good time to go out around here, so we put our night waste inside them. My job is to empty the box on the rubbish pile each morning.' He swept his hand in the direction of a midden at the forest's edge, beyond the last building. 'Mother calls it hygiene—whatever that is.'

The likelihood was all of the cottage's holes had been built in the same place. If so, the one next door would be right beside the guard. This would be of no use to Dominic as he would be seen entering, if he managed to actually squeeze through the tiny space.

'Thank you for everything you told me, you have been most helpful. I still think my best option is to go through the back window and sneak Thalia out.' A thought occurred to him as he spoke. 'You can be my sentry and make sure the others don't come back while I am inside. Can you whistle and alert me if they do?'

At least playing lookout would keep him busy and safe. Dominic thought his solution faultless, however the boy stood in front of him, hands on hips, unconvinced.

'They're not coming back until after their evening meal, so they'll be ages yet. I can do something else if you like.'

Worried if he did not find something for his helper to do, he would give the game away. Dominic sighed. 'All right, you can stand out back and help the girl out of the window. It is a long way for a girl to climb down.'

John could not know when it came to climbing, Thalia would beat a mountain goat, but he still appeared doubtful. Reluctantly, he shrugged his shoulders in agreement.

With relief, Dominic retrieved the box, and they both snuck around the back of Tahlia's makeshift prison. Noiselessly setting the box end upright, he stepped up and found the ledge mid-chest.

'Please do not see me.'

Under his breath he started his mantra before pulling himself up and over the window sill.

THE GREAT ESCAPE

It took a moment for his eyes to adjust in the dim light of the room. The figure of Thalia sitting on the bed, frowning at the window, soon came into focus. Smiling, he thought she would not be happy at her appearance. Always neat and tidy, her ordeal had caused strands of hair to escape its bindings, and her clothing was rumpled and partially untucked. Worst of all though, her face was scratched and covered with smudges of dirt. Fortunately, she seemed otherwise unharmed. That lifted his spirits.

Using his arms, he eased himself to the floor. Once he regained his balance, he sidled over to her, making sure to stay clear of the door. All the while he chanted his mantra, 'I am not here, please do not see me.'

As he approached Thalia looked around the room in consternation. Inch by inch he moved along the wall between the door and the bed, and her head turned as if she was searching for something.

'Thalia,' he whispered.

She swung her head to and fro, searching the room for the source of the sound. Confused, he stopped the chanting. Thalia's head came back around and she gasped as her eyes met his.

'What is going on?'

Thud.

Something fell to the floor, perhaps a chair as the noise was followed by footsteps heading towards them. Dominic ducked back beside the door, hoping the man would not spy him if he popped his head into the room to investigate.

'My hands hurt. Can you please come in and undo these ropes?' Thalia whined in a way most unlike her, perhaps attempting to trick her captor into believing any strange sounds were caused as she wriggled around to get comfortable.

Luckily it worked, the footsteps retreated. Bang. The seat was righted and it creaked as its occupant sat.

'Quit your whining or I will come in and tie your legs as well.' He chuckled to himself as though the thought amused him.

Pleased to have fooled the brute, Thalia grinned. In response, Dominic pulled out his knife and she presented her wrists for him to cut her bonds. Free at last, she stood and he nodded at the window. Her eyebrows flew up and she shook her head. With her hands, she indicated it was too high for her to climb. He cupped his own hands, showing how he would boost her up.

'What about you?' she mouthed.

Eyeing the height of the window, Dominic realised he would be able to clamber up, but not without making a lot of noise.

Full of bluster, he claimed, 'Easy.'

Thalia's brows remained in their raised position but, after a quick glance towards the open doorway she moved and permitted Dominic to help raise her up. He let out a sigh of relief and thanked the goddess she wore trousers rather than the divided skirt most girls preferred when riding. As she pulled herself up the rest of the way and sat astride the sill, a grunt came from the other room.

'Please, can you untie my hands? I promise not to run away.'

The trick did not work a second time.

'What are you up to?' A voice from the other room as his chair legs plunked down onto the wooden floor.

Dominic pushed Thalia through the window and she hit the ground with an oomph.

The sound of something scraping along the floor had the hairs on his neck standing on end, and it was accompanied by heavy footsteps heading his way.

Panicking, Dominic attempted to haul himself up through the opening above, while glancing back over his shoulder. A shadow loomed in the doorway, turning into a bulky male with large hands and a surly face. It took him a moment of surveying the room to take in Thalia's absence and Dominic's appearance.

At his best, Dominic would have completed his escape in the confusion, but weary from fear and physical fatigue, he froze. In a flash, the man moved to the window and squeezed a meaty hand around his ankle, yanking him back into the room.

Heroically, he struggled to maintain his grasp of the sill, while kicking out with the other leg. Ever so slowly, his fingers were losing purchase from the pressure, until a sharp bang diverted his attacker's attention. Puzzled, the man turned to identify the cause, and Dominic took the opportunity presented by the diversion to tighten his grip.

'What are you doing here, boy? Can you not see I am busy? Away with you now.'

'Is there anything to eat, mister? I'm ever so hungry and my ma will not be home for ages yet.' John snivelled for effect, and Dominic almost lost his grip in surprise.

His young friend, it seemed, had a mind of his own, and had taken it on himself to help with the escape.

'No, go away, I am busy. Ouch! Why did you do that?'

Not sure what John had done to the man, he was none-the-less grateful as, for a brief moment, the grip on his legs loosened, giving Dominic the opportunity he needed to pull himself up and out.

Dropping to the ground, twisting his arm as he landed, he glanced up. An angry face peered through the opening as the large man considered whether or not he could follow them through the gap. Next thing Thalia had pulled him up and was dragging him towards the woods. As she did the head disappeared and there was some scrabbling inside before it re-appeared as the man attempted to climb out after them.

'No. NO! We need to head to the square. To tell the guards what happened and ask for help.'

Dominic pulled Thalia back so hard she spun around, coming face to face with him, and he was able to see the anger in her eyes.

'I want to go, Dom. I just want to be away from here.'

She tugged to free herself, but he maintained his grip. Willing her to understand he rushed his words. 'If they come after us, I will not be able to fight them off. We need help.'

At that exact moment a string of words not often used in polite society came from inside. The gaoler realised the opening was too high for him to scale. With the door barred from the outside, it would not take him long to work out he needed to exit through the side window.

Thalia's gaze switched from anger to fear, and the arm he held trembled. There was no way he was going to let her be recaptured. Frantically he scanned the area, looking for somewhere to hide. It was the woods or nothing he realised.

Spotting John standing by his cottage, a piece of bread in one hand, he waved the boy away. It would be difficult enough ensuring Thalia's safety, let alone a young boy's as well. The boy shook his head and beckoned. What did he want? Could he not see they needed to escape?

His indecision allowed Thalia to make up her own mind. Not waiting for a second invitation, she pulled at Dominic and they tailed the young boy around his home and through an open door. Once they were in, a stout bar was lowered place.

Somewhat safe, Dominic suddenly felt drained and sunk to the floor. As he leaned back against the wall under a window, Thalia joined him. John pulled out a chair from the table, sat himself down and began eating his stolen food. Hopefully anyone looking in would think the boy was alone.

Dropping her head onto his shoulder, Thalia closed her eyes and relaxed against him. As she did, he felt a surge of protectiveness, and something else he could not quite place. All he knew was everything was better now she was back with him.

FREEDOM

The guard's cursing grew louder as his search drew nearer. The door shuddered but stood firm. Next thing a face peered through the window. John stared back, unblinking, while placing small morsels of bread in his mouth.

'Why you little... just you wait,' a gruff voice threatened. 'And if I find out you had anything to do with those two, well... you and your mother will realise we're not such friendly neighbours after all.'

'I am sure I don't know what you mean.' Although the words were innocent enough, the young boy's eyes twinkled with mischief.

'Argh, you need to be taught a lesson boy, but you will keep until later.'

Scratching and scraping noises penetrated the wood near Dominic's head as Thalia's captor continued to hunt for his missing charge. While they waited for the man to leave, he took the time to survey their hiding pace, and came to the conclusion John's family had fallen on hard times.

Apart from a rickety table and two mis-matched chairs, the only other furniture in the room was the bed in the corner. The comforter over top was skilfully made, but well worn in places. With no cover-ings on the windows, come winter, their home would be cold and damp. Still, someone had scrubbed the place until it shone. You could eat a meal off the floor it was so clean.

Turning his head, he found John's dark eyes watching him. The boy coloured with embarrassment as he realised Dominic was assessing his home, but raised his chin, whispering, 'My da died from the flux last autumn. My mother works sewing and doing laundry when she can, so we get by.'

Unmindful of the risk of being seen, Thalia leaned forward and took his hand. 'Your mother is doing a grand job looking after you, John. You are a fine young boy. Tell her when she gets home Lady Thalia visited and there is work for you both on Lord Ericsson's estate if she wants it. A cottage comes with the jobs. On six-day morning I will come back and arrange everything with your mother.'

Knowing his father would never help anyone who had sunk so low made Dominic a little sad. The duke believed those who fell on hard times did so because of their own mismanagement, and he would not raise a finger to help John and his mother. After all he had done that day, their helper deserved a reward, and Dominic glowed inside as his childhood friend offered assistance.

'Do you think I would be able to work with horses, miss? I do so love them.'

Prompted by John's excitement, Dominic had an idea.

'I borrowed one of Thalia's geldings to get here and I left him in the woods behind. Perhaps you and your mother might return him to the Ericsson estate and discuss possible employment a little sooner.'

His friend's smiling approval lifted his spirits, and a grin split John's face as he agreed.

'Do you know the way?'

The boy nodded he did.

Silence fell over the room, broken only by the banging and clunking caused by the guard's furious rummaging. Waiting until the sounds became more distant, Dominic spoke to Thalia.

'We need to move soon, before the others come back. First, I will slip out and check the coast is clear, then we need to run like mad to the guardhouse.'

Waiting until John slipped the bar from the door, he exited between the smallest of gaps. *Please do not see me.* Out front was deserted. He took a deep breath, stopped silently repeating his lucky words, and signalled for Thalia to follow him. Wordlessly, he led her between the ramshackle buildings until the streets widened, and the houses became more prosperous.

Before he entered the market area, a tug on his arm pulled him back into the shadows, nearly taking him off his feet. Pointing, Thalia drew his attention to a group of men sitting outside of one of the taverns on the edge of the square.

'My gaoler you have already met, and those other two helped kidnap me.'

Rather than showing fear, Thalia's face gave the impression she wanted to march over and give them all a piece of her mind. Not trusting her to control her temper, he kept an eye on her while he surveyed their surroundings. Whichever way they crossed the empty area, the men would spot them.

'There is no other way, we must wait until they leave,' he informed her. 'Unless... umm, maybe I should go across alone and hope I am not recognised.'

'You are not leaving me here by myself.' Her near-black eyes flashed as she rounded on him. Throwing her long dark curls back over her shoulder, she devised her own solution.

'If you do that thing when you disappear and hide me with you, we can stay together. Can you do it to more than one person?' Thalia asked, almost as an afterthought.

'Sorry?' His brow creased with confusion.

'You know, like when you came into my room. I heard noises and I was unable to find the source. Moments later you appeared out of nowhere. Then, when you went out to make sure my kidnappers had gone, you faded out of sight again.'

'You mean you actually couldn't see me?' Dominic's eyes widened in astonishment.

'Of course not.' Thalia glanced at him, her head tilted to the side, trying to decide whether or not he was teasing her.

'Wait, you didn't realise you made yourself invisible?' Now it was her turn to be surprised.

Still bewildered, he shook his head. 'No. Anyway, even if I can hide myself, which I do not believe, it won't help us.'

'Why not?'

'Because I am unable to do it again.'

'Why?'

'Think, Thalia. I'm unlikely to be able to do something again if I didn't even know I was doing it in the first place.'

'Oh....' Understanding dawned. 'Hold on, we can work this out.' Thalia's gaze went blank, the way it did when trying to solve a problem.

'Mmm, let me think. Before you went out the door you were definitely there. As you walked through the door, you were gone from sight. What did you change as you walked over the threshold?'

Dominic thought back, attempting to replay his actions. 'Nothing,' he said. 'No, wait a moment, I only prayed no one would catch sight of me, like I always do when I am trying to sneak somewhere. It cannot be that simple?'

'We can find out.' Thalia's eyes bored into his. 'You must try to do it again now.'

Blushing at her intense scrutiny, certain she was playing a prank, he agreed. 'All right, if you insist.'

He dropped his head, focussing on the neatly cobbled ground, and murmured, 'I am not here, please do not see me.'

Dominic's head snapped back up as Thalia gasped. She clapped her hands with glee.

'Wow, that is *amazing*. You faded right before my eyes.'

'Really?' Dominic lifted a sceptical eyebrow.

Ignoring the sarcasm in his voice, she moved on.

'Now let's try something else. Hold on to my hand and attempt to hide both of us. Only, you should watch this time so you can tell if I disappear.'

Instructions delivered, she held out her hand. Sure she was pulling his leg, he tentatively took hold of her fingers and began his prayer, only to drop them like a hot potato a moment later. Her hand was still visible, but his had disappeared. Shocked, he stopped his chant and breathed with relief as his fingers, then his palm, slowly reappeared.

'Oh, I thought that would work.' Shoulders slumped as she ran out of ideas.

'Wait a moment.'

Dominic hated to disappoint his friend, and he thought he understood how to fix this. Clasping Thalia's hand again, he began, 'Please do not see us.'

To his surprise, his hand faded away, and so did Thalia.

'Oh, that is good... very good. Now we can walk across without being seen.' Her voice reflected the smug expression on her face, but her smugness was short lived. As Dominic lead them into the square, their bodies began to reappear, a little at a time.

'Mmm, let me think for a moment,' Thalia said as they ducked back behind the building. 'Perhaps there is more effort involved in making two people disappear. When you move your concentration is split. So, how about you tuck your arm in mine. Let me worry about where we're going. You focus on whatever it is you do to hide us.'

Using her command voice to ensure Dominic complied, he did so without question. Experience told him arguing now would be pointless.

A few moment later the uneven cobbles under his feet announced their entrance to the marketplace. Thalia took things slowly so he did not stumble; a little too slowly. A pressure built behind his eyes signalling an oncoming headache of mammoth proportions, warning him there was a cost to doing whatever he was doing.

'Thalia,' he muttered. 'Thalia, I cannot do this much...' He stumbled and opened his eyes in time to watch the girl beside him blink into being. In the background the shocked faces of the men in the tavern warned him they had been spotted.

'RUN.' He grabbed at her dangling arm and pulled her towards the guard house. Thudding feet sounded closer and closer, and Dominic pushed himself to run still faster, his lungs working so hard his breath came in short gasps. Just when he thought they would be caught, the door opened and a soldier stepped out to identify the source of the hullabaloo disturbing the evening.

Dominic stopped in his tracks and half-turned in time to glimpse the last of their pursuers as they melted into the side streets.

'What have we here?' the guard demanded. 'A couple of street urchins causing mayhem.'

Dominic drew himself up to his full height before replying. 'I am Lord Dominic, and this is Lady Thalia. I have just rescued her from kidnappers and we need your help.'

'And I am the king. Pleased to meet you.'

All the pride and relief he had felt at rescuing Thalia fell away, replaced by anger and fatigue. Before he exploded and made their situation worse, Thalia stepped forward.

'Our appearance may be a little unkempt, sir, but perhaps on the off chance we are who we say we are, and that we are actually in danger, you might let us inside until things are proven one way or another. I mean, it won't hurt will it?'

The guard do not move a muscle, so Thalia pressed even harder. 'Imagine the furore if you turned us away, then something horrendous happened to the children of Duke Pierre and Lord Ericsson. Your career would be stopped in its tracks.'

While Dominic beamed in admiration at his friend, the soldier considered her words.

'I guess it won't do any harm to hear the two of you out,' he conceded as he moved aside to let them in.

HOMECOMING

Once safely inside the guard's room, he and Thalia had explained why local ruffians chased them across the square. Disbelieving, the captain questioned them closely until Lord Ericsson turned up moments later with one of the kidnappers in tow. The dim-witted fellow came to his door making demands for the safe return of his daughter, and soon found himself bound and on his way back to the village.

The guard locked the villain in a cell, where he was questioned. Not satisfied with the answers given to the captain, Lord Ericsson also took it on himself to grill the man. Both times he refused to name any of the others involved in the kidnapping, and he looked genuinely surprised when it was suggested Duke Pierre might be the leader of the group.

When it was obvious he was a hired minion with no real information, they returned to the office and there was a long, heated discussion about what to do next. Thalia and Dominic kept silent, content to leave the adults to decide the best course of action.

The two men agreed the captain should pursue the other kidnappers as he had some idea of who they might be, but they could not agree on how to deal with Duke Pierre. Eventually the captain agreed with James Ericsson's insistence they let the king deal with the errant duke.

Lord James promptly dispatched a messenger to Bannock to request the king's intervention, then the now weary man took his daughter by the arm, ready to leave for home. Thalia briefly hugged Dominic goodbye, whispering her thanks and promising they would meet again soon. Dominic was left with the guard captain to escort him home.

From under the cover of his long, dark fringe, Dominic watched his father's face, attempting to gauge his reaction to Homewood's Captain of the Guard's formal report of the proceedings earlier that day. Having been given the job of returning Dominic home, the man found himself being asked to describe the rescue of Lady Thalia from the clutches of some undesirable kidnappers, and their efforts to find all of those involved in the plot.

It was not an unreasonable request from the man responsible for ensuring the safety of all who lived in the area, but tightening around his father's mouth betrayed Duke Pierre's displeasure as the story unfolded. Still, he hid his feelings well as he congratulated his son for his brave actions. The guard finished his story without giving the slightest hint he knew of the duke's own role in the affair. Dominic sagged with relief, hoping that would be the end of it as far as he was concerned. His duty done, the captain had no option but to return to the village, leaving Dominic with his father.

Once they were alone Dominic tried to slip away before his father could turn his barely concealed anger towards him. The duke grabbed his arm and swung the boy around to face him, his pleasant demeanour disappeared as lips curled with distaste.

'I suppose everyone else has commended your bravery. I, on the other hand, know while you were out playing hero, you should have been attending dance instruction with your master. For your disobedience, you will be sent to bed without supper. Maybe your empty stomach will remind you to focus on what is important, and keep your nose out of other people's business. Manage that, and maybe you'll not be such a disappointment to me.'

Abruptly, his father realised his arm, turned and entered the study, slamming the door behind him. He was not quick enough to hide the worry and fear in his eyes from Dominic.

Rubbing his arm, Dominic grinned as he climbed the stairs to the room he shared with his brother. He had been fed a hearty stew at the guardhouse, by now Thalia would be at home, and Duke Pierre and his accomplices would soon be brought to justice. All in all, it was not a bad day.

A KINGS'S JUDGEMENT

Dominic hid in the shadows as King Terion entered with a tall, striking woman holding the hand of a young girl. They paused, waiting for the occupants of the carriage behind them to alight, before proceeding. Gasping in surprise, his mastery of the skill keeping him hidden slipped as Thalia and her father entered the hall and formally greeted their host.

His newfound trick back under control, he slipped into the ducal reception room behind the others, his trousers just about getting caught in the door. Finding a viewpoint behind one of the pillars spanning the room, he settled in to watch his father's punishment decided, hoping that finally his excesses would be curbed.

Formalities completed, the chamberlain led the woman and the child out of the room. As they left, the king took his father's throne, looking down on the two men standing before him. Duke Pierre fidgeted with this clothing, uncomfortable in front of his monarch, who was a man he loathed with every fibre of his being. Because of his Natarian heritage, his father would always consider the king an outsider, no matter how many generations had passed since their conquest of Aria.

'Firstly, let us address your recent tax levies. As a rule, I do not interfere in local issues, but the rapid rate of growth of your demands bothers me—especially as I cannot see additional money spent on improving the state of the duchy.'

Standing tall, the duke looked King Terion in the eye. 'I let things lapse a little after my wife's death.' His voice caught a little as he spoke of Duchess Gamina, 'I need to set the lands back to rights, and then there are some additional expenses, I can show you the accounts. I also need to provide a suitable dowery for my youngest son if he is to marry someone of the correct social stature...'

Dominic's heart skipped a beat. Had his father found a match for him already? It was too soon.

'I am letting you know, here and now, if there are further levies in the near future, I will permit your people to bring a case against you in the highest court in the land, and you will be judged by your peers; the other dukes.'

Lord Pierre did not move a muscle at the king's words.

'As for your methods of tax collection, I am not sure what has been happening in your duchy, sir, and I am not sure I want to know the details. Suffice to say, I would look unfavourably on anyone sworn to me, coercing their subjects into accepting additional taxes when they are clearly unable to pay.'

Dominic's father puffed his chest and swaggered forward. 'I am sure I do not know what you are talking about—' he started, but his monarch swiftly cut his excuses short.

'And I am equally sure you do. Fortunately for you, there is not enough proof to convince your peers of your guilt. If there was, you would be on your way to Bannock for trial instead of having this chat with me. So, let us at least not lie to each other in these walls, even if we cannot bring ourselves to speak the truth.'

The duke's face turned scarlet, but he wisely bit back whatever denial he had prepared.

'I cannot punish you personally for your actions, but I do need to do something to make sure Lady Thalia's life is a long and happy one. One without fear of retribution from you. Here is what is going to happen. Thalia will be marrying your heir, Hubert. This is not her choice, but she is not unhappy about it either.'

Dominic gasped and started to move forward to tell everyone this could not happen, before remembering he was not meant to be there and stopping himself. Until that moment he had not realised his feelings towards Thalia were anything more than friendship. Now, he would never find out what might have happened between them. His head buzzed so much he almost missed the next part of the proceedings, but refocussed in time to hear the king issue a warning.

'I want to make myself clear. This is the only match I will approve of for your heir. Should anything happen to his intended wife, he will not be allowed to wed anyone else. Your second son's line will not inherit. Your line will die when your firstborn does, and the Council will bestow your lands on another.'

Duke Pierre's back stiffened and his fists clenched and unclenched. In his vision of the future, Hubert married far higher than a mere lord's daughter, thus increasing their family's power and influence.

'And...' Pausing to ensure everyone in the room was listening, King Terion continued. 'To doubly guarantee your loyalty to the crown, your younger son will be returning to Bannock with me.'

'But... but this is unheard of,' his father exploded, his face beetroot with anger, spittle flew from his mouth as he spat out his objections. 'You let the rabble in the south do as they please, yet you force my son to marry low, and would take his brother from me—as if I have not lost enough already. Your actions leave me no way to advance myself or my family.'

The expression on the king's face remained stern and unaffected by the outburst, but his voice contained a thread of steal. 'That "rabble" do not flout the laws of Aria, and do not indulge in kidnapping for personal gain. Rather than worrying about what you lost today, perhaps you should focus on what you kept in spite of your heinous actions.'

Unable to take the perceived abuse any longer, the duke expelled a curse, turned on his heel, and stormed out of the hall. The doors shuddered as he slammed them closed. Dominic watched him in shock. It was a near treasonable offence to walk away from the king when you did not have leave to do so. King Terion showed restraint by not calling the man back and taking him to task for this breach.

'Well, James, it is done. With the information and witnesses we had, I could not do better. For your daughter's sake, I hope it is enough.'

Lord Ericsson drew his gaze back from the still vibrating door.

'Hubert is a good boy, Thalia could do worse. Although, I think if given the choice, she may have preferred the second son.

'Anyway, she is young so will be under my care for a few years yet. It is my hope by the time they wed, Pierre's animosity will be much reduced.'

'It is my hope as well.' King Terion ran a hand through his dark, wavy hair.

'With your leave, I would like to take Thalia to visit with Hubert before we head home.'

'You may go.'

Lord Ericsson bowed as he left the room. Dominic, who had been watching his departure, experienced an uncomfortable tingle down his spine. He turned to find King Terion staring directly at him.

'You may come out now, young man.'

TENTATIVELY, Dominic stopped saying his chant and left the shadows. When he reached the steps below the dais, he bowed before his monarch.

'You thought yourself well hidden no doubt, but I knew where you were. You let your guard down for a moment when the Ericssons arrived.' King Terion's voice exuded warmth as he spoke to Dominic.

'You might be interested to hear, before coming here Lady Thalia and I talked for quite some time. She told me a little about you and your adventures. She was extremely excited about a peculiar talent you displayed during her rescue.'

Dominic kept silent. Today's outcome was far less than he hoped for, but he worried he did not have the right words to voice his frustration to the most powerful man in Aria. At least not in a way that would not result in him being severely reprimanded.

'I understand you wished for things to be different today. Maybe you believed I would take your father away to be tried for his crimes? You are young; perhaps you cannot understand that my taking away exactly what he wanted to achieve with his foolish plans is perhaps the worst punishment I could give him.

'Maybe you also think I should let Thalia make up her own mind about who she marries, rather than dictate her future partner?'

Having his thoughts voiced out loud broke Dominic's fragile control, bursting the dam holding his animosity in place.

'Why did you not charge him under the law?' The words tumbled out. 'He is a bully and a brute. Everyone would be better off if he disappeared, and Hubert took his place.'

King Terion rose and stepped down to Dominic's level, placing a hand on his shoulder.

'You are angry at your father now, and I can appreciate how his actions have hurt you. Especially as you no longer have your mother for support. However, you may look on things a little differently once some time has passed. Although he went overboard with his treatment of Thalia, he believed he was making a better future for you and your brother. He does care for you, however he is perhaps not accustomed to showing it.'

Dominic said nothing, his hurt was still too raw to speak without anger.

'Maybe in time you will also come to understand Aria's stability relies on me not removing people merely because I do not approve of their actions. I need the law behind me when I make such bold moves, and I require the support of the other dukes.

'What I did today was the best I was able to given the circumstances. Your brother will partner with a strong woman, and he gains a stalwart supporter in Ericsson. In addition, I offer you an opportunity to live a productive life, if you will take it. Not only will your hurts mend faster if you aren't here, I believe your talents will flourish more under my guidance than they will if you remain.'

'I am coming with you as a prisoner.' Dominic studied the floor as he uttered the words, unable to stop the bitterness coming out.

'Look at me, Dominic,' the king commanded. 'I want you to look in my eyes so you can know I speak the truth.'

Dominic warily raised his dark eyes to meet a set of steely blue ones.

'I am taking you with me because I believe there is something in you more worthwhile than marrying for wealth and political gain. I believe the people of our nation will benefit greatly from your talents, and I would like to help you grow into the good man you promise to be.'

A glow spread through Dominic at the unexpected praise, and at that moment he would have done anything Terion asked of him.

FAREWELL

So, you truly aren't mad at me?' Hubert asked as Dominic placed more clothes in his pack.

'It is not your decision, so how can I be upset with you?'

Although he meant the words he spoke, he kept his face hidden from his brother lest he glimpse his hurt at losing his chance with Thalia. His mother's words stayed with him still, and he wanted to protect his brother from any more guilt over things not in his control.

'I... I...' Hubert started. 'Though I go on about her a lot, I always thought you... and Thalia ...' The sentence remained unfinished as if Hubert did not want to say the rest of the words out loud. Yet, they hung in the air between them regardless.

'Mother made it clear to us when we were little, we will not choose our futures nor who we spend them with,' Dominic reminded him as he closed his pack. 'No matter what, we will always be brothers, and friends. Besides, Thalia will make a wonderful duchess, and the ideal confidante for you when I am gone.'

Turning, he caught tears in his brother's eyes. 'I shall miss you, Dom. This place will be unbearable without you.'

'Finally you will get a room to yourself, at least that is something to be thankful for.' Dominic attempted to lighten the mood, afraid if he did not, his fears about leaving home might spill out, making his departure harder on them both.

'I would give it up, and everything else, if only you could stay. This place is glum enough without you. I fear I will not have the confidence to keep up old friendships once you are gone.'

Dominic's stomach lurched. His shy brother most likely would hide himself away in his room when not at lessons. Then he remembered something, and he studied his brother, deciding whether or not this was the time to tell him.

'No one told you?'

'Told me what?'

Deciding this was the perfect time to give his brother some happy news, Dominic elbowed him in the ribs. 'From what I understand, from now on you are to live half the year with the Ericssons.'

Before agreeing he would learn to serve his nation, he wrangled this one additional concession from the king, ensuring Hubert was not left alone at their father's mercy. Dealing with their father's bulling for only part of the year clearly made his brother happy. The grin plastered over his face made the sacrifice of his own future worthwhile. Dominic also believed his brother would be a better duke for spending time under Lord Ericsson's influence.

Hubert's face clouded again. 'It is not fair. I am doing well out of this, and you will be a prisoner. Goodness knows what will happen to you if father strays again. There is no certainty your being held by the king will stop him from doing whatever he wishes.'

Dominic laughed as though he found this funny, although he was secretly pleased by the show of concern.

'Hugh, I will hardly be kept in a dungeon. I am to travel to the estates of Lord March, near Bannock. Until I turn of age I will be treated as one of his family. Once I turn eighteen, I will be commissioned into the Arian forces until I find a wife and am ready to settle down.'

'March? Is he not the one they called the King's Spymaster?'

'So I have heard.' Dominic lowered his head to hide his embarrassment. Spy-craft would never be considered a suitable occupation for a gentleman, yet part of him was excited to be learning a useful skill, even if he could never discuss his work in polite circles.

'Oh, Dom, are you sure about this?'

Sighing dramatically, he opened the door, 'A spy? Or a peacock to be sold in marriage? Which do you think I would prefer, Hugh?'

Hubert trailed him to the stairs. 'I cannot bear to say goodbye.' He clumsily hugged his brother. 'Take care of yourself, and I will never forget what you gave up for me.'

'I don't know what you are talking about.' Dominic chose that moment to check his boots for dirt, attempting to hide his fear of the future from Hubert.

'Thalia and I talked for quite a while before she left, and she explained to me much of this was your doing. We may not meet again for some time, but you will always have a home with me, or with her family, if you change your mind about what you want to do.'

No trusting himself not to cry, Dominic said, 'Bye, Hubert.' He hastily hugged his brother. There was a wrench inside, as though he was tearing his heart from his chest, and he ran downstairs before the water welling in his eyes made tracks down his cheeks.

At the bottom of the steps stood the woman who arrived with the king earlier that day, and the girl, who was so like her she could only be her daughter. One hand surreptitiously wiped the tears from his eyes as the queen took the other and tucked it into her arm, tactfully ignoring his distress.

'I am honoured you are joining us on our journey home, Lord Dominic.'

Acceptance and warmth radiated from her, lifting his spirits a little as he sniffed back the last of his tears.

'Who is he, mama?' A pair of bright blue eyes curiously stared up at him.

'This is Lord Dominic, and he is to travel back with us. Your father says he is a special boy. A boy who will someday grow to be an exceptional man.'

The woman placed her hand on the girl's shoulder, urging her towards the door, but the girl did not budge.

Her hand reached up and pushed a stray strand of blonde hair behind her ear. 'I like him, mama.'

CHAPTER 6
YOU MAKE A GOOD POINT

Her father stopped speaking, and the room fell silent. As he placed his mug on the table, he knocked the cake plate, pulling Mina out of the story world he created as he spoke. 'You were quite daring when you were younger.' Mina laughed. 'I understand why you didn't tell us that particular story before. No parent wants to encourage their child to go gallivanting off after criminals.'

'As I've already said, I didn't know then what I know now. But that wasn't actually the point of my telling this to you.'

Her father raised an eyebrow, a signal to Mina that she wasn't going to get away with only discussing the adventurous elements of his tale.

'I guessed that, but your situation and mine are hardly the same. Firstly, you didn't become the plaything of a wealthy woman—you married someone who respected your abilities and became joint ruler of Aria. Also, you *chose* to marry Mother, and only after taking control of your life.'

Her father cocked his head to the side and studied her. 'Mm, I

hadn't quite thought of my life along those lines, and you're right. In my mind, the parallel with your situation was more about both of us having responsibilities thrust on us because of our parents' positions, and I know how difficult that can be to live with.'

Mina nodded. 'It *is* hard.'

'What about boys and girls born to poor parents who have to give up school to go to work simply so their family can live, or a child growing up in a fishing village who has few options but to crew fishing boats or process the catch? Are the challenges they face any easier than yours?'

Tensing, Mina wondered if this was going to be yet another discussion on how lucky she was to have been born a princess.

'I guess, as I grew older, I learnt every person is born into a situation they may or may not like, and who they are limits their options as they grow to adulthood. Some accept their position, but many like you and I, and your mother, cannot help but rebel.'

Mina laughed, releasing the tension. This was not what she expected.

'I've never said I am unwilling to give service to the crown. The only sticking point is how I spend that year.'

'True. We tried what your mother and I wanted. At least now we're letting you have some input.'

'To be fair, you demanded I go to the Wizard School for the year —I was never going to be able to stay somewhere like that for the full amount of time.' Mina actually enjoyed these debates with her father, but she had to be careful, as he always seemed to be one step ahead of her.

'Yes, we thought that would be a good option, because we listened to you and knew you wanted to join the guards. We also knew if you developed your magical abilities, every guard troop would be vying for your services. So, it actually met your needs and our own desire to promote girls being able to attend the Wizard School. Perhaps our biggest mistake was not fully explaining our reasons to you, but we weren't sure you would have liked it any better if we had.'

'Mm, maybe, maybe not. And I think your reasons weighed more heavily on the side of getting girls into the Wizard School than considering my future.'

'Touché. Perhaps you're right. It was a little unfair of us not to fully take into account your feelings on the matter. In our defence, you have to consider we had no alternative, because the wizards on the isle are the only ones in Aria who can provide you with a licence to use magic.'

A knock sounded at the door. Her father frowned at the interruption before saying, 'Yes.'

The doorman entered. 'Your next appointment is here, sire.'

'Thank you, please ask him to wait a moment.'

The guard withdrew, and when they were alone again, Mina said, 'I have a lot to think on. I should let you return to your kingly commitments. Besides, I'm meeting with Mother for lunch and more of these discussions.' Mina couldn't help the grimace that crossed her face as she thought of her lunchtime commitment.

'Admina?'

She stopped, her hand almost on the door handle. 'You know we both love you and only want what's best for you, don't you?' her father prompted, running a hand through his hair, leaving a few unruly strands sticking out in a most unking-like way.

Her heart melted a little at the gesture, and she said, 'Yes, Dad, I know. That's what makes this all so much harder.'

As she slipped through the door, the guard stood to attention. She nodded, acknowledging the sign of respect, then smiled hello when she recognised Tom, one of her sparring partners. Turning down the corridor, she slammed straight into a man she hadn't even noticed was there. He was dressed entirely in grey and had almost blended into the shadows the way her father's magic allowed him to.

'Pardon me, Princess,' he mumbled as he moved past her, keeping his face averted.

Walking briskly back through the corridors to her room, she could not stop dwelling on the incident. It bothered her that, if asked, she wouldn't have been able to describe a single thing about the man. She took some comfort from the fact that he was visiting her father and was probably one of his intelligence gatherers, so he was not likely to be up to anything nefarious.

By the time she reached the family quarters, her mind was back on her own problems, preparing herself for an uncomfortable lunch with her mother. Now that her father had proven he wouldn't support her joining the guard, she needed to regroup and plot her next steps. Stopping in front of her door, she changed her mind, turned on her heel, and headed farther along the corridor to Gabriel's room.

CHAPTER 7
TIME FOR A NEW PLAN

'Gabriel, why can't they understand they aren't actually giving me a choice at all? I can't become a guard until I learn to master my magic, and I can't do that without the wizards. They get everything they want, and I'll still be the number one freak on Wizard Isle.' Mina flopped onto her bed. 'I simply want to be normal. Why can't they see that?'

Gabriel left the book he had been studying when she entered and took a chair by the fireplace.

'Aren't you going to say anything?' Mina popped back up, frustrated at the absence of her brother's answering support. She was about to blast him again, but the forlorn look on his face gave her pause.

'Gabriel? Are you all right?'

'Yes, I guess.' Gabriel's tone did nothing to reassure her.

'Where were you this morning?' Mina frowned, trying to remember if he had mentioned last night what he was doing today. 'Has somebody upset you? Shall I have words with them?'

'Honestly, Mina, why do you always assume someone is picking

on me? And, just because I don't spend all my spare time in the practice yard, it doesn't mean I can't stand up for myself.'

'Right, sorry.' Mina chewed her lip. It was unlike her gentle-
natured brother to lash out like that. Then she remembered—Father
had asked Gabriel to volunteer at the infirmary and offer to write
letters home for the injured guards from Casey's new troop.

'It must have been tough for you today, spending time with the
wounded.'

'It was. Some of them have lost arms and legs. One girl may lose
her sight from a head injury, and she's worried about how she will be
able to send money home for her family. If her eyes don't improve,
she can't remain in the guard. And when I come here for some peace
and quiet—'

'All you got was me, whining about my woes, which even I can
appreciate are nothing compared to what those people are facing.'

'Exactly, Mina. Most people would give their right arms to have
to make your choice, in fact to have any choice at all.'

'You make me out to be a selfish, self-centred person, Gabriel.'
Mina stopped, wondering if the reason her brother saw her that way
was because that was exactly how she sounded. She hadn't told him
anything about her experiences on Wizard Isle, but maybe if she did,
he would think differently about her behaviour. *If I'm going to ask him
to help me, I should tell him what went on*, she thought before continuing.

'Mina? Are you still with me?'

'Sorry, I was thinking. I want you to understand this isn't me
throwing a tantrum so I get my own way.'

'I didn't say—'

'You didn't see how those wizards looked at me when I went for a
tour of the school. They didn't want me there any more than I
wanted to go. They don't think women are capable of wielding
magic, and they hated Mum and Dad for forcing them to admit me
as part of the first class.'

Gabriel sat forward in his chair. Knowing she had his attention,

Mina continued. 'Even though I was only there for a couple of days, I got a chance to speak to some of the girls training to be full wizards. Gabriel, their lives are miserable. Most of the other students are always trying to trip them up, and many of the masters aren't much better.'

'Funny, normally that would make you want to show them just how good a wizard you can be, make them eat their words.' A smile tugged at the edges of Gabriel's mouth.

'How well you understand me. I have to admit part of me does want to show them how wrong they are. Unfortunately, my magic isn't very strong, so I'm afraid I will never amount to much of a wizard. What I was most worried about was that I might actually prove them right, that women can't be trained, and then I would have let so many people down.'

Gabriel stared at her, wide-eyed, as if he didn't believe what he was hearing. 'You truly think if you failed, you'd be letting down every other girl in Aria who has magic?'

'I wouldn't put it like that.'

'Well, how *would* you put it?'

Mina thought for a moment, then shrugged. 'Just like that, I guess.'

'Why haven't you told Mum and Dad? I'm sure they'd be supportive.'

'What? Tell two of the people who saved Aria from a god that I'm too scared to fail because I can't bear to let people down? Yeah, I'm sure they'll completely understand my point of view.'

'They might, you know.'

Mina shrugged. 'Perhaps, and I might find the strength to take on the wizards if I actually wanted to master my magic... and pigs might fly.'

'So the talk with Dad hasn't changed your mind on that front?'

Mina shook her head. 'The wizards can't teach me how to use my specific abilities. The best they could do is help me learn to control my magic. I don't want to endure their scorn and loathing to gain so little.'

'Mm, difficult. And you're sure you can't be a guard without your unique talent?'

'Casey said as much.'

'What a pickle.' Gabriel leaned back in his chair and stared at the unlit fire.

Mina threw a pillow at him. 'Thanks for the great advice.'

He dodged the pillow, then bent and picked it up from the floor. Hugging it to himself, he said, 'Maybe if you can't solve the problem before you, you have to redefine the question.'

'What?' Sometimes Gabriel's brain went off on such a tangent she found it difficult to follow his line of thought.

'You want to join the guards, but to be of use to them, you must learn to use your magical abilities. The wizard school can't train you, because they don't have tutors with your expertise, even if you would consider returning to their school. If you contemplate those two things from a different perspective, the question becomes, where else can you develop your skills so you can join the guards?'

Mina sprang to her feet and flew across the floor to hug her brother. 'Gabriel, you're brilliant. What would I do without you?'

'The simple answer is you wouldn't last for long without me around.' He smiled at her as Mina took the seat opposite, letting him have his moment of glory. As she half listened to him listing the ways in which she would not survive if he were to leave, she thought to herself, *Now if only I can get over my fear of using my gift, perhaps I can find somewhere I can learn to be a scout.*

So lost was she in her own thoughts, it took her a moment to realise Gabriel had stopped talking.

'Mina, you've gone all pale. What's wrong?'

She was saved from having to answer by a tap at the door. She rose and opened it, surprised to find it was her mother's maid, Sharma.

'The queen sends her apologies, Princess Admina, but she cannot take lunch with you today. Something urgent has come up. She asked to meet in your sitting room for afternoon tea.'

'Excellent, do you want to eat with me today?' she asked Gabriel.

'I'm sorry, but you parents request your presence in the king's study, Prince Gabriel.'

The maid bobbed a curtsey and disappeared. Mina closed the door and turned to her brother. 'Any idea what that is all about?'

'I think maybe it has something to do with my going on a diplomatic mission with Dad. He's been making noise about it being time I did something more "hands on",' Gabriel said, standing and checking his clothes to make sure they were appropriate for a meal with his parents.

Mina surveyed the plain linen shirt and leather trousers he had worn on his visit to the infirmary and shook her head. 'If this meeting is in Dad's official office, goodness knows who might be there, so you'd best make an effort to dress appropriately,' she advised.

Gabriel grimaced. 'You're right. I'd better change. Sorry to rush you out, but....'

She smiled. 'You've been summoned, and I'm stopping you from getting ready. Thanks again for your help,' she said as she left the room.

⁂

'I ran into Casey in the stables. She said the two of you gave Mina a few home truths today,' Aliah said to her husband as she flicked her plait over her shoulder, dislodging a stray twig caught in her hair as she did. She picked it up and walked over to the rubbish bin to dispose of it.

The request to join Dominic in his study was waiting for her when she returned from her ride. With little time to meet with him and change before her lunch with Mina, she elected to remain in her riding clothes.

'Let's say I gave her food for thought.' Dominic's nose wrinkled. 'I know I said we needed to talk immediately, but you could've bathed and changed first.'

'Why? Is someone else joining us?' She dropped into a chair.

Ignoring her question, Dominic passed her two letters. He waited patiently while she scanned their contents.

'So, Hubert's mission failed to make contact at all, and Liam is concerned about escalating activity within Sanctuary's borders.'

'Did you read the bit about the prisoner Sanctuary's guards captured?'

Aliah sent him a withering glance.

'All right, you did. After the great magical wars in Malloria decimated the population, the number of people left outside of Sanctuary's boundaries was small. Now, it appears they're being pushed from their lands by something... perhaps an influx of new people. Some of the newer reports mention halflings.'

'People fleeing for their lives require a bit of tact and diplomacy... so... we need to consider this border situation in a whole new light.'

Dominic sighed and ran a hand through his hair, and Aliah noticed the few strands of grey were multiplying. 'I have no option but to go and broker a peaceful solution between the border communities and the incomers. While I'm there, I will also look into what can be done for the people being forced from their homeland in Talagria. It seems like we have finally relocated the last of the Carsten refugees, and now we will have to find places for a whole new group of homeless people.'

Aliah reached across the desk and covered his hand with hers. 'I would go if I thought I would be of any use. Although my people-handling skills have improved, you are still the best at managing impossible situations. And you may also need your other talent to help bring about a peaceful solution.'

He smiled at her. 'I haven't used that in a while. I am not sure I would be able to hold it for long enough to be of any use.'

Aliah laughed. Her husband's magical ability to disappear, blend in with the scenery, was legendary, and she knew he had been practicing his disappearing act quite recently. 'You forget, I can tell when you are in a room, especially when I have my sword on me.'

Dominic's eye's sparkled. 'And when was it you think I... um... spied?'

'Last six-day, when I met with the delegation from the Eastern Duchy to discuss new road tolls. You didn't trust me not to get angry with them, so you snuck into the room before we arrived and hid yourself in the corner by the door.'

'Maybe if you hadn't dressed as Aria's Warrior Princess, I wouldn't have been worried about your intentions.'

'It doesn't hurt to remind them their road taxes fund the guards who keep the peace and ensure their goods travel freely throughout the realm.' Aliah flicked her plait over her shoulder, annoyed at Dominic for questioning her judgement.

'There are far more subtle ways to do that.' Dominic was still smiling, but his tone was serious.

Aliah considered her words before responding. 'Did it occur to you that I was aware of exactly what I was doing when I selected what to wear for that meeting? I chose to be The Warrior, because sometimes our people need to be reminded our prosperity and peace came at a cost, and we need to be vigilant to ensure we maintain it.'

Dominic nodded. 'I didn't go solely to check up on you, in spite of what you think.'

Arching an eyebrow, Aliah leaned back in the chair. 'Really?'

'Yes, really. It may surprise you, but sometimes I use my gift to move around and go to meetings for no other reason than to make sure I don't lose the knack. I chose that meeting to test my skills, because I thought it would be entertaining to watch you deal with those grumbling old men, but I also wanted to find out if you could still see me with the sword on after all these years. I mean, you hardly ever use the sword's magic anymore except when talking with Seamus, so I wondered how strong your connection still was.'

Contemplating her husband, Aliah could find no signs he was deceiving her. 'Why haven't you told me you still sneak around like a spy?'

'Mm, perhaps because you use words like sneak and spy with such disdain. You've never been comfortable with my previous job.'

Leaning forward to meet the challenge, Aliah thought better of it and relaxed. There were more important things for them to focus their energies on; besides, he was right. Years ago, her mother's death had been at the hands of a spy who infiltrated the castle, and she had never fully reconciled that part of Dominic's life with who he was now.

'Fair point,' she said. 'And I can hardly complain now that I am hoping you might be able to slip into the Talagrian camps and find out what you can. If you can use those skills to help resolve our current border skirmishes....'

'I thought I might take Gabriel with me. It is time we started involving him in matters of state. In fact, I have taken the liberty of postponing your lunch with Mina and organising for him to join it so we can discuss it.'

Aliah froze, not quite sure she heard correctly, or perhaps she didn't want to believe her husband was actually considering taking their son to a border skirmish. 'Gabriel, but he is too young.'

'No, he isn't. When I was his age, I was touring the country, spying for your father, and you were fighting a god. He can only learn so much from studying books. Now is the time to find out if he can put all that knowledge to some practical use.'

'But it might be dangerous.' Her protest sounded weak even to her own ears, and she didn't even know why she was arguing. She and Dominic had often spoken of their concern that Mina might refuse the Heir's Ring and how they needed to prepare Gabriel to take up the role of future regent. Still, he was her youngest, and she wasn't quite ready to let him go.

While she worked all this through in her head, Dominic came round from the other side of the desk and sat beside her. Taking her hands in his, he said gently, 'It is time, Aliah. Our children are grown, and we must let them find their own way; otherwise, we will be leaving Aria defenceless if anything happens to us.'

'I appreciate that, but—' The room disappeared from view as Aliah's consciousness was given an almighty tug.

Aliah, good, you're here.

As if I had a choice?

Sorry for being so rough. I only have a little time, and I need to speak with you urgently.

Amelia? Aliah was more than surprised. The seer was usually so scrupulous about following correct protocol when mind speaking. For her to pull Aliah into a conversation in this way could only mean one thing—something was very wrong.

Again, I can only apologise for being so abrupt... so many things to do and so little time. Seamus has been sent to the borders to deal with some incursions. You must hurry and meet him there. You and he must face this threat together.

Dominic and I were discussing arrangements for him to go and do just that. He can certainly meet up with Seamus. I'm sure, between them, they can get this situation sorted.

No! You are required. I have seen it. The Wizard and The Warrior must do something to make sure everything turns out right, and you need to do it soon. Something big is about to happen, and it will be worse if you don't deal with the border issues first. Amelia spoke with her great-seer voice, the one she was used to having obeyed immediately.

However, Aliah was no longer the young girl who would jump to on a mere command.

Can you tell me about your full seeing?

All I have are fragments at the moment. Walter and I have been looking through some old scrolls, trying to find out more, but we haven't had much luck. All I can give you is, I'm certain you and Seamus must meet at the border, and you must do it soon.

All right, let me talk with Dominic, and we'll see what we can arrange.

Amelia left her consciousness as abruptly as she had entered. Shaking her head, Aliah found herself sitting back in the chair in Dominic's study. On the desk in front of her was now a tray of steaming pies, Gabriel's favourite, and a carafe of caffe. The door clicked behind her, and Dominic returned to her side.

'Someone needed you urgently, I see.'

'Amelia,' Aliah said, while her brain sorted through everything the seer said during their brief conversation. 'She says it must be me to go to the border. She's had another seeing.'

A knock at the door prevented Dominic from responding.

'Yes,' he said.

The door opened, and the guard entered. 'Prince Gabriel is here, sire.'

'Thank you, send him in.'

The door swung inwards, admitting their son. The guard closed it as he withdrew.

'Come in, we have your favourite lunch here,' Dominic said, indicating the chair beside Aliah. As Gabriel kissed her on the head, Dominic retook his place behind the desk.

'Your mother and I wanted to discuss your accompanying her on a diplomatic mission to the west.'

Her son's eyes widened in surprise. Then he frowned, but before he could voice his thoughts, Dominic said, 'Come, let's eat while we talk.'

Gabriel and Dominic helped themselves to food and caffe while Aliah sat watching them, unable to force even a single morsel down her throat. When they finished, Dominic wiped his hands on a napkin and looked towards her, a single eyebrow raised in query.

'So, I am going? Just like that? No discussion, no considering other options?' she asked.

'Amelia is rarely wrong, and she must be quite certain of the necessity of your being there to contact you in that way. If you're the one who has to go, I can accept the change of plans.'

'I thought I was done with The Warrior stuff.' She looked up to find her husband nodding towards their son, and she realised Gabriel finding out how worried she was about this strange turn of events was not good, especially given he was about to leave on his first official mission. What he needed was to see a strong leader who was capable of dealing with a skirmish on their borders.

'Is this something more than a trip sorting out some border problems?' he asked.

Aliah forced herself to shake her head. Pulling herself together, she turned to explain. 'Nothing bigger than that. Your father was going to go and deal with it. Unfortunately, Amelia has told me we will have more of a chance of resolving the situation if I go as The Warrior.'

Gabriel returned her gaze, but she could see from the confusion in his eyes that he was not convinced. Her youngest was an old soul who often saw through to the heart of matters. She smiled wanly at him, silently begging him to let it go.

He shrugged and said, 'Are you sure you wouldn't rather take Mina? This is exactly the type of thing she would enjoy doing as part of her year of service.'

'Oh, Gabriel,' Aliah started, but she caught Dominic shaking his head and stopped.

'Gabriel, we're sending you along, because you haven't had the opportunity to join a diplomatic mission, and it is time you did,' Dominic said.

'But my going does not mean Mina can't come as well,' Gabriel argued.

'True,' Dominic conceded. 'But there are other things we must take into consideration, not the least of which is what Mina would learn if we sent her on this mission with the two of you given her current situation.'

Gabriel looked down at his hands as he considered what his father was saying. 'Well... she'd be relieved not to be going to the Wizard School. She would be happy to be out with the guards—'

'Yes, son, but what would she have learned?' Dominic pressed.

'She would think she has gotten her own way. So perhaps she will believe if she holds out for long enough, she will always get what she wants?' This was more of a question than a statement.

Across the desk, Dominic's face relaxed. He knew, as did Aliah, that Gabriel was loyal to his sister, but if he understood why she could not come with them, he might be a useful ally when it came to calming Mina down when she learned what was happening.

'She has been set a task to find something she can do to benefit Aria. If she can convince us of how her going along will achieve that, she may join you,' Dominic said.

Another knock sounded at the door.

'Enter,' Dominic commanded.

'Guard Captain Madigan,' the doorman announced.

'Send him in,' Dominic said before turning to Aliah and winking. 'Bet you're wishing you had dressed more appropriately now.'

The man who entered the room seemed familiar. Aliah searched his face, trying to place where she had seen him before. Noticing his hair was still damp from a shower and a nick on his chin told her he was recently shaven, she looked into his eyes. Turning to Dominic, she said, 'One of yours, and you have promoted him to a guard captain?'

'Your powers of observation are improving, my dear. Madigan has been in Carsten for some time. When he arrived with their delegation, I took the opportunity to bring him home. I thought his particular skill set would be useful in dealing with our little problem on the border.'

'What skills would those be?' Aliah asked.

'Oh, they aren't magical, unfortunately, at least we don't think so. He has the ability to learn languages quickly, and also to mimic accents, which allows him to blend in and gather information in a number of difficult situations. I have asked him to lead the guard until you reach my brother's place. While you sort out fresh horses and replenish your stores, he will ride ahead and see what he can find out, and then catch up with you and Seamus at Breacher's Pass. Hopefully he will pick up something useful to help with your negotiations.'

'Pleased to meet you, Captain Madigan.'

'Your Highness.'

Throughout the conversation, the captain had remained at ease, but the flickering of his eyes told her he had taken in the fact that Dominic was no longer leading this mission. Standing, she said, 'You have a lot to catch the captain up on, and Gabriel will need to know how he fits into the company. I, on the other hand, have a more pressing matter—tea with our daughter.'

Nodding to them all, she left the room, already planning how to deal with the expected outburst from Mina when she heard her brother was going to the borderlands and she was not.

PART THREE
ONE STEP FORWARD, TWO STEPS BACK

CHAPTER 8
I'M NOT LIKE FATHER, OR YOU

Aliah sat sipping her tea as Mina paced and listed the reasons why she was the worst parent ever—taking off across the country instead of working through Mina's problems, being The Warrior again, choosing to take Gabriel with her when she knew Mina would like nothing better than to go, and simply just being who she was. As her daughter's anger wound up, she dug deep for every past grievance.

It would be pointless defending herself, because Mina was in no mood to listen. While her daughter ranted, she made some token attempts to interrupt; after all, Mina would expect her to protest a little. Meanwhile, she was actually thinking about what she needed to do to prepare for her departure in two days' time.

As she mentally reassigned her meetings to others, she realised the room was silent. Placing her cup on the table, she raised her eyes to her daughter. Mina stood in front of her, hands on hips.

'You haven't been listening to a word I've said, have you?'

Thinking of all the possible answers to that question, Aliah rubbed her forehead and chose to go with the truth. 'No, not really. Although, to be fair, I certainly got the gist of what you were saying from the first few sentences. I obviously will never measure up as a mother.'

Mina opened her mouth, and Aliah braced herself for another round of abuse. Unexpectedly, Mina frowned and sat down in the chair across the table.

'Mother, you look... well, you look exhausted.'

'Um... I guess I am,' Aliah admitted, flicking a piece of thread off the dress she had hastily changed into. 'With the Carsten delegation still here, your father was going to deal with the border dispute himself. Not only was my going unexpected, but it's come at the worst possible time—for many reasons.' Lifting her head, Aliah found herself under intense scrutiny.

'If I understand this correctly, Gabriel was going on a diplomatic mission to the borders with Dad. How is it you ended up going instead?'

Aliah sighed. Knowing Mina's dislike of her being The Warrior, she didn't want to discuss this, but her daughter deserved the truth.

Trying to inject some enthusiasm into her voice, she said, 'Amelia's had a seeing. The Warrior needs to go to the border if we are to resolve the problem of new people setting up homes on Arian lands.'

Mina stared at her mother for a long time, and Aliah wearily met her gaze and braced for another outburst.

'You don't want to go. You don't want to be The Warrior and go and save Aria again, do you?'

Surprised by the form of her daughter's attack, Aliah stood up for herself. 'I will always defend Aria, but the weight of destiny is sometimes hard to bear.'

Shaking her head, Mina said, 'No, no, that came out wrong. I always see you on the dais during public events, your god-given sword on your hip, being The Warrior saviour of the people. They adore you, and it annoys me, because it is difficult being the daughter of a hero.'

Aliah pursed her lips. 'You make your feelings on the matter of my past clear on an almost daily basis.'

Shaking her head, Mina said, 'I can't seem to find the right words today. I never thought about you having to do things you don't want to do. I never considered you might not have had a choice about whether or not you did all those things the entertainers sing about in their songs.'

Eyes wide, Aliah thought about Mina's comments and chose her own words carefully when she answered. 'Doing my duty for Aria is a part of who I am, but I won't deny a lot was asked of me back then. I also thought that time of my life was over and being The Warrior was now more standing as a beacon of hope for our people. So yes, it is difficult to go out in the field and be Aria's Warrior again.'

'But you will do it, because you believe you must,' Mina said, nodding her understanding. 'You know, I'm not like you. I don't think I could place my life at the feet of Aria.'

'And as your mother, I don't want you to become Aria's slave either,' Aliah admitted. 'I've never wanted you to sacrifice your happiness for your country like I had to for a time.'

'I do want to do my year's duty, Mum. It's just... a year on Wizard Isle... I can't. And magic... if I'm being honest, it scares me. I'm not like Dad. I can't use what I have to help me find my way in the world. I didn't ask to have magical abilities, and I don't feel like they're truly a part of me.'

'All right,' Aliah said, letting her daughter's revelations sink in. How should she handle this? This was one of the few times Mina had revealed something of herself to Aliah since she had moved out of the nursery and into her own room. Not wanting to bowl right in and ask more details about why Mina was scared of her gift, she asked, 'Is it Wizard Isle, or fear of your gift holding you back?'

Mina's fingers worried the fabric of her blue woollen dress. 'Both,' she whispered.

Her daughter's answer was unexpected, because once she had spoken of her worries, Aliah expected Mina to gloss over it. Most people she knew, including herself, had a healthy respect of magic, but it wasn't as unusual as Mina thought for people to be scared of their gift. Taking a deep breath, Aliah told her, 'Magical powers can be quite scary. I mean, once you're used to it, it can be amazing, but when you're learning to control it and develop your skills, it can definitely be overwhelming. The great wizard Seamus blew a hole in our boat when he was learning to use his.'

Aliah was relieved to see a smile on her daughter's face, and it brought one to her own when she remembered the incident. 'Would it surprise you if I told you one of the greatest magical beings of our time never wanted to use her magic?'

'Are you talking about you?'

Aliah laughed. 'Honey, my magical ability is very small, and I can only channel it when I have my sword. I'm not sure I even rate as a minor magical power. I am talking about The Great Seer, Amelia.'

Mina poured herself another cup of tea and sat back. 'Do I sense another story coming on?'

Smiling, Aliah refreshed her own drink. 'Indeed, you do. And for once, it's something you might be able to relate to. This story isn't about sacrifice or duty. This tale's about a young girl finding her place in the world.'

CHAPTER 9

AMELIA'S TALE

FAREWELL

'Please just come and look at it, Amalie,' her younger brother begged. 'You might love it and change your mind.'

'Me? On a farm? I cannot see it, Damon.'

Amalie carried on sorting through her wardrobe. After throwing the beautiful court gowns to one side, she selected only the most serviceable of her clothes. Even without a final destination, the finery women wore at the ducal court was not going to be of any use in her new life.

'There is an orchard, a garden, and plenty of berry bushes in the surrounding forest.' Her brother plonked himself on her bed, dislodging garments already folded in preparation for packing.

'Damon!' She allowed her exasperation to cut through her voice as tears came to her eyes.

Her decision to leave had not been her own—well, not totally—and it was difficult enough without her brother's attempts to change her mind.

'Come on, Amalie, you know I feel responsible for this. After all, if

I had not told Father about your foreseeing my accident this would never have happened.'

Sighing, Amalie paused before delivering a carefully worded response. 'You did not make the rule that said no one could remain on the Isle of Hand who is able to use magic.'

'But you used it to help me, to warn me. I did not have to tell Father.' Damon pressed.

'You were younger then, and scared. At the time you believed you were doing the right thing. In the end my foresight saved your life, so it all turned out for the best.' Thinking the subject closed, Amalie continued sorting through her belongings.

'But—'

Holding up her hand to silence the boy, Amalie turned and faced him. 'I knew my options when I turned eighteen. I decided I did not want anyone to take my magic away. Not only because I was concerned I would never be the same again, but because it is a part of me, part of who I am whether I like it or not.'

'I understand, but—'

'No, please let me finish, Damon. Again, it was my decision not to stay in the Southern Duchy. By remaining here I would still be able to see you all, but I would have to promise not to use or pass on the taint of magic. Someone might still want to take me in to their family under those conditions, but I fear few men want a wife who will not bear children. You have nothing to atone for. So quit worrying.'

'Will you find someone to train you how to use your gift?' Damon changed the subject.

This was something Amalie had not made up her mind about. On Hand, her gift was shunned, but she was not sure how people outside of her home island felt about women with magic. As the daughter of the Duke of the Southern Realm, her life had been quite sheltered, and besides—no one ever discussed magic on the Island of Hand.

'I am not leaving because I want to learn how to use my magic. I am leaving because I want a life as me.'

'You can do all that and remain close by, in the Southern Duchy.' Damon pressed his point.

Amelia rubbed her hand across her forehead, attempting to relieve the growing tension. 'If I remain close by people might recognise me, and they will know why I have been banished from Hand. If I go further away I can forget who I was—forget I even have magic altogether.'

'Perhaps you can do that, but look at what you have to give up to take that chance. Look at it this way, Ami—you have no plans, so why not just come and look? This is the best of both worlds. You can build a life of your own, but still be close enough for me to visit. After you have seen it, if you really do not like the idea, if you really feel you cannot build a life there, I promise I will not say another word. I will escort you to the ship for Bannock myself.'

Worn down by the nagging, she sighed. 'All right. You win.'

EARLY MORNING DEW hung heavy on the trees as they left the gates of Port Marden, heading towards the Tangled Woods. Having taken the boat over from the Isle of Hand at sunrise, they were met at the docks by a groom holding the reins of two horses. As she mounted, Amalie marvelled at Damon's confidence. Everything they needed was waiting for them when they disembarked, even though she had only agreed to go with him the afternoon before—leaving him no time to organise anything,

Once away from the confines of the city streets, Damon spurred his horse ahead, almost as though daring her to keep up. Still feeling drained from her farewells earlier that morning, Amalie was not interested in meeting the challenge.

Slowing his horse, her brother dropped back to walk beside her. 'You Father declaring he has no daughter and turning his back on you it nothing more than tradition. Neither he nor mother really meant it.'

Surprised he had accurately guessed the source of her sadness, Amalie attempted a smile. 'Knowing it and feeling it are too very different things.'

'True. I believe father said his real farewell last night.'

Looking up in surprise, Amalie caught her brother's smirk.

'He and I discussed your finances. I am tasked with seeing everything is set up to run smoothly for you.'

'It was... um... generous.' Girls banished by their families sometimes received the amount of their dowry, but the sum gifted to Amalie was far in excess of what would be expected even for the daughter of a duke.

Remembering the tears glittering in her father's eyes as he'd spoken the formal words of banishment, Amalie's heart broke at how her family was being pulled apart because of a stupid tradition.

'Damn the stupid laws of Hand. Come on, Damon, race you.' With the wind in her hair, she rode away her tensions and sadness.

Sometime later, when they had again slowed their horses to a walk, Damon said from nowhere, 'I will change the laws once I am crowned duke.'

'Damon, that is your guilt talking. You will no more be able to change the laws than our father was able to. He saw our uncle banished from the family, and now me.'

'I will. You just wait and see.'

The stubborn set to her brother's jaw brought a smile to her lips. You just might as well, but it will be far too late for me by then.

'We're almost there,' Damon said, again racing ahead.

Amalie kept to her leisurely pace, allowing the ever-present guards who shadowed the heir to the Duke of Hand to keep them in their sights. Damon had requested they stay a little behind to allow him this last ride with his sister, and they had complied. In return, Amalie promised them they would not ride off too far.

The gentle rocking of her horse, combined with the fresh

morning air, soon had Amelia almost asleep in her saddle. That was until Damon, who was riding a little ahead, stopped before a slight bend in the tree-lined track.

'Close your eyes,' he commanded.

'Damon, come on. Let's just get on with this.'

'Please, Amalie. Let me lead your horse. I promise it will be safe.'

Amalie indulged him as this was likely the last time they would be together. Closing her eyes, she held on to the front of her saddle, allowing Damon to escort her round the bend. Once her mount came to a stop, she waited a moment, listening to the birds chirp in the trees, before gazing on the scene her brother presented.

'Ta-dah.' He swept his arm out, encouraging her to take it all in.

She gasped with audible surprise. Damon had been right; the cottage was perfect. With its thatched roof and whitewashed walls, the two-storey dwelling was perhaps better described as a house. Nestled in behind was a stable and barn and, was that an orchard?

Her excitement welled as her eyes found a garden plot to the left of the house in which both vegetables and weeds poked through the soil, fighting for space, decorated in droplets of dew the early spring sun turned into sparkling jewels.

'See? I told you it was amazing.' Damon's face glowed with pride.

Amalie agreed. It was a great property. The garden might be expanded for herbs and the like. The gentle buzzing of bees as they flittered from flower to flower told her there must be hives close by. Making a living from this property was a real possibility. Although the idyllic rural scene, while easy to admire, did not immediately sing home to her.

'Damon, I'm not a farmer—'

'And this is not a farm. I mean, it once was, but the man who owns it sold the fields off to his neighbour when he grew too old to till them. He and his wife carried on selling produce from the gardens, orchards, and hives until recently.'

Damon dismounted and led his horse over to the well. Amalie followed and tied her own mount to an iron ring in the stonework.

Damon leaned against the cold stone and continued. 'A couple of moon turns ago, his wife passed on. The farmer could not bear to live here without her.'

'That is a sad story, but I still cannot see myself earning a living here.'

'Our factor assures me continuing on in the same vein as the previous owner will allow for a reasonable standard of living. We negotiated a great price for you, leaving you with some savings from the money Father bestowed. You could have a great life here, and Mother and I will visit ...' Damon stopped suddenly, his face a mask of concern. 'Amalie, what is wrong?'

Wiping the tears from her eyes, Amalie smiled a trembling smile. 'Damon, you may be able to sneak away, but Mother? You forget; she banished me.'

The heir to the Duke of Hand looked down at his sister, a mischievous grin on his face. 'Amalie, you should have more faith in us. Who do you think brokered the deal for this farm? Certainly not me. Our factor in Port Marden did it ... at Father's request.

'They may not be able to openly show their love and support, and Father being Father does not want to influence your decision one way or the other. Surely, though, this shows how much they want you near?'

Amalie searched his eyes for the truth of his words, and found it there. Although part of her wanted to rejoice at her family's support, her thoughts were still troubled. Almost more than anything else, she wanted to stay near her family, almost ... but at what cost? Was she prepared to give up a full life for that?

Unwilling to disappoint her brother after everyone had gone to so much trouble, she put on a brave face. 'Come on. There is no point in making a decision until I have seen the entire holding.' She slipped her arm through his and allowed him to lead her over to the door.

CREAKING OPEN THE DOOR, Damon said, 'We will need to put a little oil on the hinges for you.'

He stood back and allowed Amalie to enter her potential new home alone.

The external door opened into a single kitchen and living area dominated by a large wooden table. On the left, two doors led to other rooms. In front of her were stairs disappearing into a loft above. To her right was a cooking fire big enough for a large stew pot, with a built-in bread oven. Beside her stood a well-crafted bench with a copper bowl inset below a window, framing a view of the road.

'Perfect,' she mumbled under her breath as Damon slipped in beside her.

Moving inside, she opened the first door, which led to a decent-sized pantry room with a cellar opening in the floor near the back. Excellent—there would be a place to store root vegetables from the garden for winter.

'I'm sure we can bring you treats from the palace to keep in here when we come and visit.' Damon smiled as he herded her towards the next room.

Amalie peeked in to find a sun-filled room dominated by a huge wooden bed. Her eyes were immediately drawn to a delightful hand-crafted dresser inlaid with shells. Trailing her fingers over the intricate geometric design, she admired the craftsmanship. 'How is such a beautiful piece of furniture in a farmer's house?'

'The owner made the furniture for his wife. He could not bear to take it with him, said they contained too many memories. They were for sale, so I bought them for you.'

'You bought them for me?' Amalie marvelled at how thoughtful her brother was to spend his own money on her comfort.

Damon beamed smugly, before continuing, 'Mother says you can have the pick of the furniture at the Port Marden house for the other rooms. And did you see, there is a loft room upstairs where the farmer's children used to sleep? I can stay there when I come to visit. That is if you decide to stay.' Her brother stopped dead as he caught her face in the mirror. 'What is it?'

'It is just … this place was a family home …' Amalie's voice trailed off as she considered how best to put her thought into words. Until this morning, she had grown up with an extended family. Her mother's sister had been a lady in waiting to the Duchess. Her three children had grown up with Damon and Amalie, forming an almost inseparable group. Going from rarely ever being alone to living by herself in a home intended for a family was almost beyond her imagining.

She did not need to say a word.

'There is more than one way to build a family,' Damon said. 'We will still be here, and there are neighbours around who I understand from the previous owner have quite the social life. Then, once you are up and running, you will need some help. There are plenty of children with no home in Port Marden who would leap at the chance to live and work in a place like this.'

Amalie sighed. 'When did you get to be so smart?'

Her brother laughed and gave her a hug. 'I always was; you just never noticed before. Look, I will go outside and wait. Take as long as you need to make up your mind.' Shutting the door to the yard behind him, Damon left her by herself to walk through the rooms.

Someone had cleaned the whole house and made sure there were no outstanding repairs. The place was well made and cosy—she could imagine herself sitting by the fireside in the evenings after a busy day working the land. Of course she would need some comfy chairs to place by the hearth.

Returning to the bedroom, she looked out the window. It would not be a bad view to wake up to each day, although framing the glass with some fresh, floral curtains would improve the image.

Sighing, she went in search of her brother—Amalie had been bested

---

A NEW HOME

After a night staying in the family house in Port Marden, Amalie rose early the next morning and headed for the attics.

Although her mother had said she could take anything she liked, the furniture there was far too grand for a farm house. However, in the relics from the past relegated to the storerooms in the attic, she found exactly what she needed. Two old but comfortable armchairs for beside the fireplace, and a worn but still serviceable rug to place between them. A mismatch of wooden chairs for around the table, and enough curtains to cut down and make coverings for all the windows.

From the main house she took the feather mattress and quilt from one of the spare beds, and a painting of Hand from the living room. Her bedroom was to be her one concession to luxury.

Having chosen everything she needed, she arrived at the dining room in time for breakfast with Damon, who excitedly rushed her along, bursting to sign the paperwork to make the farm hers. Impatient to get going, he went to arrange transport of the furniture while she enjoyed her tea.

On the way to the meeting, the two discussed how the exchange would work as Amalie could not begin her new life as the daughter of a duke.

'What will you call yourself?' Damon asked. 'It needs to be something close enough to your name that you do not forget what you are called.' Damon started the ball rolling.

'Really? I hadn't thought of that.' The laughter in her voice took the bite from her response.

'I know. What was the name that master from Maloria called you? You know, the one who could never remember our names? I was Damien to him. My head still turns when someone calls out that name.'

'Yes, I remember him. For two years I answered to Amelia. That is perfect. What was his last name?'

'He was Master Brown. No... Amalie... you can't be thinking...' Damon was laughing so much he was not able to finish his sentence,

Amelia's mouth broke into a grin. 'That's it; I shall be Amelia Brown.'

Once the formalities were completed, Amalie found herself the owner of a property on the edge of the Tangled Wood in her own name. After the price was deducted, she still held a sizeable balance in cash lodged with her father's factor under the name of Amelia Brown.

The factor explained her money would be held like any other citizen who invested in Hand businesses. While it stayed with the company, it would earn interest, but it was there for her to call on at any time. On the way out, the factor handed her two sets of papers. The first was the deed to her farm, and papers identifying her as Lady Amalie; the second were the papers confirming her deposit, the rate of interest, and a letter confirming Lady Amalie was also known as Amelia Brown.

On the way out of town, Damon stopped by a blacksmith's and purchased a chest with a solid lock for her to keep her papers in, and then she left Port Marden for the last time as Lady Amalie.

Excitement mounted as her brother rode with her to her new property. Rounding the corner she rode into the garden and she was met with a bustle of activity as the cart was being unloaded. She was filled with an enormous sense of joy, which rose to nearly bursting point as she rushed forward to assist. Picking up a bundle she noticed a number of items she had not packed.

Cook had sent a variety of kitchen utensils, and a selection of pantry items to get her started. The housekeeper, Bessie, had added blankets and linen, along with a sewing kit and a selection of wool and some needles.

Tom, the cart driver, blushed as he said, 'Miss, I wasn't sure you'd have everything you needed for the garden, so I raided my shed for you. I hope that was all right.'

'Oh, Tom, you are so thoughtful.' Amalie hugged the man who had driven the family when they were on the mainland for as long as she could remember.

'Begging your pardon, miss, but you rushed out so fast this morning, Cook and Bessie didn't get a chance to say goodbye. They told me to pass on their best, and to tell you they understand you cannot visit via the front door anymore. They said whenever you are in Port, there is always a cup of tea for you in the kitchen, and some friends to sit a while with. You're welcome any time.'

Tom coloured again, and Amalie wiped the tears from her eyes. 'I will visit, Tom, but only if you all remember to call me Amelia. In fact, when I come, I will bring produce from my gardens and you can tell people I am Amelia the market gardener.'

Asking someone who had known her since she was a baby to call her by her new name was disconcerting, but the sooner she made the transition the better.

After placing the new chest securely under her bed, Amelia went out to help bring in her belongings. An afternoon's work saw the house furnished to her satisfaction, and she was ready to finally relax for a while when Damon and Tom departed.

As the cart rolled out of sight, Amelia turned to her new home. She hugged herself, buoyed by a strange mix of elation and fear as she walked inside. After closing the door behind her, she added wood to the already blazing fire and, reaching for some needles and wool, she sat in one of the chairs. She cast on some stitches, and in the firelight began listing in her head all the items she needed to make her home comfortable; a lamp, some plant seedlings, and perhaps lessons in bread making from Cook.

As her fingers worked the wool, she planned her next few days. I shall start on the garden tomorrow—find out what is ready to be used and clear some weeds for planting. Oh, and I must check out the cellar and see what I need to purchase for storing food for the winter.

Living alone would be tough, but if she kept herself busy and stayed strong, she would work through. Then, in no time at all she would be looking forward with anticipation rather than back with longing. That approach worked for the next two six-days. Then her precarious hold on her new life began to crumble.

THE DREAM STARTED PEACEFULLY enough with her floating on her back in the sea, mesmerised by the stars and being gently rocked by the waves. Content merely to lie there, she enjoyed the solitude, allowing her body to drift.

Slowly, the sea turned choppy. The waves grew in size and she began to fear for her safety. Righting herself, she treaded water while she searched for land. There was none to be found, and no boats on the water to come to her rescue.

As the waves increased in size. She became anxious and a knot began to form in her stomach, demanding she act—now. Striking out, she followed the waves, hoping they would lead her to land. Cold soon crept through her body, and she began to tire. Although she fought it, eventually the sea wrapped her in its inky embrace.

Just as she was about to black out, she woke up in her bed, her pillow wet with tears and her body trapped in the blankets. Unable to go back to sleep, she dressed and stoked the fire. After making herself a mug of chamomile tea, she sat knitting beside the fire until the sun rose.

Later that day the dream nagged at her as she planted some leafy greens, beans, and carrots. Yesterday she had gathered some early apples from the orchard out back to stew for her breakfast. The days were fine. Working in the garden took most of her time. Evenings were when the loneliness hit her.

Too tired to work after only a few candle-marks, she plucked some vegetables from the garden for her dinner. Distracted by her visions the night before, she had gathered way more than she needed.

She plonked the vegetables into the sink, cleaned them all, and put some to the side. After cutting the rest, she added them to the pot of stew sitting by the fire. She set the pot on to simmer and went into the pantry to fetch a little of the barley cook had sent and some mushrooms she had gathered the day before. Throwing the additional items into the pot, she gave it a gentle stir before taking a chair outside. She picked up her knitting basket and went outside to enjoy some fresh air.

Relaxing, Amelia let the early spring sun warm her through. Her eyes began to close and her head dropped to her chest only to jerk up in time for her to prevent her knitting from falling to the ground. Lack of sleep last night had resulted in her feeling a little off all day. A frown creased her brow as she relived the previous night's dream for the hundredth time.

Although the nightmare was a product of her gift, Amelia was smart enough to realise her own actions, or inaction, had brought on this particular dream. For the last two six-days she had not left her new home, and her only visitor had been her brother.

She could make excuses. It had taken a while to tidy the garden. The existing plants had needed thinning and weeding, and the produce she had culled was laid down for winter in bins Damon had brought her from Port Marden. Then it had been time to prepare the ground for her spring planting.

At the end of the first six-day, Damon had led her horse from the stables in Port Madden when he visited, announcing he was returning to Hand for a while and she would have to run her own errands from then on. Taking the pannier off his own horse, he had left it in the barn when he stabled Blaze for her.

'You will need this to bring supplies from Port Marden,' he told her when she wandered in to see what was taking him so long.

'I have everything I need her,' Amelia answered, her voice sounding a little sulky even to her own ears. Damon had merely raised an eyebrow, and she squirmed under his gaze. 'Come, I have some supper ready,' she said to change the subject.

Used to Damon's almost daily visits, she now found herself quite alone on the farm. The realisation that this was what her life was going to be like slowly set in and she told herself that if this was to be her life now then she had best get used to it. Sitting in her chair as the sun sunk below the tree line, she gave herself a stern talking to.

Amelia Brown, it is past time you stopped relying on your brother to be your contact with the outside world and started doing things for yourself.

Remembering the vegetables she had pulled from the garden that very morning, she went to the barn to find the pannier Damon had left. Using some hay, she packed the vegetables inside it. Finding another smaller container, she gathered some berries from the hedgerow as the sun set, and added them to her package.

She brought the chair inside and checked on the stew for her supper before making sure the house was prepared for her early departure in the morning. Tomorrow she would take her wares to her old home and find out if it really was possible to become friends with the people who had served her in her previous life.

Butterflies in her stomach flittered agitatedly at the very thought. As the daughter of their master, the servants had always treated her with respect. How would they treat Amelia Brown?

In the early morning light, Amelia saddled her horse and attached the basket securely to its back before leading Blaze to the mounting step by the well. Before pulling herself into the saddle, she double-checked her door was locked then, unable to put it off any longer, she headed into Port Marden.

After tying Blaze to the post in the backyard, Amelia smoothed her clothing and tidied her hair. Releasing the load attached to her saddle, she gave her horse one last pat for good luck and strode over to the back door leading to the kitchens. The knock had barely sounded when the door opened, revealing a smiling Bessie.

'I thought that was you I glimpsed through the scullery window. Come on in.'

The door swung back as Bessie made room for her to enter. After hanging up her cloak in the boot room, Amelia followed the house-keeper into the kitchen.

Although none of the family was in residence, the kitchen was still a hive of activity. The upstairs maid was just finishing breakfast and vacated her place so Amelia could sit. Bessie sat opposite and poured them both a mug of tea as she asked Amelia about her trip. Thoughtfully sipping the brew, Amelia waited for someone to ask the reason for her visit. Everyone acted as though it was perfectly normal for her to drop in this way, so she soon relaxed.

'Have you had breakfast?' Cook asked, as she took the empty seat beside Bessie and helped herself to some tea.

'I had some fruit before I left.' Amelia was uncomfortable being offered food by the people who had once served her.

Cook rose and retuned with two bowls of porridge with honey and fresh cream. 'It will be a sad day when we are unable to offer food from our table to our friends,' Cook said. Then added, between mouthfuls, 'Fruit is not enough to begin the day with.'

'Thank you,' Amelia said. 'I haven't found a source of milk yet so my breakfasts have been limited.'

'What about making bread?' Bessie asked.

Amelia shook her head. 'I always helped out in the palace gardens, so I had little time for learning more than basic cooking skills.'

'You are in luck then. I have some dough proving, and another lot to make today. Maybe you would like to try your hand at bread making with me? I have also had some extra milk delivered to make some soft cheeses. You may want to learn how to do that as well,' Cook offered.

'I'd be really grateful for the chance to learn, if you have the time to teach me that is.' Amelia pointed to her pannier. 'I can repay you with some produce from my garden.'

'Pfft,' Cook said. 'Your help will be payment enough.'

'Cook, perhaps we might take a look at what she has. If Amelia is able to pay her way, we should respect her wishes,' Bessie interrupted. 'And you never know, it might be to our benefit.' She winked at Amelia.

Cook coloured a little. 'Of course, yes.' Pulling the basket over she said, 'Let me see what we have here then.'

Having pushed her empty plate aside, Amelia wrung her hands in her lap as Cook and Bessie went through the items in her basket.

Popping a berry in her mouth, Cook smiled, then added a few to her plate. She then proceeded to feel and smell each of the vegetables on the table.

'Do you have more like this?' she finally asked.

'I have some more carrots and a few potatoes, and there are plenty of berries around. I planted a variety of vegetables over the last two six-days, some of which will be ready soon.'

Cook queried her about her planting and what would be ready when, then disappeared before returning with some baskets. 'Do you think you can fill this one with potatoes, and this with carrots and have them here this time next six-day? We will pay market rates.'

Amelia nodded, and agreed a price.

'And can you bring more berries?' Bessie asked, holding up the container which had miraculously emptied while Cook and Amelia had been talking.

'Yes, there are plenty more on the hedgerows. Is there anything you find difficult to purchase from the markets?' Amelia asked, this was a great opportunity to provide something different to the other local farmers.

Cook thoughtfully tapped her chin. 'You know your mother

brings fresh herbs over, but we really could do with a regular supply here rather than relying on dried herbs the rest of the time.'

Amelia smiled. She had already marked out an area for a herb garden for her own use. She would just make it a little bigger.

'And how are the apples going? Bessie asked. 'Willard, your farm's previous owner, had some of the best apples.'

'The early ones are just ripening. I can bring you some next six-day.'

'Excellent,' Cook said. 'What about the hives? Are they producing yet?'

Frowning, Amelia answered, 'The bees have certainly been active, but I do not know how to get the honey out.'

'Oh, we can't have that, can we?' Bessie asked Cook. 'The honey from Willard's hives is sought after. I am popping out in a few minutes. Perhaps I could call in on Willard and see if he would have time to teach you how to look after the bees and collect the honey. That is, if you would like me to?'

'Would you mind?' Amelia asked shyly, 'I would love his help if he could make the time... and if it would not be too much for him to return to his old home.'

'I am sure he could spare you a couple of days. He is not too busy, he spends most of his days down at the docks, chatting and occasionally fixing nets. And those bees were his pride and joy, so I am sure he would relish the opportunity to check up on them.'

After Bessie had departed, Cook bundled Amelia into the kitchen and they began making bread.

'Cook, this is a lot of bread given there are only four of you to feed,' Amelia commented, then covered her mouth with her hand, sure she had overstepped the mark.

Laughing, Cook placed the loaves of bread in the oven. 'I am not offended. This is not all for us. For some time now, your mother has had us making bread for the local orphanage. It is how she ensures there is plenty of food for the children without stepping on the town council's toes. It also gives us a little something to do while the house is empty.'

Amelia frowned. She had not known her mother was so involved with politics in Port Marden, nor that she was so sneaky.

Cook then moved on to showing her the beginning of the bread-making process, before demonstrating a simple way to make soft cheese from milk. Soon Amelia was working alongside the older woman, making her very own batch of herbed cheese. By the time they had finished and were tidying up, Bessie had returned with Willard in tow.

Over a midday meal of fresh bread and cheese, Amelia arranged for the man to come and stay for a couple of nights to show her how to look after her bees.

Bessie had offered her a bed for the night. Amelia was tired and tempted by the offer, but she had work to do at home. Cook loaded her up with bread and a little fresh butter, then reminded her of her commitment to return the following six-day.

As Blaze picked a path through the streets Amelia smiled to herself as she ran through the things she would bring on her next visit, already looking forward to spending time with Cook and Bessie.

———

STOMACH GRUMBLING, Amelia turned the fresh loaf of bread onto the cooling rack. It was not as light and airy as Cook's, but she found a certain satisfaction in having produced it using her own hands. After covering the loaf with a muslin cloth, she checked the gently bubbling pot of stew hanging over the fire before heading back into the garden.

As the sun rose in the sky, she paused from tying up the beans and was distracted by a movement near the track to Port Marden. A cow emerged from the side of the road, followed soon after by her brother without his normal retinue of guards.

She followed Damon and the cow around to the barn, where the new animal was moved into the stall beside Blaze. 'Damon, what am I going to do with that?' Amelia asked, gesturing to the black and white dappled animal, who turned and looked at her with mournful eyes.

'Cook said you needed a source of milk so you can make your own dairy products. My guards are following behind with a butter churn.'

'But where will she live? She cannot stay in the barn, and the one paddock I have is beyond repair.' Amelia reached out and fondled the cow between her ears.

'I have that in hand too. My men are also bringing some fence posts. If you will feed us, we will stay the night and fix your paddock up tomorrow.'

Shaking her head, Amelia took a deep breath before she spoke. 'Damon, while I appreciate your thoughtfulness, it is past time I stood on my own two feet, and I cannot do that while you drop by so frequently and bring such extravagant gifts.'

Glimpsing the hurt in Damon's eyes, she almost faltered. She steeled herself, then took his hand and softened her voice before continuing. 'I need a little time to get settled. Perhaps it would be best if when you leave tomorrow, you do not come back for a little while. Say, maybe six moon-turns.'

Her brother withdrew his hand. 'I worry about you being out here, Ami.'

'It is true the farm is off the beaten track, but that also means few people travel this way. I have a stout door with good locks. If someone does break in, I am hardly a shrinking violet. All the years of drilling with father's soldiers mean I am unlikely to forget my self-defence training. I do still occasionally practice the forms—when I have the energy that is.'

'But—'

'Damon, I'm serious. If I find I need your help, I can always pass word through Cook and Bessie. Please, I have to prove I can live and work here—alone. Besides, you should be getting back to your own duties.'

'All right. We can try. Look, here is the rest of my gift.'

As he turned to direct the guards and their cart to the barn, she avoided Damon's eyes. The hurt lurking in his gaze was melting her resolve. Fortunately, by the time he and the two men joined her for dinner, he was back to his normal self and she was able to relax.

The next morning, she was up early checking on the new addition to her farm. Upset by the journey the day before, the cow produced very little milk. Taking the animal outside, Amelia directed her to a grassy patch in the old paddock, and tied a rope to one of the few fence posts still standing. As she returned to the house, she heard the clamour Damon and the men were making as they made breakfast.

While they worked on the paddock, Amelia finished her gardening and checked her hives. Willard had told her she should visit the bees regularly so they would get used to her, so she did a little something nearby every day.

She collected a couple of pots of honey. Placing the honey pots on the edge of the well while she took off her protective clothing, Amelia started at the sound of a voice close by.

'I'm impressed,' Damon said. 'When did you learn to do all of that?'

'Bessie organised for Willard to spend a few days here last six-day to teach me about the bees. I am still new to it, and a little nervous, but I think the bees are finally accepting me.'

'Perhaps you do not need me around so much after all,' he said as he wandered back to help with the fencing.

Clutching the pots to her chest, Amelia allowed the glow of her brother's praise to warm her, before almost floating inside.

ADMINA'S ARGUMENT

MEETING THE NEIGHBOURS

True to his word, Damon had not visited for a full six-day, and they were some of the loneliest days of Amelia's life. It took all her willpower not to run into Port Marden to sit by the fire and drink tea with Cook and Bessie. Instead, she made herself wait until she was due to deliver her produce. Tomorrow was the agreed day, and Amelia had added a special gift of a pot of honey to thank the women for their support.

She was proud of her herself. Not only because she had managed to make it through a six-day without speaking to another soul, sanity intact, but because her garden was also coming along nicely. Soon she would have enough produce to begin selling at the markets, which was a relief as her only source of income was from Cook and that was not enough to keep her going in the long run.

She smiled to herself as she turned the soil, spreading cow and horse dung on it, getting another bed ready for a winter planting of potatoes.

'It's always nice to find someone happy in their work.'

The voice startled Amelia from her daydream, and she shaded her eyes with her hand to see who had spoken.

A tall figure emerged from the shadows by the barn, removing his hat to reveal a smiling tanned face with twinkling blue eyes.

'Sorry, miss. I did not mean to startle you. I am Peter; I own the farm next door.' He stuck out a large, work-worn hand.

Amelia hastily wiped her own hand on her skirt before accepting. 'Amelia.'

'Well, Amelia, I meant to come and visit sooner to welcome you, but my wife has not been well. She wanted to come and say hello with me, but she sent me out today saying we had waited beyond what was acceptable.'

Amelia blushed. Not knowing the protocol for such a situation flustered her. 'No, no really, your timing is perfect. I have been so busy getting things sorted here, I had not even had time to consider meeting my neighbours.'

'Well there are not many of us living near the Tangled Woods. Just Maisie and me. Oh and the boys and their families next door. Then there is George and Hilda on the other side of us. They are expecting their first young'n. We tend to look out for each other as we are so far from the port.'

'I am sure I will get to meet you all eventually. Would you like to come in for some tea?'

'You are nice to offer, but I need to head back—always plenty of work to do and those boys of mine will slacken off if I am not around to keep an eye on them. The wife thought it was time for you to meet some of us and sent me to ask you to dinner tonight.'

'Oh... that is very kind, but are you sure she is up to it? I do not want to put her out.'

'You have to come, please. She is fine now, and looking forward to some company. Besides, if I go back without you having said yes, she will make my life a right misery.'

His forlorn face caused Amelia to laugh. 'Well, if you put it like that, I would love to come and meet my closest neighbours. Can I bring anything?'

'That is not usually how it works around here, but if I passed up the chance for a few of your apples, once again my Maisie would chew my ear off.'

'I will bring some with me this evening.'

'Expect my youngest boy just before sundown to show you the shortcut. Is that a good time for you?'

Amelia nodded and with the arrangements finalised, Peter plonked his hat back on his head and disappeared around the side of the barn.

The thought of a meal with her neighbours put a spring in Amelia's step for the rest of the afternoon. She finished preparing the garden for planting, packed her produce ready for her trip to Port Marden the following day, and washed up in the water from the well.

Once inside, she placed her pot of stew to the side and banked the fire. Moving the loaf of bread into the pantry, she then filled a basket with apples to take with her. After closing the door, she allowed herself the luxury of warming some water and giving herself a proper clean before going into her bedroom to change.

Choosing a simple cotton dress to wear, she dressed then twisted her thick black hair back into one long plait. Her reflection in the small mirror showed working outdoors had turned her face a darker shade, which strangely made her black eyes appear deeper and more luminous. Tucking back a stray hair, a knock at the door interrupted her preparations.

Thinking it must be the neighbour's young son come to get her, she grabbed her shawl, and pulled the bedroom door closed behind her, turning to find herself face-to-face with a strange man standing in her open doorway.

'Who are you? What are you doing in my house?' Amelia drew herself up to her full, though still diminutive, height.

Confusion covered the man's face as he answered, 'I have been knocking for some time. I thought something might have happened to you, so I let myself in.'

'Do you often let yourself in to stranger's houses?' Amelia asked, furtively searching for something close by she might be able to use as a weapon to fend this man off long enough for Peter's son to arrive and help.

'What? No! I was led to believe you were expecting me. I am Anders.' When there was no flicker of recognition on Amelia's face he added, 'My father, Peter, sent me to fetch you.'

'Anders. Peter's son? Oh. Ohhh.' Unable to help herself, Amelia burst out laughing. 'When Peter said he was sending his youngest ... oh, this is too funny.'

Anders stood in the doorway, bewildered and, if his expression was anything to go by, he believed the girl his father had invited to eat with them was completely mad.

Calming herself, Amelia explained, 'When your father called you lad, I imagined he was sending a boy—someone maybe ten or eleven years old. Then you burst through my door...'

Understanding dawned, and a slow smile brought a twinkle to blue eyes which were so very like his father's. 'That must have been a bit of a shock then.' Anders laughed. 'I think he sometimes forgets I am a grown man.'

'That's parents for you.' Picking up the basket of apples, she said, 'Shall we go?'

Peter and Maisie welcomed her into to their home. Their table was a noisy one with Anders, and his two brothers, and their families all gathering to meet the new neighbour.

As his family had grown, Peter had added the farmland around her homestead to his own, and the family were doing well. Easily twice the size of her dwelling, with a smaller cottage out the back for the oldest son, it was a place full of love and laughter.

Rather later than she had anticipated, Anders escorted Amelia to the door, and Maisie yelled out over the noise for her to not be a stranger.

Closing the door on the noisy gathering, Anders said, 'Well, you have done it now.'

'Done what?'

'My mother likes to adopt strays, and she took a shine to you tonight.'

Stopping mid-stride, Amelia frowned and was about to give Anders a piece of her mind, but something prevented her. She had told the family very little about herself and so they had assumed she was alone in the world. Not sure what to say, but feeling the need to say something, Amelia wove a potted version of her story on the spot. 'I appreciate you were all too polite to ask why I am out here all by myself, but I am not alone in the world. I have family living close by. I did not want the life they saw for me, so my being here is a compromise. They visit, but I want to show them I can make my own way.'

'I was not prying,' Anders told her.

'I know, but I don't want anyone worrying needlessly about me, or deciding I need to be rescued.'

'I don't feel sorry for you. If anything I admire you. I think you're brave to be doing what you are doing, and I wish I had half your guts. But your wishes on the matter will mean nothing to my mother. She adopted you into the family already, and there is nothing you can do about it.'

Leaving her at her door, Anders departed, throwing back over his shoulder, 'I really do admire you.'

A warm flush spread through her as she shut the door and slid home the bolt. Curling up under the covers, for the first time Amelia believed this place might actually become her true home.

⸺

As the spring turned to summer, Amelia became a regular visitor to Peter and Maisie's home. Being the middle of the three properties, theirs was the natural point to get together. She met George, who had taken over his father's farm, and his wife, Hilda. The couple were devoted to each other and were about to have their first child

Now Maisie was better, she suggested they return to their habit of spending sixth-day dinners together. Each family contributed something to the meal, and Amelia found each of the women were happy to share their recipes with her.

Although she got on well with everyone, it was Maisie she most often gravitated to. The woman had indeed taken her under her wing as Anders had suggested, and seemed bent on making sure she had all the skills she needed to succeed in her life on the farm.

Their common interest in knitting led to Maisie showing her how to card, spin, and dye her own wool. Amelia enjoyed it so much she even considered the possibility of getting some sheep of her own. Peter promised he would loan her one of his boys to help with the shearing. Anders immediately offered his services.

'I am the best shearer after all,' he boasted. His brothers laughed, each exclaiming why they were the better choice, until the tales grew so outrageous Amelia could not tell fact from fiction.

Along with her regular visits to Port Marden, these gatherings dispelled her loneliness and drew her into a new community. She still missed her family, of course, but the ache was not nearly as strong.

As the summer grew hotter, Anders appeared to be taking a special interest in her. He would sit by her at dinner, or offer to walk her home, or help her clear the table. At first, she had thought they were spending more time together because they were the only unattached people in the group—it did get a little awkward when all the couples were sitting and laughing together.

Recently, though, he had taken to dropping over on one excuse or another, showing his intent was more than a casual friendship. While she was flattered by the attention, she was not sure how she felt about Anders himself. He was handsome enough, and kind, but she was not sure there was any actual attraction there.

Still he was good company and, until he tried to take things further by declaring his intent, there was no point in worrying about it.

'Would you like to stay for some tea and bread with honey? The honey is fresh from my own hives,' Amelia offered shyly to thank him for coming over to fix the gears that brought her well-bucket up and down.

'You are turning into quite the market gardener, what with your hives in full swing now.'

Anders' praise caused heat to rise to her cheeks, and she turned to hide it. 'If you just give me a moment to finish picking these berries, I will put the kettle on.'

He placed a gentle hand on her arm. 'If it were up to me, I would love to stay, but Father wants the hay brought in before the weather change.'

Anders reached out and tucked a stray strand of hair behind her ear, causing her to tense. She was happy to explore where her friendship with Anders might lead, but his touching her in this intimate way was a little too much too soon. She pulled back from his hand.

'Perhaps you will take some honey with you by way of thanks,' she said, and hurried to the house to fetch a small crock.

He took the offering and said, 'I hope you are not disappointed I have to leave. After all, we are still on for market tomorrow. You will have the whole day to thank me for helping fix your well.' His eyes twinkled. 'I will definitely be expecting some of the bread and honey for my noon-day meal.'

Before she could say anything he was off, walking briskly with his long, easy stride until the trees took him from view. A strange mix of excitement and foreboding overwhelmed her as she turned back to her garden. In frustration, she pushed the feeling down deep. She was not in the mood for one of her visions today.

'Good afternoon to you.'

Amelia jumped at the voice beside her. Turning slowly, she came face-to-face with an elderly woman dressed for travel, her eyes hidden by a wide-brimmed hat. Wary, more because she was taken by surprise than because she felt any threat, she answered the woman,

'Good afternoon to you. You are a long way from anywhere.'

'I am indeed. I travelled through the Tangled Woods, I am heading to Port Marden. I wonder if I might trouble you for some water.'

Aware of the common courtesies given to all travellers, Amelia led the woman over to the well. As she moved the water skin attached to the woman's pack sloshed. Amelia immediately went on alert—why would someone with a full water skin ask for water? Attempting to appear as though she were tidying up, she grabbed the shovel as they walked by.

'There is no need for that, my dear. I mean you no harm.' The woman continued on to the well and placed her load on the grass. Pulling up the bucket, she then found two tin mugs in her pack and proceeded to fill them before offering one to Amelia.

Placing the shovel down, Amelia took the offered drink. 'I thought you meant to fill your skin. I didn't think...'

The woman removed her hat and smiled. 'It is always best to be safe when you live this far away from others. Though if I might make a suggestion?' The woman clearly did not intend for her to answer, as she continued before Amelia was able to speak. 'If you used your skill, you would sense a person's intentions towards you.'

'My skill?'

'Yes, I felt it just then, when you were watching your young man leave.'

'He is not my...'Amelia started then stopped. Part of her wanted to protest that Anders was only a friend, yet she could not deny something growing between them, something still too new for her to be discussing with a complete stranger. Changing the subject, she asked, 'My skill? I am sure I have no idea what you mean.'

'My dear, anyone with an ounce of magical ability can sense your talent. It flared a moment ago. I may not be able to tell what type of ability you have, but you have not mastered it otherwise I would not have been able to sense it.'

Amelia hid behind the cup as she sipped her water, contemplating the woman in front of her. In turn, her guest busied herself refilling her mug while she waited for her hostess to speak.

'The tattoo on your wrist tells me you are from Hand. Those from the island often have no one to teach them how to control their skills. Am I right?'

Amelia looked down at the half-finished marque on her wrist— the one telling everyone who knew of such things what clan she belonged to. It was unfinished. She would never marry someone from her home, so her future-husband's family sigil would not be added to complete the process. Self-consciously she pulled at her sleeve so it covered the offending image.

'Do not be embarrassed. There are a few girls in our group from the island. Although they arrived with little more than their belongings and a few coins. I am sure they would be happy to help you become accustomed to life away from Hand, and teach you how to better live with your new skill.'

Caught off guard, Amelia could do little but stare at her visitor as jumbled thoughts tried to sort themselves out in her head. Other girls had left Hand? Ones with magic? Until that moment, she had believed only the ruling family was tainted with the curse, and then only one person in every generation.

Biting her lip, she considered whether or not she could remain hidden if those close by could sense her abilities. She continued to gnaw on her bottom lip as her mind processed the news that there were people who might teach her how to use her gift. Would she be able to get help?

Boys could receive magical training at the Wizard Isle. Although, to the best of her knowledge, no one from Hand had ever actually gone there. However, she had never thought about what happened to girls who showed magical abilities—who taught them how to use or hide their magic?

It was all too much to take in, especially with a complete stranger staring at her, waiting for her to work through all she had learned. 'Um... I am not sure...'

'Oh dear. Look at me barging in, asking questions, not waiting for answers, and we have not even introduced ourselves. I am Nene, hedge healer and teacher for the Woods Coven.'

'Woods Coven?'

'Yes. We're a group of women with magical abilities who support each other, learn from each other, and teach the younger generation to manage and develop their abilities.'

Amelia had not known such a group existed. 'I thought only those taught in approved schools may apply for a licence to practice magic in Aria.'

'That is so here, in Aria, but as the schools will take only boys, what are we to do?'

Amelia nodded, agreeing with the logic.

'We have our own set of rules to live by, just like the wizards. We witches use our magic for the good of others. Of course we do not openly acknowledge our abilities, or use them in public.'

Nene took a breath and Amelia took the opportunity to ask, 'There are more of you?' It was as if the flood-gates had opened and more questions spilled out of her mouth one after the other. 'Do you all live in the woods? How many of you are there? What types of magic do you practice?'

Laughing, Nene held up her hand, and Amelia stopped.

'Goodness me, you want to know it all. Let me see, there are around a hundred of us. We mostly live in the communities in the Tangled Woods, although there are a few of our group who live in some of the southern towns.

'Most of us are strong in healing, or have learned the basics of the healer's craft, and we are well thought of in our communities. We do not like to advertise our skills, which is why I was surprised when your magic touched me not long after I left my home. It was one of the things that drew me off course here today.'

Amelia, who had been surprised to learn there were so many magical practitioners nearby, was even more surprised to learn she had been broadcasting her abilities so far away. 'How far away were you when you sensed me?'

'Mm, I should say about two candle-marks.' Nene answered.

'Your magic was very loud. I should think most people with magical skills in the vicinity of the Tangled Woods would have heard you.'

Well, that changed everything. The safety net she had built the last moon turn or so suddenly felt shaky. Would Maisie and her family still accept her if they knew of her taint? How could she live here if anyone might discover her secret? 'Can you teach me to hide my magic so no one else can sense it?' Amelia asked.

The woman frowned, seeming to choose her words carefully before answering, 'If that is what you wish to be taught, yes I can. I am also able to teach you how to access and use your abilities.'

Amelia shook her head. 'No, I just want to learn how to hide myself from others.'

Understanding crossed the woman's face. 'So, if you merely want to hide your magic, can I take it you are still in contact with your family then?' When Amelia nodded, she continued, 'That is unusual. I will teach you but I am expected in Port Marden tomorrow, so I must be on my way as it is a long day's journey walking from here. I am there a six-day, but can stop by on my return.'

Once her mind was made up, Amelia wanted to move quickly. 'Perhaps you can stay the night here. I have a lift to the markets in Port Marden tomorrow—you could ride with us. It would be an easier journey for you and you might teach me a little of how to hide my magic.'

Cocking her head to the side, the woman stared at Amelia. After what seemed like an age, she slowly nodded. 'I would enjoy not having to walk, so I will take you up on your offer.'

Picking up the woman's pack, Amelia led her inside.

'Perhaps if I am to stay the night with you, you might tell me your name?' her guest asked as they approached the house.

'Amelia,' she said as she opened the door. 'Amelia Brown.'

THE QUESTION OF MAGIC

Amelia showed Nene to the upstairs room, and helped her make up one of the three beds. Leaving her to settle in, she returned to the kitchen and moved the stew pot over the fire to begin heating. After cutting the fresh loaf of bread in half, she wrapped one piece ready for the promised lunch tomorrow, and placed the other in the centre of the table beside the butter she had made the day before.

By the time Nene joined her, the stew simmered away over the fire, the table was set, and Amelia sat in one of the chairs by the fire knitting the shawl she had almost finished making for winter.

Her guest took the other chair, which creaked beneath her weight as she sighed and relaxed. 'I am getting a little old for my wanderings,' she admitted. 'I do so miss my own fire and bed.'

'Why do you travel so much if you prefer being at home?' Amelia asked.

'It is my job. When I took on the role of coven teacher, I knew it would involve finding those who needed educating and matching them to those looking for apprentices. I teach basic skills, and then the girls are apprenticed to another with a magical ability in a similar area. I am on my way to Port Marden to ask one of our sisterhood if she will take on training one of our girls who is ready for the next step.'

'It must be lovely having a group of women supporting you in what you do,' Amelia mused.

Nene barked out a laugh. 'Yes, and no. Every group has its problems, but by and large, we provide a support network, and hopefully instil in our girls a good set of values to govern their use of magic.'

Even though she was still afraid of her own talent, Amelia understood how sharing knowledge and being able to master your skills alongside other like-minded people might be nice. Shaking those longings away, she placed her knitting back in the basket beside the chair and rose. 'The stew is ready. If you would like to wash up, I will serve it.'

Nene filled the metal bowl in the bench with water before

washing and drying her hands. By the time she sat down at the table, the simple meal was served, and the woman sighed again. 'This smells delicious,' she said as she dug her spoon into the vegetable and rabbit stew and slowly chewed a mouthful. 'Do I taste thyme?'

'Yes, from my own garden.' Amelia was ridiculously proud at having served up a meal she had made herself from food she had grown or trapped.

'I noticed your garden. Not all the herbs planted there were for cooking. Do you know some herb lore?'

Helping herself to some bread, Amelia determined how much she would tell her guest of her past. Because she had asked this woman to help her, she decided she owed her honesty, if not the complete story. 'Where I grew up, our cook kept a herb garden, and she taught me some of the more common uses for them when treating ailments. I used to love reading the book she kept all her recipes in. I learned a little more from some of the scrolls and books in our library. Occasionally she even let me add a little piece of information I found to her personal herb lore.'

'It is useful knowledge. Even those among us who have healing skills only use those as a last resort, preferring to try natural methods first,' Nene said.

They continued their meal in silence. Nene insisted on washing up as payment for Amelia's hospitality, and while she did, Amelia set a kettle to boil over the fire, and prepared two mugs with relaxing herbs.

A little while later, sitting beside the fire with steaming mugs of tea cupped in their hands, Nene approached the subject they had avoided since entering the house. 'Now we are a little more comfortable with each other, shall I teach you how to contain your magic?'

'Contain it?' Amelia frowned. 'I want to be able to hide it.'

Nene took a sip of tea and smiled a slow smile. 'It is almost one and the same thing. Before we start, perhaps I should tell you a little something about the nature of magic.'

When Amelia nodded her agreement, she continued, 'The energy we use to perform magic is all around us. It is made by all living things. Some of us are more able than others to trap that energy, hold it inside, then use it to alter the elements around us. We channel magical energy by using spells and incantations, or sometimes a series of gestures.' Pausing to take a sip of her tea, Nene looked over the top of her cup and caught Amelia's eye.

Feeling the urge to show she was still listening, Amelia said, 'I understand that, and it is interesting, but it does not tell me how I can hide my magic from others.' Sitting forward in her chair, she waited for the other woman to answer.

'We will get to that in a moment. First, I want you to understand completely hiding your magic from everyone is not possible. The best we can do is teach you to contain and control it. Once a person's magic is contained, most other people cannot sense it. However, those with very strong magical abilities appear to be able to sense others' magic no matter how hard they work on hiding it.'

Amelia's alarm must have been written on her face because Nene paused.

'Do not fear. Not many people are strong enough to sense contained magic. They generally need to be physically close to a person, and looking specifically for traces of magical energy.'

Relaxing a little, Amelia said, 'I accept there will be limitations. Can we begin?'

'Fine. First you need to relax. I find closing your eyes helps.'

Amelia closed her eyes and calmed her breathing as she had been taught to do by her father's soldiers when learning self-defence.

'Excellent. Now, can you feel the heat of the fire on your skin?'

Amelia nodded. 'Yes.'

'All right. I want you to search inside of yourself and try to find a similar heat.'

Focusing on her own body, Amelia searched internally for any sign of warmth. The beating of her heart pounded in her ears, blocking out all other sensations. The only heat she sensed was the fire on her face. 'Are you sure I have real magic?' she asked in frustration.

'Mm, this approach works for most forms of magic, except those that are more, shall we say, internal. Most magic-users have subconsciously been reaching for their magic and using it to affect the world around them, so looking inwards and finding the source of their energy is instinctive. If a person's skill is more internal, this process appears to get a little muddled.'

'Internal skill? Like perhaps seeing into the future?' Amelia queried.

'Yes, that would be one of the types of magic I am talking about. Can I assume your skill is along those lines?'

Amelia hung her head and whispered, 'Yes.'

Her guest reached forward and took her hand. 'I know in Hand magic is banished, but this seems like something more. What happened to make you so ashamed of your talent?' she asked gently.

Gazing down at the gnarled hand holding her own, Amelia was unable to say anything.

Nene encouraged her to speak. 'Whatever happened could be a block to your learning. Slowly, Amelia managed to force the words out. 'Just before my sixteenth birthday, I had a dream. My younger brother was to have the honour of dealing the killing blow to the wild boar on a hunt for the first time. I dreamt the boar would severely wound him and he would not be able to walk again.

'He was only a little over a year younger than me, and we were close. I could not stand by and let him get hurt. I crept into his room the night before the hunt and begged him not to go. He considered me a silly girl for worrying about him. Goaded to anger, I told him about my dreams, thinking it was the only way he would listen to me and stay safe. I thought he would understand, and keep my secret.

'He grew frightened and went straight to our father. I had not counted on my family's abhorrence of what they call mage-craft being stronger than their love for me. My father locked me in my room for being "hysterical", and the hunt went ahead as planned.

'My brother never dealt the killing blow. The boar attacked him, as I predicted, and it was only because my foreknowledge prepared him that my father killed the animal before it did any lasting damage.

'Ironically, I managed to save my brother, but the boar charging as in my dream sealed my fate. My family were forced to disown me because those with magic cannot live on Hand. My brother feels guilty because he thinks I am banished because of his actions—'

'And part of you believes your dreams bring about the future, rather than letting you glimpse what might happen,' Nene finished for her. 'It is not your fault, Amelia. You do not cause things to occur; you simply see a possible future, and that can be a good thing. In the end, your brother did not lose the ability to walk, and you would likely have been banished eventually for some other incident.'

Taking Nene's cup, Amelia rose and refilled it along with her own. Talking about the incident that changed her whole life was unsettling to say the least. Nene was not ready to let it go though as she continued when Amelia was settled back in her seat.

'I understand why you want to hide from your talent but I hope someday you will be able to embrace it for the goddess-given gift it is. Until then, I will help you control it so your foresight does not interfere too much with your life.'

Nene gave Amelia's hand one last squeeze, then sat back. 'Let us begin again. Relax and feel the heat of the fire.'

'I am ready,' Amelia said as the blaze warmed her skin.

'Now, I am going to try something a little different this time. Turn away from the fire. Let your senses reach out and find the same warmth again somewhere in the room.'

Imagining herself standing in an open field, head tilted back, searching for warmth, Amelia used all her senses to find heat. There, she found the fire, but what was that? She directed her senses back to a small ball of heat just before the fire.

Opening her eyes, she looked directly at Nene. 'What was that? I felt something warm just there?' She pointed.

Nene's eyes sparkled in the light of the flames. 'Good, you found it. That was me. You found my energy. Close your eyes. I am going to move farther into the room. Try and find the heat of my energy again. Open your eyes when you do.'

Repeating the entire process, Amelia found the warmth of her teacher's magic in front of her, by the sink, then to the side by the door to her bedroom.

'One last time,' Nene told her, and Amelia turned in her chair. The heat was so close she was certain the woman now stood behind her. There was no one there. Something moved near the table and Nene stood.

'But... but if you were there, what did I feel?'

Smiling broadly as she sat, Nene told her, 'That was you. You found your magic. Can you do it again?'

This time, Amelia stilled herself and focussed inside, and she managed to find the ball of fire nestled around her heart. Throbbing in time with her heart-beat, the flame flickered in tones of yellow and orange. 'It is beautiful,' she said in wonder.

'And nothing to be afraid of.'

'No, it is not.'

'It is getting late,' Nene said as she looked at the candle on the table. 'Perhaps we can work for a candle-mark on containing your magic.'

After teaching Amelia to imagine pouring her magic into a bottle and putting a stopper in it to prevent leakage, Nene made her student practice until she could do it while holding a conversation. When Nene deemed her competent, they took a break and had another cup of tea.

'So, now you can contain your magic perhaps I could show you a little magical skill to help you with your life out here,' the teacher offered.

Amelia hesitated before saying, 'I told you, I do not want to use my magic.'

'I know you did, but you will be better containing your magic if you know what it feels like to use it. And this is only a small thing.'

When Amelia did not answer, she continued, 'Perhaps you can learn it to experience the feeling of releasing your magic, whether or not you use it after tonight it entirely up to you.'

Seeing sense in the proposal and being a little curious to find out what it felt like to use her magic, Amelia nodded her agreement.

Nene demonstrated some gestures and spoke the words that activated the magic. Once Amelia had mastered the gestures, she repeated the ancient words out loud, 'encasse firmee', while cupping her hands around an imaginary ball. Then she pulled her hands apart and said, 'relesse' to allow her all her magic free or 'ceerelesse' to allow a small portion to trickle out.

Nene explained with practice her body would learn the spells and thinking the words would be enough. 'Now, one last lesson before we sleep. Release a little of your magic and direct it towards me. Keep your eyes closed and try and follow it with your thoughts.'

Amelia did as she was told. 'Cee-re-les-se.' She said the word slowly and as she did, she imagined a trickle of the energy she contained reaching out to touch Nene. Before she had completed the word, her magic came up against something solid and Amelia was encompassed in warmth.

'What happened?' Nene asked.

Opening her eyes, Amelia attempted to describe her experience. 'My magic hit some sort of barrier and I felt … this is going to sound odd, but I felt warmth and acceptance.'

Nene grinned. 'You are an excellent student, Amelia. Your magic touched the very edge of me, and, I guess you could say it tasted me. It is a little magical weapon should you choose to use it to find out the intent of others you meet.'

'Thank you, but I am not sure I would ever feel comfortable using it on another person.'

'You live alone here. I am sure it will come in handy checking the intent of strangers who happen on your place.'

'I am sorry. You misread my intent. I am not sure I ever want anything to do with using magic at all... ever,' Amelia explained.

'It is your choice, my dear. Now, I suggest a snack before we go to bed. Practicing magic uses your body's energy, and you must be careful never to expend too much at one time. Also you must always replenish your body's resources after prolonged use.'

Finishing off the loaf of bread with some honey, the women sat in an easy silence. As she rose to go to her room, Amelia turned to her guest. 'When you come back this way, maybe you will stop by and check on my progress? Perhaps you could even stay a while and teach me some more?'

'Perhaps.'

———

ANDERS ALLOWED Nene to pass then blocked the doorway before Amelia could exit. Looking into his face, her stomach clenched—had she misjudged Anders' willingness to take her guest with them to market today?

'Is there a problem with Nene coming with us?' she asked. 'There is plenty of room in the back.'

'She is a witch.'

'Sorry? How can you tell?' Did Anders have some magical ability himself? Did he know she could use magic? Tensing, Amelia searched his face for some clue.

'Just look at her. She dresses like one of those women who live in the Tangled Woods, and everyone knows they are all witches,' Anders whispered.

Amelia's shoulders slumped with relief. 'Tosh! She's an elderly traveller who I offered hospitality to last night, and a lift into Port Marden today.'

'I'm telling you, she's a witch.' Anders' lips curled in distaste. 'If she's caught with us then we will be tainted by association.'

'And I am telling you she's nothing but a woman travelling to visit friends in Port Marden. I offered her a night's accommodation, and a lift to the port.'

'You are too trusting. You shouldn't let strangers sleep under your roof,' Anders told her.

Angry at being instructed on how to behave in her own home, Amelia turned and glared at the man now loading the baskets Nene had carried from the barn into the back of his wagon.

Waiting for the woman to return inside to gather her own things, Amelia hissed, 'That decision is mine to make. As is the decision whether or not to come with you today, or to travel to the markets under my own steam. So you have a choice too, Anders. Either we both come with you, or you go alone.'

Dismissing her threat, Anders finished stowing the baskets and asked, 'And how will you get all this food to market?'

He was so sure of himself. Amelia stiffened her spine and clenched her fists. 'I only need to take one basket of goods to Port today—the one to fill my order. I have not yet paid for a stall, so the other can stay behind. My horse can carry one basket as well as the two of us.' She raised her chin and met his gaze with defiance.

'You would do that? You would go against... risk your livelihood for a stranger?'

Amelia did not move a muscle and she did not miss the slip-up. If she and Anders were to remain friends, he needed to understand her life was her own, and so were the choices to be made.

'Fine. She can come.'

'Thank you, Anders.'

Now she had her own way, she was ready to be conciliatory. After returning to the house, Amelia picked up the lunch basket and placed it on the table, ready to add a few extra apples just in case. As she entered the pantry to get the crock of honey she had promised

Peter as her payment for sharing a lift to market, she turned to find Nene had come downstairs and was thoughtfully studying her.

'What?' She was in no mood for further arguments.

'Was that wise?'

'I'm not sure what you mean.'

Nene paused. 'I think you need to think seriously about what you want from your future, and whether or not you see that young man as part of it.' Her teacher picked up her travel pack and left a stunned Amelia standing by the door. Their argument had been in whispers, so how had the woman known what had been said?

Anders turned to take Nene's pack from her and stowed it in. He then helped the older woman into the back. The mask of pleasantness he wore slipped as he climbed into the front seat and took up the reins, showing the anger in his eyes as he raised the tailgate.

Without thinking it through, she cupped her hands, opened them a little towards Anders, and said, 'Ceerelesse.'

Waiting a moment, she was certain she had done something wrong. Then it hit her—a mass of hurt and anger—and it was not directed at Nene, but at her. However, when he assisted her into the seat beside him, he showed no sign of what he was truly feeling, hiding it behind a courteous smile. Disconcerted, she sent him a wan smile in return.

They set off at a brisk pace. Anders explained the earlier they got to Port Marden, the better the place they would be able to secure at the market. As they travelled, no one spoke and Amelia took the time to process the morning's events.

Was Anders like so many other people? Was it only the unregulated use of magic he feared, or was there more to his reaction to Nene? The older woman was right; she had to find out before she allowed their friendship to change into something else. She also needed to discover if his feelings were shared by the rest of his family.

More worrying though was the anger she had gleaned behind

the mask he wore. It unsettled her how easily he was able to hide it. Had he been hiding his true thoughts all along?

Shaking her head, she attempted to dislodge the discomfort in the pit of her stomach. Firstly, this was only the second time she had tried to read someone with her magic. She had no idea whether the reading she had gotten was Anders' deepest feelings or just his feelings at that moment. Secondly, she had never needed magic to read people before, so why should she start now?

Having taken herself in hand, Amelia began looking forward to her first market day in Port Marden as they joined the line of farmers' carts entering the township.

Tired of the uncomfortable silence, she struck up a conversation with Anders. 'How is your brother Ben doing? Is he excited about the baby?'

Anders laughed. 'It is all he ever talks about. Although I would not call it excited—perhaps a little more like scared out of his mind. I am sure once the baby is born he will have some time to help find some sheep for you, if you still want some.'

They continued talking about what Amelia would need to do before she purchased livestock and their cart rolled up to the gates. Just inside, Nene asked to be let out as her friend lived close by.

Amelia hopped down from the cart to say goodbye and wish Nene well. As the older woman hugged her, she whispered, 'Heed my words. Take some time to decide who you want to be before you fall into something with that young man. It is not fair to him or you to become more than friends before you make up your mind about your magic. I will return in a six-day. See you then.'

Once Nene had departed, Amelia grabbed the basket containing the goods for her old home in Port Marden. Feeling the need for some time to think, she said, 'Anders, I am going to deliver this first and meet you at the markets. That way I will not be rushing at the end of the day.'

Frowning, Anders said, 'I do not understand why your special buyer cannot come to market like everyone else, but I guess now is as good a time as any to make the delivery.'

Shaking her head at Anders' behaviour this morning, Amelia refused to explain her actions to anyone, and headed off along the street, not waiting to see what Anders did.

Cook was pleased to see her, and Amelia added the payment to the purse she carried with her market fees and a small amount of coins for day-to-day purchases. Foregoing a cup of tea because she did not want to leave all the work at the market to Anders, especially not in his present mood, Amelia said her goodbyes.

Bessie popped some freshly made strawberry jam into her basket as a treat just as she was leaving, and Cook stopped her as she opened the door. 'Young Damon asked me to give you this.' She handed Amelia a letter.

'Thank you. I will see you in two six-days.'

Opening the envelope as she walked, Amelia read: "I know it has not been the agreed six moon-turns, but I would like to meet with you. Unless you tell Cook otherwise, I will come visit you tomorrow."

Her mood lifted as she stopped and tucked the letter in her pocket. Rather than making her brother wait the full time they had agreed, she would allow him to visit. She wanted to see him, especially after the last couple of days.

Turning the corner into one of the streets lining the market square, she scanned the shop windows as she passed. An item caught her eye—a handsomely bound leather journal. It reminded her of the old herb lore she used to write in for the cook on Hand, and she just had to have it. She wanted to study herbs, and the journal would be perfect to record her thoughts.

After entering the shop, she spent almost the entire contents of her purse on the book, some writing implements, and a candle lamp so she could continue working once the sun had set. Tucking everything into her basket, she hurried on to the market.

Anders had finished setting up his stall and was unloading her produce when she arrived. 'I planned to place a blanket on the ground and lay your goods out here,' he told her as she placed her basket in the back of the cart parked behind his stall.

'Thank you, Anders, but I have coin to rent a table for the day.'

'You need not waste your money,' he informed her. 'I am sure our regular customers would be interested in buying your honey and dried fruits. I can send them over to you.'

Her deal with Anders' father was for a ride to market only, and although her driver's offer was genuine, Amelia did not want to be reliant on others for her livelihood. Starting out with customers Peter and his family had been servicing for years would leave her beholden to them.

'Thank you again for the offer, Anders, but I would prefer my goods out where everyone can see them in the main marketplace.'

As they spoke, the market manager passed by calling for day traders to come and pay for their tables. Amelia smiled at Anders, and, balancing her two baskets of produce very carefully, she followed the manager to the day-trader section.

The morning was hectic. Amelia's honey and dried fruits sold out before lunch, and she even took some orders for the next market day. Happy with her success, she packed up the stall and returned to the bustling market area where long-term traders like Anders' family sold their wares directly from their carts. Slipping in behind, she stowed her baskets and picked up the lunch she had packed for them this morning.

Smiling, she rounded the wagon and tapped Anders on the shoulder. 'Are you ready for something to eat?'

'Really, Amelia, you should not leave your stall unattended. There are thieves everywhere, not to mention you might miss a sale.'

Her smile faded. 'Sorry?' She raised her eyebrows questioningly.

A blush rose from under Anders' collar. 'It is just you are new to this, and I am trying to help you out here.'

'Anders, I have nothing left to sell.' Amelia laughed, hoping Anders might join her in celebration of her success.

'You sold out? Already?'

'Yes. Isn't it wonderful?'

Anders looked anything but pleased as he turned to his own half-empty stall. 'Oh.'

'After I eat, I am happy to help you this afternoon.'

'Are you sure? You don't want to go and waste some of your hard-earned money—maybe buy something like a useless book?

Amelia froze, anger rising inside her. 'You went through my things?' She glared at the boy in front of her.

Anders back-pedalled, mumbling, 'Of course not... I would never. I was hungry and only looking for something to eat. I went into the wrong basket.'

With her anger still burning red-hot, Amelia drew herself up to her full height and placed her hands on her hips. 'You also think it is all right to lecture me about what I spend my money on. My money, earned by me, to be spent by me. Who do you think you are?' After turning on her heel, Amelia strode over to the cart and loaded her baskets in the back. She took some of the bread and fruit from the lunch basket and placed it on top of her packages from this morning. Slipping the basket over her arm, she swept passed a speechless Anders, and left the markets. 'I will find my own way home,' she threw over her shoulder.

Half-hoping her neighbour would follow her and apologise, she stopped by a clothing stall. Under cover of looking through the coats, she turned to find Anders distracted by a customer. He caught her eyes over the woman's head, a pleading expression on his face.

Stubbornly turning away, Amelia made up her mind. It was still early enough in the day at this time of year for her to make it home before it got too dark. Leaving the market, she headed through the crowds towards the gate.

The sound of hooves striking cobbles caused those on foot to move to the side of the road just as she spied the gate. A horse stopped beside her and Damon leaned towards her as if to speak, then glanced around. Appreciating this was not the place for a reunion, he nodded to a side street and, when she was sure no one was looking, Amelia slipped down the alley behind him.

Halfway along, she found herself pulled into a bear hug as Damon swung her off her feet. 'What luck. I thought you would be tied up at the markets all day.'

'Put me down, Damon. I sold everything and I finished early.'

'What? So you decided to walk home? Cook said you shared a ride here, surely you could have waited?'

Amelia's brow creased in a frown. 'Let us just say I prefer to walk.'

Damon placed his hand on the sword hanging at his side. 'What did he do? Do I need to defend your honour?'

Placing her hand on his arm, Amelia laughed. 'Damon, no. Amelia Brown is no one to the Duke of Hand's son, and it must remain that way. Anyway, he did nothing to offend my honour, just my independence.'

'Sorry. I'm not sure I understand.'

Amelia paused. If she told her brother what had happened, he would likely decide to defend her, and that would not help anyone. Still, he expected some sort of answer.

'Life is different outside of the palace. You would never consider a woman was not able to decide things for herself, but there are many who believe I need protecting because I am young and I am a female. Not only protected from others, but protected from myself as well.'

Damon burst out laughing. 'Anyone who thinks you need looking after has never attempted to beat you in an argument, nor seen you best me sparring at arms practice.'

Finally letting go of her anger, Amelia joined her brother's laugh. 'There is not much call for arms practice out here, but I still carry my knife just in case.' She patted the handle of the blade that hung at her waist. 'And I guess others do not know of my little nest egg, so I do not have to make the sacrifices they do.'

'What you are saying is they do not know who you are, which is as you wished. You are going to have to find some other way to teach people to respect your independence.'

Amelia looked thoughtfully at her brother, reviewing her day from this new perspective. 'It's odd you know, I used to give you advice and now it is you counselling me. Anyway, changing the subject, your note said you wanted to see me about something.'

Her brother coloured under her gaze. 'Umm, well, why not come home and stay the night and I can tell you all about it. Then I can escort you back tomorrow.'

'Damon, I am not sure... We are supposed to be keeping our distance.'

'Please. You are selling produce to Cook so you visit all the time. Just go in through the back door like you normally do, and leave the same way tomorrow.'

Amelia stopped arguing. After her miserable day, it would be nice to be pampered in her old home.

A GROAN ESCAPED Amelia's lips as she slumped in her chair. Almost as though she had known Damon would bring his sister back, Cook had presented all her favourite foods for dinner and Amelia had stuffed herself silly.

Talk over the meal had been light. Damon had asked about the farm, and with pride Amelia told him about her success at honey production, and in drying apples and pears from her orchards. She had also pointed out the vegetables served with the meal were from her own garden.

'Although I believe I could get by with market gardening alone, I do have more ideas. I am thinking about getting some sheep for their wool, and I have some skill with herbs. Cook has ordered fresh herbs from me, but I also thought about growing and drying some, and perhaps selling some tea blends. I would need to try and remember some of the recipes I made before, and I thought maybe next time you visit, you might bring me some books on herb-lore from the library in Hand.'

Damon smiled as he finished his dessert of spiced apples and cream. 'Of course I can, and there may even be some in the library here if you want to look before we leave tomorrow. Do you need me to bring you some parchment and writing things as well?'

'You are sweet to ask, but I bought a book to keep my recipes in today, and some writing supplies, and a decent lamp. My one luxury since I left home, but it will be worth it when I set up my new wares.'

'Excellent. You have come a long way since I last visited. I have one question though—are you sure about the sheep? It would be quite an expense and time commitment merely to have your own wool.'

'I do quite enjoy spinning and dyeing, and not all of my endeavours have to be moneymaking.' Amelia defended her position.

'All right. It is your decision. Perhaps you might humour me though, and when you are at the markets next, look at what it costs to purchase fleece, and weigh that up against the cost and hassle of owning your own animals'

'If it will make you happy,' Amelia said without any intention of doing it at all.

'If you are finished with dinner, shall we take tea in the living room?' Damon asked.

'I could not eat another thing,' Amelia said as she followed her brother into the next room.

Damon sunk into a chair by the fireplace as the housemaid poured their tea. Amelia waited for him to speak. Whereas he was quick to talk about her life, he was more reluctant to talk about his own.

Leaning forward, elbows on his thighs, his tea cupped between his hands, he started. 'I missed you, Amalie, Amelia—it will take me some time to be comfortable calling you that. I was so lonely after you left and I could no longer visit. Everyone behaves as if you never existed, and they tiptoe around me.

'I moved permanently over here about two moon-turns ago, using the excuse I wanted to learn more about the family holdings in Port Marden.'

'I had no idea,' Amelia said, somewhat hurt that no one had mentioned it to her, and annoyed with herself that she had been so caught up in her own life, she had not noticed the signs someone was living in the house when she visited.

'That is not surprising. I asked everyone here to keep it to themselves to let you concentrate on your own life, and to allow me to get used to not having you around.

'I began working with Father's manager and his son, who is learning the business as well. A few days after I arrived, I was invited to their home for a meal, and I met her there—Elise.

'She was the first person to ask me about you, and how I was coping without you. She is so warm, and smart and funny, and she does not talk to me like I am the future duke. I would like you to meet her.'

Amelia hid her smile behind her cup. So Damon was in love. She was happy for him; he needed someone to share his life with. 'Did you speak to Mother and Father yet?'

'I went home last six-day. Elise's mother is sister to Baron Liam, whose holding is just north of Port Marden. Her connection to the baron allows Mother and Father to consider Elise as a suitable match. They are coming here this six-day to discuss things with her parents.'

'Oh, Damon, I am so pleased for you.' Amelia placed her cup on the table beside her, and rose to embrace her brother.

'I worried about telling you, since... well, you know...'

'Damon, I made my choice and am happy building my life where I am. Besides, I have not completely ruled out a future with someone else.'

Shoulders sagging with relief, Damon smiled and began to regale Amelia with all Elise's amazing accomplishments.

Laughingly, she told him, 'Perhaps it is best I never meet her. I am sure I will pale beside such a goddess.'

Damon blushed. 'Too much? Sorry, it is just I so want you to like her.'

'I was only joking. I would be happy for you and her to visit me any time. To keep my identity secret, it is best it is done at my place, away from prying eyes. I cannot wait to meet the person who finally stole my brother's heart.'

DETENTE

Amelia's horse sped ahead and she grinned as the wind whipped her hair. Riding with her brother, with his guards trailing a ways behind, was a treat she was going to make the most of. Damon insisted she bring her possessions in a travel pack rather than her basket, which he had then carried for her. The two books she had found on herbs, a leg of venison, and her purchases from yesterday were clearly weighing him down—either that or he was letting her win the race back to her cottage.

She turned the corner and her home came into view, but she pulled up short as she saw a familiar figure waiting outside.

Damon joined her a moment later, and leaned over to speak. 'Your problem from yesterday?'

Sighing, Amelia nodded.

'Would you like me to deal with him?' he asked.

Pushing him away, she said, 'When did I ever need you to fight my battles?'

'Jean, when he kept trying to kiss you.'

'I had it under control.' The anger she experienced when the son

of a local baron had cornered her in the stables and tried to force himself on her threatened to return.

'You were going to kick him somewhere no boy likes to be kicked.'

'So, you were doing him a favour rather than defend my honour?' Amelia grinned as she dismounted, thankful Damon had managed to restore her equilibrium. Reaching up, she took the pack Damon handed down to her. Passing him the reins to her mount, she said, 'I look forward to seeing you and your intended the six-day after next. Now go. I need to handle this, and you hanging around will not help.'

'Go easy on him, and remember no boy appreciates being kicked there.' Damon winked as he turned his horse and rode away.

Anders stood and met her in front of the door.

'Good morning,' Amelia said as she unlocked the padlock that had secured her premises in her absence. 'I did not expect to see you today.'

'I arrived back too late to return your baskets yesterday. It took some time to load up after the market, and I got stuck in the masses leaving Port Marden afterwards. I expected to catch you up on the road and return them then, but now I find you had a better offer,' he said as he placed her baskets on the table.

Once again, Amelia found herself annoyed by Anders' veiled comments on her life. He was a good friend but, no matter that he believed he was helping her, they could not continue to spend time together if he thought he could run her life.

Shrugging her pack off her shoulders, she turned to tell her neighbour this, only to find him right behind her, his brows drawn into a frown.

'I do not know what happened yesterday. It was nothing like the plan I had made for our first market outing together,' Anders said, sounding like a child whose favourite toy had been taken from him.

Amelia raised an eyebrow. 'What did you plan?' she asked neutrally.

'I thought we would go to market together, set up our stalls, and sell our wares. Then Mother said to invite you home for an evening meal. I planned to show you how well we worked together. Instead, you wanted your new friend to come along, and everything fell apart from the moment I arrived.'

Not sure where this conversation was going, and not even sure she wanted to have it, Amelia moved around Anders to fill a kettle with water. After raking the coals in the fireplace, she added some kindling to start the fire. A nice mug of tea might calm things down. 'Would you like something to drink?'

She hoped he would say yes to give her an opportunity to sort out her thoughts while she pottered around the kitchen.

However, Anders grabbed her arm and swung her around to face him. 'No, Amelia, I would not like a cup of tea. I would like to talk to you about what happened yesterday, and hear your apology.'

'My apology?' Anger boiled inside her. For the sake of neighbourly relations she held it in check. 'What exactly am I to apologise for?'

The thunderous look on Anders' face warned her this conversation was not going to end well. 'I would like you to apologise for bringing a stranger with us to our first market. For leaving me before we had even set up. For setting up your stall so far away, and for storming off and not telling me where you were going.'

The unfairness of the situation was not lost on Amelia, but she did not want to argue with Anders and sour her relationship with her neighbours. Attempting to smooth things over, she asked, 'And if I apologise for the things you accuse me of, will you apologise for presuming to tell me how to run my business and my life?'

Anders' brow furrowed. 'I do not understand what you mean? I was merely looking out for you. As you are a woman alone, it is my duty to help you make better decisions. Everything I said was for your own good.'

Enough was enough. With her temper barely under control, Amelia used her self-defence training to twist and jerk, breaking Anders' hold on her arm. Moving around the table, she glared across at him. 'I am sorry I gave you the impression I was alone in the world, or that I needed anyone's help and advice on how I live my life. I am sorry you planned a day yesterday and did not ask me what I wanted. I am sorry you thought the business arrangement I made with your father was something more than it turned out to be.' Amelia's hands trembled as she tamped down the angry words forming in her head.

'I guess that young pup you spent the night with treats you so much better. If you believe someone of his status will ever make an honest woman of you, you are dreaming.'

'How dare you assume... I am not that type of....'

Anders had the grace to blush in shame. 'I am sorry, Amelia.' He held out his hands, beseeching her to forgive him. 'That just slipped out. I let my jealousy get the better of me. Can we talk about it?'

Taking deep breaths to calm her frayed nerves, Amelia chose her words carefully. 'We are both obviously upset at the moment. I value your friendship, but if we are to remain friends you need to appreciate I am my own person. I make my own decisions and I answer to no one. I think it is best if you leave now, and think about what I have said. If you want a friendship on that basis, next time we meet we will forget these last two days ever happened. If you choose otherwise, I will understand.'

He took a step towards her. 'I thought we were more than friends—'

Holding up her hand to warn him to come no closer, she said, 'We do not know each other well enough yet for you to assume something like that. Now please go.'

Anders took a nervous step towards her as if he wanted to say more. Then, seeming to think better of it, he turned on his heel and left. Overtaken by exhaustion, Amelia sank into the chair behind her.

Later that afternoon, she opened the door expecting Anders had returned, but instead found herself face-to-face with his mother. She stood aside to let Maisie in.

'I apologise for the mess. I am just testing out proportions for a thyme honey. Please take a seat and I will put the kettle on.'

'If I am interrupting, I will not stay.'

'No, no, I am nearly finished. I will make some tea in a moment, come in and make yourself comfortable while you wait,' Amelia encouraged the woman inside as her brain ticked over. Why had Maisie had come to visit—today of all days? Had she come to tell her she was no longer welcome in their home?

The very thought of being excluded caused a tightening of Amelia's stomach. Not only would she lose the friendships she had so carefully built, it would be difficult to live this far out from Port Marden without the support of her neighbours.

Taking a seat on the other side of the table, Maisie watched as Amelia finished cutting fresh thyme into a muslin bundle and tying it to a stick. Placing the knife back into the sheath that hung at her side, she then positioned the wood over a crock of honey, allowing the bundle of herbs to submerge.

Her neighbour stood and moved around the table to get a better look at what she was doing. 'That is an interesting way of making honey.'

'I got the idea from the market. One of my customers said she bought local honey to help her daughter's allergies, and it reminded me of honey I used to eat as a child. The thyme can help with breathing difficulties as well as allergies, but I needed a way to infuse the liquid and I came up with this. Hopefully people will buy some. I will take some to the next markets I attend.'

'You are a very clever girl, and perhaps my son does not appreciate your finer qualities.'

'Please, Maisie, let us not talk of Anders anymore.'

Job done, she carried the crock into her storeroom and covered it with another muslin, before returning with a container of her everyday tea.

Sighing, the older woman pushed the basket she had placed on the table towards Amelia. 'I made a blueberry pie for dinner last night, and I brought some today as a peace offering. I am afraid Anders, being my youngest, has always been a little indulged. He wanted for very little growing up, and when he set his cap on you, it never occurred to him to ask if you felt the same. For him, it skipped from intention to reality.'

Amelia busied herself pouring water over dried leaves to make their drink, allowing Maisie to get things off her chest.

'Please understand, I am not apologising for his behaviour. In fact, his father is having a word with him now about the proper way to court a girl. What I came to say is please do not judge us by the eagerness of youth. We are and will remain your friends, whatever you decide to do about Anders.' Maisie sat back in her chair, hands folded in her lap.

Sitting across from her guest, Amelia placed two steaming mugs on the table between them. 'The thought never occurred to me. Anders may have been a little ahead of himself, but there has been no real harm done. And, if I am honest, my parents were also a little remiss. Bringing me up the same as my brother did not prepare me for a world where women are not always considered to be independent.'

Maisie laughed. 'I know what you mean. I am sure Anders' view of women is a little skewed. He has only ever seen me looking after our family, in a very traditional role.

'I have only been able to do that because in our early years, Peter and I built up the farm together. We shared both the physical work and hardships; we were equal partners. It is Peter's pride I am now able to take it a little easier in my later years, spending more time looking after our extended family.'

Sipping her tea, Amelia's stomach unclenched as she was now back on her usual footing with her neighbour. 'Maisie, if Anders and I are meant to be it will happen. If not, I am pleased you and I will still be able to be friends.'

'Always. While I am here, might I suggest you try making some lemon honey. I use it often to ease summer colds,' Maisie said, moving their conversation away from more emotional subjects.

'What a good idea. Do you know where I can get some lemons, as I am sure I have not seen any trees around the farm.'

'Of course. I grow lemons in my garden. I will trade you some for some of your thyme honey. Also, I am happy to help you grow a tree for yourself from a cutting. I have a couple extra at home for you if you like, and if you plant them soon they will have time to bed in before winter.'

When Maisie left some time later, saying she needed to be back home for dinner, Amelia's new life was no longer crumbling around her.

TWO DAYS LATER, Amelia was washing up after having spent the day extending her herb garden, when she caught sight of a figure emerging from the woods. Anders approached the house, carrying a bouquet of wildflowers. She opened the door for him, but he would not meet her eyes.

'Amelia, I am sorry. Can we start again?' he said, holding the flowers out towards her.

As far as apologies go, it was simple and to the point. Amelia was tempted to forgive him on the spot. However, given recent events, she allowed a little of her magic to touch Anders and whispered, 'Ceerelesse.' She read confusion and regret, and perhaps a tingle of embarrassment. Satisfied his intentions were genuine, she took the flowers and invited him in.

'Mother asked me to see if you wanted to join us for dinner and meet her newest grandchild, who arrived last night. We are having something of a celebration. Of course, one of us will walk you home after.'

Amelia considered her muddied clothes and asked, 'Have I time to change?'

'You look fine to me.' Anders smiled. 'But I understand these things are important to women. I will wait.'

Amelia quickly slipped into her best dress. Checking her hair was tidily back off her face, she picked up her shawl and returned to Anders.

'I am ready,' she announced.

The evening was pleasant, with just the beginnings of a chill in the air as summer moved into autumn. Anders seemed in a happy mood, and Amelia took the opportunity to raise something that had been bothering her as they strolled through the woods between the farms.

'Anders, the other day you seemed quite put out by the very thought the traveller I helped might be a witch ...'

'I thought we were not going to ever talk about that day again.'

'It is not the day I wanted to talk about, but I did want to ask why, if magic is not outlawed, you found the idea of that woman having it so abhorrent.'

Her companion stopped in this tracks. 'Why do you ask?'

'I am just curious about local thoughts on the matter,' Amelia said in an attempt to find a reason that would not give away her secret.

'Well, I am not against the use of magic. Like everyone else, I am happy to be around magic users who have been properly trained, been authorised by the crown, and follow the laws laid down for its use.'

'So you mean anyone trained by the wizards at the school on the Wizard Isle?'

'Well, I guess so.' Anders nodded as he spoke.

'Have you ever heard of them admitting girls to the school on the isle?'

Again Anders stopped walking to look down at her. 'No, everyone knows the school only takes on boys as students.' He continued walking.

'Hold on. How do girls born with magic obtain their licence from the crown?' she asked. Although she already knew the answer, she wanted Anders to think about this.

'They do not.' There was not even a pause in Anders' step as he announced this fact.

'But without a licence ...'

'They cannot practice magic. That was why I worried you might be aiding a witch the other day. You do not seem the type who would enjoy breaking the law.'

'You are right; I am not. I am interested to know, though, what happens to girls who display magical abilities?"

Anders did not answer immediately, frowning as he seemed to consider her question. 'There cannot be many as I have not heard of any near here. The few women who practice witchcraft are reported to the guards, as unlicenced magic is illegal. I guess magic is something only males can control, otherwise the school at the Wizard Isle would take female students as well.'

Amelia was a little disturbed by Anders' acceptance of this double standard, and a little disappointed he did not even pause to question it. However, if his attitude was common, it explained why Nene took girls from their homes and trained them in the Tangled Woods. Away from the general population they could be taught to manage and use their magic without fear of discovery.

At least on Hand everyone knew where they stood. Magic was never discussed, and the law stated anyone found to have magical abilities was to be stripped of their magic or banished. Perhaps if more people had talked about the use of gifts, she would have known in the rest of Aria the law had been set up so no woman would ever be able to use their talents, and she would have been better prepared.

'Why this sudden interest in magic?' Anders asked, startling her out of her reverie.

She could never tell him of her skill, and this saddened her. It also firmed up her initial suspicion that they would never be anything more than friends. Not wishing to start yet another argument, she reached for a non-contentious reason. 'You know I am preparing some herbal teas to sell at market, and women healers are considered witches in some towns. I just want to be clear on the customs and laws around here.'

Anders laughed. 'We are not so backwards we think healers and those skilled in herb craft are magic users. I think you will be fine.'

Pleased she had thrown Anders off the scent, she continued to mull over what she had found out and what it meant for her. Nowhere in Aria was safe for her to use her gift, so it became even more important to her that she learn how to control it.

As Maisie opened the door to welcome them, Amelia forgot her concerns as she was wrapped in the warmth of the neighbouring family. Greeting the newest member, she held the girl in her arms, and for the first time Amelia knew, with the certainty of her gift, she was not destined to be a mother.

With a world that did not treat women the same as men, and who vilified females who displayed magic, there was no way she would risk a child of hers being placed in the same position she found herself in. For some reason that did not tear her heart out the way she had thought it would.

Enjoying the experience of holding the tiny soul, she rocked the baby to sleep. As the baby's eyes closed, Amelia looked up and found Anders watching her, a rather possessive look on his face, almost as though he saw their future. She resolved to tell him she could never provide the future he wanted—soon—before it was too late. He deserved to find someone who would bear him children and add to this wonderful family—someone who better fitted into the mould of his ideal woman.

That was a conversation for another time. Tonight was a night for celebration and enjoying herself.

Once the baby was safely tucked into its cradle, Amelia went to help Maisie serve the meal. Later, Maisie and Peter walked her home, declaring they needed the fresh air, instructing the youngsters to clean up as they left.

Peter was impressed with the improvements she had made to the farm, which caused Amelia to blush with pride. As they left, Maisie agreed to bring over the lemon trees she had promised the following day.

After sliding the bar of the door into place, a contented and weary Amelia made sure her fire was well-banked before falling into bed.

Too much of Peter's special mead the night before made it difficult to get herself out of bed the next morning. Snuggling deeper into the bedclothes, she rolled around until she found a comfortable spot and tried to go back to sleep. Unfortunately guilt overcame lethargy. Kicking the blankets off, she forced herself to get up.

Making herself a cup of reviving tea, Amelia avoided looking at the dishes she had not washed yesterday. After taking a chair outside, she sipped her tea in the sun and planned her day. Having closed her eyes for a moment, she jerked them open to find Anders standing in front of her, a big grin on his face

'Good morning,' he said cheerfully, and she grunted in response. 'I see you are not doing too well this morning. Dad's home brew can do that to you.'

Her stomach sunk a little, she needed a frank talk with Anders about her expectations for the future. Now was as good a time as any. 'Would you like some tea? The water is still hot.'

'We were all a little late getting started today and Dad said I was not to dally as the winter potatoes will not plant themselves. Mum asked me to drop these off to you,' he said, pointing to two small lemon trees he had placed beside her. 'She would have come herself, but she is still tidying up after last night.'

'Oh dear. She was going to help me plant them so I would be able to find the best place for them to grow.'

'I know, that is why she said to tell you they need to go in a sunny place with well-drained soil, north-facing is best.'

'Thank her for me. I will plant them this evening.'

'I see you have a new bed dug. Is it for your winter crop?' Anders leaned against the wall, clearly not in too much of a hurry to return home in spite of his refusing a drink.

'Not exactly. I plan to gather some wild herbs and see if I can get them to grow in my garden. I have enough potatoes, beets, carrots, and turnips planted in the other two beds for my own use and to meet the needs of my special customer.'

'But there is not enough there for you to sell at market as well.'

'I know. I looked around the market and found there were enough vendors like yourself there selling vegetables. People liked my apples and honey because this farm has a reputation, but it would be hard for me to compete against larger, established farms selling vegetables. So I am trying something different.'

'That is very wise of you.'

Amelia smiled at the almost-compliment. It seemed taking Damon's advice and proving she could stand on her own two feet by showing Anders she had her own plan to make a go of the farm was working. 'My ideas will take a little while to put into place, and I told your father last night I will not be going to market for a moon-turn so I can fully stock up on the things I want to sell.'

'Will you be all right without the income over winter?'

Although Amelia bristled inside at the question, she did not jump down Anders' throat. 'I have my regular customer to keep coin coming in, and I am well-stocked for the winter. It will be tight, but I will manage.'

'I admire your resourcefulness. I tried to convince Mother and Father to increase our lemon grove so we can start selling them at market, and maybe even venture into selling some of Mum's curd and cordials.'

'That sounds like a great idea.' This was the first time Anders had spoken to her of his own plans for the future.

'It is, and Mum thought so too. But Father said we make a good living with what we do already, and lemon trees take a lot of tending.'

Anders' tone was surly, and Amelia braced herself for another of his outbursts—but it did not come.

'Finally Mother and I wore him down last night, after they returned from taking you home. Seeing how well you are doing softened him a little. He told me I could fence off some of the top field, the one by the house, and see what I could do with the trees. Of course I have to keep up with my other work, and it will take time to establish the new trees, but it is a start.'

'That really is good.'

'It is just...' He shuffled from foot to foot. '... I may not have time to help you out so often. I mean, your arrangement with Dad about going to market with us still stands, but I'll have other pressures on my time.'

'Anders, it is fine. You need to look to your future, and I have taken advantage of your generosity for long enough. I was thinking about hiring someone to help me fix things up over the winter months anyway. I will just have to look into it a little sooner.'

The tension left Anders' body and he visibly relaxed, before tensing again. 'Looks like you have company.'

Amelia turned and raised a hand, shading her eyes to find she did, indeed, have a guest, as a young woman brought her mount to a halt at the edge of the path from Port Marden.

'Another one of your fancy friends?' Anders commented.

Her hackles rose and she prepared to defend herself, but the twinkle in his eye suggested he was teasing her, so she relaxed and merely said, 'She is no friend of mine. I have never seen her before in my life. Perhaps it is someone who got lost on the road.'

The girl dismounted and walked confidently over to them. 'Amelia? Amelia Brown?'

'I am she,' Amelia answered.

'I am Elise.'

For a moment, Amelia could not place where she had heard the name before, then it all came back to her. 'Elise. Damon's friend?'

Seeing his company was no longer required, Anders excused himself and headed back to work.

As he drifted out of earshot, Elise said, 'Sorry, I did not mean to interrupt anything?'

'You were not interrupting. He had to return to work anyway. Would you like to come in? I am afraid I was not expecting, um, visitors today. So it is a little untidy.'

Amelia led her guest inside and placed her mug on the bench before she went over to stoke the fire to make another cup of tea. She turned to find Elise, sleeves rolled up, stacking dishes ready to wash up.

'You do not need to do that,' Amelia told her. 'I do not normally leave a mess like this, but we had a bit of a celebration at the neighbour's last night, and I find myself quite behind today.'

'Between the two of us we will get you back on track, and then perhaps we can visit for a while,' Elise said as she walked to the fire, picked up the still-warm kettle, and proceeded to fill the sink with water.

By the time the girl finished the dishes, Amelia had lit the fire and reboiled the kettle. She then swept the main rooms and took another chair outside. Making the tea, she asked Elise to take a seat while she finished up.

After checking the pantry to make sure she had something to offer for the noonday meal, Amelia joined her guest in the morning sun.

'I love your place,' Elise said. 'It is just as Damon described it.'

'It suits me,' Amelia answered, and an awkward silence fell.

'I must apologise for dropping in like this,' Elise started. 'And without even Damon to introduce us. It is just I did not know what to do with myself today. Of course it is all right for Damon. He is able to work to take his mind off things. What was I supposed to do? Just sit around and wait while our parents talk?'

The girl's words nudged something loose in Amelia's mind—the big meeting between the parents. Today must be the day.

'I decided to go for a ride. Then I thought, what a great opportunity to meet you. Of course, I never thought you might have work to do. I mean, they bring us up to be so useless when it comes to everyday things, so of course I would not have thought I would be interrupting your workday ...' she trailed off, perhaps realising she was babbling.

Amelia smiled reassuringly. 'Fortunately I only have a little planting to do today, and that can wait until late afternoon.' Amelia attempted to help the girl relax, but her efforts fell astray.

'Of course I do appreciate you make your own living, and I am happy to do anything I can to help. It may even take my mind off things. Oh, and I brought you a present I thought might be of some use.' After placing her cup on the ground, Elise went back over to her horse, which she had tied to the well post, and retrieved something from her saddle bag.

She handed the gift to Amelia, who opened it to find a book on the medicinal use of herbs. If Elise had not fully won her over when shed helped with the dishes, she did now with her thoughtfulness. 'Elise, while this is lovely, it is too much. Books like this cost a lot of money.'

'I am not a spendthrift, if that is what you are worried about.' Her words were terse as her brow furrowed.

Amelia placed her hand on the other girl's arm. 'I was not suggesting you were. It is just, books are precious, and expensive, and...'

'Honestly, Amelia, at home there is a library full of books no one except me ever reads. Uncle sent some books from his library for my mother, and they are valued so little they have sat in the chests they arrived in for years.

'When Damon told me about your interest, I searched through them and found this. I asked Mother if I might lend it to a friend, and she said I might give it to her. So I am.'

'Well, if you're certain, I would love to accept it. Thank you.'

'Of course it is obviously a bribe to buy your goodwill.' Elise laughed, and Amelia could not help but join her.

'It's worked,' Amelia told her. 'On a more serious note, I can see you make Damon happy, and I can also see you really care for him, else you would not be working so hard to win me over. That is all I ask of the person my brother marries.'

'Let's hope your parents think the same way.' For a brief moment, Elise's confidence wavered, then she took a breath and carried on. 'What can I do to help you today?'

'Apart from the planting, I planned a wander in the woods. I found a patch of wild garlic, and another of late-season blueberries. I want to gather some cuttings of the berry bush, and pull some garlic bulbs. Then I was going to plant them along with my new lemon trees this afternoon, after lunch.'

'Sounds perfect. Let us get started.'

The girls spent a relaxing day gathering and planting and getting to know each other.

Later, as they tidied themselves up, Elise asked a question that threw Amelia off balance. 'So, the man this morning—is a friend? Or perhaps something more?'

Amelia thought for a moment, unsure what to say. She longed for someone to confide in, but she had only just met this girl. 'I am not sure. I enjoy his company, but recently his actions have me wondering if we can ever be more than friends.' Unable to fully express her true feelings, Amelia carried on putting the garden implements away.

'Do you think maybe he is too low-born for you? No, you are too much like Damon—that thought would never occur to you. Is this something to do with your talents? You do not need to hide anything from me. I already promised Damon to take your secret to the grave.'

'What if my secret was about me actually practicing magic?' Amelia asked. 'I am not sure even Damon would be able to countenance that.'

Elise paused for a moment, showing her chatty exterior hid a very thoughtful mind. 'Of course then I would be placed in a difficult situation. I will never lie to Damon, but unless he asks me outright, I do not see any problem in not saying anything to him. And as they do not like talking about magic on Hand, the chances of the subject ever coming up are slim.'

'I would be breaking the law and you would be helping me cover it up.' Amelia pushed.

Elise snorted. 'A stupid law that allows men to use their magic and offers no way for women to do so. That is one law I would be happy to ignore. Now we have that out of the way, do you feel more able to clarify who your friend is?'

Sighing, Amelia told her, 'At one stage I thought we might have had the start of something ... um ... special. I found out he does not feel the same way about women and magic as you do. I think it will be for the best if we just remain friends.'

'Oh, what a shame. I can tell he likes you, and you both looked very comfortable together when I rode up.'

'I am not sure I would say he likes me, more that he likes who he thinks I am. Actually it is worse than that, it is as though he has this ideal of the perfect woman and he is trying to fit me into the mould,' Amelia explained.

'Definitely not someone you want to become involved with then. Though, if you want to use your magic then it is all for the best.'

'I have not decided either way about my gift. There is a friend arriving in the next day or so to finish showing me how to hide and control my magic. She also offered to teach me how to use it if I want.'

Elise cocked her head to the side and studied Amelia before answering. 'Talking with you places my worries about today into perspective. I wish I could give you some direction, but I think you need to work out yourself what you want from this life. I will tell you this though: Damon and I will be there to support you whatever you choose.'

The future Duchess of Hand hugged her, and for the first time since she had left home, Amelia allowed herself to be comforted.

A short time later, Elise rode out with some honey and a packet of special tea in her bags, promising to visit Amelia at the markets in two six-days' time.

'I shall look forward to it,' Amelia said, not just to be polite, but because she really was looking forward to seeing her brother's intended again.

DECISION TIME

'Finally.' Amelia let out the breath she had held. 'That took way too long to learn.'

'Perhaps it was not long at all, my impatient friend. After all, you spent the last six-day just learning to control your magic. Taking only two days to use your ability to scan a body and find an ailment is actually quite quick,' Nene told her.

'Are you sure it is your aching knee I was meant to find, you are not just saying that to encourage me?'

'Believe me, I am sure. All this walking around I have been doing recently has caused an old injury to flare up. I am happy to confirm you have the skill to find internal problems with people. Do you want to learn more?'

Amelia did not know how to answer, so she asked a question herself. 'Have you met others who can see the future?'

'One, once. Although I have heard of more who live beyond the Tangled Woods, and even more residing over the mountains.'

'Can you tell me what good their magic has been used for?'

'That is a difficult question to answer as it depends on how you define good. The skill used on a macro scale can help people prepare for times of famine or war. However, most people do not want to find out about their own individual futures, and very often they will not thank you for telling them.'

'It is as I thought.'

'Now you have control of your magic, you should be able to prevent all but the most invasive foresight dreams. Although, if you release your magic, your ability to see into the future should return. I take it you do not want any further training?'

'I have never been comfortable about my particular skill. It did save my brother from serious injury, but the end result was having to leave my family. Recently it showed me I will lead a long and happy life, but I will never have children of my own. It is a double-edged sword, and I cannot really see any good coming from using it.

'However, you taught me another use for my magic when you were here before, the ability to sense another's true feelings, and I did find that useful. Are there other things you can teach me like that? If there are, then I would be happy to learn those.'

'There are. I can teach you some tricks to help with your herbal medicines. Things that can help you diagnose illnesses. You will need to be careful when and with whom you use them, but it is a useful skill if you want to help others.'

'I would love to learn, if you have time to stay and help me.'

'I have the time, but ... there is no delicate way to say this. We in the coven share our knowledge with each other. If I am to share our lore with you, I would need to be sure you will do the same when called upon by one of our sisterhood.'

When Amelia did not immediately answer, Nene spoke again. 'If that is too much to ask ...'

'No, it is not that.' Amelia was quick to reassure her. 'I am happy

to give back, but what can I possibly teach someone else? I do not intend to use much magic often, or spend a lot of time studying it. I am unsure of how I can keep up my end of such a bargain.'

Nene laughed. 'Our teaching is not all about magic. You are already quite knowledgeable about herbs, and I can see you are studying to understand more about them, and to develop your own medicines and cures. Perhaps one day one of our healers might want to learn about herb craft, or even something as simple as how to grow them. At the moment though, because of where you are placed, having members of our coven stay here when we travel would be more than enough payment.'

Amelia sighed with relief. 'I hope to bring someone in to help around the farm, but I will always ensure there is a bed here should anyone from the coven pass by.'

Since that night, Amelia had been applying herself to learning how to diagnose illness using magic. By the time Nene left, Amelia was confident in being able to use her abilities, but was sad to see her new friend go.

Once her teacher slipped safely into the woods, Amelia turned back to her home to find Anders standing by the well, his face a thunderous cloud.

'Good morning, Anders.' Amelia chose to ignore his anger.

'I thought we agreed she was a witch, but you chose to let her stay anyway.' Anders did not take his eyes off Nene's back.

'I think, if you remember correctly, we did not agree she was a witch. And even if she were, it is my choice whether or not to let her stay here. Was there something else you wanted, Anders?'

He handed her a basket of lemons. 'Mother asked me to deliver these in payment for your thyme honey.' His job done, he turned on his heel and left.

I really must have that talk with him before things get totally out of hand. I must tell him once and for all that we are only friends, Amelia said to herself, before moving on to the day's tasks.

THE DAY HAD STARTED out quite promising. She was excited about taking her flavoured honeys and medicinal teas to market, and she had loaded her extra baskets onto the cart along with her usual produce, then jumped up beside Anders.

Even though the autumn air was chilly, the early morning ride was still pleasant. Anders chattered excitedly about the progress he had made with his lemon trees, and cheerfully let her off at the gate to drop the vegetable order at her old home. Cook had given her a parcel from Damon—the books he had promised to find—before shooing her out the door.

While she ran her errand, Anders had managed to find her a rented table close to his site, which she was grateful for as it made setting up much easier.

The day got better as, halfway through the morning, Amelia glanced up from her restocking to find Elise and Damon looking through her teas.

'Hello, Amelia.' Elise beamed, and before a stunned Amelia could say anything, the girl continued, 'Mother liked your tea so much she asked me to come to the markets and get some more. I think she should try some of your thyme honey as well, or do you think the lemon one, Damon?'

Mechanically, Amelia moved to look for the tea she had given Elise to take home, while her brother leaned in and said under his breath, 'Mother and Father came to an agreement: Elise and I are betrothed.'

'Here you are. This is the same one you got from me the other day,' Amelia said as she handed the package to Elise, smiling as she did. Then she whispered, 'congratulations' as she picked up the two honey pots Elise was looking at. 'The thyme honey is good for respiratory problems, whereas the lemon honey is better for those colds.'

'I really am not sure which one Mother would prefer. Perhaps I should take a jar of each. Damon, I might need another basket to carry all of this.'

'Perhaps you could borrow one of mine and return it next market day,' Amelia offered.

'Oh, you are too kind,' Elise said as Amelia slipped behind the stall to get one of her baskets for them to load their produce into.

Damon moved in behind her, as if to help. As she placed the honey and tea in the basket, making sure they were safely stowed, Damon quietly said, 'We will visit one evening soon and give you all the news.'

As she handed him the basket, his eyes darted round and, seeing there was no one looking at them, he kissed her on the cheek. When Amelia returned to the front of her stall, Elise handed over the price of the goods, and with a cheery wave, led her betrothed away.

Later in the day they were both weary as they packed up after a busy day. Flushed with the success of her new products, Amelia's mind brimmed with ideas as she watched the trees as they passed. Port Marden was well in the distance when Anders broke the silence.

'So now your boyfriend brings his fiancée to your stall as if there is nothing wrong with it. You treat me as just a friend, although I am someone who you could build a future with, but you allow him to kiss you with his future wife nearby.'

So many thoughts raced through Amelia's head, so many possible answers, but she was smart enough to realise any of those tart retorts would only fuel his jealousy.

'He is our future duke. Is that how he turned your head? Promising you wealth? A better life?' His eyes flashed. 'Did he purchase your farm for you? Is that why you have enough money to waste on books?'

Refusing to dignify his accusations with an answer only seemed to stoke his anger.

'I thought to offer you a future. I still would if you would promise to call off your affair with that... that... *spoilt child*.'

Taking a deep breath, Amelia said, 'I will say this once, and once only—I am not having an affair with Lord Damon, and nor will I ever. He is dear to me and stood by me when others did not. His future wife is my friend, and if you think I would act one way to a person's face and another behind her back, then you do not know me at all.'

Amelia did not say another word all the way home, unable to trust herself not to spit out something sharp and hurtful. On the other hand, Anders apologised repeatedly for his jealousy and attempted to cajole her into talking to him.

By the time they reached the turn to her cottage, Amelia had made up her mind: she needed to tell Anders they could only ever be friends, and she had to do it now. It was the only way she might still be able to salvage her friendship with her neighbours.

As the cart came to a stop outside her door, Amelia jumped down. Pulling her empty baskets from the back of the cart, she then carried them to the house and placed them on the ground while she undid the lock. Behind her, something scraping across the wagon bed told her Anders was removing her two partially full baskets.

She walked inside and dropped her baskets on the table, leaving room for Anders to put the others. Still fuming, Amelia admitted she had to tell Anders how she felt about him now. Turning to ask him in, she found her baskets beside the open door, and just caught a glimpse of his cart heading back down the road. Once again, he had left without her being able to tell him they were not compatible and had no future together.

Sighing, she went to shut the door, and caught a glimpse of shadows moving near the path. Two figures emerged from the bushes beside the road and ran towards her.

'Nene? What is the matter?' she asked as the woman drew near, dragging a young girl behind her.

'I will explain in a moment. Can we come in?'

'Of course.'

Moving aside, she allowed the woman and young girl past,

closing the door behind them. She allowed them to settle while she placed her baskets in the pantry and raked up the fire. After placing a kettle and the stew pot over the flames, she turned to her guests.

'What is the matter? How come you're back so soon?'

'A runner came for me. It seems Kayla here used her magic in front of the wrong person. She needs to go into hiding for a bit. Can we stay the night? I would not ask, but the girl is exhausted. We will be on our way tomorrow.'

'Of course you can.'

'Before you agree, I should tell you that man of yours saw us as he passed by. His face turned to thunder as he rode away.'

Not stopping to even consider what that might mean, Amelia told them not to worry; they would be safe there for the night.

She fed her guests, then Nene tucked Kayla up in one of the beds upstairs, coming back down to join Amelia for a tea before she too retired.

'I am so sorry to put you in this position without warning.' The woman took a mug from Amelia.

'I would not hear of you both spending a night in the open when there are extra beds here,' she told her.

'I hope it doesn't cause any problems between you and your young man.'

'The problems were there already, and it is past time I dealt with them. I am afraid I've been putting it off, hoping it will go away.'

'That boy is smitten, and people in love sometimes do funny things. You need to be careful with...' She stopped mid-sentence as the sound of hooves filled the night.

Amelia rose and went to the window over the bench. In the moonlight she made out two horsemen, followed by Anders' cart.

Without thinking, she flung open the door. 'Anders, what happened? Is everyone all right?'

'Amelia Brown?' one of the men on horseback asked.

'Yes.' She was more cautious now as she glimpsed a look of triumph on Anders' face.

'I believe you are harbouring a known witch and user of magic.'

'I am not. A friend and her niece are staying the night on their way home.'

'Lies,' Anders yelled. 'That woman is a witch.'

'It is an offence against the laws to harbour a user of magic. Please ask the woman in question to come out,' the guard threatened as another cart pulled up at the end of the road.

Amelia stood firm in the doorway, but Nene slipped past her.

'That is her.' Anders pointed accusingly.

'I recognise you. You are Nene Goodson, wanted by the guards to answer an accusation of unlicenced use of magic in Port Marden.' Turning to Anders the man said, 'You were right, young man. This woman has had a charge of witchcraft laid with us by a very prominent citizen. We have been looking for her for sometime.'

'It is true; I am Nene Goodson,' the woman admitted. 'And I can tell you I have never used magic in Port Marden, but I am sure you will want to verify that.'

'I must take you and Amelia Brown into custody,' the guard responded.

'Amelia has no knowledge of any use of magic, or that I was wanted by the guards. I will testify to that.'

'I told her you were a witch,' Anders accused.

The guard turned and looked at the young man. 'You told us you suspected a magic user had wormed her way into your girlfriend's house, but she would not believe you.'

'But I told her.' Anders stood on the cart, unable to control his anger.

'You also told us you had not actually seen the woman use magic, so could not lay a charge. We agreed to come take a look, and if it was a known magic user we would take her into custody.

'Mistress Brown, you are free to stay as it seems you had no idea you were harbouring an actual witch. Mistress Goodson, you must come with us and answer the charges against you.'

'Look after Kayla. Someone will come and pick her up in a few days' time,' Nene whispered as she walked past, head held high.

The other guard dismounted, carrying a rope.

'I will come peacefully,' Nene said as she walked over to the other cart and hoisted herself up.

'What about the girl? She must be a witch too,' Anders protested.

'Mistress Brown?'

'The girl has come to help me out on the farm over winter and has shown no magical ability to me, sir,' Amelia answered truthfully.

'As Amelia said, she has not shown any magical ability in front of either of us,' Nene confirmed. 'And I will testify to that.'

The guard frowned. 'I think I had better see this girl for myself— just to make sure.'

'She is sleeping,' Amelia said.

He dismounted. 'Take me to her. I promise to try not to wake her.'

The man followed Amelia into the house. She picked up a lamp and showed him to the room upstairs. Kayla stirred as the light illuminated her face enough for the guard to see her, but did not wake.

Shrugging, the guard handed the lamp back to Amelia and returned to his men. 'All right, we can leave her behind.'

'What will happen to Nene now?' Amelia asked the guard.

'She will be held in a cell until she is called before a magistrate.'

'When will that be?'

'It normally takes about two days to arrange a hearing.'

'I will come in the morning,' Amelia called to Nene as they took her away. 'I'll arrange an advocate for you.'

'You would help her?' Anders spluttered. 'Even knowing what she is, you would still help her?'

'You yourself said there is no way a woman can legally practice magic in Aria. I say if she did actually use her gifts as charged, then the laws of the land forced her to become a criminal, and I cannot stand by and do nothing while she rots in prison.' Amelia turned to go back inside.

'Wait.' Anders jumped down from the cart and went to follow her in.

Standing in the middle of the doorway, she blocked his entrance. 'Anders, your actions tonight mean I no longer consider you a friend, and you are no longer welcome in my house.'

'You cannot keep me out.' He moved to barge past her.

In a flash, Amelia's defensive training came back to her. She took a fighting stance and reached for the knife she always wore on her belt. It appeared the same as the small knives all women carried to help with everyday tasks. However, hers had been made from the finest steel and as well as being useful for cutting vegetables, it was perfect for close hand-to-hand combat.

Holding the blade in front of her, she said, 'I told you, you're not welcome here. Do not make me hurt you.'

Anders laughed down at her. 'Please, a slip of a thing like you cannot hope to stop me from doing whatever I want.'

The tone of his voice and the implied threat caused a trickle of fear to form in Amelia's stomach, but she held her ground. Anders moved to pass her and, once more she blocked the doorway, jabbing out with the knife, just nicking the skin below his shirtsleeve and drawing a little blood. 'The next one will do harm. I do not want to hurt you, but be aware I am trained and I have bested bigger men than you.'

Something in her tone must have convinced him she meant business.

'I will not stay where I'm not wanted. But do not come crying to me when you realise what you have lost.' He sneered at her.

'Goodbye, Anders.'

She closed the door before dropping the bar in place with a loud thud and leaning back against the solid wood, her body trembling with relief.

HOW TO SAVE A WITCH

Amelia did not even wait for the sun to wake her the next morning. In the predawn light she milked the cow and saddled her horse. Amelia opened the door and was met by Kayla, who was up and stoking the fire. The girl jumped at the sound of the door opening.

'Where is Nene?' she asked, her voice barely carrying over the scraping of the coals.

As Amelia recounted the events of the previous night, the young girl huddled in a chair, wrapping her arms protectively around herself.

Amelia made them some breakfast and, as the girl ate, she outlined her plan. Kayla's hands shook as raised the spoon to her lips. She placed it back in her bowl with a thunk before she announced, 'I will come with you. I can help.'

'No, please. You will be safer here.' Amelia would not be able to get what she needed in Port Marden without becoming Amalie again, and the fewer people who knew her by that name the better.

Kayla's mouth took on a stubborn set, and her voice was a little more confident. 'Nene helped me when I was in trouble. Now it is my turn to help her. Please, you must take me with you.'

Worried if she forbade the girl from coming Kayla might just follow anyway, Amelia took a mouthful of food before pushing the bowl aside. She did not know how to answer, then she had an idea. 'I am not sure how long I will be today. If I get delayed there will be no one to milk the cow and take care of things here. Also, if I do manage to free Nene, it would be nice if we came home to a warm fire and a cooked meal. Can you cook?'

'Yes, and I can make bread.' Kayla paused then, wrung her hands and said, 'If you think I can be of more help here, I will stay. I must admit, I was not looking forward to going back into a town after my last experience.'

Relieved she had agreed to stay behind, Amelia showed Kayla where everything was. Once she was done she asked, 'Can you read?'

Kayla nodded.

'If you get bored, there are some books on herb-lore in my bedroom. Please be careful with them though.'

'I will, I promise.'

'Drop the bar behind me, and do not open the door until Nene or I return. I should be back before the cow needs milking again at sundown.'

Instructions delivered, it was time for Amelia to leave.

RIDING her horse into town made the journey so much quicker, but still Amelia was impatient. Even so, it was very early when she rode round behind the family house and dismounted. A surprised Tom came out to meet her and took the reins of her horse. Opening the door to the kitchen, Cook welcomed her in. 'Oh, my dear, what is wrong? You look like you have been chased here by the furies themselves.'

'Cook, I need to see Damon urgently. Is he still here?'

'He is. He does not go home 'til the boat today. Look, take yourself into the kitchen and I will nip up and get him.'

Amelia sat herself in a free chair. The upstairs maid brought her a cup of tea, then placed a bowl of oats full of dried fruit and topped with a generous dollop of cream in front of her.

Riding in the fresh morning air had returned her appetite, and Amelia wolfed down the meal as she waited for her brother to appear. Finally, Damon slipped into the seat beside her, eyebrows raised questioningly. 'What emergency prompted this early morning visit?' he asked as he picked up the mug of tea Cook had placed in front of him.

'I need an advocate, and a good one,' she blurted out.

'What?' The mug almost slipped from his hand.

As Amelia explained the situation, Damon visibly relaxed.

'I do not know of anyone suitable. I use an advocate for business purposes, I cannot see him taking this sort of thing on.'

'If I may,' Cook interrupted them, 'I hope you do not mind, but I overheard what you were talking about, and I may know someone who can help.'

Damon looked up in surprise. 'How?'

'I am not sure you realise, but some of the staff here in the house and at the office are people from Hand who have been found with skills, making it difficult for them to remain on the island.'

'Really?' Amelia was unable to hide her surprise.

Cook smiled. 'Yes, really. Your parents were not able to persuade enough of the nobles in Hand to change the laws about magic, so instead they made it easier on those they banished from the island. In return for not using our magic, we are given employment. Why do you think we went out of our way to help you settle here? We all went through it and decided to support you through this difficult time.'

'So you...' Amelia started then stopped.

'Yes, and that is also how I met the advocate. I am sure you realise women who use their gifts often fall foul of the law, given there are few legal ways for us to practice magic. My sister was one of them. Advocate Brunel helped her, and his name is well-known by the women of the woods.'

'You are part of...'

'No, dear, not me, but my sister is. She informed Nene of your presence, and asked her to look out for you when she was nearby.'

Damon had not moved during the conversation, and he continued to stare in disbelief. Turning to her brother, Amelia explained the coven's existence, and why women needed to be so careful about using magic.

'That is outrageous,' he said when she finished. 'After I become duke, I shall change this.'

'Bless you, young sir. This has been the law for generations and cannot be undone in a day, or even a moon-turn. Many hearts and minds need to be altered before that law can change.'

'Besides, that is a long time off. We need to do something for Nene now. Cook, where can I find Advocate Brunel?' Amelia asked.

'His office is on market square, beside the Grey Goose Tavern.'

Amelia rose to leave, but Damon placed a restraining hand on her arm. 'Wait, I will come with you.'

'You cannot do that, Damon. People may place us together and realise who I am.'

Cook chuckled with genuine amusement. 'You can call yourself Amelia and try to blend in with others, but most of the people in Port Marden know exactly who you are, and may even suspect why you are here. Over time, they will likely as not forget your past, but for the present there is no risk to Master Damon.'

'All right. Give me a minute to finish dressing and we will be off,' Damon said as he left the room.

IMPRESSED with a future duke turning up in his office, Advocate Brunel cleared his day to spend on Nene's case. The short, rotund man had calmly taken down all Amelia knew, then he had disappeared for a candle-mark or so to talk to the guards about the complaint they had received.

'Right, let us go,' he said upon his return.

Amelia's stomach grumbled as she stood.

Damon remained in his seat. 'Where to?'

'Why to the prison of course. I need to talk to the accused to see if I can mount a defence. Come, come.'

'Do you need us there?' Damon queried.

'I would not normally take you with me. But time is of the essence and sometimes the guards there like to follow procedures to the letter. I should have placed a request in writing with the prison clerk, and well—'

'Having the future duke turn up with you might grease the wheels a little,' Amelia provided.

'Why yes, exactly.' The man smiled.

'I am meant to be catching the boat across to Hand today,' Damon said.

'Write your apologies, and my clerk will take it to the ship.' The advocate slipped behind his desk and pushed some paper and a pen over.

Head down, Damon wrote furiously for a moment, then folded the letter. Before he was done, Advocate Brunel held out an envelope then was already at the door summoning a clerk.

'How can he be so portly when he is always rushing?' Damon asked grumpily under his breath as he stood to follow Amelia out the door.

At the prison, Damon's presence was the only reason the advocate was able to see Nene. However, it was not enough to get Amelia and Damon in as well. They had to wait in the clerk's office while the advocate spoke to his client.

Damon paced, and the poor clerk watched his every move, no doubt unable to work with so esteemed a visitor in his office. Amelia was about to suggest they find a tavern for some lunch when Advocate Brunel returned.

'All good,' he said, sweeping into the room. 'I have a few people I need to talk to. Should we meet back at my office in, how about two candle-marks?' Without waiting for a reply, he left the two of them standing there.

Amelia thanked the clerk for his hospitality as she and Damon departed to look for somewhere close by to eat.

Settled in a dark corner of the Grey Goose Tavern, they ate their pies in silence. Once her hunger was vanquished, Amelia sat back and looked out the window, thinking.

'What do you make of it all?' she asked Damon.

'I am not sure. Advocate Brunel is certainly hard-working, but I guess we will not know where we stand until we meet with him again.'

'Mm, I guess not. I am going to visit a bakery. The prison clerk said the food is not very good, and I want to get something for Nene.'

Sighing, Damon wiped some gravy off his plate and leaned back. 'I was hoping to wait here in comfort for our appointment, but I guess I can come with you.'

They were a little early for their meeting, but Advocate Brunel was happy to see them when they arrived. 'I have spoken to the people Nene was with the day she was accused of using magic, and I believe we have a better-than-average change of getting the charges dismissed as malicious.

'It seems the man who accused her has a grudge against the women from the Tangled Woods as his daughter ran away there. He recognised Nene, and accused her of performing a spell, a curse, in the street. The people she was with are good citizens, and they say they saw no such thing. And as no one else came forward to support his accusation, it is his word against all the others.'

Amelia slumped with relief, but Damon sat forward on his seat and asked, 'If that is the case then how did things get this far?'

Advocate Brunel sat back in his chair and steepled his fingers, 'This is quite common I am afraid. When it comes to accusations of unlicensed magic it is a case of guilty until proven innocent.'

'That is outrageous,' Damon started, but Amelia placed a restraining hand on his arm.

'What do we do now?'

'I have the dismissal request to draft to place before the magistrate tomorrow. You can go home now and wait.'

'Thank you so much,' Amelia said, but the advocate brushed her words aside with his hand.

'You can thank me tomorrow when your friend is free,' he said, his attention already back on the paperwork on his desk.

BECAUSE OF THE LATE HOUR, Damon insisted on escorting her home and she was grateful for the company. Wearily, they returned to the farm, the light from the lamp Damon's guard carried flickering as it lit their way.

While they rode, Amelia's tired eyes began to close, only to fly open in alarm. In her tired state she must have released control of her magic, and she had been overwhelmed with a sudden sense of foreboding. Digging her horse in the ribs, she sped off, trusting Damon and the guards to follow.

Arriving at the clearing in front of her house, she was surprised the door to her cottage was wide open. As she dismounted, Amelia could just make out the embers of the fire, a pot of stew hanging forlornly on the hook above it. Taking a deep breath to calm her rising panic, Amelia called out, 'Kayla? Kayla, where are you?'

Amelia rushed around, checking all the rooms and calling for the girl. There was no one inside. She picked up her lamp. Stopping by the table to light it with a taper from the fire, her hands trembled. Finally the flame caught and she was ready to resume her search.

'Amelia, what is it?'

Amelia jumped at the voice, having forgotten all about Damon and the guards in her worry. She raised frightened eyes and answered her brother. 'Kayla, she is not here.'

She picked up the lantern as she ran past Damon and into the night. Heading towards the barn, her brother's guard tried to stop her.

'You do not want to go in there, miss,' he told her, grasping her arms to prevent her from moving.

Shaking him off, she strode into the barn and immediately wished she had not. In front of her Anders was on his knees on the floor, cradling the still body of Kayla. The young girl's blood-soaked hair trailed in the straw, her body as limp as a rag-doll's.

With tears streaming down his cheeks, Anders looked up at her. 'I did not mean it, Amelia. You must understand. I was so angry. She would not open the door, and she would not tell me where you were. No matter how many times I knocked.'

'So how did she end up here, Anders?' Amelia asked, her voice gentle, masking the turmoil inside.

'So, I waited in the woods. I watched until she came out with a pail to milk the cow. I followed her into the barn and asked her where you were.

'At first she would not tell me; she asked me to leave. I shook the information out of her. She told me you had gone to help the witch. I would not believe you helped a magic user. And she taunted me, saying you were a magic user yourself so of course you would help others like you.'

'But Anders—'

'She told me such lies,' he spat. 'I was upset ... and so angry. There was this... this red haze. I think I threw her to the floor. I must have. When the red cleared, I found her like this.'

Amelia's hand flew to her mouth, 'Oh Anders... no,' she whispered.

'She banged her head. She won't move. I shook her, but she won't open her eyes.'

A strangled cry forced itself from Amelia's lips. 'Anders, what have you done? She was just a child.'

At the sound of her voice, Anders flung Kayla from him and launched himself at Amelia. Roughly grabbing her arms, he yelled, 'Tell me it is not true. Tell me you are not a witch.'

Amelia struggled to get free, but Anders' grip on her arms tightened. 'Tell me!'

'Leave my sister alone.' Damon's voice came from behind her.

'Sister?' Anders' fingers dug into her arms; the anger in his eyes sent icicles of fear through her. 'You are his sister?'

The guard moved behind the young farmer, and he placed a hand on Anders' arm. 'Come on now. You do not want any more trouble. Leave the mistress alone.'

It was as if the words fanned the flames of Anders' anger. 'Sister? Mistress? You are the duke's daughter? You lying, scheming witch. Was anything about you, about us real?' Anders flung Amelia from him and ran into the night.

'Oh, Anders,' Amelia whispered, tears streaming down her cheeks. The weight of what he had done stealing the breath from her lungs.

CONSEQUENCES

After Damon left to notify the Port Marden guard of what had happened, Amelia went to Kayla. Her body was cold; she'd departed this world some time ago. Before she could move the body, Damon's guard stopped her.

'Best leave her where she is, miss, until the men from Port Marden see her. They have ways of telling how she died, and they like things to stay just as you found them.'

He helped her to her feet and led her indoors where he stationed himself by the doorway. He refused any food or drinks, preferring to keep an eye on their surroundings.

Sitting by the fire, a mug of tea in her hands, Amelia lost herself in her thoughts as the sun rose through the window over the kitchen sink. Her heart weighed heavily as she pondered how things had come to this. Was there something she could have done to prevent Anders' breakdown, and Kayla's death?

Not long after dawn, Damon rode in with Elise. When Elise found Amelia had not slept a wink, she led the older girl to her room and helped her to bed.

Sinking into the mattress, Amelia said, 'I cannot sleep.'

'I am sure they will find Anders.' Elise sat beside her and took her hand.

'No, it is not that.' Amelia sprang upright. 'It is all my fault. If I had been honest with Anders, then none of this would have happened.'

'Amelia, I thought you were more sensible than that. Anders made his own choices for his own reasons, as did you. We cannot change what happened; we can only learn from it.'

Sure she would not be able to rest, Amelia lay down, and within a heartbeat was asleep.

A GAP in the curtains revealed the setting sun had turned the sky purple and orange when Amelia finally pulled herself from her slumber, stirred by voices from the other room seeping through the door. She kicked the covers back and dressed in the cool evening air. Opening the door between the rooms, she was surprised to find Nene sitting in a chair by the fire, chatting to Elise. In the excitement of the night before, the woman had slipped her mind.

'Nene.' The name came out almost as a sob as she ran to the woman, who rose to meet her embrace.

'Thank you, Amelia. Thank you so much for your help. I am a free woman; all charges were dropped.'

'But Kayla... I'm so sorry.'

Sadness clouded the woman's eyes. 'Poor Kayla. It is a sad day when a young girl loses her life in such a manner.'

'But you tried to warn me—'

'About the danger to you. Nene shook her head. 'No one could have predicted this.'

Amelia plucked up the courage to ask the question that would shatter her heart. 'And Anders?'

Elise's hands gripped hers. 'The Port Marden Guards found him in his parents' barn. They were too late to save him.'

Amelia closed her eyes. 'Peter and Maisie, they must be devastated.'

'They are heartbroken, not only to lose a son, but also to find out what he had done,' Damon said. 'I sat with them a while. They are proud people and, much like you, they believe they bear blame for what happened. They were talking about leaving—they did not want to stay here to be reminded daily of what their son did.'

'Oh, no. I can move if it means they will stay.'

'I am not sure they would want that. They were proud of their position in the local community and feel they can no longer fulfil a role here. Not just because of what he did in a fit of madness, but also because he did not have the courage to face up to his actions,' Damon explained. 'I offered to find them a place on Hand where they can move away from prying eyes. Their other sons will take over the farm for them.'

'How horrid for them. Maisie spoke of how much she had looked forward to retiring and spending more time with their grandchildren.' Amelia felt empty inside. Maisie and Peter were giving up so much, and after all their years of hard work. 'If this is the devastation love can cause, I will never open my heart to anyone again.'

Elise and Damon's eyes met. 'This is not what true love looks like.' Elise's words were filled with certainty. 'True love is not about one person trying to make the other into what they desire; it is about bringing out the best in both people. I hope one day you might find such a love.'

Silence fell over the room, as if no one knew exactly what to say. Amelia's thoughts wandered back to Kayla. 'We will need to tell Kayla's family what happened,' she said quietly.

Nene place her hand on Amelia's. 'They abandoned her some time ago. Tomorrow I will return to our community and arrange for the coven's farewell.'

'I want to come with you, to meet the others and say goodbye to her,' Amelia told Nene, and as she spoke it was as if she had placed a key piece in a puzzle, completing the picture. By uttering this one sentence, she was taking the first step towards a new future.

'Are you sure?' Damon asked. 'It is a dangerous path you take when you choose to practice magic.'

'While I do not think I will ever use my foresight to predict the future, there are other sides to my gift I would like to explore. I also want to find a way to support the women who are forced to practice magic in secret.'

Elise smiled. 'Besides, she has a special relationship with the future duke, and knows an advocate who will help should she encounter any trouble.'

Nene was more sceptical. 'There is a risk in what you do. Once you join the coven and begin using magic, your life will change forever. It is likely you will become more isolated from the people who live around you for fear of your secret coming out.'

'If I stay here, I am not sure Peter's sons will want to have any more to do with me anyway.' Amelia's heart was heavy with sadness as she uttered these words.

'Closing yourself off from having close ties in the community is also why most of our number never marry. It is a solitary life you will be choosing. I do not want you to look back in years to come and regret your decision.'

As the older woman gazed into the fire, Amelia sensed Nene was talking about herself as well as warning Amelia of the pitfalls of becoming a practicing witch.

Suddenly weary to the core, Amelia took a seat at the table opposite her brother. 'Damon, I think this path is the one I am meant to take. Recent events have shown me I am destined to spend this life alone.'

Elise leaned over and took her hands. 'You will never be alone while Damon and I draw breath.'

'And you will never be completely alone with our sisters to support you,' Nene added.

Sitting there enveloped in their warmth, Amelia said nothing. She silently pledged to make Kayla's death mean more than a tragic loss. Without thinking she let go of a little of her magic and allowed it to touch everyone in the room. Although still heartsore, the love she experienced from her new family started the healing process.

As their love washed over her she caught a glimpse of the future she now faced, one where she supported other magically talented women learning to live with their gifts and the crack in her heart closed a little more.

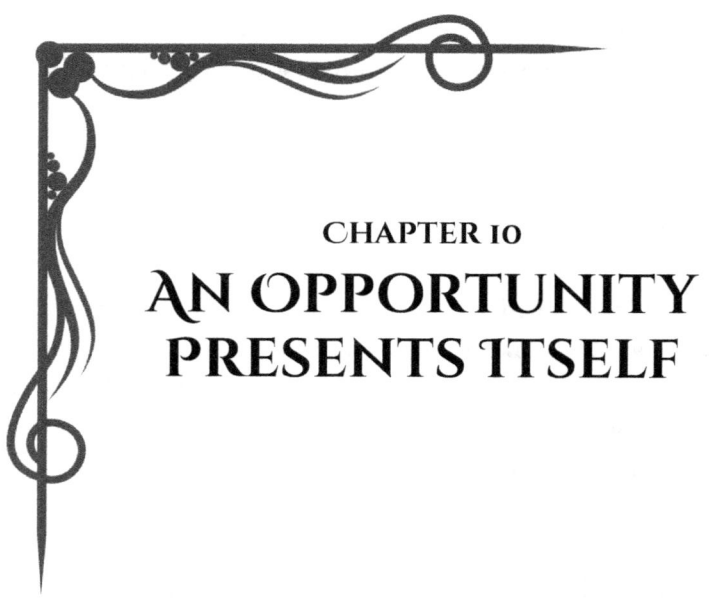

CHAPTER 10

AN OPPORTUNITY PRESENTS ITSELF

'Many years later, Amelia left her cottage, helped us fight a god, met Walter, and moved to Sanctuary, and that whole time, she never forgot her promise to help Arian women use their magical talents. She spent many years with the witches around Port Marden and in the Tangled Woods, developing their skills, as well as teaching them how to help their local communities,' Aliah finished off.

'She was quite brave, especially as she could have been found guilty of practicing magic without a licence,' Mina admitted.

'She's an amazing woman. When Walter started his school helping both boys and girls learn to control their magical gifts, she used to teach classes along with him. I believe she still teaches herbal healing from time to time, in addition to training her own apprentice seers. Once she was accepted for her foreseeing abilities, she persuaded the council in Sanctuary to allow girls from Aria to attend the school Walter set up.'

'And the wizard Seamus went to help Walter establish his school?'

Aliah smiled sadly. 'Yes, he did.'

'Do you miss him?'

Tilting her head to the side, Aliah gazed into the fire. 'I do. We went through so much together that he became like a brother to me.'

'But you talk to him all the time, don't you?'

'Yes, but mind speak is not the same as physically being with someone.'

'You must be looking forward to seeing him again.'

'I am. It's the one good thing about going to deal with this border dispute,' Aliah admitted, as she wondered if he would recognise the girl he saved the world with after so many years.

'Why didn't he come and train at Wizard Isle?' Mina asked, and Aliah got the feeling she had been working around to this question since the end of the tale.

'Many reasons. One of them was because he didn't want to embarrass his father or brother by remaining in Aria. But I think the overriding factor in his decision was that he was never accepted by the wizards there. His gift is different to everyone else in Aria, and I believe they were afraid of what he could do.'

'He was the son of the Duke of Hand, wasn't he? Didn't he have to leave home because magic is outlawed on the island? And he's Amelia's nephew, so he would have been treated the same way she was when people found out he had magical abilities.'

Mina grinned as Aliah's eyes widened in surprise. 'I've done my research. Just because I don't spend a lot of time in the library reading doesn't mean I can't look up information when I need to. I've also spent some time looking into why many people in Aria still don't want to get their magic licences even now, and not all of them are from Hand.'

Aliah's shoulders slumped. The people on Hand still banished those with a magical gift, in spite of the work she and Duke Damon had done to open people's minds. She and Dominic had tried so hard to reform Wizard Isle after many of their numbers had fought with the Carsten army to overthrow the royal family. They had not been successful, and many people still despised their elitist attitude and wouldn't send their children to be trained by the wizards. She sighed; sometimes she wondered how much she and Dominic had actually been able to change in the ten years since her father died.

'When your grandfather handed the throne of Aria over to your father and me, we encouraged some of the more forward-thinking wizards to visit the school at Sanctuary to see what they had achieved. Those men came back full of praise for what Walter's school was doing, and they lobbied along with us to have girls admitted to Wizard Isle. Finally, two years ago, the wizards admitted the first girl to their ranks. We thought more would come, but there are still only a handful attending.'

'But they have to study for years to become full wizards,' Mina pointed out. 'The first ones won't graduate for another three years.'

'Yes, which was why we were happy when they started the school this year focussed solely on teaching magical control and how to use each pupil's specific abilities. Males and females would attend the school for a year. Then, at the end of that time, they would sit an examination, and those who passed would receive their magic licence.' Aliah hoped this step, perhaps more than any, would change people's views of magic... and Wizard Isle.

Mina frowned. 'It always comes back to this, doesn't it? I can be a pioneer, pave the way for other girls to be accepted, be seen to be a leader before I accept the Heir's Ring—'

Taking a deep breath, Aliah deftly avoided the argument. 'If you had told us your fear of magic, we would not have pushed you to attend the school.'

'What?' Mina's face was a study of disbelief.

'You're surprised? Do you really think we would force you to do something you are terrified of, for the sake of Aria?'

'Yes.' Mina's answer was little above a whisper.

'Then I guess we have both been misunderstood,' Aliah conceded. 'Maybe we should both remember things are not always as they seem.'

'Does the same principle apply to my accepting the role of your successor? If I am not confident enough to agree to be first in line to wear the crown, will you force me to become heir?'

Aliah considered her answer carefully. 'Your father and I have made some headway towards setting up an advisory council made up of key people, but we are a long way from changing Aria's form of government.'

'The barons would never allow it,' Mina said.

Aliah nodded. 'At least not in my lifetime. So, for better or worse, we're members of the royal family in a country ruled by a monarchy. It's our duty to be trained to lead our people. Either you or Gabriel will have to take on that responsibility.' She held up her hand as Mina made to object. 'What I find funny is, you think he's better suited to the role, but it may surprise you to know he says the same about you. He thinks you inspire people to follow you.'

Pausing to give Mina a chance to take this in, Aliah made herself more comfortable in the chair before continuing.

'You're both still young, and your father and I want you to explore who you are before we ask one of you to take on the role as heir. Stability in Aria is important, so one of you will need to take up the mantle of regent-in-waiting, but that is a discussion for the future. As I keep saying, we need to settle your year of service first.'

As dusk settled and a servant came in to light the candles, the mother and daughter fell silent, each lost in their own thoughts. When they were alone, Mina again began picking at her skirt.

'I have no idea how to move forward now. I mean, I was so sure I should become a guard. Now I know I cannot join as a trainee because of who I am, and my one way into a guard company requires me to develop my magical abilities. I'm at a bit of a loss.'

Aliah waited until she was sure Mina said all she was going to before responding. 'Are going to the Wizard School or becoming a guard your only options? I mean, is there nothing else you can see yourself doing?'

Mina coloured, and Aliah mentally kicked herself. Things had been going so well, and now she had angered her daughter all over again. However, Mina's fingers stopped their work, and she smoothed the material of her dress before responding in a calm voice.

'I guess I can think of other things: a diplomatic post, a secretarial role here at the palace, or perhaps even a year teaching at one of the new schools opening up in the cities. However, this is about using my skills to benefit Aria, and almost anyone could do those jobs better than me.'

'I would have said they could do them as well as you,' Aliah conceded.

Mina smiled. 'They would be better, because they'd want to do the work, whereas I would be counting the days until my release.'

Aliah bit back a chuckle. 'I wouldn't write off joining the guard just yet. Amelia overcame her fear of magic, and so did Seamus. Their experiences have me wondering how many other people are frightened of the power inside them.'

Mina's eyes widened, and a smile tugged the corners of her mouth. 'Mm, I guess I might not be the only one.'

This was a huge breakthrough, and Aliah was reluctant to speak lest she say the wrong thing or indicate she favoured a particular path. For if there was one thing she had learnt this afternoon, it was that she did not know her daughter as well as she thought she did. She also had a feeling Mina was not telling her everything about her reluctance to return to Wizard Isle.

'I have a lot of thinking to do,' Mina eventually said.

Taking this as a polite dismissal, Aliah stood. 'If it would help, you can miss the formal dinner tonight. I can make up some excuse for you.'

Mina grinned appreciatively. 'Thanks, Mum.'

Leaving her daughter sitting thoughtfully by the fire, Aliah wished she could remain with her. Unfortunately, queens did not have the luxury of missing court functions, and she still had to be dressed and primped before making her appearance.

Sharma, her maid, placed the final clip before checking Aliah's attire. The boned bodice of her blue gown flared into a wide skirt, which was covered in lace. Her hair had been tamed into an elaborate plait laced with flowers circling her head except for a few recalcitrant wisps, which curled around her face. She thanked the girl and dismissed her before sitting on the edge of the chair to wait for her husband.

Exhausted, she wanted nothing more than to lean back and relax, but she didn't want to risk wrinkling the gown and having to change again before dinner. Perhaps it was because she was tired, or maybe because she wanted to talk to him, but Dominic seemed to take an age to emerge from his dressing room. When he finally appeared, he was tugging at his cuffs, unable to sort the row of three tiny buttons on his left hand. Aliah stood to help him.

'Where's Julius?' she asked as she finished the job Dominic's valet normally did.

'I had some letters I needed delivered discretely. Besides, he's more use as a secretary than helping me put clothes on—that I can do myself.'

Aliah's eyebrows rose. 'Clearly, that isn't true.'

Dominic barked out a laugh as he slipped his arms into a long tailored jacket that matched her gown. 'All right, you caught me out. I was able to do it before the court fashions grew so elaborate. Perhaps we could have a word with some of our more fashionable courtiers and ask them to tone things down a bit. Are you ready to go down?' He held out his arm for her to take, but Aliah didn't move.

'Can we talk before we go? I wanted to check your real feelings about my leaving to meet up with Seamus and sort out the issues on the border.'

Dominic dropped his arm and took her hand in his. 'In this

instance, my thoughts on the matter don't come into it. Amelia said you have to go. Having a long conversation about how I feel won't change that.'

'It matters to me.'

Shrugging, he placed her hand on the crook of his arm and moved them towards the door. 'Would I prefer to be riding to my brother's palace and meeting up with Seamus? Of course I would—getting away from the pomp and ceremony here is always a welcome break.'

'I knew it.' Aliah stopped them by the door. 'We can always move the court to the Western Duchy, and then you could come too.'

'You're sweet to think of moving more than one hundred people just so we can be together, but we can't do it.'

'The royal coffers can compensate your brother for the costs of accommodating the court,' Aliah said, knowing Duke Hubert ploughed most of his spare coin back into trying to repair the damage his and Dominic's father wrought during his time in charge. There was no way he could afford the cost of hosting so many people.

Her husband leaned over and kissed her cheek. 'I love you for being so considerate, but coin is not our main problem—logistics is. It takes a month to move the entire court, and we don't have that sort of time to waste. Besides, we have a delegation on their way from the Southern Duchy to meet with the Carstenites, and we still need to find a solution for Mina.'

Aliah turned to face her husband. 'Of course, you're right. On the good-news front, we may have had a breakthrough with our daughter.'

'Oh?'

'I think she has accepted she must learn to use her powers if she's to join the guard.'

'So she's going back to the wizard school?'

'Not exactly. In fact, when I return, we must spend a bit more time investigating things at that school. Although they've opened their doors to women, it seems they're giving the female students quite a hard time.'

Dominic stroked his chin, which normally indicated he had an idea forming. 'I have been working a little with Wizard Alric—'

'Isn't he the one who convinced some of the council to vote with us to have girls admitted to the school?'

'That's him. He's worried things are not changing quickly enough on Wizard Isle. His biggest concern is if they drag their feet, then another school of magic will petition for a charter, which would weaken the council's position in the long term.'

'That's interesting.' Very interesting, in fact, and perhaps indicative of the school's view of women that Alric took this matter to Dominic and not to her, or both of them together. 'Did your wizard friend have a solution in mind?'

'He did, actually. He's looking for a new teacher in his faculty, one able to teach magical medicine, and is having problems, because his graduates prefer field work to passing on their knowledge.'

'I don't blame them. If what Mina says is true, the school's not such a great place to be,' Aliah interjected dourly.

'Back to the subject at hand—he asked if I would contact the school in Sanctuary to see if they have anyone interested in the post, and he specifically asked for a female tutor.'

'Really? He wants to bring a female teacher here? From another school? And the council agreed he could?'

Dominic laughed. 'Initially, he proposed asking one of the hedge witches, but the council of wizards wouldn't countenance that. I think he knew the outcome when he suggested it. His next move was to propose they request a teacher for Sanctuary, and the council leapt at the chance.'

'They agreed to a woman?'

'Not specifically. Alric pointed out they didn't stipulate it had to be a man either, and once she arrives....'

Smiling, Aliah said, 'A case of better to ask forgiveness than permission?'

'Exactly.'

'Perhaps once Alric has some help, you could petition the wizards for him to become one of our advisors. He's obviously a politically astute young man.'

'He is indeed, and what a great idea to invite him onto our advisory council.'

'I've always believed that only once Arian students and wizards see a woman using magic in their own environment, would they change their minds about it being an abomination. I hope that is still true. And maybe this new teacher will also give the girls already studying at the school some heart.' Aliah attempted not to sound as despondent as she felt about the wizards and their treatment of women.

'Once females begin to graduate and return to their communities, public opinion will also change, and the wizards will no longer be able to hide their heads in the sand.'

'You always try to look on the bright side, Dom. Unfortunately, these changes will come too late for Mina. Besides, healing isn't her discipline.' Aliah could not lift herself from the slump she had sunk into since talking with Mina.

'Maybe I can persuade one of the teachers to tutor her while you are away. I'm sure I can convince them she wants to return to complete her course, but I forbade it because I need her here to help with diplomatic duties. That way they still get to claim to have trained a princess, but without any of the disruption of her actually attending classes.'

'And what will you tell Mina?'

'That this is a compromise, and hopefully by the time you all return, she may be skilled enough to join the guard as a scout... if she applies herself.'

Aliah loved the way Dominic could see unique ways around a problem and find the benefits for everyone. 'I knew there was a reason I married you.' She planted a kiss on his cheek. 'When will we tell her?'

'Perhaps you can tell her in the morning. You've put in the time with her the last few days; you should reap the rewards. Now, I guess we need to go face the court. We're already more than fashionably late.' Dominic opened the door and led her through and down the corridor to the wide staircase leading to the formal function rooms below.

As they walked, Aliah schooled her face into its queen mask, but inside, she still fumed quietly that she and Dominic had to use stealth and trickery to change the lot of women in Aria.

MINA SNUGGLED her face into Brownie's neck. The horse she had learned to ride on was now too old for the long treks she favoured to escape the confines of the castle and had been put out to pasture. She had not yet chosen a replacement mount, and often visited her faithful companion when she was feeling down.

This evening, she had a lot to think about, not the least was how she was going to overcome her anxiety about using the magic inside her. Once she figured a way around her fear, she still then had to find a way to learn how to use it before applying to join the guard as a scout.

Brownie's coat shone with care and attention, and the horse nuzzled her jacket near the pocket Mina normally kept his treats in. As she reached for the apple, she and the animal both froze. The air around them tingled as if it was charged like a magnet.

Magic. Someone is using it nearby.

She had thought herself alone in the stables by the pastures, as few people from the castle ever ventured down here. Clearly the building wasn't as empty as she believed. She offered the apple to her horse before silently slipping out of the stall, her hand moving automatically to the knife she always wore attached to her belt when she was out of the castle.

Keeping to the shadows, she crept past the other animals. Drawing closer to the end of the block of stalls, she could hear a low, soft crooning. She could not make out the words, but she was almost mesmerised by the sound. She crouched down by the door the sound seemed to be coming from.

There it was again—the tingle of magic in the air. A horse nickered, and the low singing continued. After a brief pause, a voice said, 'I know you're outside. Show yourself.'

The accent was strange, and Mina started as she realised it belonged to a Carstenite. Standing up, she leaned around and looked over the stall door, finding herself eye to eye with a slim, weathered man dressed in the manner of someone from Carsten. His brownish-red skin was creased about the eyes, and his long dark hair was tied back in a ponytail similar to her own. He had one arm round the neck of a chestnut mare. The other was rubbing her coat in a rhythmic motion.

No one from the delegation would have a legitimate reason for being in the stables reserved for the guard's horses. All her instincts said she should leave. Still, she was curious about what the man was up to.

'What are you doing here?' Mina asked, hand still on her knife.

'I am tending to my friend. She ate something, and it did not agree with her. I think some of your rich grasses have given her the most terrible wind.' He laid his forehead on the glossy hair of the horse's neck.

Mina still had not relaxed her stance. 'I wasn't aware the delegation from Carsten brought any horses with them.'

The man smiled, a big toothy grin. 'You are observant for a stable girl.'

'You can't be too careful.' Mina's tone was guarded.

It was like she and the man in front of her were dancing around, each wanting to find out about the other without asking direct questions. They could be at this all night and she would be none the wiser as to who he was and why he was here.

Then again, to admit she felt his magic would tell him she herself had magical abilities, because only another magic user could sense when someone was using their gift. And, without knowing exactly who this person was, she wasn't going to give that piece of information away. On the other hand, he seemed wary of her—almost as though he was not comfortable with her being here.

At a shuffle from behind, Mina turned and was relieved to see Jack, one of the stable hands, enter carrying a bottle of tonic his master used to settle horses' stomachs. He nodded to her, respecting the informality she requested while in the stables.

'Here you go, Rinnard. It's a good thing you thought to come down here. They don't have anything like this at the castle stables. This is what we use on our horses when their food causes them problems.'

'Can you please tell me what is in it?' the man in the stall, Rinnard, asked.

'Of course. It is mostly camomile tea mixed with a few other common herbs to help relax the stomach. Hopefully she'll get used to the grasses around here and the problem will pass. Master says you can pick up some more before you ride out.'

'Thank you, young man, and thank your master for me.' He took the bottle and returned to tending his horse.

'Who is he?' Mina whispered to Jack, jerking her head to indicate the man in the stall.

'He rode in with Captain Madigan yesterday. Apparently, he's the new tracker. Was he bothering you?' Jack frowned, ready to swing to her defence should he need to.

'No. No!' Mina shook her head. 'I was being nosey.'

'Do you need anything else before I take my dinner break?'

'No, I'm fine. Thanks, Jack.'

She waited until the stable hand departed before leaning over the stall door and whispering, 'What you did before... for your horse...?'

'I used a little magic to make a connection with my friend, to let her know she isn't alone.'

'Well, you shouldn't do it here in Aria. The wizards don't like it.'

The man looked back over his shoulder at her, as if sizing her up, before leaving the side of his mount and walking to the back of the stall. Moments later, he returned and held out a bronze metal band. 'I spent all morning with some of your wizards, and I earned this. Will I have to show it each time I use magic, or just when I do it around another magic user? Should I be asking for yours?'

This was not what Mina had expected, and she now felt like she had lost control of the situation. 'Um... no... sorry. You don't have to show it all the time. I was worried. I didn't want anything to happen to you.'

Rinnard cocked his head to the side. 'You don't have one, do you?'

'I'm not a witch,' Mina blurted out.

'Yes, I hear women here are not trained to use their gifts.' He nodded as if reaffirming something to himself.

'Are you a tracker like Jack said?' Mina changed the subject.

'Yes, I have joined your Arian guard for the period of one of your years.'

'And you track using... using your gift?' Mina felt a flutter of excitement.

'I do.'

In all her years, Mina had never met another farseer, and all the questions she had bottled up inside threatened to spill out, if only she could risk talking so openly about herself. Perhaps she could work out another way of gathering information without exposing her secret.

'I've never met an actual magical tracker. Is it difficult to learn?' Mina asked.

His black eyes studied her carefully before answering. 'It does not take long to learn the technique, but like everything in life, you improve the more you do it.'

'Did you attend a school on Carsten like our Wizard Isle?'

'No, we have no school of magic. In Carsten, once a magic user has been identified, an experienced teacher is found for them, and they are apprenticed for a period of two years. At the end of their apprenticeship, the magician is graded by a panel of five magic users and, if they pass their tests, are given a licence much the same as the one I received from your council.' Gently rubbing the horse's neck, he stared at her again. 'Are you asking these questions for yourself?'

'Oh no.' Mina thought quickly. 'I'm curious. This is the first time I have seen people from Carsten. I haven't had much of a chance to speak with any of them, and I wanted to find out a little bit more about your people, that's all.'

'Mmm.' The stare did not waiver. 'Well, if your next question was going to be whether or not females are apprenticed, the answer would be "yes". Now, if you will excuse me, I'd like to finish up here so I can go and find some supper.'

Mina had been dismissed, and in realising that, she relaxed a little. No one would treat a princess like that; her cover remained intact.

'Thank you for talking with me. It was surprisingly interesting,' Mina said as she turned on her heel and walked quickly back to her own horse, who was cheerfully munching on some hay. After tidying away the brushes she had been using, she hugged her Brownie goodbye and headed back to the castle. All the while, her mind was only half on what she was doing; the other half was processing what she had learned. There were other places she could learn magic; she was not limited to Wizard Isle. And while Carsten was not a possibility at the moment, Sanctuary certainly was.

PART FOUR
THERE ARE RISKS YOU DON'T UNDERSTAND

CHAPTER 11

SANCTUARY IS NOT WHAT YOU THINK

A*liah?*

Seamus? Give me a moment.

Aliah glanced up from the papers she was studying and spoke to the merchant standing patiently by her desk. 'Everything looks in order here. I will pass the documents on to the king, and he will add them to the offers being discussed with the delegation from Carsten.'

The rather rotund man managed an awkward bow and stammered, 'Thank you, Your Majesty,' as he backed towards the door, which the guard opened for him.

'Can you ask the others to give me a few minutes. I'll let you know when I am done,' Aliah told the woman assigned as her daily protection. The guard nodded curtly and closed the door behind her, leaving Aliah alone.

Seamus, I am all yours.

Sorry to bother you. You must have an awful lot to organise.

I do, but I am certain it will be all cleared up by tomorrow, or at least handed off to Dominic to deal with. How can I help you?

I wanted to make sure you were on target for a rendezvous at...

Seamus? Seamus, are you still there?

Sorry, we're on the move... lost you for a bit. Not used to... on horseback. I want to check on when you think you might... Breacher's Pa...

Yes, we arrive in three days' time.

We?

Yes, Gabriel was going with Dominic to take part in his first diplomatic mission. We decided it would still benefit him to come along with me —not that I can teach him much about diplomacy.

He'll... company. Kahal is on his first field assignment for the guards and...

Is it safe for them? Amelia contacted me yesterday and demanded I be the one to sort this out. This is turning out to be more than the meet and greet, agree on a way for us all to live together, and return home situation that Dominic and I originally thought it was.

For my part, I have no option. Kahal's unit is rostered to this duty... embarrass him by requesting he stay behind. As for Gabriel? That's your...

Aliah doodled on the paper in front of her as she tried to piece their conversation together. There were so many things jumping round in her head it was difficult to concentrate on what was important, and it was obviously hard for Seamus to keep this communication going. If only she had her sword handy.

What if we have to fight? I haven't thought to bring healers. She opted for the thought yelling the loudest.

I have that covered. Walter is leaving... the next day or two with a group of healers from the school... need is for you to get here.

We are setting out early tomorrow, so stop worrying.

Did you resolve things with Mina... offer for her to come and learn here still stands.

Not sure how to word her answer without giving offence, Aliah chewed on her lip.

Aliah? I lost you again.

No, I was thinking. As an outsider, she would have to undergo a trial to see if she is suitable for her field of study...

Aliah, what happened to you... and to Emer is not common.... the trial outsiders go through to obtain entry to the school is not a major one, ... less likely to happen. Most supplicants don't even see a god.

Years after her own trial to become The Warrior, Aliah still broke into a sweat when she thought about the door to the cave closing the moment she reached it, locking her inside. Seamus had negotiated for her release and always swore this was part of his trial—to cement his commitment to working as a team—not due to any failure on her part. Whether that was true or not, Aliah had spent much of her life feeling she hadn't truly proven herself as The Warrior.

Can you promise me she won't end up trapped inside a trial cave?

It isn't likely....

But you can't promise.

Of course not. I can't predict the will of the gods any more than you can.

Hey, you must have got the hang of this. You're not breaking up anymore.

I learn more quickly than I used to. Seamus laughed.

We're not going to make any decisions about her future until I get back. Dominic will take her under his wing while I am away, and the rest can wait.

I'm sorry, Aliah. I didn't mean to upset you. The paths our children choose are often difficult to navigate. When Kahal decided to join the guards rather than finish his magical training, I didn't know what to do. And without Emer being here...

Seamus and Emer's son was their oldest, and he'd been close to his mother. He hadn't recovered from losing her, and it had broken Seamus's heart when he left his studies and joined the guard in an effort to honour her memory.

Kahal's magical gift allowed him to sense the intention of others and sometimes glimpse the outcomes of their actions. As this was often a precursor to seeing the future, there had been strong opposition from Amelia, as Great Seer, to his course of action. A distraught Seamus had to fight long and hard for his son to be able to choose what he wanted to do with his life.

Well, at least we both have one child who does not make waves. Aliah laughed, hoping to lighten the mood. *How are Orla's studies going?*

Orla was about six months younger than Gabriel. Having inherited a healing gift from Emer's mother, she was quite content to apply herself to becoming the best healer she could be.

She is doing well. At the moment, she spends much of her free time with Amelia, learning traditional herb lore. Amelia thinks she may have the rare gift of being able to fix troubled minds. She won't be allowed to explore this until she is quite a bit older. Until she has a strong sense of herself, there's a real risk she might become trapped in someone's fractured mind.

Aliah sighed. *Is nothing ever easy?*

Seamus laughed, and Aliah could picture his dimpled smile. *If life were easy, you'd be bored.*

She shrugged; he was right. Life's challenges were what kept things interesting. There was a knock at the door. Checking the candle on her desk, she saw it was already midmorning, and she knew who had interrupted her time alone in spite of her instructions.

Sorry, Seamus, I've got to go. Mina is here, and I should spend some time smoothing things over with her before I leave tomorrow.

All right, bye, Aliah.

I'll see you in a couple of days.

Aliah tidied her desk and composed herself before calling for the guard to allow her daughter entry.

Mina took the chair across from her and placed her hands demurely in her lap.

Oh no, Aliah thought, *I get the distinct feeling I'm not going to like this conversation one bit.*

'I'VE BEEN THINKING about our talk yesterday. I still want to join the guard in the long term, but I can't go back to the wizard school. The girls are treated appallingly there, and it was worse for me, because everyone assumed I was only accepted because I'm a princess.'

There, she had finally said it. Clasping her hands more tightly, she waited for her mother's lecture on how she shouldn't allow what other people thought of her to hold her back.

She watched as her mother fiddled with her pen, placed it down on the desk, and then picked it up again. When her eyes met her own, she was surprised to find sadness.

'Your father and I were so excited to finally have girls admitted to the wizard school that I guess we didn't spend a lot of time thinking about how those girls would be treated. Looking back, it was probably too much to ask that every teacher and student welcome them with open arms and simply treat them the same as male new entrants.'

Mina reached out and took her mother's hand. 'You can't change everything in a single day, Mum. And like you always say, you shouldn't let that stop you from taking the first step.'

It was odd being the one delivering the lecture, but the pleased smile on her mother's face sent a rush of warmth through her body.

'You're right, Mina. Your father and I, along with Wizard Alric, have some ideas in mind to speed up those changes. Unfortunately, that doesn't help you in the meantime.'

Grinning to herself, Mina said, 'I know you're working hard to find a solution for me, but I might have come up with one myself.'

'Oh?'

'I think you and Father should send me to the school at Sanctuary. They have experience with my type of magic, they already teach girls, and I'm sure I will fit in better and learn more somewhere where I am not known as Princess Admina. Then I can come back here and petition the wizard school for a licence. I can then be one of the first females to earn a licence to practice magic that way.'

When she had thought through the problem last night, and

finally accepted she needed to overcome her fear of her gift to get to where she wanted to be, this seemed the only reasonable solution. She then spent most of the night preparing arguments to counter all her parents' concerns.

'Oh no, Mina. No.'

All right. She hadn't prepared for a simple no. She opened her mouth to launch into the speech she had worked on, when she noticed Aliah had turned white as snow. Mina peered closely at her mother and realised the look on her face was one of fear.

'Mother, what is it?'

Her mother dropped her trembling hands into her lap and took a deep breath. 'When an outsider goes to Sanctuary to learn how to use their magic, they must undergo a trial to ensure they are proficient in the magic they wish to study and for the gods to assess their intent. The gods check the supplicant will use their magic for the good of all.'

'I know that,' Mina said, not quite sure where her mother was going with this.

'Your father and I discussed getting you a tutor from the wizard school to train you, by yourself, while I am gone. I am sure he will choose someone sympathetic to your situation, perhaps even Alric himself.'

Mina hadn't seen that one coming. Then again, how could she? The wizards had never allowed private tutoring before. She took a moment to consider the offer. It was better than attending school on the isle, if the council would agree to it; there was only one problem.

'There aren't any wizards on the isle who have experience in farseeing, but there are in Sanctuary.'

Her mother frowned. 'How can you be so sure?'

Mina wrinkled her nose in disgust as she remembered the conversation with her magical control tutor. 'One of my teachers delighted in telling me they couldn't teach me how to best use my gift, that they hadn't had a farseer on the isle in years. He did say they have a few in Sanctuary, because they need tracking skills more in the wilds. He made it sound like that was because they were less civilised or something, and like farseeing was a lesser sort of magic.'

'Oh, well I guess there are still more than a few other prejudices lurking on Wizard Isle. That doesn't mean a good teacher can't show you the basics of managing your magic and at least train you to the level required to earn your licence.'

Again, Mina considered her mother's point. What she proposed was reasonable, but she sensed something else was behind her mother's reluctance to let her go to Sanctuary to study. If she wasn't going to offer it up easily, she would have to make her annoyed enough to let it out.

'You won't let me go, because you don't trust me, do you? You don't trust my intentions and commitment. You don't trust me to pass my trial.' There, that should do it.

Her mother actually looked stricken, and Mina's stomach clenched with guilt. It was too late to take it back now, though.

Composing herself, her mother took up the pen again and began twiddling it as she spoke. 'You have no idea what a trial is. I nearly did not pass mine. They leave that bit out of the histories, because it isn't very hero-like. I almost ended up stuck on a plane in between worlds—' Her mother's voice was strangled, almost as if she were forcing the words out.

'But you didn't. You're here now.' Mina wished with all her heart that her mother would stop speaking, that this interview was over, and she could go back to her room and reassess her plan.

Her mother's voice lowered, and Mina had to strain to hear her next words. 'Not everyone is as lucky as I was.'

'What do you mean?'

The pen stopped twirling, and her mother looked up. 'Some people don't return from their trial.'

Mina couldn't believe what she was hearing. She couldn't tell if her mother was serious, or whether she was merely finding reasons to object to her plan. None of the books she read on the subject discussed people not returning from their trials.

'Who are "some people"? How many, and how often?'

'Seamus's wife, Emer, for one.'

'You and Father said she died suddenly from an illness.' Disappointed, Mina glared suspiciously at her mother, certain now this was some sort of trick to put her off going to the school at Sanctuary. She had thought they were getting along, that they were past those sorts of games, but perhaps she had been wrong.

'That was what we told everyone here. It was easier than explaining when she entered the trial caves to speak with the gods that she never returned. Trials are dangerous and have consequences beyond your imagining, Mina. Whatever happened during Emer's trial, not even Seamus could save her.'

'Tell me; tell me what really happened with Emer,' Mina demanded, her need for information overriding the obvious distress this conversation was causing her mother.

The room was silent for a long time, but finally her mother spoke. Her voice started off shaky but grew stronger the more she said. 'This is not going to be like the other stories you have heard over the last few days. Much of it, I have pieced together from Emer herself, as well as from Seamus and Amelia. If you're sure you really want to hear it?'

Mina almost faltered; her mother's words sounded like a warning. In spite of her misgivings, she nodded.

'All right then.'

CHAPTER 12
THE TRIAL OF EMER

DESTINY CALLS

The perfect blue sky shimmered and sparkled as the spring breeze lifted her high above the treetops. Soaring over the forest, she enjoyed the freedom of flight before flattening out and riding the currents to where the trees met the plains.

Below the canopy, miniature figures moved into attack formation. Relying on her eagle eye to identify the disturbance they had been called to deal with, the guards had paused, waiting for her report before proceeding.

Do you see anything? Commander Borrick's voice filled her head, bringing her thoughts back to focus on the task at hand.

Some fires in the distance, near the mountain passes. I think they are camping there.

Details, Emer. I need details. Report! her commander snapped.

Sorry, sir. Details are hard to hold in my head in this form. Twenty fires—so upwards of one hundred men.

Any sign of the ones who attacked our hunting party?

No sir. Hold on. Emer circled around. *Wait a moment.*

A slip of blue near the forest's edge caught her attention. She changed direction to take a closer look. Flying over the area a second time, she saw everything was normal. As she was about to leave, she saw it again. This time, the flash of blue was followed by a beam of light.

Climbing higher, she glimpsed an answering yellow burst from the base camp. Following the line of communication, she sped towards the mountains, skimming across the prairie grass until she caught a new current.

As she flew, she sent a message. *They're hiding in the bushes at the edge of the forest, about 45 degrees left of your current position.*

Number?

I can't make them out particularly clearly, but no more than twenty would be able to hide well in that small a space.

Excellent, return to base. We'll take it from here.

I am just on my way to scout their camp, Emer informed her commander.

You have your orders. Return to base. Borrick's tone was sharp and angry, but Emer ignored the implied threat.

We need to...

Are you disobeying an order, Guard?

No, sir.

We will speak when I return.

Following a wind current that swept her high in the sky before turning her back towards Sanctuary, the exhilaration flight usually brought Emer was drowned out by bitter disappointment.

Far below, she watched with eagle eyes as the company circled the raider force, ready to deal retribution for an earlier attack on a hunting party, which wounded many and resulted in two deaths. She turned away before they engaged, saddened at her exclusion from the coming fight.

When the company set out this morning, she had been filled with a sense of purpose. Someone invaded their lands, and she was doing what needed to be done to protect her people. Even when

Borrick asked her to take to the sky and scout for them, she had not protested—her being able to shape-change and scout made her all the more useful to the guard corp. What angered her was being sent back before the fighting began. She was more than capable of holding her own in a battle.

As a child, her father, the Great Seer, had foreseen a momentous destiny for her. As a result of that vision, her life altered dramatically. Everything she did was aimed at preparing her to play her part in the prophecy. In fact, she had only been allowed to train as a guard, because her father believed the skills she would acquire would be useful later in life.

When The Wizard and The Warrior met with the gods and received their tokens of power, the gods revealed Emer was one of those who should accompany them on their quest to defeat the enemy who threatened their lands. Since returning, her father had left her alone to live her life as she pleased, believing her destiny fulfilled—until two moon turns ago.

He and his apprentice, Amelia, both received great seeings within days of each other. Amelia's appeared to have something to do with a growing storm from the west, whereas Caraig, her father, was warned the time his daughter would be called to serve was drawing near.

The seeings were presented to the Sanctuary Council, and Emer was withdrawn from the rota of guards. They did not want to risk the life of someone so critical to the future well-being of their people.

It was only because of the increased activity on their boarders stretching the guards so thin that she had been allowed to resume her normal duties, but they treated her like something precious and easily broken.

As a trained soldier, it was her duty to follow orders and do what was necessary to protect the people of Sanctuary, and her ability to track their enemies was a vital part of their defence. What upset her was once again, she was not in charge of her own life. Everyone had a say in what she was capable of doing—except her.

If only her father had not had a new vision, or if it had been about someone else. No, if only he had spoken to her and they had discussed it before he revealed it to the ruling council, perhaps she might have had some influence over what happened after, had some control over everything that happened next.

By the time she landed back in Sanctuary, her anger had reduced to a slow burn. Turning back into human form, she changed out of her uniform and headed home. As she walked, she attempted to put the frustrations of the day behind her. It wasn't fair to take them out on her family.

THE SCENE that greeted her as she entered her living quarters was utter chaos. Seamus, her husband, stood in the middle of the room, hands on hips, staring at on overturned pot on the floor. Her oldest child, Kahal, was ducking the swinging arms of her daughter, Orla.

'How could you?' Orla shouted, a tear escaping from the corner of her eye. 'She told us how worried she was about the test.'

'We were trying to help her lighten up a bit. If you tense up before linking with someone, it won't work.' Kahal defended himself both verbally and physically as Orla howled and threw a potato from the vegetable basket on the bench behind her.

He ducked, and the potato carried on into the main living area and hit the back of one the chairs by the fire before thudding to the floor.

'Well, your prank had the opposite effect. She failed and won't be able to apply for a resit until the new moon.' Orla slumped into a chair.

Emer caught her husband's eye and raised an eyebrow in query.

It seems Kahal and his friends thought they would "loosen" Bali up before her linking assessment by sending a little shock along her link in practice. The poor girl had no idea what was happening and panicked. She burst into tears and lost control of the link. She was so upset she wouldn't try again with the teacher.

The children must have sensed their mind speak, as both looked towards her. The room was silent for a moment until, as if on some sort of cue, they both started recounting their side of the story, each competing to be heard over the other.

Emer closed her eyes and rubbed a hand across her forehead.

'Enough!' Although Seamus's voice was low, it had immediate effect—they both closed their mouths. 'Your mother just walked through the door. Give her time to catch her breath.'

'But—'

'No, Orla. Your mother and I are going for a stroll. When we return, I expect the kitchen to be clean. Dinner is probably inedible, so the two of you can pull together a cold meal for us from the pantry, and I want to hear no more about this until after we've all eaten.'

Kahal smirked, and another tear slipped from Orla's eye. Although her daughter was strong and resilient, the one thing that wouldn't fail to upset her was the mistreatment of others. Her empathy would stand her in good stead should she become a healer as she planned.

As for Kahal, her mischievous firstborn, although he caught glimpses of how actions might affect the future, he was somehow blind to how his pranks could hurt others.

'Before you help Orla clear up, you need to go apologise to Bali. And you will offer to help her prepare for her next assessment, which I am sure your father can rearrange for next six-day,' Emer instructed her son.

His eyes dropped to the ground. 'We didn't mean any harm,' he mumbled. 'I would never do anything to hurt Bali. How were we to guess she would react that way?'

Orla snorted, and Emer raised her hand to silence the girl.

'Try to think, Kahal; is there anything you can think of that might have indicated Bali's reaction to such a prank might not be positive?' Emer asked and waited for her son to reason this one through.

'You don't mean I should have used my gift?' He still would not raise his eyes from the spot on the floor.

'Do you believe it might have helped?' she asked him.

He shook his head. 'No, my visions aren't that accurate yet. If I can't look into the future, how else would I be able to tell what would happen?'

'Bali has been your best friend since you were both in nappies. Next to her family, you know her better than anyone,' Emer said.

'I guess.' Kahal's head dropped farther.

'Has Bali ever enjoyed being pranked?' Emer asked.

Finally, Kahal raised his eyes. 'Zac said it worked for him when he was worried about his assessment.'

'And are Zac and Bali alike?' Emer pressed.

'Zac said it would help her. I wasn't so sure,' Kahal mumbled. 'I was about to say maybe it wasn't such a good idea, and Zac just did it.'

'So, you didn't really think it would work, yet you said nothing?'

Kahal face turned red. 'No. After, she looked so funny I couldn't help but laugh.'

Emer waited patiently for the lesson to sink in. Kahal took a deep breath and raised his gaze to meet hers, the guilt in his eyes telling Emer he finally understood the depth of his betrayal.

'I need to go apologise to Bali... find some way to make every-thing right.'

She nodded, and he headed for the door.

'Great,' Orla said, 'now I'm left with the cleaning up.'

Seamus moved to stand beside her. 'And perhaps that is as it should be, my darling girl. It might remind you hurling things across the room at your brother is not the only way to make your point.'

Before she could object, Emer said, 'To make up for it, Kahal can do all the dishes after the meal. Now, your father and I are going to take that walk he mentioned.'

ADMINA'S ARGUMENT

Having shut the door behind them, Seamus pulled her hand through the crook of his arm and led her along the indoor corridors of the cave system they called home and others called Sanctuary. When they reached the enormous three-story hall of the main entrance, they stopped, leaned against the second-tier balcony, and gazed out into the almost circular hall Emer's ancestors had hewn from the mountain. The late afternoon sun bronzed the rocks, softening the usually imposing feel of Sanctuary's vestibule.

'Not a good day?' her husband and best friend asked.

'I've had better.'

'Still on the bench then?'

She took a deep breath and released it slowly. She waited for the tension to fully leave her body before she answered. 'I can't do my job while they insist on wrapping me in cotton wool. I'm so frustrated.'

'Do you want to talk about what happened?'

She squeezed his arm. 'It won't help. We both know what the real problem is, and getting annoyed at the symptoms does not help anyone.'

'Perhaps it is time,' Seamus said, turning to look out the doorway, and she joined him, leaning her arms on the cool stone of the balcony.

The sun was setting, turning the sky brilliant oranges and reds. The opening carved from the mountainside framed the trees at the edge of the main clearing, turning them to ominous shadows before her eyes. The entranceway was quiet at this hour. Only a few inhabitants rushed through, heading home for their evening meal. Some nodded to Seamus and Emer as they passed, for everyone knew everyone else in the small community they lived in.

Emer looked up at the high vaulted ceiling and marvelled at the place she had grown up in. When her ancestors carved this home out of living rock, creating a safe haven for their people, they used a magic so ancient the skill had been lost many generations ago.

Corridors spread out from the entrance deep into the mountains, like spokes from the hub of a wheel. Doors dotted the walkways, and behind each one lived an extended family group. Most homes had a communal area consisting of a main room—used for family gatherings and cooking meals.

Rooms would then span out from the shared areas so each smaller unit could have their own living area and sleeping rooms. Sometimes, the internal spaces were divided by wooden doors, but in most homes, they were divided by curtains. The inside of each cave was light and airy, even though few had windows to the outside world.

Being surrounded by rock made Emer feel safe and cocooned, but she was well aware Seamus felt differently. Born on the Island of Hand, he had learned to live in Sanctuary, but he still preferred to be able to see the outdoors—hence their destination tonight.

'Emer?'

'Have you ever really thought about the amazing skill it must have taken to build Sanctuary?'

'Yeees... it's incredible, but what—'

'Our way of life here has not changed for hundreds of years.'

'I know.' Seamus frowned at her, and she could almost hear the cogs of his mind whirring, trying to catch up with her thoughts. 'So, if nothing is going to change, you finally think it is time for you to move on?'

She did not have to ask "move on from what?" Over the last few moon turns, many of their conversations dealt with whether or not she should stay with the guard. Any other soldier with her skills and length of service would not only have had their own platoon by now but would likely have been invited to join the council's defence committee.

Her role in prophecy had stalled Emer's career so many times it was unlikely she would ever reach her goal of sitting on the committee and helping others plan Sanctuary's security.

She sighed. 'I guess so. I'm just not ready to take that leap yet.'

'We would take you on at the school in a heartbeat. You have a knack for handling children, and we could certainly use someone with your talents.' He hugged her, and she leaned into him.

'I don't know, Seamus. It is probably time for me to move on, but I need to find my own path, not follow in yours.'

The look of hurt flashed across Seamus's face so quickly she was not sure she read it correctly.

'Of course, you must do what is right for you.'

She hugged him. 'I appreciate the offer, I do, but I need some time to think about my next moves before making a decision.'

'In the meantime, you can resign from the guard. You have enough leave to take some time off and figure out where you want to be.'

Everyone in Sanctuary was expected to contribute to the community in some way to earn credits for necessities, and Emer knew Seamus's words were intended to reassure that no one would pressure her to find her new niche immediately. Also, the credits in their ledger would allow them to live in comfort for quite some time.

A movement behind her husband caught her eye, and she leaned round him to find Jojay, her father's scribe, trying to attract their attention.

'I'm sorry to be a bother, Guard Emer, but Amelia asked me to fetch you.' The painfully thin girl spoke from behind a curtain of hair, and Emer thought, not for the first time, that Jojay would prefer never to leave the scrolls she spent most of her life working with.

'Now?' Seamus asked.

'I believe it... it's urgent.' Jojay twisted her fingers around each other, and Emer's stomach clenched.

Her physically fit father had always been such a powerhouse, but in the last month or so, his health had taken a turn for the worse. Each time she approached the subject, he brushed her off, asserting he was fit as a fiddle. However, words could not hide his growing frailty, and now this summons increased her level of concern.

'Lead the way, Jojay.' Seamus slid Emer's arm back through his, and they followed the scribe to the upper hall. As they arrived at her father's dwelling, the door opened, and Amelia moved aside to allow them entry.

Seamus's aunt had moved into her father's suite of rooms with her husband, Walter, a moon turn ago. Her father insisted he invite them to join him, because he and Amelia wanted to spend time exploring the new great-seeings, but Emer suspected it had more to do with her father's state of health.

Caraig invited Amelia and Walter to take over the master bedroom and make it their own, while he moved into what had once been Emer's childhood room.

'I will be going home now,' Jojay said as they entered, escaping before anyone could waylay her.

'Is my father all right?' Emer's stomach knotted even more as she asked the question.

Amelia took her hand and led her over to a group of chairs by the fire. The irony of the blind woman leading her brought a smile to Emer's lips. When Great Seers successfully completed their trial, their sight was taken from them to facilitate the development of their inner sight. Their other senses adjusted, and most of the time it was difficult to tell Amelia or Caraig could not see as others did.

'Your father fell asleep soon after we called for you,' Amelia said as they sat. 'He didn't sleep much last night, so it is best we leave him to rest now.'

Emer attempted to keep her tone even, but she was tired of everyone skirting round the subject of her father's health. 'That is not what I asked, Amelia.'

The older woman turned to Seamus. 'Walter is in the study if you wish to join him.'

Emer felt Seamus's relief as he kissed the top of her head and left to join his friend and mentor.

'There is nothing you could say that can't be said in front of Seamus,' Emer told her.

Amelia laughed. 'Even without my eyes, I could tell that boy would rather have been anywhere else but in this room.'

'Amelia, just tell me what's going on.' Emer's exasperation finally spilled over, and her voice sounded sharp even to her own ears.

The woman tensed. 'It's nothing but age,' she said. 'Unfortunately, growing old for a seer is more difficult than for others. It is like the gods want to pass on all they can before you move on to the afterlife, so Caraig has been plagued with visions almost every time he closes his eyes.'

'Oh, I had no idea.' It seemed she and her son had more in common that she cared to acknowledge—neither could see what was right under their nose until it was pointed out to them.

'Caraig should have talked to you about this.' Amelia ran a hand through her hair, and Emer realised the older woman was weary.

'Look, you don't have to explain,' she said. 'Father was already quite old when I was born, and his time to move on to the next life is here. It is the circle we all tread.'

Amelia took a deep breath. 'Your father and I speak often about how much to tell you about what's been going on. I believe you should be told everything, but your father says that could affect what is to be. When all is said and done—'

'He is still the Great Seer, and you are only his first apprentice.' Emer finished the thought for her.

Amelia's head dropped. 'It's not only that; he is the one whose seeings involved you. I have only been catching glimpses of how we here in Sanctuary will be affected by what is coming.'

Emer's anger began to bubble deep in her gut. 'Don't you think I should know what's going on if it relates to me?'

Amelia took her hand. 'I believe so, child, but really that is a matter for you and your father to discuss.'

Tugging her hand back, Emer spoke low and firm. 'I cannot go on like this. I'm living half a life while everyone watches and waits to find out what will happen to me.'

'The truth is, we cannot say for certain what is meant for you. Even piecing together Caraig's visions, and with all of us checking the past prophesies and histories, we cannot even begin to guess what is in store for you.'

'Can you even say for a certainty father's seeings are about me?' Emer asked.

Amelia nodded. 'You appear as an eagle and a wolf in his visions, and there is no other who shape-shifts into two forms, let alone those two specific ones.'

Emer slumped into the sofa. 'Amelia, what am I to do? I cannot wait indefinitely for destiny to find me.'

'You know as well as I do there is only one other option.'

Amelia was right. She and Seamus had skirted around the subject since her father announced she still had an important role to play in the future of their land—should she go to the trial caves as a suppli-cant and ask the gods to reveal her future, or should she wait for destiny to find her?

'It's a gamble, Amelia, and I am not sure I'm prepared for the consequences. People are generally reluctant to go before the gods to ask about their future, because the outcomes are so often not what they expected. Most come out changed and leave their old lives behind. Some lose their minds when they glimpse their future, and a small few never return at all.'

'You're correct, Emer. There is considerable risk involved, but the alternative is to carry on as you are.'

There was nothing more to be said. Emer knew her options, had known them for some time, truth be told, and now the next move was up to her.

Unfolding herself from the sofa, she walked over to her father's room. As silently as she could, she opened the door to check on him. Her heart leapt. Caraig was tangled in his sheets, curled into foetal position and shaking like a leaf.

'Amelia!' She managed to cry the seer's name as she rushed to her father's side.

She reached out for him, and he grabbed her hand, pulling her close. 'Emer, there is fire, so much fire... and it burns.'

Gasping in pain as his grip tightened, she said, 'Father, it's all right. I'm here. Just try to relax.'

Still, his grip tightened again. 'Fire and children. You must guide the children. But beware the fire... no, you must go towards it... for the children....'

His grip slackened, and his body went limp. He was so still Emer leaned over to ensure he was still breathing. A faint touch of air tickled her cheek, and the knot in her stomach loosened a little.

She sensed Amelia's presence, then Seamus's strong arms were around her, leading her out of the room.

'Walter went to fetch a magical healer,' he said as he guided her to a chair.

She sat down, vaguely aware she was shivering. Someone placed a blanket over her and a warm cup of caffe in her hands. While one part of her brain reacted to these things, the other part repeated *fire* and *guide the children.*

EMER ANSWERS

After her father's death, no one expected Emer to return to work right away, and, if she was honest, defending Sanctuary was the farthest thing from her mind. Of course, there had been the family funeral and then the public memorial service to keep her busy. After that, everything went quiet.

Amelia had taken charge of organising Caraig's office, keeping Jojay on to deal with the extra workload. And as for clearing out her father's home, Amelia offered to deal with packing up everything there as well. This made sense, as the dwelling came with his duties of Chief Seer, and it was likely Amelia would be given permanent residency when she formally took over this role. Of course, that would not happen until Amelia completed a trial before the gods and they ratified her appointment, which would happen at the next full moon in two days.

So Emer had time on her hands, and not much to do to fill it. Dwelling on the loss of her father and her frustration about the fact that his death left her future in limbo was getting her nowhere. To quieten her mind, she needed activity.

First, she cleaned their apartment and even went through the children's clothes, returning the stuff they had grown out of to the clothing store for repurposing. Then she turned her attention to the kitchen, clearing out cupboards and scouring pans to within an inch of their lives. Now she sat down with a cup of strong caffe and wondered what to do with herself next.

Should she go and help Amelia clear out her father's possessions? She didn't want to offend her or suggest she didn't trust her. The older woman had always treated her like one of her own family, and in fact she was closer to Amelia than she had been to her father. She just needed something to do to keep the thoughts running through her head at bay. Her father's words ran back and forwards through her mind, and she didn't know what to do with them.

Washing up her cup and leaving it on the bench, she grabbed a jacket and headed out. She had no destination in mind; she just needed to be moving. Avoiding the more popular walkways, she wandered through the corridors and out into the courtyard in front of Sanctuary.

The afternoon wind was bracing as she lifted her face up towards the early spring sun. Closing her eyes, she allowed the rays to warm her before she slipped into the shadows and transformed. It had been far too long since her last run through the forest, and today she needed to clear her head.

She wasn't sure how long she had run for—wolves marked time

in a different way. The sun was high in the sky when she finally tired and flopped down beside a stream to drink. Aware it was getting late, she turned back towards her home. She took her time, reluctant to face the decision she had made.

It would be wrong to say she thought through her problems while in wolf form. It was more that, as a wolf, emotions were removed, and she viewed things with a little more clarity. Filtering out her feelings enabled her to focus on the core issues. By the time she transformed back into herself and emerged from the woods, she knew she needed to discuss her decision with Seamus, but it was Amelia she went in search of.

She found the seer in the main library, helping her reader roll up the scrolls they had been working on. On sensing Emer's approach, she dismissed the young boy.

'Emer and I can finish up with these. You run along now.'

The boy did not need to be told twice. There was still some daylight left, and he would no doubt be joining the other children his age playing some game or other in the safety of the natural arena out the back of Sanctuary.

'I've been expecting you.' Amelia picked up a scroll and began rolling it up, and Emer joined her at the table. As they carried the documents over to the librarian a little later, the older woman whispered, 'Come, let us go watch the youngsters play while we talk.'

Emer drew Amelia's arm through her own, and they walked through the maze of corridors, exiting into the enclosed space where the youngsters met up after their chores were done. The noise they made as they played bounced off the walls and was interspersed with laughter and whispers from the parents sitting in the shade, using the excuse of keeping an eye on their offspring to socialise a little before the evening meal.

Wending her way through the occupied seats, Emer found a quiet space for Amelia and her self opposite the three doors leading to the trial caves. The irony of their position was not lost on either woman.

'I know why you came.' Amelia took her hand.

Emer chuckled. 'You wouldn't be much of a seer if you didn't.'

'This has more to do with human nature than foretelling. You have been unsettled for some time, and I believe you have now chosen a course of action.'

Emer frowned. 'You can foresee that?'

'You have the scent of wolf and forest on you.' Amelia laughed. 'I find wolves are very pragmatic creatures, and I'm sure your wolf-self cut through all the emotions and focused on the crux of the matter.'

She squeezed Amelia's hand. 'You're right.'

'And I believe you would like me to talk to Seamus—'

'No. I mean I would love it if you were the one to tell Seamus my decision; it would certainly be easier on me. But I think it's important I'm the one who breaks the news to him.'

'Of course, that is what I would have suggested to you anyway. So, what do you want of me, dear?'

'I wondered if you could invite the children over for dinner tonight so I can have Seamus to myself, without distractions.'

Amelia laughed a full-bellied laugh from deep inside her stomach. 'And with Kahal and Orla halfway across the other side of Sanctuary, they won't be able to hear Seamus's response. I expect he will want to express his opinions quite strongly, and perhaps... loudly.'

'I see you and I understand each other completely,' Emer said, spying her children on the field and calling them over with a wave of her hand.

'Are you sure about this, Emer? You could wait until the next new moon, or even the one after that.'

'Not really, but it is the right thing to do.' She pulled her hand from Amelia's and stood as she saw Orla and Kahal peeling away from their group of friends. 'I just hope Seamus feels the same way,' she said under her breath as she thanked Amelia for her help and went to meet her children.

THE LOOK on Seamus's face vindicated Emer's decision to eat alone that night. As soon as she mentioned she could no longer sit around and wait for destiny to find her, his features hardened to an inscrutable mask. After fifteen years together, she knew him well enough to realise he was holding his explosion inside until she finished talking.

'At the moment, I feel like I am living half a life. I'm not allowed to do my job just in case something happens to me, and at home, I always wonder if this is the last time I will read with my children or eat a meal with all of you.'

She sat back in her seat and watched as his expression change from confused, to worried, to downright scared. Finally, it settled on concerned, and the only sign of his internal stress was the white of his knuckles as he placed his clasped hands on the kitchen table.

'I'm sure, once Amelia's named the new Great Seer, she will lift the ban on your guard activities if you ask her.'

'She might well do so,' Emer admitted somewhat reluctantly. In her mind though, relying on Amelia to fix things still meant someone else would be controlling her life. Besides, it would simply put off their facing the underlying issue. 'But that won't solve the real problem—the prophecy hanging over my head like a sword waiting to fall.'

The silence that followed was heavy with the thoughts running through both their heads and of words unsaid. Emer didn't need to explain to Seamus the crushing weight of her decision; he understood her dilemma, because he had been through it himself.

As The Wizard sent to save them all from the wrath of a god, he had wrestled with the demons of his destiny in the past and had fretted over the fall out of those decisions ever since. It was because of his experience that Emer could not sit back and let prophecy take control of her life—she would not allow the gods that much power over her and her family.

Seamus stood and took their plates into the kitchen. He returned a few minutes later with two cups of caffe, and she braced herself—the real argument would start now.

'This type of trial is unpredictable and dangerous. There is a chance you may not return to us, or if you do come back, you could be completely changed.'

Ouch. Straight to the core of his fears. He was not going to take it easy on her.

'You know it is rare for that to happen,' she countered.

'The gods almost kept Aliah with them, even after she had completed her trial and been named as The Warrior. So it is not as rare as you would like to think.'

'You always believed the gods kept her from leaving the trial caves as part of The Wizard and The Warriors' test. Are you now telling me you believe differently?'

Seamus sighed slowly, as if releasing tension. 'No, I am not. I still have nightmares about not being able to convince the gods to let her leave with me.'

She reached out and took his hand. 'I'm the one who sits up with you until you have calmed down after you have those dreams.'

He forced a smile and squeezed her hand. 'So, if I feel that way about what happened to her, the sister of my heart, imagine the panic I'm feeling now at the thought of that happening to you—the half that makes me whole. I'm not sure I could bear to carry on if I lost you.'

The force of his fear surrounded her, and Emer found her resolve faltering. She had no desire to hurt the man she loved almost more than life itself. And what if she did not return, and Seamus actually fell apart? What would happen to Kahal and Orla? They were still young enough to need someone to guide them through to adulthood.

'Then what am I to do, Seamus? I have only two choices—to live my life as if it could all be taken away at any moment, or to ask the gods what they want from me.'

Letting go of her hand, Seamus stood and walked around the table. Lifting her to her feet, he enveloped her in his arms. Leaning into him, her one thought was *I want to stay here forever. Damn the world! And damn the gods!*

Fire, a voice in her head said. *Guide the children*, it whispered.

No, she couldn't hide from her duty; it would find her eventually, no matter what she did. Gently, she pushed Seamus away and stared at the face she had woken up every morning beside for almost half of her life.

'Is there another option I'm missing?'

He shook his head. 'None that is not a variation of those two.'

'What would you do if it were you?'

He stiffened and frowned. 'That's not playing fair at all, Emer.'

'Sorry, Seamus, I don't want to hurt you or the children, but I think I'll go crazy if I don't at least try to find out what's in store for me.'

'This is big, this decision. Too big for just one discussion. It isn't only that the trial may find you unworthy and you may be held on the plane of the gods—or worse. It's also that you may be told what you have to do, and that might change our lives forever.'

'Yes, that is possible, even probable.'

'On the other hand, you may not be called to action for years yet, and our children are still young enough to need both their parents around... at least until Kahal finishes his training and is accepted for an apprenticeship with the library and Orla starts studying as a healer.'

Emer jerked away. 'Do you think I don't know that? Do you think I want to leave our children without a mother, for whatever reason?'

'Umm, Emer—'

'What sort of mother will I be if I hide from my own future until I can no longer avoid facing it? What lesson will I be teaching them?'

'You're going somewhere?'

Emer swung round to find herself face to face with Orla.

'Who's going where?' Kahal's voice came from the other room.

Emer froze. This was not how she expected the evening to go. Her head was spinning with multiple options to explain away what the children overheard, but what she said was, 'What are you two doing here?'

'The council sent for Amelia and Walter, so we finished supper and came home,' Kahal answered.

Although she attempted to appear calm, the nervous tremor in her voice was obvious when she spoke. 'All right. Well, your father and I need some privacy for a while longer, so if you could both go to your rooms, I would appreciate it.'

Over his sister's shoulder, her son stared at her with eyes so like her own it was unnerving.

'What's going on?' Kahal asked.

'Mum's going somewhere, and she and Dad are fighting about it,' Orla spoke, her head tilted to the side as she considered her parents. Eventually, her eyes rested on Emer, and she frowned.

Emer turned to Seamus for support. *I think our daughter's empathy might turn out to be a god-given gift,* she sent.

Possibly.

What should we tell them?

'Your mother asked you to go to your rooms,' Seamus said in the no-nonsense voice he used to such great effect in the classroom but seemed to have no impact at all on his children.

Kahal squeezed past his sister and confronted his father. 'Is this about the prophecy, the one they think is about Mum?'

'How do you know about that?'

'Everyone's talking about it, Dad,' Orla said. 'They discuss it when they think we aren't around, but we've heard enough to piece together what's going on.'

Emer dropped into a chair, overwhelmed and unprepared for the entry of her children into the discussion. She wanted to protect them as much as possible from this unpredictable part of their lives.

Rubbing her temples to ease the building pressure in her head, she sensed Seamus move closer, as if to protect her. 'And just what are they saying?'

'They mostly discuss whether or not Mum will choose to go to the trial caves with Amelia, or whether she will wait until a new vision is sent to Amelia now that she is Great Seer,' Kahal told them.

'And what do you think?' Seamus's his tone was casual, but Emer sensed the tension in his body.

'Trial,' both children said together.

'Really? Why?' Seamus spoke as if this was a typical evening conversation.

'Amelia may not get another vision, and the scholars haven't been able to come up with anything more for moon turns now,' Orla said.

'And it would be horrible just waiting around not knowing,' Kahal said, then added, 'And most people say she will join Amelia this week, because it would be auspicious to have your trial at the confirmation of a new Great Seer.'

'Besides. Mum has been acting weird since Grandad's visions. And it's been worse since he died.' Kahal nodded as Orla spoke. 'We just want our old mum back, and this is the quickest way for that to happen.'

'All right, I think you've made your point of view quite clear. Now please, your mother and I would like to talk about this alone.'

The sound of retreating feet told Emer her children had left the room, and she slouched across the table, her head hidden in the crook of her arm.

'Before they came in, I thought I knew what I was going to do,' she whispered almost to herself. 'Now, I am not so sure. They think this is like a great adventure—go talk to the gods, find out what is going on, then come home and everything will return to normal. They don't comprehend the dangers.'

A bitter laugh escaped Seamus's lips as he rubbed her shoulders.

'Of course they don't. They are young, and they haven't experienced the joy of living through a prophecy before.'

'Before he died, my father told me I need to guide the children. What if fulfilling the prophecy has something to do with *our* children, with saving them from something evil?' Emer turned her head to the side so she could see Seamus.

His hands stopped their movement, and he gnawed at his lower lip, something he only did now when he was forced into making a difficult decision. 'So, this is what you've been wrestling with? You're worried that you are meant to save *our* children?'

'Yes,' she whispered, then sat up straight. 'Sometimes, I think it may not be our children, but then I worry it doesn't matter whose children the visions refer to. If I have to guide or save anyone's children, then I want to be as prepared as I can be.'

'Oh, Emer.' He knelt beside her and took her into his arms. 'Why us? Haven't we done enough?'

'It would seem not.' She hid her face in his shoulder, the scent of him offering additional comfort.

'I understand why you need to know. Does it need to be this moon turn?' Seamus's voice pleaded with her to say no. It didn't, but she couldn't even give him that much. His body shook as he sighed. 'Yes, it does, doesn't it? This weighs heavily on you, and you will not rest until you have answers.'

Her heart hurt so much she couldn't speak. She wanted nothing more than to tell Seamus she had made a mistake; she could wait to find out her destiny, and in the meantime, they could carry on as if nothing happened. No matter how hard she tried, the words just wouldn't come. The lie could not pass her lips. All she could do was hold on to him and gather some ease from the arms that held her.

A TALK WITH THE GODS

Seamus did his best to turn the dinner into a celebration, but there was no hiding the fear and concern everyone felt for Emer and Amelia entering the trial caves the following morning. Walter would not leave his wife's side for fear it might be their last night together.

Kahal and Orla picked at their food and gave monosyllabic answers to any questions about their day. Finally, unable to keep the exasperation from her voice, Orla said, 'Mum, all of that is so unimportant considering what you face tomorrow.'

Emer covered her daughter's hand with her own and gave it a squeeze. 'It is precisely because of what I am facing tomorrow that I want tonight to be as normal as possible. It is the time I spend with you all that gives me the strength to face the gods.'

Orla stared at her plate, but Kahal understood. He sent a meaningful look towards his mother before telling a story of a prank played over their lunch break. Soon, Orla joined in, and Seamus placed a comforting hand on Emer's leg under cover of the table.

Things lightened up for a while, until a knock at the door echoed through their cave. Amelia paused midsentence and looked towards Emer. 'It is time,' she said.

The atmosphere in the room changed immediately. Everyone stood almost as one. They took turns hugging Amelia and Emer goodbye. As was tradition, those facing the gods would spend the night of the full moon in a special room so they could meditate and contemplate their trial the following morning.

Attempting to remain light-hearted for the sake of the children, Seamus played it as if Emer was leaving on one of her normal patrols. She followed his lead and admonished the children to listen to their father and not to slip up on any of their chores, before she gathered them both into her arms and gave them a hug.

Seamus walked with her to the door. 'Stay safe for me', he whispered into her hair as he wrapped his arms around her. 'My heart beats heavier until you return.'

She stood in his embrace, drinking in the smell of him, until

Walter coughed discretely behind them. Pulling away, she stood on tiptoes and kissed her husband goodbye. 'Whatever happens, please believe that you and the children are my life. I am only whole when I am with you.'

Before he said anything else, she opened the door and ushered Amelia through before closing it firmly behind them. As they moved down the corridor, she didn't look back. She knew if she did, she would not be able to find the strength to carry on.

The procession silently walked to the contemplation rooms. Upon their arrival in the common area outside, Emer thanked their guide. Once they were alone, she led Amelia to the closest door before making sure the seer was settled, then retreated to her own spartan cell.

All the rooms were furnished the same. There was a simple wooden bed covered in a colourful wool blanket, a table with a carafe of water, and a single comfortable seat. The folded robe she must wear tomorrow sat on the chair. All those requesting an audience with the gods were expected to present themselves unadorned and penitent.

She took a deep breath and closed the door before making her way to the bed. Sitting down, hands in her lap, she wondered what to do with the rest of her evening. She was not tired, and she was not one given to introspection. Her room had a single window above the bed. Climbing up, she was just able to peek out and catch a glimpse of the colours of the setting sun as it turned the evening sky crimson and purple.

Smiling, she made a decision. She grabbed the robe from the chair and bunched it into a ball. Pushing the window open, she placed the robe on the ledge to prevent the opening from closing. She changed into an eagle and perched on the ledge before manoeuvring her body out of the window, careful not to damage her wings.

As she rose into the night, she caught a glimpse of her cell and realised getting back in was not going to be so easy. Still, not to worry now. She caught a current and rose into the sky, bathed in the light of the setting sun. When it was too dark to fly, she dropped to the ground and switched to wolf form.

Keeping to the shadows, she made her way to one of the lesser used entrances. Lesser used unfortunately did not mean unguarded, and she waited until the guards were distracted by a couple of children before slipping back into the halls and making her way slowly to the cell.

Keeping to halls rarely used at night, she made it back to the common room without running into anyone. Before changing back into human form, she sniffed the air down the hallway to make sure no one was heading her way. She then tiptoed to her door and opened it quietly before slipping through the gap.

'Nice flight?'

Emer's heart leapt into her mouth, then she grinned. 'Seamus, you shouldn't be here!'

'And you shouldn't be out flying around.'

'I can clear my head when I fly, but I can't concentrate on tomorrow with you here.' She closed the door.

'I only popped in for a moment to say a proper goodbye. Why the need for flight?'

'I needed to clear my head.'

'And sort something out?'

She nodded.

'Anything I can help with?'

'No, not really It's just my brain is telling me I need to do this tomorrow, but my heart saying not to. It's like I am placing prophecy first—before our family.'

Seamus hugged her. 'I think you're looking at this the wrong way. I have been doing a lot of thinking over the last couple of days, and I believe you must do this tomorrow. If you don't, you won't be in a position to place us first, because part of you will always be wondering how long you will be with us; how long before the prophecy kicks in and takes you away.'

Emer sighed. Even though Seamus also summed up her own

feelings, knowing they were on the same page did little to ease her worries.

'When you come back tomorrow, you will be able to fully be with us, and you will have some idea for how long we will all have left together. I surely believe that will be better for everyone.' He squeezed her tight, as if he didn't want to let her go. 'That was all I needed to tell you and why I risked coming here. When you meet with the gods tomorrow, you can do so with our full love and support.'

'Seamus, what did I do to deserve you?' she asked.

'You supported me when I doubted myself, when I couldn't believe anyone in their right mind would choose me to save the world,' he said matter-of-factly.

'The way I remember it, I gave you a hard time—told you to get over yourself.' She chuckled at the memory.

'You did, and that was exactly the type of support I needed. Now, I must go so you can rest and be ready for tomorrow.' He kissed her and opened the door, before saying, 'Don't forget to retrieve your robe before you close the window.'

This time when she sat on the bed, her tired limbs relaxed immediately, and soon sleep sent her to a blissful oblivion.

Waking early, Emer forced herself out of bed and slowly changed into her penitent's robe. Neatly folding her clothes and placing them on the end of the bed, she was ready to go. For a few moments, she attempted to pace out her nervous energy, but there was not enough space in the small room to work off her tension. With a sigh, she sat on the chair and took some deep breaths in an attempt to control her anxiety.

Her hand automatically went to the silver bangle around her

wrist and began twisting it, as was her habit when nervous. *Oh no. I can't take this with me.* She worked at the bracelet until it finally popped off, leaving angry red marks on her hand. Gently, she placed it on top of her clothes and returned to her seat.

Instead of trying to calm herself for the coming ordeal, Emer now stared at the bracelet, remembering the day she and Seamus said their vows and exchanged tokens as an outward sign of their commitment. Taking off the bangle today was like severing her ties with Seamus and their children. If she did not put these thoughts from her mind, she would never get through her ordeal and return home.

There was a knock on the door, and it opened to reveal a girl in a guard's uniform. Not much older than her own children, the girl's trembling hands betrayed her tension.

'Are...' She cleared her throat and tried again. 'Are you ready?'

Emer stood. 'As I will ever be.'

'Do you come wearing only the robes of a penitent?'

Glancing back towards her bracelet, Emer took a deep breath and returned her gaze to the guide. 'I do.'

'Shall we go?'

The early morning sun was low on the horizon when Emer entered the amphitheatre at the back of Sanctuary. The last time she had been here, the space was filled with the shouts and laughter of children and the conversations of their parents. Today, there was utter silence. Not even the birds chirped their usual song.

The guide led Emer to the lone figure standing in front of the three trial cave entrances. The role of trial adjudicator had fallen to her father as Head Seer and would now belong to Amelia. However, as Amelia was undergoing her own test today, the position was filled by Angus, the elderly head of the Guild of Scholars.

As she approached him, she wondered if Amelia was already in the caves, or was she still waiting back in her room? Having been a guide in her younger days, she knew the answer she would be given if she asked the girl beside her—*that is not your journey.*

'Ah, Emer, welcome,' Angus said, taking her hands in his. She had known this man since before she could walk. He was a kind soul with a wicked sense of humour. With her nervous stomach churning, she hoped today he would keep that side of himself in check.

Almost as if he sensed her unease, he bent forward, kissed her on the cheek, and whispered, 'Good luck.' He straightened up and drew an air of formality around himself.

'Emer, you have requested to speak with the gods to ask their intentions for you. As is tradition, you must enter the caves wearing only the clothes you stand in now. Can you please confirm you have no other items with you?'

Her hand automatically went to her wrist, feeling for the bangle that usually rested there. She felt naked and alone without its comforting weight. Shaking her head, she clasped her hands behind her back and stood in the guards' "at ease" position, drawing some resolve from years of discipline and training. 'I have nothing with me,' she answered.

'It is time to begin. You must choose a cave. When you enter, the candle will be lit. You have twelve candle-marks to complete your quest. The bell will toll at six candle-marks, then again at the ninth candle-mark, and every mark after that until the twelfth. If you are not out of the cave at that time, you will not return. Are you clear?'

'I am.' She almost added "sir" but stopped herself in time.

'Please choose your entrance.'

She was not sure if she believed the often talked about meanings of choosing a cave, but like many people in Sanctuary, she would not totally discount them either. In her mind, Emer had already chosen —she walked towards the middle cave.

Just before the entrance, she hesitated. Was she disrespecting the gods by not choosing the left-hand cave? Those petitioning the gods usually went there as a sign they were making a decision with their heart. No, choosing the entrance to her right would be showing disrespect. She believed circumstances forced her to come here today, but she could not quite bring herself to make such a bold statement of her feelings by selecting that cave. She continued through the entrance she had originally chosen.

The cavern was dark and cool inside, and when she turned to look back out into the arena, she found only solid rock. Standing in the centre of the darkened space while her eyes adjusted to the lack of light, she took up her at-ease stance again and waited. Her legs cramped, she shook them out, and she waited some more.

Eventually, she sat cross-legged on the ground and continued her vigil, and as she did, she wondered if she had misjudged the signs. Had everyone? Was she being too proud by assuming she was at the centre of a new prophecy?

Time passed, and Emer, used to a more active life, became bored. Closing her eyes, she relived her flight as an eagle just a few days ago, when she had flown the skies the day after her father's funeral, before moving to a memory of running in wolf form.

The six-hour bell chimed. She stood and walked around, feeling for a gap in the walls, which would indicate an entrance had appeared and she could leave. Nothing. She had no option but to wait. Dropping to the floor, she lay on her back and stared at the ceiling. She couldn't have been wrong. If she wasn't meant to be here, why had the exit disappeared?

Like all those who grew up in Sanctuary, as a child, she answered a dare to sneak into the caves, only to be disappointed when she found they looked like any other cavern in the area. Later, her father explained they only took on special properties when the veil between their world and the realm of the gods allowed, and that was why ordeals were only held the day after a full moon.

If she was meant to be here, her only option was to wait until something happened or the cave opening reappeared. Closing her eyes, she allowed her mind to take to the air. This time, she replayed a flight over the forests surrounding her home. To help herself relax, she imagined the smell of the trees and the salty tang of the wind blowing from the sea. It was bliss. She flew over Sanctuary herself and, just as she had done on that day, she spied her children with their class participating in an outside lesson. Picking out Orla and Kahal with her keen eyes, the magic of the memory fell away.

When she first shape shifted as a child, her teacher warned of losing too much of herself to the animal. Shape shifters who did that often became trapped in their animal form. She was advised to find an anchor, something more important to her than the freedom she found as an animal.

Initially, she had been too scared to change into animal form for long periods. The mother she adored died when she was very young, and her father was always more of a seer than someone she connected with on an emotional level. Then she met Seamus, and she found her link to the world.

Later, when the children came along, she knew in her heart she would never desert them for anything—not even the exhilaration of taking to the skies or running free through the forests. One thought of her family changed her back to being human without any regrets.

The scene in her mind altered, and she found herself in the forest with Seamus. The first time she had taken him through these woods, they were fleeing from soldiers attempting to kill them, and she had not wanted that memory to put him off making his home here with her.

Now, her thoughts took Emer to the time she planned an overnight hunting trip to show Seamus the true beauty of her home. It was not long after they had defeated the god who threatened their world, and they had returned to Sanctuary to make a home for themselves.

Soon after they arrived at the camping spot she had chosen, Emer turned into wolf form to find their dinner. Seamus followed her for a while as she showed him all her special places. As the sun sank, she left to hunt their dinner while he made camp and built a fire.

The freedom she experienced running through her second home as she hunted her prey was intoxicating. She ran for hours and lost track of time before her stomach rumbled and she remembered

Seamus. Picking up the two rabbits she caught, she turned back towards their campsite.

The look of fear and worry on his face wrenched at her heart as she turned back into human form before handing over their dinner. They talked about his fears while the rabbits cooked. He not only worried that something happened to her, but also that she might decide to stay in wolf form forever. He did not want to lose her, but he would understand if the life of a wolf appealed to her more than being with him.

'I will always return to you,' she promised as he held her in his arms that night. 'Nothing is better than being here with you.'

She sat upright in the cave, her heart pounding, overwhelmed with remorse. Why had her mind been drawn to that specific moment?

THE ATMOSPHERE in the cave had changed, and the ghostlike form of a goddess appeared in front of her. Emer recognised her as the one the people of Aria worshipped simply as "The Goddess". Emer moved into a kneeling position, not as a sign of worship, but as a precursor to standing.

'I think you have already guessed, haven't you?'

Emer nodded as she moved to her feet to look the god directly in the eyes. 'This is some sort of choice between my family and the freedom of my animal forms.'

The goddess raised both her hands palm upwards, gesturing for her to continue.

'Are you telling me to keep one I must give up the other?' Emer's voice trembled. To never be able to change form again was like cutting off a limb. Her life would be completely different. Would she still be the same person if she did? But it was no choice—she would always choose her family.

A slow, sad smile transformed the goddess's face, and Emer remembered nothing was ever that simple when it came to the gods, and her stomach knotted. What was coming was going to be worse than losing her ability to transform.

'No, Emer, the decision you must make is more complex than that. Your world faces an enormous threat, one substantially bigger than the one my brother posed.'

'Are you talking about the danger he came here to fight?' Emer asked.

'I am, I'm afraid. He thought he could mould the people of your world into a fighting force strong enough to overcome this foe. Unfortunately, a battle of that nature would likely have destroyed everything, leaving only a barren wasteland.'

'The prophecies my father and Amelia are sensing, they tell of a new threat and are directing us on how to combat it?'

'Of course. Unfortunately, this conversation has come about sooner than we anticipated. His love for you drove your father to reach further for answers than he was safely capable of doing, and the messages he received were a little bit... shall we say... less than gentle.'

Emer's eyes widened. 'Are you telling me you killed my father?'

The goddess placed a hand on her shoulder, and she fought the urge to shrug it away in anger.

'I am sorry, my child. His worry for you drove Caraig to try to find out more and more about what will happen. He wanted to spare you from coming here yet, to give you as much time with your family as possible.'

Tears welled in Emer's eyes, and she cried for the first time since her father's passing. Caraig had always found it difficult to show his emotions, but in the end, her father tried to find out her future for her, and it had killed him.

'Caraig wanted to spare you this, but we gods can only speak

clearly to mortals here in the caves. I am sorry we were unable to give him more information. The burden of his death must be borne by both you and me.'

Although the words were intended to provide comfort, guilt and anger vied for space in Emer's heart. The hand on her shoulder tightened.

'I don't care about your sorrow. All I am interested in is whether or not you can tell me my role in upcoming events.'

A frown creased the goddess's brow, and Emer remembered who she was talking to, but it was too late to take her angry words back now. Fortunately, the goddess ignored the tone of her outburst.

'Our conversation with you was always scheduled for the ascension of a new Great Seer, and Caraig's unfortunate death accelerated events. Because of this, we cannot tell you as much as we would like to be able to, to help you make your decision. But we are where we are.' The goddess shrugged.

'Can you tell me anything at all about my role in the new prophecy?' Emer asked, attempting to control her feelings, but it proved to be difficult in light of the gods' inability to speak plainly or provide any real information.

'Yes and no.'

A sigh of frustration escaped from Emer's lips, and the goddess held up a hand to prevent her from speaking.

'We cannot tell you what form the threat will eventually take, but we can tell you it is definitely coming.'

'All right. What about my role in this?' Emer's tone was clipped.

'That, I can say. You will need to guide the ones identified to defend your people against whatever is coming.'

'So I am not needed until the threat emerges?'

'Not exactly. We need someone to commune with the ancient inhabitants of this world, someone to take them back to the dawn of time and identify what we are facing. Then you must use what knowledge you gain to help the actors in the prophecy.'

Emer digested the words and put them with what had been found out about the prophecies to date.

'You believe Seamus and Aliah—I mean The Wizard and The Warrior—are to play a part in all of this, don't you?'

The goddess nodded. 'Though their contribution is still not clear, they have a role in events.'

'So this will happen soon, in our lifetime?'

'We believe so, yes.'

Emer chose her next words carefully. 'Let me make sure I understand you correctly. I am to learn what I can about an ancient threat, after which I will become a guide of sort. My father said something about children. Do you know anything about what that might mean?'

The goddess's face went blank, her eyes became unfocussed, and she was silent for a while. *Probably talking with the other gods,* Emer thought. Finally, her eyes refocused, and she said, 'I am not sure what he saw in his last moments. What we can foretell is, should you choose to take on this role, the lives of many children will be saved.'

'My children?' Emer was quick to ask.

'Specifically?'

She nodded.

'We are uncertain. Your children may be involved, but it might also mean the entire next generation of children.'

'Well, if children are involved, of course I will do this,' Emer said. 'Just tell me what I need to do and when.'

The goddess stood eye to eye with Emer, although she had not appeared to move.

'I will not take that as agreement yet, because you are not in possession of all the facts. You cannot communicate with the Ancients from here. I must take you to them.'

'All right.'

The goddess's tone sent a snake of unease through Emer.

'Also, they are not human, so you cannot be in human form when you speak with them. I cannot tell you how long it will take you to learn their history, and I cannot say whether or not you will be able to return to your life here when you are done.'

Emer froze. She was correct; it had been too easy before. Now she had to decide if she had the courage to leave her children, perhaps forever, to save their future.

'Will I be able to say goodbye to my family?'

'If you agree to take this on, I will need to transport you to the home of the Ancients before the veil closes.'

'Then can I come back next full moon and give you my decision?'

The goddess shook her head. 'Perhaps I was not clear before. The anointing of a new Chief Seer gives us a unique boost in magical energy on this world, a boost we must have to get you to where you need to be. Of course, your father dying prematurely altered our plans somewhat, and normally you would have been aware you were leaving your family when you entered the cave... but I am afraid it is now or not at all.'

'And if I chose not at all?'

The goddess paused for the bell signalling the ninth candle-mark.

'Then our chances of the next generation living in the world as it is now drops dramatically. Are there any other questions?'

Emer had hundreds, if not thousands, but none of them would make this decision any easier. She closed her eyes. 'No.'

'I will leave you to make your decision.'

When Emer opened her eyes, she found the goddess gone, and the entrance to the cave had returned. Angus sat patiently in the distance. Someone had brought him a chair so he would be comfortable while he waited for the trials of this day to end. Her father would have been able to leave the arena, as he could always sense when a person's test was complete in time to return to greet them. No such luxury for Angus.

Emer dropped back to the ground and crossed her legs. Clearing her mind, she went through all her options. Well, not all, there were only two—return to her family and hope they would find another way to survive the future, or leave them to ensure their future survival.

The bell struck the tenth candle-mark. Angus stood to meet Amelia. Sanctuary clearly had a new Great Seer. Emer smiled.

She stood and paced. Was she strong enough to do this? Could she really leave her family to become their hope for the future? Did she have the strength to do this without Seamus at her side?

The eleventh bell tolled, and Emer sank to the ground, facing the entrance. Having made her decision, she resolved to stick by it. Only one more candle-mark to wait now. She would do this, because it was the right thing to do, no matter the cost to her or her family.

Amelia returned and stood by Angus, who had abandoned his chair.

Clasping her hands, she stared at them, sure she was doing the right thing. The time passed slowly.

Then Seamus joined his aunt. Somehow, he must have found out when she went in and came to meet her. Her heart was tearing apart. She couldn't do this without Seamus by her side. But she had no choice.

'I love you, Seamus, now and forever.' She repeated the words she had said at their binding as her hand reached for the place where her bangle usually sat.

Tears streamed down her face, reading Seamus's concern as he moved towards the caves. Angus and Amelia tried to hold him back, but he would not be stopped. The final bell tolled, and the entrance disappeared moments before he reached it.

'You cannot do this!' she heard him yell. 'Have we not given enough? Send her back. Take me instead.'

The air changed again. Emer stood and turned to face the goddess. The deity held out her hand, and on it sat Emer's marriage bracelet. 'I understand we ask a lot, but we are not unaware of what you are leaving behind.'

As tears streamed unchecked down her face, Emer took the piece of jewellery and slid it back onto her wrist before following the goddess from the cave.

THE DISAPPEARANCE OF EMER

Seamus? Seamus?

Would she get through this time? Seamus's grief had been so intense when she attempted to mind speak with him soon after her departure that she had not been able to find a way through it to contact him. Reluctantly, she waited another two full moons before trying again to reach him.

Seamus? A little louder this time. She sensed his mind waking and reaching for her.

Emer? Seamus cried out. *No, she's gone. It can't be her.*

It is me, my beloved. It is really me.

Emer? Where are you? Tell me, and I will come for you.

No, my beloved, where I am, you cannot go. I just wanted you to know I'm alive. I am where I have to be, and I miss you all so very much.

We miss you too. When can you come home? The pain in Seamus's voice wrenched at her heart.

Not for a very long time, if at all.

Emer....

Please believe me, Seamus. I had no option. I am doing this for our future and the future of our children.

Oh, Emer. The loss in his voice fractured her already broken heart into even smaller pieces.

We may not be able to be together, but at each full moon, we can talk for a little while. Tell me about the children.

Emer?

Yes, my love, I'm here. Tell me, did you manage to talk Kahal out of joining the guards?

No, you know when his mind is made up, he cannot be budged. Seamus chuckled.

From the first time we took him to the library, he talked about becoming a librarian. Emer's voice softened as she remembered the day.

I know, but he now says that was the dream of a child. If his mother can sacrifice her life for the good of our people, how can he do any less?

Oh. No. Emer had not considered her sacrifice might tempt her children to similar feats or heroism.

I think he wants to honour your memory, and this is the only way he knows how. Seamus's voice was almost a whisper.

Oh, Seamus, I am so sorry. This is not the future we wanted for him.

In the end, it is his choice, Emer.

My sword is under our bed. Can you give it to Kahal please?

There was a pause before Seamus asked, *What if you need it when you return?*

I can get another. It would please me if he uses it. She did not have the heart to tell him things with the Ancients were going so slow it would be years before she would need a sword again.

Orla has been accepted into the healers' order and will begin classes in the fall.

Finally, something to smile about. *That is fantastic. Her gift of empathy is well suited to the life of a healer. I am so proud of her. I hope she knows that.*

She does. How are you doing? The question was tentative, almost as if Seamus was not sure he could bear to hear the answer.

It is harder than I thought. I'm lonely, and I miss you all.

ADMINA'S ARGUMENT

We miss you too.

Emer?

The voice came as it always did on the full moon.

Emer!

Emer? Was that her name?

I hear you.

Emer, my love. I think the time is coming when we will be together again. It's been more than two years. I bet you won't recognise the children.

My love? Home?

Children? she asked the voice.

Yes, Orla and Kahal were so excited when Amelia told us the prophecy is becoming clearer. That means your job is almost done.

The voice did not belong to an Ancient, but it was familiar. Somewhere in the back of her mind, a thought wriggled to break free. A thought of him, of who he was. Yes, she knew him. He was.... She struggled to find the name. No, it was gone.

She meant to ask him about something. Someone? Was it him, or was it someone else?

Who...? What?

She couldn't find the words.

Oh, Emer. I love you, now and forever.

The voice disappeared. A tear formed in her eye, and she felt a tug of sadness, but she could not quite grasp why the voice in her head had that effect on her.

EMER?

She barely stirred when she heard the strange voice now.

Emer, I'm not sure if you're even there anymore. I haven't heard you speak for more than a year, but I will talk with you every month until I find you or I find out you're.... Amelia believes the time the prophecy spoke of has come. It won't be long now. Please wait for me.

She closed her eyes and went back to sleep, not even pausing to wonder who Emer might be.

CHAPTER 13
ALL RIGHT, I'LL THINK SOME MORE

'Wow, Mum, that story's a little dark, isn't it?' Mina raised an eyebrow. 'It sounds like you are trying to scare me out of going to Sanctuary.'

Aliah tensed, then forced herself to relax. It had been difficult discussing her fears with Mina, and recounting Emer's demise brought all her own ghosts to the surface. She had to remember that her daughter had no idea what the trial caves were actually like. Also, she had never met Emer, so from her perspective, this was merely a story.

'You asked me to tell you what happened. It wasn't my intention to upset you, Mina. But I hope now you can understand how my own experiences, and the fact that I lost a good friend when she went through her own trial, makes me more than a little bit nervous when you said you are quite happy to put yourself forward for such an ordeal.'

Mina's hand was cool and strong as she reached across and covered Aliah's.

'I understand, Mother, but you can't protect me from everything bad or dangerous forever. Besides, can't you see Emer had to do what she did?'

Aliah nodded. 'Of course I can. You can't escape your destiny, especially when the gods take a direct hand. It's just... well, I lived through the devastating affect her disappearance had on Seamus and his family.'

Mina's brows drew together in a little frown. 'I can't imagine how hard it would have been for Orla and Kahal to lose their mother. I can't imagine my life without you... or Father.'

Aliah chuckled. 'I would have thought you would have enjoyed the freedom of making your own decisions.'

'Mum! I'm not totally self-centred. I appreciate that you and Father think you have my best interests at heart, even if we might disagree on what that is.'

'And because we want the best for you, we don't want you to rush into a decision about your future. That's why we want you to stay here until I return. Not only does your father actually need your help with the trade delegation from Carsten, but it's also an opportunity for you to come to terms with using your gift.'

Mina stood and began pacing. 'You're worried about the dangers of my going to Sanctuary, yet you're happy to take Gabriel with you to deal with an unknown foe. Does that mean you have decided I will be heir, and Gabriel is expendable?'

Aliah's fists clenched, and she concentrated on relaxing them before she responded to her daughter.

'Neither of my children are "expendable"—ever. And your father and I have never made any secret that we would prefer our oldest child to wear the Heir's Ring unless they proved to be totally incompetent.'

Mina huffed, but Aliah carried on. 'As your father and I have already explained to you, Gabriel is coming as part of his training, just as you went with your father to Hand last year. If our scouts deem the mission to be too dangerous, he will remain with your uncle while I continue on to meet up with the delegation from Sanctuary.'

'You should take him with you. If he proves himself in a border skirmish, the people will welcome him when you place the Heir's Ring on his finger.'

'Mina!' Aliah could not keep the exasperation from her voice. How did this conversation get away from her so quickly? 'The ring is rightfully yours as the eldest, and although you have come close, you have not yet done anything to make us think you can't learn how to rule Aria.'

'But I haven't done anything to make you believe I can either.' Mina mumbled the words as she plonked back down in the chair.

Poised to deny the accusation, Aliah stopped herself. Mina was right, and offering her platitudes would not help her relationship with her oldest child. 'No, you haven't. You are young and untried, as is Gabriel, and have not yet had the opportunity to prove yourself. Sometime in the future, we will have a discussion about whether or not offering you the ring is our best way forward—for Aria and for you.'

'But I don't want it.' Mina glared at her mother. 'I don't want to rule Aria!'

Taking a deep breath, Aliah reined in her frustration. Growing up, she wanted to be considered for the role of Heir, but because she was a woman, no one thought her capable. Hers and her sister's duty was to marry a man who the people would accept as ruler. Still, Mina was not her, and she was entitled to her own thoughts on her future.

Aliah studied her daughter. They had come so far, and here they were fighting again, and about something that did not need to be decided right now.

'We have a duty as the ruling family of the nation to provide good leadership. Part of that is making it clear who will lead Aria if something happens to your father or me, which is why it is important for us to name an heir. But we are still young and healthy, and we have time to make that decision.'

'But you still want it to be me.' Mina pressed her point, although her tone was less belligerent now.

'I can't deny I hope it will be you. But we will decide that when the time is right.'

Mina shrugged and leaned back in her chair. 'Which is not now, because you have bigger things to worry about?'

Aliah's eyes widened in surprise, and Mina smiled.

'I am not completely stupid. Something big is going on at the border; otherwise, you and Seamus wouldn't be going to deal with it. You especially, because it would take an extremely good reason for Aria to send its monarch into danger.'

Shaking her head, Aliah attempted to focus. Her daughter's mood and thoughts seemed to change with the wind, and she allowed herself a moment to wonder if this was a ploy to keep her off balance.

'We have some intelligence about what is going on in the borderlands, but we won't have the full picture until we get there. On the good-news front, we're taking very capable people with us, and we'll get to the bottom of whatever is going on.' Aliah reassured her daughter while she wondered how much more her children had picked up from castle gossip about what she was riding into.

'I know enough to realise part of ruling is about choosing the right people for specific jobs and that you shouldn't place your leader in danger unless the situation is dire,' Mina said.

'I think you're forgetting your father is co-regent, and he was preparing to go deal with this.'

Mina shrugged again. 'You are the regent with the royal bloodline, and you were The Warrior. I doubt the people of Aria would allow Father to continue to rule alone if something happened to you.'

The pen stopped twirling between her fingers, and Aliah regarded her daughter carefully. For all her denials about her abilities to lead Aria, Mina was demonstrating a good grasp of Arian politics. She resisted praising her, not wanting to give away what her daughter revealed.

'We are not on the verge of an invasion, Mina. I am not going because there is a grave threat to our nation, but because Amelia had a seeing that the situation will be resolved if The Wizard and Warrior turn up to deal with it.'

Mina snorted again. 'It always comes back to that, doesn't it—the Warrior thing?'

Taking a deep, calming breath, Aliah wondered how it was all right for her daughter to bring up the subject of her being The Warrior, yet when she did, it was like she was bragging.

'Unfortunately, sometimes it does. It doesn't matter what else I have done with my life; people still see me as The Warrior. Not the person who brought about changes to the position of women in Aria, or the person who brokered a lasting peace with Carsten, or someone who has overseen one of the most peaceful and prosperous periods in our history.'

'You sound bitter?' Mina's voice lifted in surprise.

Aliah said, 'I didn't choose to be The Warrior. Don't get me wrong; I don't regret it, and I certainly learnt a lot. It's just... that was who I was for a mad few moon turns when either by good luck or good fortune a group of us managed to save Aria. I have done so much since then... and—'

'And since you defeated the god, the people of Aria have tripped over themselves to do what you wish in thanks,' Mina said.

'I can't deny, at times, being a legend has come in handy, but mostly it's frustrating. I work hard to be a fair and good leader, but most people assume everything falls into my lap because I'm god-touched. Sometimes, I want to be seen as me, Aliahanna, and be appreciated for what I have achieved.'

Mina sank back into her chair. 'I never thought about it that way, but I think I understand. I hate people seeing me as "The Princess" and assuming everything is easy for me because of who I am. You want not to be known only as The Warrior.'

Taking a long, hard look at her mother, Mina leaned forward and was about to say something, when she was interrupted by a knock on the door.

'Sometimes I feel like my whole life is orchestrated around door knocks.' Aliah sighed.

'I know what you mean.' Mina laughed.

'Come,' Aliah said.

'I am sorry, Your Highness, but the king requested your presence as soon as possible.'

Aliah looked towards her daughter; Mina nodded for her to go.

'I have some thinking to do. We can finish this later, Mum.'

'AND SHE SAID she hated being The Warrior sometimes.' Mina flopped back on Gabriel's bed, arms outstretched.

'Well, yeah, that's obvious.'

Gabriel moved her right arm so he could place a pile of clothes on the bed. Mina slapped his hand away.

'Why is it obvious, oh great, wise one?'

Mina rolled, sat up, and swung her legs onto the bed. Sitting cross-legged, leaning her chin on her hands as she watched her brother pack, she waited for him to enlighten her.

Sighing as if it was too much trouble to educate his dense sister, Gabriel said, 'No one is only one thing. I mean, Father was a duke's son, then a spy, and now a king. But he's also a husband, a father, and a friend.'

Gabriel opened his travel pack and began rolling his clothes and placing them inside. Mina punched his arm, frustrated at his ability to put his thoughts into words.

'All right, Mr I-Know-Everything, why would Mum hate being "The Warrior" when the people would not have made her queen and allowed for her to co-rule if she had not saved Aria from certain doom?'

Pausing, Gabriel turned and looked at her as if she was mad. Mina shifted in discomfort and felt obliged to answer her own question.

'Because it was like they were asking The Warrior to rule, not Princess Aliahanna,' she said, and Gabriel returned to his packing.

'So, are you almost ready?' Mina changed the subject.

'When I've packed these things, I'm done.'

'You must be excited.'

Again, Gabriel stopped what he was doing and frowned into his bag.

'No. I mean I was when I thought I was going with Father to negotiate a border settlement. But Mum being called to go as The Warrior means it is likely to be dangerous, and, well, you know I'm not much of a fighter.'

'Huh, you sell yourself short. True, you've yet to beat one of our trainers in a fight. But you understand we're taught by members of the elite guard, and you're travelling with a regular troop, so you're likely to be one of the best swordsmen there.'

'Mm, they will still have one advantage—they will have fought for real.'

'You may not like fighting, Gabriel, but if you have to, I'm sure you will do better than you think.'

'If I am even allowed to get involved. I mean, Mother has said if the reports are too bad, I'll be left with Uncle Hubert. How's that for confidence in my ability?'

Mina laughed. 'As I have had pointed out to me on numerous occasions over the last few days, the guards do their job better when they don't need to worry about protecting one of us.'

'I guess. Anyway, what about you? What are your plans?'

Mina picked at a loose thread on the blanket. 'Father wants me to take Mother's place at his side over the next couple of moon turns so I can improve my abilities to handle matters of state.'

It was Gabriel's turn to laugh.

Ignoring him, she continued. 'In return, they will find me a tutor to help me learn to work with my magic.'

'I take it you've decided to become a scout for the guard then?'

'I have.'

'And you are happy with a tutor?'

'It's better than the alternative.'

'I have never heard of a person being trained to use their gift by a wizard tutor though.'

'I met this guy in the stables, Rinnard, from Carsten. That is the way they teach their gifted people there. They're sort of apprenticed to someone with a similar skill.'

'Sounds interesting, but the Wizard Council here would never go for that. I'm surprised they're considering it—even for you.'

'I'm not sure they have yet. Father will make the request once all the ruckus around your departure dies down.'

'But you sounded as if.... Never mind.'

'No, what were you going to say?'

'Well, you sounded like you've someone willing to teach you already.'

Mina chewed at the edge of a nail and wondered how much of what was going round in her head she should share with Gabriel. He had enough to worry about with his own issues. Still, she would love to have his counsel; on the other hand, he might feel compelled to tell their parents. She was saved from making that decision when a steward entered the room, informing them they were late for the farewell dinner.

A MESSAGE FROM SEAMUS

Leaning forward, Aliah kissed her husband on the cheek. 'You look dashingly handsome this evening,' she said.

'I wanted to remind you what you're leaving behind.' He pulled her arm through his and escorted her from their rooms. 'In case you had any thoughts of straying while you're away.'

Aliah laughed. 'As if I could ever find anyone to replace you.'

'Flattery is exactly what I need at the moment.'

Aliah.

Aliah stopped mid-step, and Dominic halted beside her. 'What is it?'

'Seamus.'

Seamus, what's happening?

I needed to warn you; we may have a problem.

Not fighting already? Not so close to Sanctuary?

No, no one's attacked us. But I think we're being watched.

Someone's following you?

Not physically, but I keep getting this feeling that someone is... you know—

Scrying?

295

Yes. That's exactly it. Do you remember Walter describing what he felt when our old enemies were watching us in the palace on Hand? I believe I'm experiencing something similar now. I think I have managed to hide us, but I wanted to warn you to be careful.

'Seamus says someone is scrying them. He is worried they might also try to watch us when we leave Bannock.'

Dominic unlooped her arm from his. 'I'll go and check on the skills of the magic users in your party. Maybe one or more of them can create some cover. I'll meet you at dinner.' He kissed her before heading off.

Aliah?

Yes, I am here. I was updating Dominic, and he has gone to ensure we're prepared.

I am going to call back to Sanctuary for a farseer to join our group. In the mountains, there are many places to hide, and we will be safer with someone who can sense the presence of other people.

I believe one of our scouts is a farseer. Do you think you might need more than one?

Ah... wait a moment... no, the guard captain says one should be enough. He asks if you could bring any recent maps you have of the area though.

Already packed, and I will check with Hubert before we leave his palace. He might have something more up to date.

Good.

I need to go. I have a farewell state dinner. We're on target to leave at first light.

See you soon.

Seamus left her mind, and Aliah took a moment to compose herself before heading to the main dining room.

ALIAH WAITED in the antechamber for Dominic to join her. As they entered the dining room, all those assembled rose as the co-monarchs made their way to the head table, where their two children and esteemed guests stood. Dominic took the seat beside Gabriel, and Aliah sat to his left. To her left sat the two highest ranking representatives from the Carsten delegation. Once the king and queen were seated, everyone else was able to settle down and enjoy the feast.

The ensuing meal was strained. Aliah encouraged the Carstenites to talk with Dominic, but they were only interested in dealing with The Warrior. It seemed they had all but forgotten her husband's role in saving their world from disaster.

Halfway through the meal, she and Dominic swapped seats, and Aliah hoped for some light relief while talking to her children. It was not to be. Gabriel was distracted by remembering things he might need on his trip, and Mina picked at her food, saying nothing.

'What's wrong with Mina?' she asked Dominic as the servants cleared away the last savoury course.

'I managed to squeeze in a chat with the head of the Wizard Council today. The tutor they've suggested for Mina is one of the ones who made her short time at the school miserable. I have asked Alric if he would mind taking the job on, but I haven't heard anything back.'

'Do you think they're making a point?' she asked.

'Indeed. We have changed so much with regards to the teaching of magic; this might be a step too far for them. I think they want to make it as unpleasant as possible to stop others from requesting a tutor for their offspring.'

Aliah bit back a sigh. *Why must everything be such a battle?*

'If Alric cannot take on the role, Wizard Mayborn works with a trainee teacher. They have suggested he might be trusted to carry out most of the instruction under Mayborn's Guidance. So this might still work out.'

'Mina doesn't think so, though?'

'No.' Dominic smiled wryly. 'I have suggested she knuckle down and make the best of a bad situation.'

'I'm not sure that'll go down well. She's getting such a raw deal at the moment. We were working through her issues and coming up with a plan for a future, then all this had to happen.'

'Life doesn't always go to plan, and it won't hurt Mina to find that out sooner rather than later. Besides, there is a little bit of sugar coming to help the medicine go down. I haven't told her yet, but the delegation from Hand arrives in two days' time, and Duke Damon has included his heir, Jonas, as well as Jonas's daughter, Dahlia, in his party. She and Mina got on well together when we were in Hand last year. Dahlia showed her the sights, and I'm sure Mina would love to return the favour.'

Chuckling, Aliah asked, 'Isn't she the one who introduced Mina to her first tavern?'

'That's the one.'

'You should tell her. That news is certain to bring a smile to her face.' Aliah paused a moment before asking mischievously, 'Are you sure you can handle the two of them loose in Bannock without me?'

Aliah missed her husband's answer as a servant leaned in and placed an ornate, sugary confection in front of her. *A good thing I will be spending a few days in the saddle,* she thought. *I will need the exercise to work this off.*

As soon as the dessert course was cleared, Gabriel excused himself. 'I haven't finished packing, and I've thought of a couple of other things I need to take.'

'I hope the extra things aren't more books,' Aliah said as he leaned down to kiss her cheek.

'Um...'

'All right. Remember, we depart at sunup. Don't be late.'

Mina also stood to leave. 'I'll help sort out Gabriel. He needs someone to make sure he doesn't overpack and send his poor horse lame.'

'Remind him there isn't much room for books on the trail. Try to limit him to one. He can exchange it at his uncle's library if he manages to finish it,' Dominic told her.

Mina smiled. 'I saw at least three go in his bag before dinner, and I bet he has thought of another one or two he simply must take with him.'

'See you in the morning,' Aliah said to her daughter's departing back.

With the children gone, Aliah concentrated her attention on the two remaining guests at their table. The talk was mainly about trade goods, and Dominic was attempting to interest the Carsten delegation in attending the next market in Bannock.

'I am afraid, Your Highness, the locals do not care much for us. We would not get a chance to discover what your good country has to offer when the traders are so hostile.'

'Leave that to me. By the time I'm finished with you, no one will have any idea you are not local.'

The men glanced questioningly at Aliah, who grinned as she remembered some of the disguises Dominic had her put on so they could attend markets alone together when they were first married.

'My husband has a different approach to things, and I'm sure you will be well looked after as I leave you in his hands.'

She stifled a yawn. 'If you will excuse me, gentlemen, I have an early start in the morning, and a long ride to my destination. Hopefully we will have a new leader appointed quickly and I will be able to return before your departure.'

'Of course,' the younger of the two men said. 'I hope your trip is successful and your subjects listen to sense.'

'I am sure they will,' Aliah said as she stood to leave, relieved Dominic had come up with unrest in a local community to explain her hasty departure. It would not do to let their previous invaders in on the fact that they had border troubles in the west.

'I won't be long,' Dominic said as she left through the back door of the state dining room.

CHAPTER 15
A FORMAL FAREWELL

Her mount impatiently danced across the cobblestones as Aliah searched again for her daughter in the gathering crowd. Dominic stood on the steps leading up to the castle's main entrance, surrounded by court dignitaries and officials. No matter how hard she looked, Mina was nowhere to be seen.

The last of the garrison was lined up behind her and Captain Madigan, and the rising sun was turning the morning sky a brilliant purple. Out of the corner of her eye, Aliah saw a hand waving. She turned in her saddle to find Mina's maid trying to get her attention.

The trembling woman wrung her hands, even more distraught than she had been earlier when she informed the royal couple their eldest offspring had elected to go for an early morning ride rather than attend her mother and brother's farewell. Dominic had sent the woman in search of Mina, but the shake of her head told the queen her daughter could not be found.

Dominic's face clouded over with suppressed anger. Aliah overheard him say, 'Go look again. And when you find her, tell her to get herself here immediately, or I won't be held responsible for the consequences.'

Catching her husband's eye, Aliah pushed her disappointment to the side as she waited for him to join her. She had thought she and Mina were making headway, and it hurt her that her daughter had not come to say farewell.

'We can't wait any longer for her to appear. I am afraid dealing with her rudeness is another thing I will have to leave with you,' she said.

Dominic squeezed her hand. 'All right, let's get this show on the road.'

Aliah sat tall and proud in the saddle as her husband returned to the farewell party and smiled as he drew the mantle of king around himself. He wished the troop safe travels and success in their endeavours, finishing with 'May the goddess travel with you and bring peace back to our lands.' Having completed the formalities, he walked down the steps to rejoin her.

Taking her lead rein, he led the departing company towards the gate to Bannock town.

'Don't be too hard on her, Dom. Watching Gabriel head out on a mission she would love to join would be difficult for her.'

'I'm not promising anything,' he said through clenched teeth.

'Please, for me.'

'Don't worry about it. I want you to concentrate on keeping yourself and Gabriel safe. We don't know exactly what's going on in the mountains, but I would rather give up the Ariel border garrisons than for anything to happen to you or Gabriel.'

'Dom, what if this is bigger than I can handle?' Aliah's stomach twisted at the thought. Did she have it in her to face down another invasion?

'You will have Seamus with you, and I'm only a few days ride away, and Hubert is even closer.' He placed his hand reassuringly on her leg. 'Promise me you'll look after yourself and Gabriel.'

Looking down into her husband's face, Aliah wanted more than anything to leap from the saddle and tell him she didn't want to go, didn't want to leave him. But she was not riding out as Aliah. She was Queen Aliahanna—Aria's Warrior, and she couldn't let the people see her fear. So she simply said, 'I promise.'

He let go of the reins, and her horse took her through the gates and into the city.

MINA LEANED over and fiddled with the bridle of the mount she was riding, averting her face as she rode past her father, trying to appear as one of the last in a long line of guards. As she did so, she caught a glimpse of the anguish on his face as his eyes followed her mother. For the second time that morning, she almost faltered, almost pulled her horse up and declared her presence.

The first time had been when she saw the disappointment on her mother's face when she realised Mina had not come to wish them farewell. She had not counted on her mother minding her non-appearance quite so much, and her stomach somersaulted with remorse as her mother tried to hide her pain.

Now, seeing her father's concern for her mother, she regretted leaving him to face the next few moon turns alone. He had advisors aplenty, but he would have no one to relax and spend family dinners with. Biting her lip, she raised her head and trotted on. She had given her bond, and she must honour that commitment for the next twelve moon turns—come what may.

As they passed through the town gates and headed towards the western duchy, the pace quickened, and the new captain of the Guard rode back along his company. He pulled up beside the man riding to Mina's right.

'Rinnard.'

'Captain.'

'It appears I have one more guard than I had last night.' The captain's steely grey eyes raked over Mina before turning back to his scout.

'I have been persuaded to take on an apprentice,' the scout answered.

'Given your knowledge of our mission, do you believe we should be taking on an untried scout?'

'We fought last night, and I find her more than competent with the weapon she carries. I am confident she can fend for herself should we end up having to fight, which you will no doubt test for yourself over the next few days. In the matter of her scout training, she has a strong gift, and I have contracted to help her develop her skills. That is my business, as we agreed when I bonded with you.'

Mina gritted her teeth but said nothing while the two men discussed her abilities as if she was not there. When she begged Rinnard to accept her as an apprentice, she had sworn to follow his every order without question for the next twelve moon turns. His first demand had been to let him deal with the captain.

The scout had explained to her, 'He is young for his position, but he is a good commander in spite of his age. He will allow me to train you if I handle this right.'

Resisting the urge to raise her head and meet the captain's gaze as he assessed her, she was somewhat relieved when he turned his attention back to Rinnard. 'You have earned the right to choose an apprentice, and if you say she can fend for herself, that is good enough for me. Remember though, we have no capacity for freeloaders on this trip. We will talk later about what we do with her when we leave the main force.'

He turned to Mina. 'Welcome to the company. Day to day, you will do as Rinnard asks, but should it come to a fight, you will follow my lead. In all things, even your right to stay with Rinnard, my word is final. Understand?'

'Understood,' Mina mumbled, keeping her head and voice low as she realised the captain leading the troop was the man who had been waiting outside her father's office a couple of days ago. Fortunately, she had pulled her guard's cap down over her eyes so her father wouldn't recognise her, and she hoped it would also fool this keen-eyed man, at least for a while. She couldn't risk him identifying her, not this close to home.

'You look familiar. Have we met?'

'I found her in the lower stables. Perhaps you saw her while you were looking after your horse.'

Captain Madigan stared at her, and Mina moved uncomfortably in her saddle, hoping that, dressed in the guard uniform with her hair tucked under a cap, she looked like all the other nondescript female guards in the troop. The look he gave her before turning back to Rinnard told her otherwise.

'She's your responsibility. Make sure she takes her place on the duty rosters and doesn't hold us back. I must be mad to let you bring a newbie on this mission.'

With that, he rode off, and Mina's perplexed gaze followed him. She was sure Captain Madigan worked out where he had seen her before and knew exactly who she was, but for some reason of his own, he was happy to keep that knowledge to himself—for now.

Rinnard turned to her. 'I'm pretty sure the captain never came to the lower stables, so where would he have seen you, Mina?'

'Around the castle grounds, I guess.' Mina would not start her apprenticeship by lying to her master, but that didn't mean she had to tell the whole truth—unless he asked directly.

'Humph. That is not an answer. Maybe you will trust me enough to tell me the truth when we know each other a bit better.'

Relieved to have the conversation done with, Mina fell into line beside her new master but could not relax completely. At some stage, someone would recognise her, and her secret would come out. She had to hope that by then they would be far enough away from Bannock that she would not be sent home.

In the meantime, she had not become Rinnard's apprentice merely to join the border mission. She was serious about learning to control her magic and about becoming a scout. When she found out about her wizard tutor last night, she had considered all her options. In the end, she realised Rinnard was the ideal teacher for her.

Not only could he train her to use her magic, as her parents wanted, but he could do it while they were part of a guard troop. It was the perfect solution. She only wished she'd had a chance to talk it through with her parents, but they were asleep by the time she organised everything.

Actually, that wasn't totally true. She avoided her parents all morning, because she didn't want them to forbid her from doing this. That's not to say her stomach wasn't churning with guilt, not least of all because they tried so hard over the last few days to find a future she was happy with.

To make up for running away and disappointing them, she would be the best apprentice scout and tracker possible. She would soak up everything Rinnard had to teach her, and she would make her mother and father proud.

'Rinnard, when do I begin my training?' she asked, eager to get started.

'You have already begun,' he answered.

MORE FROM THE WIZARD AND THE WARRIOR

Independent authors live and die by word of mouth recommendations, so please take the time to let others know you enjoyed reading this book.

https://www.goodreads.com/book/show/56932671-admina-s-argument

To Find More Books in The Wizard and The Warrior Series
https://viviennelfraser.com.au/wizard-and-warrior

ABOUT THE AUTHOR

Vivienne has been writing books since she was fifteen years old, but only friends and family were allowed to read them. Forced to give up work because of family commitments she was encouraged by friends and family to finally put some of her writing out there for others to read.

In the real world after leaving university with a BA in History and Politics she worked as a Personnel Officer, an Office Manager, a Project Manager, a DBA and IT Manager, then as a Business and Data Analyst, adding an MSC in Information Systems along the way. Through all these changes in career she continued to write, escaping into fantasy worlds.

Born in Invercargill (New Zealand), she has lived in; Dunedin (New Zealand), London (England), Petersfield (England) and currently lives with her husband and son, and their dog ,Trouble and their mad cat, Lola in Sydney (Australia).

For future releases and current news you can find Vivienne at www.viviennelfraser.com.au
or on Facebook at www.facebook.com/vivienneleefraser

ACKNOWLEDGMENTS

I was listening to an interview with author Dan Aaronovitch, and he said some characters in his books clamour to come back, and that resonated with me. When I decided to do some novellas and short stories from the Wizard and Warrior world Amelia, Dominic and Emer were all battling for supremacy.

Then, in a conversation with my son, Sam, I asked if he was writing what happened next after series one, what would he do? (I won't tell you what he said because that would spoil the surprise) From that conversation, Admina's Argument grew.

As always there are many people who helped make this story what it is. Firstly I want to thank the team at Lauren Clarke editing (www.CREATINGink.com), Heather Bosevski and Hot Tree Editing for bringing these stories to life.This book would not be what it is without them.

I also need to thank my lovely sister Sandy. She is always such a great support. She not only reads my books, even though fantasy is not really her thing, but she takes the time to proof read them for me, as well as inspiring the revised ending for this tale. I could not do any of this without her. Or without Jim who does my maps and some of my covers, and the dishes and cooks when I am writing. This time he also fitted in a rather amazing drawing of Admina for me.

Finally to all of you who will take the time to read these stories. I love writing, but I get a real boost every time someone downloads or buys one of my books. I hope you try another some time.

You can keep up with Wizard and Warrior news
on facebook @wizardandwarrior
To Find More Books in The Wizard and The Warrior Series
https://viviennelfraser.com.au/wizard-and-warrior

www.ingramcontent.com/pod-product-compliance
Lightning Source LLC
Chambersburg PA
CBHW062115170626
46813CB00002B/463